# TRINIDAD NOIR

# TRINIDAD NOIR

EDITED BY
LISA ALLEN-AGOSTINI & JEANNE MASON

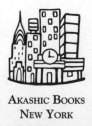

AKASHIC BOOKS
NEW YORK

Published by Akashic Books
©2008 Akashic Books

Series concept by Tim McLoughlin and Johnny Temple
Trinidad map by Sohrab Habibion

ISBN-13: 978-1-933354-55-2
Library of Congress Control Number: 2007940662

First printing

Printed in Canada

Akashic Books
PO Box 1456
New York, NY 10009
info@akashicbooks.com
www.akashicbooks.com

## ALSO IN THE AKASHIC NOIR SERIES:

CARIBBEAN
SEA

Maracas

Sant
Cru

Chaguaramas

PORT-OF-SPAIN
(SEE INSET)

San Juan

THE REPUBLIC OF

# TRINIDAD
# & TOBAGO

Caroni
Swamp

Couva

GULF
OF
PARIA

San
Fernando

Palmiste

Godineau

COLUMBUS CHANNEL

Sans Souci

TOBAGO

napuna

*ATLANTIC OCEAN*

RINIDAD

Diego Martin      Maraval
        Fort George
                  Emperor
                  Valley
        St. James  Zoo

                  Uptown
                  Port-of-Spain

                  East Dry River

PORT-OF-SPAIN

*And if somebody don't buss somebody face*
*How the policeman going to make a case?*

*And if somebody don't dig out somebody eye*
*The Magistrate will have nobody to try*
*And if somebody don't kill somebody dead*
*All the judges going to beg their bread*
*So when somebody cut off somebody head*
*Instead of hanging they should pay them money instead*

—Lord Commander, "No Crime, No Law"

# TABLE OF CONTENTS

# PART II: TOWN

# INTRODUCTION
PARADOXES IN PARADISE

People think they know the Caribbean, the white-sandy-beaches-rum-and-Coca-Cola-smiling-natives-waving-palms Caribbean—you know the one. And sure, the Republic of Trinidad and Tobago has sun, sea, beaches, the whole tourist schtick. But this southernmost country in the Caribbean archipelago is filled with paradoxes. She isn't always the idyllic tropical dream. Far from it. Sometimes she's a nightmare.

In *Trinidad Noir*, you'll trail the country's criminals, her prostitutes, her officious bureaucrats, her police, her ordinary citizens. Expect to be intrigued. Expect to be entertained. But don't expect to understand Trinidad.

It's ironic that this volume is the first noir collection to come out of this country because, in a sense, Trinidad was founded on crime. Christopher Columbus's arrival in 1498 was the start of a criminal enterprise of epic proportions: it began with the theft of the island from its indigenous Carib people, then their genocide, followed by African slavery and the importation of indentured labor to man the obscenely lucrative cocoa, sugar, and coffee plantations of the eighteenth and nineteenth centuries. Today, Trinidad's political climate of excess and corruption is buoyed by an economy bloated with oil and natural gas monies and by an element of society afloat in drugs and guns. There's fodder enough here for ten volumes of *Trinidad Noir*.

Trinidad's history is imprinted in the faces of her people: East Indian, Portuguese, and Chinese indentured laborers; descendents of African slaves; European colonials; and the Syrians and Lebanese who migrated here in the early twentieth century. Black, white, dougla, East Indian, Chinese, and Middle-Eastern Trinis—you'll meet them all in these pages.

The country's profound cultural diversity has produced a resilient people. Trinis are characteristically God-fearing, family-oriented, and generous, but despite their apparent insouciance they can also be unscrupulous and divisive. They are often deeply religious yet ridiculously carnal, living a Victorian double-life. By night they love the same neighbors whom they claim to hate by day. Tension among these groups, most notably between the predominant East Indian and African populations, makes for political minefields in almost every aspect of national life. Yet in their everyday lives Trinis coexist peacefully: they live side by side, they intermarry, they lime and fete together.

Each spring most Trinis throw propriety to the wind and strip down to soul essentials for Carnival. Carnival combines the pre-Lenten celebrations of the French planter class during slavery with African masking traditions to form what is arguably the greatest show on earth. Masquerading as characters inspired by fantasy, film, Vegas, nature, and whatever else catches the designers' fancies, hundreds of thousands of people take to the streets. Together they jump and wine—a sensual dance involving hip gyration—to calypso, soca, and pan, indigenous music created largely by the black working class.

This collection includes stories by some of today's most acclaimed Caribbean writers, and for such a small country, the Republic of Trinidad and Tobago has an impressive literary legacy. Among the endless traits that typify Trinis—depending upon whom you ask—is a graciousness which is humbling to encounter. We would like to thank our contributors for their immediate and enthusiastic responses to our requests for noir stories, an entirely new genre for some of them. In fictionalizing crime in the real crime setting of Trinidad, they have created a decidedly literary noir collection with their sometimes lyrical, sometimes humorous, sometimes nostalgic, sometimes shocking, but always inventive stories. Their quality characterizations, plots, and styles concurrently reveal the country's darkness and its appeal with an unexpected and gratifying result: the Trinidad that emerges makes *Trinidad Noir* as much a delightful crime romp as it is an exposé of the seedy side of life.

Although Trinidad has big-city aspirations in her two main urban areas of Port-of-Spain, the capital, and San Fernando, there is still plenty of country life in her cane-farming central plains, her southern swamps, and her coastal fishing villages. Set in the various parts of the country, these stories reflect the island in all her contradictions. As you turn the pages, you will experience a nation like no other. See for yourself, but bear in mind: there's nothing a Trini won't do for you, and there's nothing a Trini won't do to you.

*Lisa Allen-Agostini & Jeanne Mason*
*Port-of-Spain, Trinidad*
*May 2008*

Tabanca like that has two cures—new love or exorcism. [?] chose the latter, only because he saw her in the face of [?]ry woman he met and feared that any new partner would [?] prove fickle and desert him for another man.

Leaving her clothes in the drawers and her compact of [?]eap brown face powder on the dresser, the only things she [?] left behind, Trey took off from Diego Martin's close houses [?] cramped streets and headed north.

[?]ey pored over the small pile of dark green herb in his left [?]lm. Nimbly, he shredded the sticky, soft leaves and brown [?]wers hidden in the mass, picking out the polished black [?]eds and putting them aside. When the mix was cleaned to [?]s satisfaction, he reached into the front pocket of his col-[?]ful nylon shorts and extracted a balled-up piece of white [?]per. This he unfolded into a two-inch square and poured [?]e cleaned herb onto it. Behind his ear was a single ciga-[?]tte. Trey pulled it from its nesting spot and broke off about [?]alf an inch. He sprinkled the tobacco onto the herb on the [?]per, then placed the end of the cigarette on the smoothed-[?]ut sheet. Rolling the herb into the shape of the cigarette, he [?]eticulously straightened the emerging cylinder. When it was [?]erfectly flush, he wrapped the paper around it, put it to his [?]ps, and licked the flap shut.

"Danny!" Trey called to a similarly clad young man lying [?]n the beach in front of him. Danny had dozed off, his long, [?]encil-thin dreadlocks trailing in the golden sand. The hair [?]as almost as light as the sand itself, in contrast to the owner [?]f the hair who was midnight black. Danny jerked up, only to [?]ubside nearly immediately. "Danny," Trey said on an intake, [?]you want some of this, man?" He extended the joint and held [?]n the smoke to better absorb the THC into his lungs. Danny

# PART I

COUNTRY

# POT LUCK

BY LISA ALLEN-AGOSTINI
*Sans Souci*

She always left him, wandering off like
provocation or explanation, returning j
and without comment after a day or a we
He loved her, but it was hard to keep track of v
in her life. He kept her clothes neatly stacked
drawers and hoped for the best.

One day she just didn't come back. He only
accident after six weeks that she had actually n
another man in his—their—neighborhood. It
knew well. They had smoked together and tha
friends of a sort. Not very good friends, evident
had had no problem taking his woman away.

After that Trey lost his appetite, partly be
usually meant buying ingredients at the shop a
opposite her new home in Diego Martin's mos
class suburb of Rich Plain Road. He saw her throu
sometimes in a tiny pair of white short pants, ne
she didn't have when she lived with him, hang
towels out to dry on the lines strung outside. The
skintight and he recognized the imprint of her la
their dense denim folds. The lower curve of her
hung just under the frayed hem. Instead of wan
potatoes and corned beef, he'd taste her memory, s
He grew thin.

stretched out his hand and took the cigarette without opening his eyes. He put it to his lips and drew deep. It was his turn
to hold in the smoke. As they sucked in the heady marijuana,
passing the joint back and forth, the sea roared in the background. "Good stuff," Trey murmured, his eyes reddening and
narrowing as the weed took effect.

"Yeah, I get it from a partner in the village. Not the
usual suspect," Danny replied. He sat up and looped his waist-
length dreadlocks with one hand, tucking them into a knot.
He looked over at his cousin, his eyes as red as Trey's. "This
man have it sick, horse. Only quality weed he supplying. No
compress, only fresh." He took another hit. "I trying to get
him to sell me some more but he brakesing. Say the man who
he getting it from gone away for a week."

The waves continued to roll up on the sand. Trey's orange surfboard, leaning on the fisherman's shed next to him,
cast a long shadow across his deeply tanned face. His olive
skin was freckled across the bridge of his nose, complemented
by his short, nappy Afro, the color of brown sugar. Full lips
curved into a slight smile as he contemplated the surf. His
hand reached out to lightly caress the board, which was rough
with a thick coat of wax. "You going and hit that again before
it reach cigarette?" he asked Danny, who shook his head and
passed it back to him. Trey nursed the joint until the weed was
burned off and passed the rest of the funk back to Danny. "I
ent feeling for no cigarette right now." They were quiet for a
few minutes. "Thinking of going back." Danny said nothing.
"Two months in the jungle is enough, man." Danny smoked
without comment. The murmur of the waves continued. "I go
have to call them men to pick back up a little end in work."

"Is so you is a work jumbie, boy?" Danny finally replied.
"Two months of surf, weed, and country food, and you ready

to go back in the rat race?" He shook his head again. "Me, I wouldn't rush back to go and work in no factory assembly line."

"Is not no assembly line," Trey snapped. "I tell you, I is a technician. Is skilled work, man. And the two months was good, partner, but is time I go back. I have things to do."

"Like what? Tack back by that slut?" Danny rolled onto his knees and to his feet.

"Don't talk about she so."

"But she's a slut, Trey. She leave you for your partner. How she go play you like that?"

Trey's golden eyes, about the color of his skin, gave him a ghostly appearance. Right now they were cloudy with weed and budding rage. "She make a mistake, all right? That don't make she a slut."

Danny sucked his teeth in disgust and grabbed his own board from the sand. "I heading up the road. Later." He flicked the butt of the cigarette into the blue ocean. "Tasha real chain you up, boy," he muttered as he walked up the track leading to the main road. "If I was you, I would have shoot both of them."

Trey scowled and lit another cigarette from a pack in his pocket. "Is not Tash, is Garvin. That man is the one who is to blame," he told his cousin's broad back. Danny wasn't listening, focused instead on scaling the rocky path without dropping or dinging his board on the huge stones on either side of the track. "Is Garvin who pull she in!" Trey swiftly sucked on the cigarette. "Is he, not she. Is he fault."

Danny's blond locks disappeared over the top of the steep path. Trey was left alone with the rocks and the waves, the sand and the fisherman's hut.

Beyond the road, the Sans Souci forest towered, dim and

green and forbidding. In two months, Trey had only been in the forest twice, both times with his cousin. They had gone to find a certain spring which Danny swore had the sweetest water in the world, but they had become lost in the undergrowth and never found it. They made do with the chlorinated water piped in by the public utility, but Trey craved the fresh, untreated water of the spring. He stubbed the cigarette out in the sand and rose, grabbing his board and heading toward the forest in bounding strides.

Bareback and barefoot, his lean, muscular body quickly maneuvered the path. His calloused feet barely registered the bumpy pitch of the Toco Road before he was in the cool mulch of the forest. It was rainy season, but the ground wasn't sodden, only damp and spongy with fallen leaves and topsoil. He had no idea where he was going, but with a quick glance around for a landmark, Trey moved into the woods. He passed a giant immortelle tree, a clump of stunted cocoa trees, a dead one stretched across what could have been a track. The gloom deepened as he walked, the trees becoming larger and taller, the ground softer and cooler despite the mid-afternoon heat.

The light changed. It was somehow brighter, more airy. A sloped clearing appeared full of lime-green, leafy shrubs about a head taller than his six feet. "To ras!" he breathed, breaking into the space gingerly and leaving his surfboard behind.

The weed was planted in even rows, smelling pungent, sweet, musky. As far as he could see, marijuana trees were coming into bloom, their small orange flowers just starting to show—plants ripe for the picking. Making his way through the rows, Trey tenderly brushed the leaves and stems. He almost missed the hut in the center of the field, stumbling when he noticed the galvanized steel sheeting that made up its walls and roof. The double gate, also corrugated sheets of steel, bore a heavy iron padlock threaded through a thick steel chain looped into a pair of holes in the gates. The message was clear: *Keep out*. To Trey that was as good as an invitation.

He walked the entire field until his feet were sore and covered in mud. There wasn't a soul in sight. He picked his way back to the galvanized shed and peered through the holes in the gate. It was dark inside and he couldn't see much, just large hanging shapes. The smell, however, was unmistakable— it was exactly the same weed he had just been cleaning. Trey turned and ran for the road, leaving his surfboard behind as a bright orange marker to light his way back to paradise.

Jimmy the maxi-taxi driver was cagey, driving extra slowly on the winding country road. Though a large banner on the back windscreen proclaimed it *Jah Bus*, the real owner was a Christian who wanted no part of Rastafari. A keen business-man, he recognized that popular culture glorified all that was Rasta, from dreadlocks to Bob Marley and marijuana use, so he latched onto the trend to make his business popular. He warned his drivers, the men he hired to work the vehicle on a twenty-four-hour rotation, that he wasn't going to allow weed smoking on the job. What they did in their own time was their affair, but behind the wheel of *Jah Bus* they were to be clean and sober.

It was close to 10 and Jimmy, an occasional Rasta, had fin-ished his last trip with only $100 in pocket after oil, gas, and the $300 child maintenance he had to pay his ex-girlfriend every two weeks for their three sons. When Trey and Danny flagged him down and put their unusual proposition to him, Jimmy had been of two minds, thinking about the maxi's owner and the prospect of being out of a job. But the offer of a bonus payment was irresistible. It wasn't every day that someone offered to rent your maxi for five pounds of weed. Though he doubted the resurrection of Haile Selassie I, the late Ethiopian emperor whom Rastas acknowledge as the descendant of Christ, he certainly agreed that smoking weed was an ideal part of livity. Five pounds of it—a whole black bin liner full of the stuff—would keep him high for quite some time.

Trey and Danny directed the driver to a small house on a hill off the main road. It was where Danny lived and where Trey had been hiding out from the world for two months. The house was like most of the others around it, a humble concrete dwelling with a small front porch, a neat garden behind a chain-link fence, and three pot hounds skulking around the yard. "Rambo!" Danny shouted affectionately at the first brown mongrel to reach his feet as he pushed open the rusty gate. Hiding behind a lush ixora was a black bitch, marked like a Doberman pinscher but with none of the grace of the breed, and lounging on the front steps, just below the porch, was a dog that resembled both its parents, half-brown and half-black. Trey shot a warning look at the one behind the bush. Sarah was prone to snapping at strangers and Jimmy was already nervous enough. "Come nah, Princess," Danny was urging the dog on the step, nudging her aside with his foot. "Move and let people pass. You feel this is your house, eh, girl?" Trey stayed in the yard between Jimmy and the growling bitch.

"That is you, Danny?" a woman's voice called from the house. Aunty Zora leaned over the bottom half of the Dutch door leading to the kitchen. Her arms were covered in flour up to the elbows. Jimmy eyed her long salt-and-pepper dreadlocks with admiration. "Full some water and bring it for me, nah. This pipe giving trouble again." Trey's maternal aunt glanced at Jimmy with little curiosity. The boys were always bringing friends home. "Good evening," she said mildly before disappearing back into the kitchen.

Danny changed direction, going around the house instead of through the front door. "Give me a minute, man," he tossed over his shoulder as he headed to the kitchen, reemerging in a moment with a plastic pail in each hand. As he filled the buckets at the standpipe outside the kitchen, Jimmy edged closer to Trey.

"So, where the thing?" Jimmy asked, lighting a cigarette and peering around the yard.

"Cool yourself, nah," Trey muttered. "We go handle it. Let the man see about he queen first."

"Scene," Jimmy agreed, swiping his brow with one finger and flicking the stream of sweat off to the side. "What she making?" he asked Trey, sniffing the fragrant air that smelled of vanilla.

"Sweetbread."

"So much'a sweetbread? Is all up by she elbow I see flour. Allyuh have a bakery or what?"

Trey was growing testy. "She does make and sell. Sweet-bread, cake, drops. All of that."

"Which part she does sell it?" Jimmy was a talker. Trey was tired of it already.

"In the village there. In the shop."

"Scene," Jimmy nodded. The loaves of sweet coconut bread, full of raisins and cherries, were very popular. Aunty Zora was quite the businesswoman and had placed her products on shelves all up the Toco Road, a string of communities that curved in a rough semicircle around the northeastern tip of Trinidad from Valencia to Matelot. Danny, when he wasn't surfing, delivered the goods in their old beat-up Land Rover.

After their visit to Aunty Zora's, they stopped by the fisherman's hut on the beach to load the maxi to the roof with stuffed black garbage bags. Then they drove off to town in *Jah Bus*.

Trey lay on his back in his dusty bedroom surrounded by bulging black garbage bags. His bloodshot eyes and slack expression told his mother the story when she opened the door. That, plus the unique aroma of twenty pounds of fresh weed.

"So, is so you come home and ent offer nobody nothing?" His mother sized him up. "Didn't see your mother two months and you haven't said a word. Smoking inside here by yourself." She crossed her arms over her slender chest, tossing aside long dreadlocks with an angry flick.

Wordlessly, Trey reached into an open bag and grabbed a handful of weed. "Here, Mammy. Smoke. Have a time." When she saw the quality of the herb, she smiled.

"Where allyuh get this? Danny farming now?"

Trey shook his head. "The less you know about this ganja, the better. Trust me."

His mother hesitated, her smile slipping slightly. "Is tief you tief the weed, Tracy?" Trey took a pinch of herb from the same bag and started building a spliff. He didn't answer. "So when they come looking for you, what we go do?" Her voice grew shrill.

"Let me study that. Besides," he flicked aside a seed, "that ent go happen. The place was deserted and we didn't tell no-body nothing. Is one man know and he ent go say nothing. That is the maxi man. And we pay he off good." She looked skeptical.

"I hope you know what you doing." She paused, watching him lick the spliff and light it. "And what you going to do with all this weed?" There were five or six bags, each two feet high and two feet wide.

"Don't you worry about that," Trey said through a cloud of smoke.

From the time Trey let it be known, through a hint dropped at the corner shop, that he had product to sell, the calls started coming. *Man, hook me up with some of that* was what he heard every ten minutes on the phone. Then there were the customers, mostly men, who drove or walked up to the house at all hours asking for a ten-piece or a five-piece, conveniently measured buds rolled into tinfoil fingers, just enough for a spliff or two. His neighbors were smokers themselves, so there was little chance they would turn him in to the police. As long as he kept things quiet, he would be fine.

The talk of Trey's new hustle had to come back to Garvin, a man whose appetite for weed was exceeded only by his appetite for luxury. Lying in bed next to Tasha, Garvin inhaled the smoke from his fat, short joint. He passed her the channa pack, a marijuana cigarette resembling the paper cones vendors used to wrap channa in years before, when boiled chickpeas were a popular snack. Tasha took the cone and drew deep. The room was silent. The fifty-two-inch plasma TV was muted, showing images of gyrating bodies, rappers, and singers. Silk sheets slid noiselessly from her naked body as Tasha rose and padded across the plush white carpeting to the bathroom.

She surveyed herself in the mirror as she washed her hands after using the toilet. Same full breasts Trey loved. Same high, round butt. Same long, jet-black legs. Better makeup, definitely a better weave. Garvin wasn't pretty but he was generous to a fault. And that fault was stupidity.

Sliding back into bed next to him, she asked, "So what now?" Garvin frowned, shrugged. He smoked some more. "Antonio coming back in five days," she said pointedly. "He going to want to know where the weed is." Again, Garvin shrugged. "What you going to tell him?" She didn't wait for him to shrug again. "You going to tell him you lost five pounds of weed? Just so? Like magic?" Garvin looked genuinely troubled. His pale brow wrinkled, his thin lips folded into a scowl, even his nearly transparent ears looked upset, blushing bright red. "You forget how he get on the last time—"

"How I go forget?" Garvin snapped. "Is my ass he shoot!" Reflexively he grabbed for his flat behind, finger dipping into the round scar of the bullet wound. It was still pink and raw, a fresh reminder that he shouldn't tamper with his big brother's stock. But was it enough to stop him from "redistributing" over two Ks of compressed, high-grade Vincy weed while Antonio was on a buying trip to St. Vincent? Nope. Garvin frowned again, wiggling yellowish toes until their joints popped, a habit Tasha loathed.

She thought of Garvin's pale body against hers and shuddered. No doubt Trey, that honey-dipped lover of her past, was twice the man in all respects. Trey was smarter and more complex too. But he was also poor. He lived with his mother, he worked in a factory, and his only ambition was to surf, smoke, and "reason" with the other Rastas on the corner, talking religion and livity late into the night and leaving her home alone. Flicking a glance at her $200 pedicure as she kicked off the covers impatiently, she knew that Trey's was the wrong family for her.

Garvin's, on the other hand, was perfect. Behind the modest façade of their house was an upscale, even posh home, equipped with every modern convenience and luxury, all paid for by Antonio's job as a marijuana agent. He imported and wholesaled the stuff, keeping a relatively small amount for recreation, bribes, and retail sales. The boys lived on the proceeds of Antonio's part in the lucrative marijuana trade, sharing everything except women.

Living around the corner from them, and buying weed from Garvin, who handled the retail trade for Antonio, she had gotten to know the brothers well. It wasn't hard to see that they liked the chase, both of them, so she teased them into wanting to steal her away from her undeserving man. Though it was Garvin who took the bait first, it was Antonio she really wanted. As rich as he was, he would be able to afford a lifetime supply of the Baby Phat jeans, Timberland boots, and Gucci bags that Tasha craved. If she never wore another knockoff it would be too soon.

Sitting at the edge of the bed, she sucked her teeth in disgust. Antonio had balls. He was no Trey, who had too much damned integrity, but Antonio was a strong man who knew his responsibilities. Antonio would never have grabbed and sold his brother's weed to take her on a shopping spree. *Idiot*, she thought, tossing an annoyed look at Garvin.

"You think I want him to shoot me again? I can't take that pain. Besides, he might kill me this time." He wasn't joking. Antonio had a wicked temper, hence the bullet wound, an emblem earned a few weeks before when Garvin had accidentally-on-purpose forgotten to give him a bag of cash. Antonio had come looking for him with a grim look and a gun. When Garvin lied, Antonio hit him in the buttocks to remind him who was in charge. Although the wound was still healing, the lesson had already been lost. Garvin imagined he could take Antonio in a fight. The poor fool.

"So what you going to do about it?" she repeated. Garvin thought for a minute, sucking on the joint.

"I go have to replace it."

"With what? You feel weed does grow on trees?"

Garvin grinned. "Well, yes. Besides, you ent hear your ex-man have a new sideline?"

She was slow to respond. When it hit her, she did a double take. "Trey selling now?"

Garvin nodded. "And I hear is some real high-grade." Tasha's eyes lit up.

Danny called Trey with bad news. "The man come back. He asking questions."

Trey wasn't sweating. "Jimmy irie, right? We ent have nothing to worry about, brethren. Is cool. Nobody ent see we and nobody don't know nothing."

"They don't have to know nothing to lick we up," Danny said cagily. "He only have to suspect is me and my ass is grass."

Trey laughed at the unwitting pun. "Don't fret yourself, cousin. We safe like Selassie I briefcase, man."

On the other end, Danny was biting his lip. "Man . . ."

Trey, blowing out a thick cloud of smoke, repeated his assurances.

Danny wasn't appeased. "I coming down. We have to deal with this man or he go find we and mess we up bad bad, brother. I coming down tonight."

Trey hung up the phone just as a voice called, "Good afternoon," from outside the house. Ambling to the door in shorts and a plain white undershirt, he jumped visibly when he saw his visitors—Garvin and Tasha. He walked to the gate.

"What going on?" Trey greeted Garvin. "Tasha." He couldn't help his eyes, which drank her in. She smiled lightly and held Garvin's arm tighter.

"Trey, my brother!" Garvin was all fake good cheer but his

eyes were flint. His grip around Tasha's waist contracted. "I hear you have some excellent smoke. I was wondering if you could make a deal with us. I need two kees. Will you give it to me?"

"I don't know about give," Trey said coolly. "But I could certainly sell it to you if you want." Garvin was half-listening. His eyes were busily roaming the façade of the house, trying to bend around the corner to see what lay on the other side. In time, his brain churned the information around. "How much?" he asked. Trey called his price. Garvin whistled. "Even with the employee discount that sounding high," the drug pusher said with a small, cold laugh. Tasha stood up taller, bristling.

Trey was casually taking out a sample for them. "Smoke that and tell me it not worth it."

Garvin rubbed the thick, fragrant leaves between his fingers, pulling them apart to feel the stickiness of the plant. It was perfectly dried, and full of illegal goodness. He didn't have to smoke it to know it would be a sweet, potent ride.

They were standing at the gate in the fence surrounding the yard, Trey on one side and Garvin and Tasha on the other. Garvin jerked his head in farewell and pulled Tasha down the road after him into a black Lexus SUV.

Tasha was livid. "What the hell was that? You don't have to pay he for that weed! Just take it!"

Garvin sucked his teeth and drove faster. "Hush your stupid mouth, nah," he mumbled threateningly. "What you think I planning to do?" They reached his house, drove through the electronic gate past the half-dozen dozing Rottweilers, parked, and walked through the triple-locked front door with its alarm system. "But I had to find out if he had the weed. No sense robbing he for a ounce. And look, he have it. Nice grade too." Tasha waited in silence for him to get to the point. "So while you bulling him to distract him, I go find the weed and take it."

She recoiled instantly. "What you mean?" She pushed a finger into his face. "What you take me for? Some kinda ho?"

"Aye, take it easy. What, you can't bull the man one more time? I sure when you was living there allyuh wasn't playing patty-cake when the night come. What is one more, for this? For me?" He paused, giving her a canny look. "Or I know what it is. You want me to get lick up. You want Antonio to shoot me."

Tasha's face grew hot. She slapped him hard. "Don't be an ass, Garvin. I done tell you already, me ent no ho."

Rubbing his face, he cut her a sideways look and lifted his hand to hit her but stopped. "Why you always have to slap me, Tasha? I tell you don't do it. One of these days I will slap you down."

Instantly contrite, Tasha snuggled a hand on the reddened cheek. "Sorry, darling."

He sucked his teeth in disgust. "Anyway, you go have to distract him somehow. Whether you sex him or not is your choice. Me ent business with that. Just make sure he don't come out. I go handle it from this end."

But she doubted Garvin could. "Why you don't distract him and let me tief it?" Garvin shook his head, but before he could speak, she interjected, "I know the house better than you. I know where he does like to hide things. It make more sense this way, Garvin." She pressed her round breasts into his chest and thrust her hips forward until their pelvic regions touched. By the time she kissed him, Garvin had changed his mind.

"No scene." He couldn't maintain a blood flow to both his brain and his penis, so he aimed low.

The knock was soft. It was close to midnight. This time Trey wasn't surprised to see Garvin outside his window. "What's the scene, man?" Trey asked.

Garvin grinned. "I come to do the deal, partner." Trey rubbed his eyes. He had been napping before the visit. He yawned and stretched as he closed the window and went to open the front door. His nemesis was still grinning. "Two kilos, man. Look, the money there," Garvin said, gesturing at a small package on the steps of the front porch.

Trey didn't move from the doorway. Something felt wrong. "Look, man, I change my mind. I not selling you again." As he moved to close the door, Garvin sprang forward with surprising grace and speed.

"How you mean you ent selling me? Man, don't talk foolishness now. Two kilos. Go and bring it."

Trey shook his head. "Nah, partner. I done. You go have to get that someplace else—"

The report of the gunshot silenced them both. Blood drained from Garvin's face and he was as white as the wall he had to lean against to keep from falling.

Leaving him standing there, Trey ran to the back of the house from where the noise had come. Tasha's still body was sprawled on the ground by the kitchen door. Danny was standing in the doorway, dazed, a .38 in his hand. Trey rushed to his side and grabbed the gun.

"She was picking the lock, Trey. She was coming to tief the weed . . ."

"Boy, you mad or what? What we going to do now? Eh?" He turned to his dead ex-girlfriend. Knowing she had probably been trying to steal the ganja was no consolation. He stooped and stroked her silky, dark cheek. It was still warm, unblemished, and as soft as it had been in life.

Danny sprang to action. "Boy, we don't have no time for that. We have to move she."

Trey nodded. At least he had some garbage bags at hand.

*   *   *

When Garvin got home he was trembling and pale. Antonio found him there, still jittery and sickly yellow, four days later. Tasha was gone, and so were two kilograms of product. Antonio wanted an explanation and he wanted one quickly.

"Is-is-is Trey!" Garvin stammered, breath cut short by the fingers tightening around his throat. "He trust the weed and then tell me he don't have the money." Antonio relaxed his grip. *Trust the weed? Why would Trey want two kilos of weed on credit?* Antonio glared at his brother, but Garvin just gave an anxious smile.

They pulled up at Trey's gate in Antonio's Lexus SUV, a shiny black monster that Antonio probably loved more than he did his whiny, dishonest little brother. It was nearly 1 in the morning.

"Trey!" Garvin bawled at the top of his lungs. "Trey!" There was no answer. Antonio leaped from the van and strode up to the house. Kicking in the front door, he entered. There were no signs of life or weed, except for endless ashtrays overflowing with cigarette and spliff butts.

Garvin murmured weakly, "Like they gone."

Antonio, a stronger, larger version of Garvin, was not amused. He pulled his Magnum Desert Eagle from his waistband and put it to his brother's temple. "You go find them, right? And find my weed. If I only find out you had anything to do with this—"

"But how you go say that, Antonio?" Garvin whined.

"You like to tief too damn much. You feel I don't know you?" Antonio flicked off the gun's safety and rubbed the chrome muzzle against Garvin's cheek. "If I only find out," he repeated. Then he uncocked the gun and stuck it back into his waistband. He turned to look at the contents of the house again. It was on the dresser in Trey's bedroom that he found what he was looking for—a block of board wax wrapped in a plastic bag labeled, *Zora's Sweetbread and Cakes, Toco Road, Sans Souci.* He grinned. There was no humor in the smile.

Once again, Trey was surrounded by black garbage bags. This time they were empty. Danny, sprawled in a beanbag next to the bed, was nearly unconscious. Trey was feeling no pain himself. It was the last of the weed, a nearly impossible amount to smoke out in three days, but with dedication and a lot of help from their friends, mothers, and Jimmy, they had done it. The evidence was up in smoke. Mostly, anyway. Aunty Zora had seen her way to baking a most excellent batch of sweetbread with an unusually strong herbal kick.

Trey stumbled to his feet and zigzagged to the bathroom. As he let a stream of urine hiss urgently into the toilet bowl, he vaguely heard a car pull up outside in the silence of the Sans Souci night. Moving to the window, he saw the moonlight bouncing off the glossy surface of a familiar black Lexus. "Shit," he muttered. Danny was bleary-eyed when Trey tried to shake him awake. "Danny, boy, get up. Garvin and he brother come looking for we."

This was instantly sobering. Danny shook his head to clear it. "What the hell we go do?" he asked in a whisper.

Trey was down on his hands and knees, avoiding the windows. "Well, first thing is to get to ras out of here."

They slipped silently out the back door as Garvin and Antonio walked through the front gate. The three dogs, rushing at the strangers, kept them occupied, and at first they didn't see the two figures running down the road. It was Garvin, shaking Sarah off his left ankle, who spotted them.

"Look them running!" Antonio and Garvin gave chase

into the bush. But the dark night, even lit by a full moon, confounded them. They were soon lost. There was a rustling to their right. Garvin, who had never been in a forest before, whimpered, "Antonio, what was that?"

Antonio sucked his teeth and kicked at the undergrowth. "What you get me in here, Garvin? You's a real clown, boy. I don't know why I does trust you with anything." They kept walking for about an hour, drifting further and further into the bush. Then they spotted it—a sloped clearing planted with lush marijuana trees higher than their heads. Garvin was the first to rush in.

"So, is here he get it!" he exclaimed. In the quiet forest, his voice was a cannon.

"What you talking about?" Antonio asked, fingering a leaf with admiration. Even in the dark he recognized it was good weed.

"Trey. This is where he get the—"

Too late, he realized his mistake. But Antonio already had the gun to his head.

"I thought you say he tief the weed from we."

Garvin gave a sickly smile. "Well . . ."

"I tell you already, I go kill you for tiefing from me."

"But Antonio, listen, this is the weed, man! I smoke it myself!"

Neither of them heard the footsteps behind them. A pair of gunshots shattered the quiet of the night. Antonio never had time to turn and fire a single bullet.

The tall, bald-headed man with the smoking gun spat on the two bodies before turning on his heel, saying, "Come back to tief my weed again, you bitches. Not one fart of that."

In the fisherman's hut on the beach, Trey and Danny shivered for a few hours until dawn before creeping back to the house. Garvin and Antonio never came back for the Lexus, so eventually it replaced the battered Land Rover as Zora's delivery van. And in Zora's backyard, a new bed of ixora bloomed unusually well that year.

# THE RAPE

BY KEVIN BALDEOSINGH

*Couva*

When she first saw the jogger, Hemrajie was sitting on the porch as she did most evenings. She did not notice him until he had run past the house. He wore a white strap jersey, maroon shorts, and his back looked very straight and very strong.

"Who is that?" she asked Feroza, who was sitting with her on the porch as she did most evenings. Feroza looked up from her newspaper. The man was already past the last house of the village, running steadily down the road which snaked through the cane fields. The sun's rays reflected off Feroza's spectacles, dazzling Hemrajie, who blinked and turned her head.

"Dunno," said Feroza. "I never see him before."

"Me neither."

They watched the man run around the corner and disappear behind the rippling cane stalks. The sun was glaring but low, and the evening darkness would come suddenly. Hemrajie took a sip from her glass of iced tea. Feroza resumed reading the newspaper. She had already finished the second of the three cigarettes she allowed herself. A half-filled cup of coffee sat on the iron-fretted center table next to a clay pot with African violets. Feroza drank so slowly that her coffee always got cold before she finished, and she would never let Hemrajie reheat it in the microwave. The two women looked very different. Hemrajie was fat and dark-skinned, Feroza fair and very thin. Hemrajie had round features—round eyes, round nose, a pursed mouth. Feroza had small sharp eyes, a hooked nose, and prominent front teeth. She had married at twenty-one and divorced at twenty-five. Her husband had been an alcoholic. Hemrajie had never married, had never even had a boyfriend. And when Feroza told her stories about her married life, Hemrajie was glad to have avoided the beatings and the bad sex.

Feroza said, "A next woman get kidnap. From Couva."

"They getting closer," Hemrajie said. Couva was a town seven miles from the village.

Feroza continued reading the article. "She thirty-four. Has a restaurant. Husband is a pilot."

"Indian?"

"You have to ask?"

"I hear the last one leave the country already."

"I don't blame she. Look at what she went through."

"Was four men, ent?"

"Yes. And two was Rastas."

"Poor woman."

"I hope they find this one quick."

Hemrajie shook her head. "They will find she after the ransom pay. It always have police behind these things. Most of them in the police force black too."

"True," said Feroza. She took up her third and last cigarette, flicked her lighter, and turned to the letters page.

Hemrajie looked down from the porch at the village. She could see as far as the corner, where the village's main rum shop stood. On most evenings, the men would gather there to drink and play pool. The concrete area in front of the bar had wooden stools and three round wooden tables, each with a thick center leg and thatched umbrella over it. Hemrajie could see the usual set of men at the rum shop. There were some who only went to drink on a Friday, and on weekends there would be unfamiliar faces, especially if Feroza's family was having a special promotion. And there were those men who were at the bar most days. Hemrajie knew all of them, although she spoke to none of them save to say hello and knew some of the younger ones only by face. Jit was a truck driver who came to the bar mainly to escape his nagging wife. They had three children, and it was said that the third wasn't Jit's. Ricky, who was twenty-seven years old, had an irregular income cutting people's lawns and spent most of it in the bar. He lived with his parents in a household of grandmother, two uncles and their wives, and eleven other children in a structure which had been extended so often that it looked like a Lego-block building. Sonny was fifty-three, a primary school teacher, and had been accused some months ago of molesting a seven-year-old girl. Saleem, who was thirty and single and a clerk in a hardware store, was there for two weeks out of every month. For the other two weeks, he would be at Patricia's house in Teemal Trace, since her husband worked offshore on an oil rig every fortnight. And Sam, Tally, Vishnu, and George just liked drinking beer and talking.

Hemrajie knew all this even though she had lived in the house by herself for the past three years, ever since her mother had died. Some information she got from Feroza, some from the village women who would pass every so often to check on her. Even though she did not socialize in the village and had no husband, Hemrajie was respected because she was respectable. She was educated, went to temple twice a week, and had enough money so she didn't need to work for a living. But she had only one true friend.

"That man coming back," Hemrajie said to Feroza.

Feroza closed the newspaper and looked up. The sun was an orange ball on the horizon now, and the air had become cool. The man was running on the other side of the road, so he faced the few cars speeding along the smooth black tarmac. His pace had slowed, and as he came closer Feroza could see the sweat on his forehead and upper arms. His legs, Hemrajie noticed, were well-muscled. He did not look up at the two women as he passed the house.

"Like he training for the marathon," Hemrajie giggled.

"Nah," replied Feroza. "He breathing too hard." They watched as he reached the bar. He did not look at the men there or nod to anyone. He rounded the curve of the road and they could no longer see him.

"He must be from Bombay Number Two," Hemrajie said, settling back in her iron chair. She had replaced the bamboo furniture after her mother died. The metal was painted white and had removable lilac-and-blue striped cushions.

"Maybe," Feroza said. "I don't feel he coming from far." Bombay Number Two was the next village two miles up the road.

"Because he breathing hard?"

"He didn't look like a marathon runner."

"Maybe he in training."

Feroza shrugged, looking down at her newspaper. Hemrajie took up her glass of tea. The ice had melted, and she opened the ice bucket and put some more cubes into her tall glass.

When Feroza finished her cigarette, she got up and folded her newspaper under her arm. "I gone."

"See you," Hemrajie said.

Feroza usually left around 6, before it got dark. She lived in the house above the bar. The bar was owned and run by her family. She had come back there to live after she left her husband. But Feroza had nothing to do with the business. She was a nurse in the public hospital, and she always had a story about how demanding patients were and how most of their ailments were their own fault. Whenever Feroza had the 8-to-4 day shift, she would walk up to Hemrajie's house in the evening. Hemrajie would make iced tea for herself, and Feroza would read the newspaper and smoke her cigarettes. On Fridays, Feroza would also have a glass of white wine. She always kept a bottle in Hemrajie's refrigerator. Hemrajie didn't mind, although she herself drank no alcohol. It was only at Christmas time that she would have one glass.

After Feroza left, Hemrajie went inside and turned on the TV to wait for *The Bold and the Beautiful* which started at 6:30. This gave her time to clear the center table and wash the dishes. Apart from the soap operas, Hemrajie passed the time reading best sellers and mystery novels. Even though her mother had died three years ago, Hemrajie was still not accustomed to having so much time on her hands. After the stroke, her mother had been unable to exert herself, and Hemrajie had taken care of her for fifteen years. This was the primary reason she was not married, with children, like her three sisters. Since their mother died, her sisters had stopped visiting and called only occasionally. They were vexed that Hemrajie got all the Lotto money that their father had won two decades ago which had allowed him to quit his job as a taxi driver and drink himself to death within five years. And Hemrajie had never limed with boys. Even when she went to university, she had done her work and come home. She could have gotten a boyfriend—other girls on campus who were even fatter and darker than she had done so. But Hemrajie had always been a good girl, and if her father had not died, he could have arranged for her to meet someone.

But he had, so she spent fifteen years caring for her mother and her retarded younger brother who was now in a government hospital because none of the sisters wanted him and because a private nursing home cost too much money. Hemrajie always thought the beatings her father had given her mother were why her younger brother had come out so.

Now Hemrajie lived quietly, taking care of the house, cooking every day, drawing money from the bank every month, worshipping God twice a week, and sitting on her porch each evening.

Feroza did not come the next evening. She was working the night shift for the next three days. So Hemrajie sat alone on the porch with her iced tea, enjoying the breeze, gazing out at the rippling green blades of the sugar cane. She did not notice the jogger coming up, and saw him only when he passed the house. His back still looked very straight and very strong. He was wearing dark-blue shorts this time and a purple jersey. She didn't know what he looked like—when he had passed back the day before, her gaze had been caught by his legs. Unlike many other Indian men, he did not have thin calves. The outside crease of his thigh muscles was deep and the inner balls just above the knees were very developed. He disappeared around the corner in the distance, and a taska truck, its iron trailer looking like a cell for some huge beast, appeared from the opposite direction, turning onto the dirt track just before the village. Harvest time was starting, and the trucks would be running for the next six weeks. When the fields were cleared, Hemrajie could see all the way to the factory where the canes were processed into sugar and molasses. Even with the cane arrows tall and uncut, smoke rose fitfully from the factory's blackened chimney.

The jogger reappeared within ten minutes, which meant he had not run very far. Hemrajie thought that he had probably run up to the first side track of the road where the cane cutters walked toward the massive scales to weigh their bundles, then turned back. He was moving at a slower pace now, but Hemrajie thought he still looked fit enough to be a marathon runner. As he came closer, she looked at his face. He was not handsome, but he had a square chin. He passed the house and glanced up, and before she turned her head, Hemrajie thought she saw him raise an eyebrow in acknowledgment. He seemed to be in his late thirties but could have been older, and he was very brown but not as dark-skinned as she. He ran down the road, again ignoring the men who were drinking outside the bar.

At twenty-five past six, Hemrajie went inside to watch *The Bold and the Beautiful*. Afterwards, she made some sada roti and tomato choka for dinner while she listened to the seven o'clock news. The kidnapped woman was still missing, but the family had gotten a ransom demand. With the TV on, Hemrajie ate while she read three chapters of a Patricia Cornwell novel. She had a large collection of murder mysteries but found the Cornwell pathologist the most believable detective of all. After she washed the dishes, Hemrajie watched a drama on Lifetime about a woman who discovers that her perfect husband is a psychotic killer.

At ten o'clock, she brushed her teeth, showered, and creamed her skin. When she went to bed, she took out a dildo from the bedside table drawer. Feroza had given it to her ten years ago, for her thirtieth birthday. "Is a cobweb cleaner," Feroza had said, tipsy from the wine she had drunk that evening. The two of them had gone to a restaurant for the occasion. Hemrajie had been shocked, but treated the gift as a joke, as had Feroza. But she had kept it and used it every other week or so. She would have used it more often but felt guilty. Her orgasms were much stronger with the object than with just her fingers, and she usually had two or three before she stopped. Then she would put it away, say her prayers, and lay in the darkness waiting for sleep to come. It was very quiet this night, as always, though Hemrajie thought she could hear the grinding of the factory over the way. It was only at that hour that she felt the emptiness of the house. She had thought of getting a pet, but she did not like dogs or cats. There were a few chickens in the coops downstairs which were for eating. She had plants in the front yard, though, and she reminded herself that she had to pay more attention to them now that the dry season was here.

After falling asleep, Hemrajie dreamed she was being chased. In the dream, she was able to run very fast from whoever was chasing her and she did not get tired at all.

Hemrajie was tending her plants when the jogger passed the next evening. She had just started watering the bougainvillea when she heard shoes beating a rhythm on the tarmac. Through the spaces between the bricks of the front wall, she saw him coming. He had a full lower lip and deep-set, small eyes. As he passed the big gate, Hemrajie got a better look at him. His nose was curved with flared nostrils. Small curls of hair were plastered sweatily to his neck. He passed so close to her wall that she could hear his deep breaths. But he did not see Hemrajie in her garden behind the wall, and she felt relieved.

She had done all the planting herself in the three years since her mother died. There were bougainvillea, crotons, hibiscus, oleander, sweet lime, and even a small palm tree at each corner of the front wall. But the yard was unkempt. The back of the house was bounded by a high brick wall, with piles of old wood, iron rods, barbed wire, and other rubbish. The chicken coops were there, and every month Hemrajie would twist the necks of a few birds, pluck and gut them, and put the cut parts into the freezer. She never had to buy meat. Under the house where Hemrajie parked her fifteen-year-old car was tamped dirt, but there was a concrete walkway to the small gate in the front wall and a gravel path to the larger double-gate that was only opened on the two days when Hemrajie went to the mandir and once every fortnight when she went to the grocery store. Two shallow concrete drains, black with moss, ran alongside the yard. Weeds sprang between the loose dirt that turned to mud in the wet season. Hemrajie had thought about planting lawn grass on the sides and back of the house, but that would have cost too much. So she got plants instead which filled the front yard with greenery and color and blocked the back from people's view.

When she finished watering her plants, Hemrajie took a trowel and a watering can, opened the small gate, and went outside. She had planted frangipani, jump-up-and-kiss-me, and Easter lilies along the wall. Grunting slightly, she stooped and began digging up weeds from between the flowers. She wore a dark-blue tracksuit and felt very warm. But the track-suit was baggy and Hemrajie was comfortable to be out on the road in it. It was only when she heard the sound of running shoes that she realized the man had not passed back. She kept her head turned away as he ran by, digging assiduously, but she felt his eyes boring into her bowed back. It seemed to Hemrajie as though long seconds were passing between each footfall. She looked around only when she could no longer hear the sound of his footsteps. He was wearing the maroon shorts again and another white jersey. His running shoes were gray with red stripes. Then a movement caught her eye, and she saw Geeta sitting on her porch. Hemrajie ducked her head and began digging again. Geeta was thirty-six, a housewife who sold barbecued chicken on the weekends outside her house. She had two children, a fourteen-year-old daughter and an eleven-year-old boy, and her husband was an accounts clerk in the Education Ministry. After a few more minutes of digging, Hemrajie got to her feet, wiping her hands on the front of her pants and picking up the bundle of weeds. Geeta, still on the porch, waved to Hemrajie, who waved back. But she knew Geeta would think she had come outside to look at the man.

It was only during a commercial break for *The Bold and the Beautiful* that it occurred to Hemrajie that Geeta had come out to watch the jogger too. She was not usually out on her porch in the evening because the sun hit her house directly at that hour. And Geeta was married. Although her two children had broadened her hips, she liked to wear fitted clothes to show off her still-smallish waist. She had been on her porch in a halter top and a denim skirt that reached above her knees. But Hemrajie knew that Geeta would not have come out if her husband had been home. The thought eased her mind, and she was able to concentrate on the rest of the show.

That night, Hemrajie went to bed an hour early. She felt tired and thought this was because of the work she had done in the garden.

"I feel I should start taking some exercise," Hemrajie told Feroza.

"Why?" Feroza asked. She was off for the weekend. Hemrajie had not sat on her porch for the past two evenings, finding that she was always busy with something inside the house or in the back with the bird pens.

"I do some work in the garden, and I find it leave me out of breath."

"Maybe you overexert yourself."

"And the doctor say my sugar kinda high."

"Ent you went for that check-up three months ago?"

"Yes. He tell me I should start taking exercise."

"Gardening is good exercise."

"I always do that. I was thinking of going for a walk in the evening."

Feroza took a sip of her coffee, which was still hot. "Nothing wrong with that."

"You will come with me?"

"Girl, look at me. I thin like a rake. You want me to disappear?"

"A li'l walking wouldn't make you disappear. Besides, you yourself say you breathing hard just from walking up the stairs."

"I'se get enough exercise with them patients," said Feroza.

"Oh gosh, come nah. I want the company."

Feroza took another sip of coffee, put down her cup, and unfolded her newspaper. "Oh, all right. When you want to start?"

"Tomorrow should be a good day," said Hemrajie.

The next evening, when the shadows had grown long, Hemrajie walked down to the corner to meet Feroza. "Which way you want to go?" Feroza asked. She was already waiting in front of the bar, wearing red track pants and a yellow T-shirt. Her pale arms protruded like sticks from the sleeves. Two men, Ricky and Vishnu, were sitting at one of the outside tables drinking beer.

"Let's walk down, nah," said Hemrajie. "I don't want to walk toward the sun." They headed into the village. Hemrajie walked with a light-footed stroll. But she noticed for the first time that Feroza had an odd gait. They were walking slowly, but she extended her legs out fully and swung her hands almost up to her flat chest, as though moving at a fast clip. And as Hemrajie saw the jogger round the corner ahead, she wished she had come out alone.

"Just now," she said. "My shoe feeling loose."

Feroza stopped and waited while Hemrajie stooped and pretended to tie her shoelaces. The jogger came up to them.

"Evening," he said. Hemrajie did not look up, and Feroza did not answer. He passed by and Hemrajie rose and they began walking again.

"Why you didn't tell the man good evening?" asked Hemrajie.

"I thought he was going to make some stupid comment."

"Why?"

"He look so. You know how Trini men is."

"Oh." They continued walking until they reached the corner.

"Turn back here?" Feroza said. The stretch of road beyond had no houses, but ran through a small forest.

"Yes," said Hemrajie. "We could reach the next end of the village and call it a day. That is a good distance for the first time out."

"Hm! Like you ambitious. The jogger fella inspire you or what?"

"Don't be silly," said Hemrajie. They headed back past the bar, which already had more men, past Hemrajie's house, and toward the end of the village. Hemrajie was perspiring, but Feroza's skin looked as cool as ever. They were both breathing more heavily. They passed the last house, a wooden structure on poles with a concrete annex behind, where a family of ten lived—Ameena and her husband Paul, their four children, Ameena's mother, and Paul's younger brother, his girlfriend, and their baby. "A little further?" Hemrajie said, glancing at Feroza.

Feroza, who had begun to slow, took a deep breath. "We have to watch out for them trucks," she said. "You know them drivers does drive mad sometimes."

"We won't go too far." The man was coming back. Hemrajie put a pleasant expression on her face, but instead of saying good evening as she intended, she just watched him. He nodded at her, without speaking, and passed. He had an unhandsome face, as she had thought, with sharp cheekbones and a set mouth. He was unshaven.

"He look kinda dougla," said Feroza.

Hemrajie glanced over her shoulder, where the man was already at the curve of the road. "You find? He look pure Indian to me."

"He kind of dark."

"I darker than he."

"You Indian dark. He look dark like Negro people."

"You want to turn here?" asked Hemrajie.

"Sure."

As they began walking back, a taska truck roared by, its giant cage rattling.

It was one month later that the accident, and the rape, happened. Hemrajie and Feroza had begun walking regularly. It was only in the first week that Hemrajie's thighs and ankles hurt. But she lost two pounds, and that encouraged her to continue. Feroza cut down to one cigarette when they sat on the porch, which they now did after their walks. They knew the people in the village had watched them at first, tongues wagging, but that soon stopped. The man continued to jog and would raise an eyebrow when he passed them. He never smiled. Feroza decided she did not like him.

"But why?" Hemrajie asked her.

"My blood just don't take him," she said.

"But you never talk to the man."

"You don't have to talk to somebody for your blood not to take them."

"Okay," said Hemrajie.

This conversation occurred after the day the jogger passed them at the bar when there was a promotion for a new brand of rum, and many men who were not from the village were liming outside. Hemrajie and Feroza had been walking back, and the man passed them from behind. He was wearing a pair of green and black shorts they had never seen before.

"Like he running faster these days," Hemrajie had said to Feroza.

"Hm."

Then they'd heard someone outside the bar say, "But watch how the Gruesome Twosome staring down the fella!" Hemrajie and Feroza pretended that they had not heard. But Feroza did not go home till after dark that evening, and Hemrajie missed *The Bold and the Beautiful*. They stopped walking to the bar and began heading in the other direction, and the next time they passed the jogger he nodded as usual. But Feroza said he was looking at them funny.

The accident happened on a Sunday. There were not many cars passing on the road, but the evening sun was very bright. Hemrajie and Feroza had planned to walk, and had already put on their tracksuits, but then changed their minds because it was so hot. They sat on the porch, Hemrajie drinking iced tea and Feroza, because of the heat, drinking iced coffee while she read the newspaper. The jogger passed by. He was wearing his maroon shorts and a blue jersey.

"He good to run in this heat," Hemrajie said.

"I think he ready for the marathon," said Feroza. The man passed the last house, running steadily, and vanished around the corner. A taska truck came out from the cane field, turned onto the road, and made its way toward the distant chimney. The canes would soon be harvested and then the land would look very big and very flat.

"They find the woman body," Feroza said. "The one who get kidnap last month."

"I thought the family pay the ransom."

"They still kill she."

"Anybody get arrested?"

Feroza sniffed. "Police does arrest police?"

"They do when is a Indian officer, you never notice?"

"True, true," Feroza said. She took a last gulp of her coffee and Hemrajie drained her glass of tea. The sun eased down to the horizon, but the man did not return.

"Like we friend making some extra distance today," Hemrajie said.

"Look so," said Feroza.

"You want to make a small walk? Work out some of this sugar?"

"All right."

It took them five minutes to reach the bend. The road stretched out to the far factory, but they did not see anyone running. A car sped by, the wind of its passing making their clothes flutter.

"That strange," Hemrajie said. "I don't think he woulda go so far."

"Maybe he take a run through the cane field."

"Maybe."

"We could walk up a li'l bit again."

They continued for another five minutes, by which time the sky was getting dim. It was only on their way back that Feroza saw something out of the corner of her eye. "What is that?" she said.

They stopped, peering through the canes. Then they saw him. He was lying in the middle of the field, several feet off the road. His head was twisted back, his arms and legs cast out limply.

"Oh God," said Hemrajie.

"Come," Feroza said.

They eased their way through the canes. Feroza knelt beside the man and put two fingers to his neck. Then she put her ear in front of his nose.

"He . . . ?" Hemrajie began, but did not complete the sentence.

"He not dead," said Feroza. "He unconscious."

"What happen to him?"

"Car hit him," said Feroza. "Or more likely the taska and the driver didn't notice." She peered in the dimming light at his nostrils and ears, then ran her hands over the man's head, down his arms, then his torso, then his legs. "Nothing broken," she said, as though talking to herself. She rose to her feet.

"What's that?" Hemrajie said.

Feroza looked down at the man's body. "What?"

"Uh, that," said Hemrajie. "In front. By his, uh . . ." Feroza bent down to look more closely, then pulled at the man's clothes. "Is his intestines?" Hemrajie asked. Feroza was blocking her.

"No," Feroza said. "Look at this." She moved aside. She had pulled down the man's shorts and Hemrajie saw that his penis was full and pointing bluntly to the sky.

"What—?"

Feroza ran her fingers along the man's hair again. "Uh-huh. A depression right here. He get hit on the head."

"But how—I mean—?"

Feroza sat on the ground. "We had a patient like this three years back. Young fella, about twenty-five. Get a blow to the head, right around the same spot. Was in a coma and had a permanent cockstand." She looked up at Hemrajie. "He was in the ward for three months. You could bet a few of the nurses take advantage of that."

"Advantage?"

"Yes. It was good."

Hemrajie stared at her friend in the dimming light of the cane field. "You mean—you?"

"Yes. Was more than ten years since I get something."

Hemrajie continued to stare.

"Oh, don't watch me so," Feroza said. "Was no harm."

"What happen to the patient?"

Feroza shrugged. "He never come out of the coma." She looked down at the man's penis, then reached out and put her hand around the swollen shaft. "I tell you he was dougla."

Hemrajie laughed, then her hand flew to her mouth. "You shouldn't be doing that!"

Feroza looked up at Hemrajie. "Why you don't take something?" she said. Her tongue slid delicately over her front teeth. "You never had a man. Now is your chance." She glanced down at the jogger. "He will never know."

"I couldn't," said Hemrajie. "I couldn't do that."

"Why not?" Feroza's voice was low, cajoling.

"We have to get him help."

"We will. But his vital signs stable. No harm."

"I can't," said Hemrajie.

Feroza got off the ground, but did not let go of the jogger's penis. "Well, I going to," she said in the same low voice.

"What?" said Hemrajie. "Suppose he have AIDS!"

Feroza shook her head. "He does take care of himself."

"Feroza!"

"It dark. No one will see." She grinned. "But you could watch and learn how to do it." With her other hand, Feroza slipped down her pants and her panties, then squatted on top of the man. She eased down with a deep sigh. Her hips began to move and, underneath the hem of her jersey in the dim light, Hemrajie could see the shaking of Feroza's pale shanks. In a few minutes she stiffened, grunted, and her hands turned to claws on the man's unmoving shoulders. She stood, pulling up her underwear and track pants in one movement. "I'll go by you and phone for the ambulance. You wait here with him. Give me your house keys." Hemrajie reached into her pants pockets and handed over the keys. Feroza took them and turned to push her way out of the cane. She glanced back at Hemrajie. "It go take me twenty minutes to go and come back. And the ambulance probably won't be here in less than an hour. I mightn't even reach back before half-hour."

"All right," Hemrajie said. "I will wait."

Feroza left, and Hemrajie stood in the middle of the canes under the starry sky. After a while, she stooped down and she saw that Feroza had not pulled up the man's shorts. She reached out, then hesitated. Slowly, she put her face closer. Except for a picture from a magazine when she was twenty-three, she had never seen a man's penis. The light from the moon was enough for her to see details—the pulled balls, the thick vein on the underside, the swoop of the helmeted head, even the intimate slit at the top. Hemrajie thought how ugly the penis was, and how beautiful. She reached out timidly and put her fingers around it. It did not feel anything like her dildo. It was firm yet had give. It had a throb and a warmth. It was alive.

She looked around. The canes were a wall of black lances and the moonlit road beyond was empty and silent. Hemrajie pulled down her pants to her knees. She didn't wear panties when she walked because they rode up. She would just rub him against herself, she thought, just to see what it felt like. She moved on top of the man, feeling his hard flesh poking at her soft and secret place. She held his penis and moved it against herself. She did not intend to put it in. But he was so hard and she was so wet and it slipped so easily into her. She rested her weight on him and began moving her hips as Feroza had done. This was what she had never known, and she closed her eyes and imagined that she was in her bed on her honeymoon, and she quickened her hips and came within moments.

Hemrajie's head drooped in release. She took a deep breath. He was still inside her, still hard, as she started to ease off his body. And she saw his face in the moonlight, and the strength ran out of her legs, and she sank, helpless, back onto his erect shaft. In the clear light of the moon, the man's eyes were open and aware and staring mutely at her.

# THE FUNERAL PARTY

BY SHANI MOOTOO

*San Fernando*

Matilda Jasodhra Mansing would not wear black. Her concession to funereal tradition on the occasion of her husband's burial was blue. She had commissioned the dress from April Lang, Trinidad's finest designer, a long time ago. *Design me something*, she had said, *something spectacular for when he dies, should I be blessed with life so long, and do make me something, something less garish but certainly leaning toward the spectacular, for my own day, my own day of reckoning.*

Once the word had been given, the paper creation was put into production, a conversation in silk and satin about nature and origins—not so much the flora but the fauna of Trinidad invoked, alongside suggestions of the theater of Carnival—feathers, that is, and wings, sequins, iridescence, all of these commingling with the subtler concupiscence evoked by the Indian sari (teasing translucence, tightly bound and bound and bound, as if to influence deportment, yet an exposé, par excellence, of the wearer's physical attributes)—a provocative concoction, in short, delivered post haste, for the occasion. The fabrics, the sequins, the feathers, all shimmered in disturbing shades of blue.

For relief there was gold. An abundance of it. Gold laced her neck and dipped into the cleavage of her bodice, dangled from her ears, ringed her fingers and both forearms wrist to elbow, as if she carried on her all the pieces her now-dead goldsmith-and-jeweler-in-general husband had presented to her. (*Bribes*, she gloats, pleased that she was in such a manner bribable.) This particular excess fortified the lie in the concession to wear what one would previously have simply termed *blue*.

She arrived late to Selvon's Funeral Parlour in San Fernando. The yardman, the same one who had been employed by the Mansings for some thirty years now, walked in behind her, tied and suited—and wasn't that a gold watch chain dangling from his belt?—faintly, perplexingly recognizable-but-not-entirely so to neighbors who, passing by the Mansing house, would have seen him in his other yardly incarnation, tied and suited like a mimic lord.

The new widow was late arriving because the updo of her hair, the first time it had been styled, was to her tastes unsuitable, too austere. Her stylist had been obliged to wash, set, dry, tease, comb, and spray the do all over again until there was an upsweep reminiscent of at least one of the wings of the Nike of Samothrace, the sculpture in the Louvre in Paris where she and John had honeymooned. In seeing the headless statue, so early in their marriage, there occurred an immediate self-recognition—not the present self, but the one she would become: strong, on the wing, a soar of stone. She would have her hairdresser create the symbolic wing of her funereal costume, precisely on her very present head, a declaration that John Lucknow Mansing had not succeeded in driving her crazy.

At seventy-nine years of age, one her husband's junior, and for a while not so limber anymore, she finally gave in to the necessity of a walking cane. Hers, a gift from the yardman, was fashioned out of a broomstick, carved to resemble a snake coiled around a hibiscus tree trunk. Two rubies, no doubt taken from the dead jeweler's stash, marked the snake's eyes.

From Matilda Jasodhra Mansing's temples, neck, and wrists rose the scents of oil of geranium and ylang ylang to stem the staining fragrance of chloroform, the netherworld candle-smoke odors of a funeral parlor, and later, under the umbrella of a samaan tree at the San Fernando Lapeyrouse Cemetery, the fetid dampness of freshly dug, worm-ridden earth.

Meera Meera Johna Mansing, John and Matilda's spinster, middle-aged, son-to-her-father, daughter-to-her-mother, female-born but gender-shifting like sunlight through a leafy tree on a windy day only child, tore herself away from Vishala (or was it Amanda, perhaps it was Brianni, or maybe Carmen that time?)—to whom she had been making passionate like amongst breadcrumbs, mustard seeds, flecks of arugula, shards of prosciutto, parts of meals they fed each other between play in a Brooklyn brownstone—and traveled hundreds of miles to Bel Air, La Romain, Trinidad, not because her mother told her to come and dispense with those damned termite-pocked, moth-eaten butterfly exhibition cases in which she felt Meera Meera Johna was implicated (having caught the butterflies for her father decades ago) and not because Meera Meera Johna was curious to see who would and who would not attend her father's funeral—all reasons enough—but because it was from him she had learned the crafts she had been practicing when her mother's phone call interrupted to say that "they"—meaning she and the yardman, for it was apparently "they" who made decisions nowadays—had taken her father off the respirator, and after ten days in a coma he had slipped quietly away, and it was to him she owed debts of gratitude.

As if it were not enough that he was her father.

\* \* \*

"Me-me, come child, catch Papa a butterfly, will you?" John Lucknow Mansing would say.

"Did you see a *Morpho* today, Papa? Or shall I just get you a monarch?"

In childhood Meera Meera Johna was in awe of her father, thinking him then no ordinary indiscriminate collector but a specialist, for the ordinary orange and black monarch, and the considerably less common *Morpho*, were all he ever wished her to net him. Once, or twice, and in a blue moon, even thrice a season, mischievous rapacious wind currents twirling over the Guyanese rain forests would go after a *Morpho*, curl themselves about the unfortunate one, spin it about until it was rendered as if in a drugged state, and that wind would propel and haul, propel and haul the thing, at times like an iridescent blue handkerchief, at other times like an oversized candy foil wrapper, all the way from its native Guyana, high above the churning where the Caribbean Sea and the Atlantic do violent trade, to Bel Air, La Romain in southern Trinidad, where the wind, bored now and having spotted something else to toy with, the *Anartia amathea*—smaller, more delicate than the *Morpho*, and its simple red color a relief—the wind would drop the inextinguishably exquisite blue thing, drop it like a penny to the ground, only to sidle up now to *Anartia amathea* in the next phase of its serial-courting nature. *Morphos*, for this reason, on coming to what was left of their senses, remained rather dazed, and although they picked up their somewhat ragged, slightly ego-bruised selves, they were easy to net.

What John Lucknow Mansing did with these *Morphos*, their blue the inspiration for numerous Carnival and other kinds of costumes, what he did with these, for they disappeared soon after they were caught, remained a mystery until the day of his funeral. On the other hand, the monarchs that had been stretched and pinned were reduced by time to small orderly mounds of shiny dust in the cases that lined the walls of John Lucknow Mansing's private study, under the shut doors of which, when he was alive, seeped the disturbing stench of chloroform.

*Me-me, catch me a butterfly*, is what he would say, offering his daughter the net.

Then came a Sunday that began like any other Sunday but turned out to be like none at all.

That very net led Meera Meera Johna by her nose, caused her to skip and trip up, down, and around behind a magnificent *Morpho*, the biggest she or her father had ever seen, one the size of a small child's head, as sapphire one minute as the tropical sky at night, as silver and turquoise as the gulf the next, a butterfly-bird rising and falling on ribbons of ocean winds, a siren of iridescence drawing Meera Meera Johna through the front gate up the road past six houses and two corners, causing her to trespass up up up the high wide red-painted concrete stairs of Isabella Tatiana's shrub and flower-surrounded bungalow. There, on Isabella Tatiana's generous terrazzo-tiled veranda, Meera Meera Johna was suddenly breathless, and perched on the railing of an overly ornate wrought-iron balcony, she reached out, the net agape, for the flying thing, such a perfect present for her father, when it leaped lithely over the railing and was caught in a swirling current of air. It flapped its wings and, gaining control of itself, rose higher and higher, and once above the rooftops of the neighborhood, it stopped flapping its wings and merely glided. She had the good sense not to try and follow it.

The wall-length sliding doors to Isabella Tatiana's house were drawn wide apart.

"Mrs. Tatiana?" Meera Meera Johna whispered from the

balcony. There was no answer, so she called again. "Hello, Mrs. Tatiana? Are you there?"

She could have been a lucky thief that day, if she were so inclined. On tiptoe still, she entered and followed the net around walls and down the high-pile blue-red-taupe Afghan-carpeted corridors that ended at a closed door through which low calls and moans wafted. Meera Meera Johna pressed her ear to the door to be sure and heard. A groan. Not an urgent or ugly groan but still, a groan. If someone behind a closed door were making a sound like that, whether ugly or not, wouldn't you assume they might be in need of some assistance, she asked herself?

Meera Meera Johna called again: "Hello?" The groaning persisted, the sound of pleasure, curiously, and she, if she could be heard, was ignored. She turned the door's handle, waited, and called again. So, unnoticed, she walked right in.

Meera Meera Johna saw everything. Realizing that the two on the bed were in no hurry and were oblivious to all, and that if she were to return and in earnest concentrate on the goings-on in there, she would need a little something to eat, she left the room in search of the little something. She shut the door as she might have shut any door, caring nothing about making door-closing noises—after all, the two were oblivious to all. She located the kitchen, and the refrigerator, and found in its freezer compartment a tub of milkweed-and-chrysanthemum flavored ice cream.

That Sunday, a Sunday like no other Sunday, Meera Meera Johna returned to the neighbor's bed on the edge of which she sat, a perfect chrysanthemum-and-leaf-of-milkweed ice-cream sundae wilting, and, still unnoticed, she studied her father, his cacao-colored skin richly, steamily aglow, and she regarded the woman beneath him, hers paler than white, whose groaning

Meera Meera Johna came to understand declared, *Yes, uhuh uhuh, yes*, her eyes shut, torso arched, neatly pinned by her hands and feet atop a velvet coverlet the deep saffron color of pollen, her hair held tightly in John Lucknow's fist. An interesting situation, Meera Meera Johna pondered, the way Isabella stretched and pushed her pelvis upward, mothlike, and her father like a wasp atop, his pelvis just barely flicking the moth's.

That very night, when the Mansing family sat at the dinner table, at precisely the time Meera Meera Johna finished posing the question to her father why that afternoon when Isabella Tatiana was groaning, he continued to perch so long on top of her, Matilda Jasodhra, a pale, frail woman—as yet unwinged—who looked as if she had long been chidden by the sun, halted her gleaming brass fork in mid-flight toward her mouth and took studious note of the cube of rare agouti meat—which she herself had barbecued—skewered on its prongs. She brought her fork, agouti untouched, to rest on the brim of her fine bone china plate, an act accorded the precision and delicacy of one experiencing an awakening. She just as carefully, thoughtfully, lifted the sweating stemmed water glass, and sipped from it ice-cold water. Matilda Jasodrha Mansing, once she had set the goblet back on the table, shot up her nose and chin to the ceiling with less delicacy now, and with a flamboyant flick of her head determined that she, she had had, she had had absolutely enough. Matilda Jasodhra thawed back to life, and John was spared having to answer Meera Meera Johna's burning question when his wife belted out, "We will have a party. A big, big party with music. Lots and lots of music. Live. Cha cha cha. Cha cha cha. I shall oversee the entire thing myself, and everybody shall come to it. Including That Tatiana Woman." Matilda

Jasodhra took it into her hands that day to grow her very own wings.

The day of the party, just outside the front entrance to the house, the yardman had been clearing away the unsavory evidence of day-to-day yard existences—brown fallen leaves, weeds, a wind-borne candy wrapper—when he came upon a corner that was infested with snakes. He was, at the moment the neighborhood children led by Meera Meera Johna appeared, ramming a broomstick straight down into a hole. He had anesthetized the snakes with chloroform, a bottle of it given to him for this very purpose by his butterfly-collecting jeweler boss, and was now shoving, shoving, shoving into the hole one of these garden snakes that had minutes before been a smooth, brilliant green thing the length of a man and a bit, sunning itself on a hibiscus shrub, but was now rumpled into numerous odd angles that oozed and squirted liquids in tones of browns and reds. The gardener was shoving the snake into the hole, killing it again, and again, just to make sure, he explained when they said to him, voices full of awe, "But the thing dead already, why you beating it so? It coulda make a good skipping rope if you hadn't a mash it up so." He looked up at them, his eyes—what should normally have been the whites of his eyes, red-red-red, and the pupils, black-black-black—like jumbie beads, the children whispered among themselves later. They watched him move from hole to hole until he had tucked away five garden snakes in all. In the childrens' peripheral vision shuffled the less arresting single-file procession of fifty women marching up the street, approaching the servant's gate at the back of the Mansing house. They were all dressed exactly alike, in white servant shirts with rounded frilly collars, and black narrow knee-length skirts, black stockings, and black closed-up shoes. Each pushed a two-tiered trolley laden with dishes on which courses of catered food were artfully splayed.

"Meera Meera Mansing, inside now. Time to dress. It's late and getting later by the minute. Come now." Her mother's voice shot through the house, taut yet euphoric, from the bedroom section down to the front garden, and Meera Meera Johna responded in a flash, leaving her friends to the hands of the yardman.

Just before seven o'clock, from the front of the house an infectious *Cha cha cha, Cha cha cha, Cha cha cha* wafted up to the bedroom section. Meera Meera Johna lifted her skirt, tugged at the scratchy crinoline beneath, twisted it, and tugged some more. Her mother snapped at her, *Stop lifting your skirt.* Her scalp hurt too, her hair having been combed back velvet smooth into a ponytail. Meera Meera Johna raised her eyebrows and wiggled her ears in an attempt to weaken the grip. Her mother was leading her down to the party when they both saw the light coming from under the door of John Lucknow's studio. Forever alert to his abundant furtivenesses—for what else could one call it?—Matilda Jasodhra yanked her daughter along and they both pressed their ears to the door. They heard nothing save for the muted vibration of *Cha cha cha, Cha cha cha.* Matilda Jasodhra tried the knob of the door. It was locked. She banged, and John Lucknow's voice, it was indeed his, responded sharply, *What?* Matilda squealed at him to open the door. He did. That dreadful sweet scent of chloroform assaulted her and Meera Meera Johna, and she wondered, as she always did, why it hadn't as yet done him in. He held in his hands his jeweler's glass. *Working?* she wondered. *Working right up to the last minute before the party?* She glanced—not so discreetly, so perhaps she gazed rather than glanced—throughout the room, vision gaining the amorphous properties of air that allowed it to float and bend so that she could see around to the back of the desk and behind curtains, and seeing that he was alone, she breathed a sigh of relief. He too sighed. Then she saw a tray of butterflies on his desk. *Leave those damned butterflies alone, why don't you,* Matilda Jasodhra whispered between her teeth, *and come. Our guests will arrive any time now.* John Lucknow sent her on down with an assurance that he would be there in seconds. *Why? What for? What on earth for? How odd,* she thought, but that was her husband, and on down to the front of the house she and her daughter went.

Faces Meera Meera Johna knew from television bounced about on bodies the TV seldom showed: There was, at her parents' party, the mayor of the city (whose legs were, it seemed to her, too short for his body), the minister of health (whose feet were very small), the minister of security (whose belly strained against his white shirt), other politicians, entertainment celebrities, various neighbors, some close friends, a handful of relatives, and the president of the country, Sir Oswald Jones (whose legs were long and whose shoes were very shiny) and his wife, Lady Oswald Jones (whose calves were muscular). And yes, that was her—the Tatiana woman whom Meera Meera Johna congratulated herself for recognizing as she had only before seen her once, and she was then in a reclining position, her hair held tightly in one of John Lucknow Mansing's hands. Meera Meera Johna stared at the Tatiana woman. Matilda Jasodhra put a stiff and warning hand on her daughter's back and shoved her toward Their Excellencies. Meera Meera Johna moved forward, Isabella Tatiana trapped in her peripheral vision. *Where is my father?* she wondered. *Still in the study? Why isn't he here to meet the guests?* And then

Meera Meera Johna pondered: *She, Isabella Tatiana, known in one part of our house as That Tatiana Woman, is what must be called beautiful. She must be more beautiful than my mother or me.* Isabella Tatiana moved from Meera Meera Johna's peripheral vision to its forefront. They locked eyes. Tatiana's were greenish-gray. Her hair was dark brown. Open, it was long. Wavy. She was tall, she was slim and her skin pale. She smiled incessantly. She wore a black dress with no straps. Meera Meera Johna wondered how such a dress stayed up. Isabella Tatiana wore only one speck of jewelry, a silver ring on a finger, and from it flashed beams of iridescent blue, turquoise, black. She smiled still. Her lips were bright but, if Meera Meera were not mistaken, they were naturally so, no lipstick that is, and they seemed soft. She wore shiny black high-heeled shoes that showed her toes. Her toes were—

Matilda Jasodhra caught her daughter's distraction and dug her fingers into her daughter's shoulders. Meera Meera Johna winced. Isabella Tatiana's smile broadened, but only, Meera Meera Johna thought, for Meera Meera Johna herself to see, and . . . and. And she winked. That was a wink, wasn't it? All of this, but Meera Meera Johna, nevertheless, drew to her mother's attention.

A man, whose face was unknown to her, instructed her in a jovial, mischievous, and booming voice that she should ask the nation's president for absolutely-absolutely anything her little heart desired, and surely-surely it would be granted. The other guests laughed, raucously. Her Excellency Lady Oswald Jones, wearing around her neck a heavy silver chain (that drew attention to itself and away from her bony neck) from which hung a silver pendant inlaid with dazzling blue patterns, managed a stony smile. Meera Meera Johna's eyes grew big. As much as she was tempted to bring notice to the unfortunate fashion *faux pas*, Meera Meera Johna kept to herself this queerness. By drawing on knowledge garnered from watching and listening to the main woman in her life, her mother that is, she intuitively conjectured that mentioning the *faux pas* would surely embarrass the two women, and without any hint of her distraction she simply looked up into the president's eyes and said, "Really?"

His Excellency laughed and told her to whisper in his ear and he would do his utmost to please her. A squawking chortle erupted on the patio again. His Excellency stooped and Meera Meera Johna whispered away. The president's face stiffened and he turned gray. He pulled Meera Meera Johna to his chest, pressed her head against him, then whispered back to her, but at least one person heard him say, "I don't know why he was perched on her. I don't think that is what was happening. Are you sure you weren't seeing things?"

Meera Meera Johna understood in an instant, and tried again, "Can I ask another question then?" The president, hesitant this time but bending to the pressure of the audience around him, moved his ear to Meera Meera Johna's lips. He heard her question and pulled away as if she had spat. He peered across to the far room at his host John Lucknow Mansing, cavorting some distance away. He glanced up quickly at Matilda Jasodhra. He looked at his own wife, and then he looked back at Meera Meera Johna. He shoved his lips in her ear. They tickled her.

"But of course they love each other," he was heard to say. "How else would you have come into this world? Look at them. Just look at this lovely evening, all these lovely people. They must love each other to be able to create this sort of enjoyable occasion. Now, young lady," the president continued, "who would you like to be like when you grow up? Have you any heroes?"

Meera Meera Johna thought for a moment and then said, "My father." The guests clapped their hands in giddy agreement.

The president said, "Well, that is assured. That I can grant you. The sins of the father, et al. But a note of caution, my child. Take care of what you wish for. You may, to your delight—or horror—get it!"

The man with the booming voice said, "Your Excellency, *par excellence!*" There was laughter, and then John Lucknow Mansing finally arrived on his patio, a good few minutes after his guests. All attention turned to him.

Meera Meera Johna extracted herself from the president's grip. She inhaled until her chest was as taut as the skin of a balloon, and forced herself to give brave answers to questions like, *So, what class are you in now,* and, *Who made that lovely dress for you,* and, *What are you eating, child, that is making you grow so tall and so pretty?* She took happy note: She was a capable child, capable of all of this, and her chest, still full of air, did not split, nor did a single strand of hair escape the elastic that was now like the fastener on a bag in which her heavy brain pulsed.

Meera Meera Johna had to endure an eternity of ten minutes of adults talking to her as if she were a trick puppy, throughout which she distracted herself by watching her mother. She was impressed by her mother's administration, the way, like a concert director using the barest nod or a concentrated look, she conducted the servants. Her mother did more with the yardman though. He had been standing still with a tray of empty cocktail plates and scrunched napkins held up shoulder height in one hand (his jumbie-bead eyes indiscreetly jumped about the room, from her mother to the various guests to her father to Isabella Tatiana back on to her mother). Matilda Jasodhra Mansing went over to him and whispered briskly, orders no doubt, for he busied himself. He walked back and forth now, but with the same tray of empty cocktail plates and scrunched napkins. Then, with an equal briskness, she turned to Meera Meera Johna and ushered her back into the depths of the house. On the way, far from the presence of the guests, and outside of earshot of the household staff, Matilda Jasodhra Mansing tightened her grip on her daughter's shoulders and sternly demanded, "What did you ask Sir Oswald?"

To which Meera Meera Johna whispered, "Nothing. Honest, Mummy. Nothing."

Matilda Jasodhra, although she had not heard her daughter's questions nor the president's answers, knew her daughter well enough to reply, "What is wrong with you? Why are you always asking those horrific questions? Why can't you simply behave yourself, Meera Meera Johna Mansing? Change into your pajamas and get into your bed this instant. I don't want to hear another peep from you."

Long after she was supposed to have been asleep in her bed, Meera Meera Johna got out, crept in the shadows down to the front of the house, into the living room. The three-tiered crystal chandelier that hung from the high ceiling cast dancing prisms of color on the wood floor. The smell of the polish the yardman had applied that morning still lingered. The room had been vacated of almost all furniture except for some chairs pulled up against one part of the wall. In the low light she moved against the wall and slipped into a corner behind a tall blue-and-white-patterned Chinese vase out of which a *Monstera deliciosa* grew. She crouched down and was well-hidden. The guests had eaten dinner, and dancing and drinking in earnest were just beginning.

Matilda Jasodhra moved about the room, *Cha cha chatting* a minute here, another there, all the while catching the eyes of servers and her yardman, who seemed to only need a nod from her to know what it was she wanted. Her father was with a group of men, and Isabella Tatiana That Tatiana Woman was with them. Meera Meera Johna, peeping through one of the holes in a leaf of the *Monstera deliciosa,* wondered how her dress stayed up without any straps, and was surprised to find that thoughts on the matter made her, very strangely, dizzy, but a dizziness that she, strange to her, enjoyed. These word-less thoughts caused tickles in her mouth, tickles that felt as if they were caused by the wings of butterflies brushing against the interior contents of her chest, and around the inner exterior of her knees, and in between her toes.

A man had his arm around the white woman Isabella Ta-tiana That Tatiana Woman's waist—*Was it her father's arm, or another man's arm?*—and she, Isabella Tatiana That Tatiana Woman, had her hand on someone's back, the back of a man who closely resembled her father. And then Meera Meera Johna had to close her eyes and shake her head. *How could two women show up at the same party wearing similar necklaces and pendants?* She was sure Isabella Tatiana had worn no jewelry to the party, yet now she wore the same silver chain around her neck as Her Excellency. *Perhaps Her Excellency gave her own necklace to Isabella Tatiana,* thought Meera Meera Johna. Or then again, perhaps Isabella Tatiana had stolen it from Her Excellency. There was just too much confusion around these adults and Meera Meera Johna became tense—even more tense, that is—and felt a little bit nauseous. Flashes of irides-cent blue darted from the pendant that pulled the chain in an insistent and perfect V but stopped just short of tucking itself into her cleavage. Turquoise one flash, then full-moon blue, and full-moon blue again, then black, and back to turquoise, full-moon blue, full-moon blue, as if in time with the *Cha cha cha, Cha cha cha*. She wanted to jump out from behind her leaf and tell someone about the possibility of a theft. Anyone. But in truth, the necklace looked a hundred times better on the smooth pale skin of Isabella Tatiana. *Good for her*, Meera Meera Johna thought suddenly, *even if she stole it*. Then Meera Meera Johna saw that the man who resembled her father was indeed her father and that it was her father who was hugging Isabella Tatiana. Or so it seemed. It is not easy to see clearly through the hole in a philodendron's leaf.

The man-who-resembled-her-father-who-was-her-father's fingertips rested on the beautiful Tatiana woman's hip bone. Meera Meera Johna imagined her father perched on this woman whom he (or perhaps not he) was hugging, and with the thought came that dizziness, delightful one second, nauseating the next, and there were, too, those butterfly-wing kinds of tickles as seconds before.

She looked away to her mother who was outside on the patio. Her mother's gaze shot repeatedly to those of the guests with whom she chatted, all the way across the almost empty living room (straight past the philodendron plant) to the room in which her father, and most of the men, and That Tatiana Woman had gathered. Her mother glanced back and forth, her mouth paralyzed in the shape of a smile.

Meera Meera Johna concentrated again on her father. His fingers tapped, just barely tapped that hip bone in time, and rubbed the hip bone out of time, and then tapped it in time again to the music. He extracted himself and went to speak to the deejay. Isabella Tatiana's eyes followed him. The deejay spun in his swivel chair to reach a pile of albums. He showed them to her father and her father nodded. The music changed

from a slinky-sounding *Cha cha cha* piece to the most popular calypso of the day. In an instant, all the guests began to
move their bodies to the beat. In sudden haste, the men and
women from both sides came together into the center of the
room. The room had filled up fast and with so many people it
darkened.

Lady Oswald walked over to Meera Meera Johna's father.
They walked together, several steps away from all the guests.
Sir Oswald watched them from a distance, and his face grew
darker than the room. Lady Oswald seemed to be scolding
Meera Meera Johna's father. Her father pulled Lady Oswald
to him, gave her a small kiss on her cheek, danced away to the
light switch on the wall, and, although the room was already
dark, dimmed the chandelier so much more that Meera Meera
Johna could have stood up and waved her hands and not have
been spotted. Lady Oswald stayed still, her back to the rest of
the party. She fixed her hair, but she stayed for a good while
where she was. The men were beginning, one by one, to loosen
their ties and undo the top buttons of their shirts.

Meera Meera Johna watched her father. He was bringing, onto what had been turned into a dance floor, Isabella
Tatiana That Tatiana Woman with the black dress the dress
that had no straps the dress that had no straps that somehow
how on earth it stayed up, and her long wavy hair so wavy. He
kept his tie fastened, and did not dance like the other men
in what was called a "break-away," but in his hand he held
one of the woman's, and the other hovered on her waist. He
seemed to push and pull her with that hand. They grinned at
one another. Lady Oswald walked through the dancing crowd
to her husband and he gripped her hand and seemed to pull
her hard, to march her straight toward the stairs that exited
the house.

Meera Meera Johna's mother suddenly appeared, walking hurriedly through the mass of dancing people, bumping hard against her father as he danced with this woman. "Oh, I'm sorry, excuse me," she said, her eyes aflame and watery, her mouth still pinned in a smile, but a ragged one now. John Lucknow Mansing let go of That Tatiana Woman as if he had been stung by her hip and her hand, and in an action as smooth as a dance move he wrestled with the reluctant wrist of his wife as he pulled her to dance with them. She continued to try to wrangle her wrist from John's grip while biting the lower lip of her still smile-shaped mouth. The water in her eyes tried in vain to extinguish their fire. She pointed beseechingly to something on the patio. Meera Meera Johna looked in that direction, but there were no guests there as they were now all on the dance floor, leaving the yardman to pick up their empties. Meera Meera Johna was sure she caught his jumbie-bead eyes watching her parents, and there was that sickening feeling in her tummy again. John Lucknow Mansing did not even look in the direction of the patio in which his wife was pointing, but shook his head and seemed to insist that she stay and dance. The floor was so crowded that Meera Meera Johna couldn't now see what was happening without imposing herself, but in a second her mother had yanked her hand from her husband's and left the room. Meera Meera Johna hoped her mother would not return and interrupt everything again.

Her father reached his arm around the Tatiana woman's waist, pulled her to him, this time closer, tighter, firmer. One of his men friends shimmied up to Meera Meera Johna's father and the woman; he thrust his arms in the air and his pelvis was aimed at the woman's. Meera Meera Johna's father had a glazed grin sealed on his face. He stepped back to indicate permission, then spun around on one heel to arrive again next to the woman. The man had by this time finished his gyration, and spoke to Meera Meera Johna's father. Meera Meera Johna's father lifted his face to the chandelier, closed his eyes, and had a full laugh. He looked the man in his eyes and shook his head, as if to say, "You know!" The man backed away in time to the music. Meera Meera Johna's father and the woman put their arms around each other, and they danced side by side. The woman put her lips to Meera Meera Johna's father's ear and they moved about there. Meera Meera Johna's father did not look at her but nodded. He let go of her, slipped away from her, and spun around again.

Her mother did not return, but the following morning, by pressing her ears to the closed doors of her parents' bedroom, she heard her mother say, ". . . not divorce you, not over my dead body . . . not after all that I have . . . for you . . . and Meera Meera Johna . . ." (Meera Meera Johna was both pleased and frightened, and felt oddly guilty, to have been mentioned.) "And I want to know what your relationship . . . Lady Oswald . . . No wonder Sir Oswald . . . Sir Oswald should have . . . you . . . I will . . . you suffer . . . will have to live with me for the rest of your life." Meera Meera Johna ate breakfast alone, and then she went out into the yard with her butterfly net in the hope of catching, not her father, but her mother, one big blue butterfly.

Mee Mee Jo, as Brooklynites Vishala, Ursela, Tanya, Susana, Rhonda, etc., called her, was in a most delightful and, so, unfortunate position when she received the first call from her mother telling her that her father had, as she had long worried might happen, succumbed to the effects of breathing in an excess of chloroform.

On pulling Vishala's lavender-colored spandex strapless top up over Vishala's head in a hot and flustered state, it occurred to her that she could use the stretchy thing to tie Vishala's hands together, so she did just that as Vishala made a brilliant show of mock protest, flinging her head from side to side, and wincing, begging for forgiveness. Mee Mee Jo then reached under the lined polyester skirt to find that Vishala had worn no underwear. This so excited Mee Mee Jo she put her mouth to Vishala's and kissed her softly in gratitude. Then she held the top of Vishala's skirt and pulled it down and down, side by side, and the hand-tied Vishala struggled slightly even as she lifted herself to make the removal easy, and Mee Mee Jo, having got the thing down, used it to tie the feet of her gorgeous prey who kept on whispering *pleasepleaseplease* and *uhuh uhuh uhuh*. Mee Mee Jo lay her naked body on top of her Vishala, grabbed a handful of her long and wavy hair, and held it just tight enough to give the impression of brute force, even as one of the fingers of that same hand stroked Vishala's face in tenderness, and when Mee Mee Jo placed her hand, hard and stiff, on Vishala's neck, Vishala gave a cry of pleading and desire all at once, and Mee Mee Jo's entire body was seized by a raging desire of her own. She achingly, slowly lowered her pelvis toward Vishala's, Vishala's thrust upward impatiently wanting, and was about to flick herself at her prey when the phone rang. She would not have answered had it not been for the special ring assigned to her mother.

What Matilda Jasodhra didn't tell her daughter was that the police were about to take her into their vehicle to transport her to police headquarters to find out why certain articles of her clothing were drenched in the deathly sweetness of chloroform, and why John Lucknow (ill-luck then, really) Mansing had cotton fibers in his lungs, and markings of chloroform about his nose and mouth, and just as she was lifting a leg into the vehicle—the yardman trying desperately and in vain to insist that his madam was innocent of everything on earth, so desperately that he had to be restrained—the detective in charge received a call on his cell phone, and after speaking for ten seconds with him and ten with the forensic doctor, she was let go. Oswald Jones, now an old man who had long ago divorced his wife and who, after an initiative led by him in Parliament, was appointed President For Life, had himself, himveryself, telephoned—no one questioned how he might have known of certain details of the current situation, but his foresight in many matters had long been recognized and heralded—and the case was post-haste slammed shut.

What she did tell her daughter was that the newspaper headlines the day after her husband's, her father's, death read, *Butterfly Killer's Death Ruled, a Case of Nature's Revenge*. Ignoring the typo, she quoted over the telephone, *Yesterday morning southern jeweler and amateur lepidopterist John Lucknow Mansing, eighty years of age, fell asleep on a wad of chloroform-soaked cotton intended for live butterflies*, and immediately got on with the business of focusing on dangers associated with butterfly keeping in particular and with animal-related hobbies in general.

Meera Meera Johna Mansing flew to Trinidad in time for her father's funeral, and to clean up the butterfly mess in his study. There was not to be found there a single one of the beautiful *Morphos* she had been so proud as a child to net her father. *Oh well*, she thought, *how like him*.

The funeral service itself, at the Grant Monorail Presbyterian Church, was a gathering of mostly women, all of whom were divorced or had separated from their husbands, three-

quarters of whom wore silver necklaces, or earrings, or rings on their fingers, or belts around their waists, and—it was Meera Meera Johna who first noticed—on some part of the surface of every piece of silver at that funeral was embedded bits of blue *Morpho* wings, in patterns that varied from flower-like shapes and waves of an ocean to scales of a fish or a snake. There at the front, in spitting distance from Matilda Jasodhra Mansing, was Isabella Tatiana, winking and smiling still at Meera Meera Johna, sporting in her old age a slight *Cha cha cha* tremble, and Meera Meera Johna noticed that even in her wrinkled skin, That Tatiana Woman was as beautiful as forty or so years ago. And there was Lady Oswald, but not, of course, Sir Oswald, from whom she was long ago divorced, stern and upright as ever, a scowl growing on her face as it began to dawn on her that she was not the only silver-and-*Morpho* wearer.

The dawning was gradual, but soon each woman who thought she had at one time been one of only two women in John Lucknow Mansing's life—and of those two believed what she had been told, that she was the brighter—realized that she was simply one of many. The acoustics being what they were, the vocals inside Grant Monorail Presbyterian began to sound like the staging of an impromptu experimental piece of choral music, a concerto of staccato *sotto voce* gasps: arching whimpers, a strumming of tenor realizations crescendoing to full-blown wails, *tremolo* growls and soprano screams in a multitude of pitches. When the pastor left his podium and ran down to console the confused and enraged *ad hoc* choir, Matilda Jasodhra soared like a Venus, the Venus of San Fernando, to the pulpit to see better. From there, the casket of her husband—of these women's lover—not an arm's length from her, she waved her walking cane as if the choir's winged conductor, pointing at one woman after the other, and it was to her delight that whichever woman she pointed to complied with her conductor's command and wailed or hissed or growled appropriately. When the inevitable fight broke out, she banged her cane in glee on the casket, but wigs were already being pulled off, clumps of real hair flung in the air, and shoes, some with dangerously pointed heels, were being hurled. Jewelry was being yanked from necks and ears, and rings torn off fingers. Suddenly, the swarm of women, as if all at once, came to a slow realization. They all together ceased their fighting. There was silence. And then the ominous growl, and seconds before the move occurred—one knew it was coming, it was bound to happen—every woman, save for John Lucknow Mansing's wife and daughter, charged toward the casket. The pastor, adding a baritone drone to the affair, fled when the lid was torn right off. He didn't, therefore, lucky for him, see the devastation to John Lucknow (ill-luck now, really) Mansing. It was unpleasant and messy.

Matilda Jasodhra wished she'd had a video camera with her, thinking what a good film this would have made. Meera Meera Johna wondered just how much she had really become like her father, and thought there was indeed more to learn from him, even in his demise, for she mustn't end up like this. How awful it would be, she thought, for Vishala and Brianni and Carmen, all lovely girls, really, to behave in any way like this. She wondered if the recently dead could hear, and if they could feel.

The yardman too, like the pastor, saw nothing, but not because he had fled. He remained in the church, at the heels of his madam, looking like an ill-fitting lord, smelling disturbingly sweet. He stood behind Matilda Jasodhra Mansing, toying with the tail of her dress, counting for the umpteenth time the fortune that would befall him. He would have to find them a new gardener, someone else to anesthetize the garden snakes. And he would, of course, have to take care of the daughter now, so much like her father in any case, and from that very point of view, who would fault him, he wondered, for his intentions? *An intervention here, an intervention there, such as they are,* he assured himself again and again as he fingered the fabric of satin and silk, *are sometimes necessary, and so a good thing.* He nodded in agreement with himself. *A very good thing, indeed.*

# DOUGLA

BY REENA ANDREA MANICKCHAND

*Caroni Swamp*

erks. Jagabats. Jackasses. I never believed them. Those fools of the Scare-'em Crew, as they called themselves, had me on a merry-go-round. I hate merry-go-rounds, always did as a child and always will. They made me wanna puke. The Scare-'em Crew actually invested in some of the crimes on the crime list themselves. The only thing they did not get into was killing. The leader was a pastor who didn't want to disobey that commandment.

I shoulda known they were a bunch of jokers. I got a job just doing the small stuff like trafficking weed. It paid well and was not too much of a hassle. But then they tried to get me to pick up some of the heavier stuff. The pastor told me it would only be for two months while his son was away, and when he came back I could stop. Yeah, right. It ended up being six months even after his son came back.

God, I was a damned fool. I shoulda listened to my damned instincts. But as always, I tried to please Mother. Tried to look and be the good son she always wanted. I had to earn money in order for her to feel proud, so she could be just like the rest of the cacophony bitches she limes with. Hell, now she hates me—another dougla gone bad. Damn it, I even saw it in Vish's eyes.

I couldn't join the army. After all, it was for the Afro boys. And I didn't want to work in the garage with my older brother. I just couldn't stand them Indo boys riding along with their souped-up vehicles and gloating 'bout their drag races. I know she didn't want me to do anything illegal, but what's a dougla like me to do? After all, doesn't dougla mean bastard in Hindi? That's what they call people like me who are half-Indian and half-African.

"Hey, pretty dougla! Stop daydreaming and get ready!" the African guard bellowed.

Get ready? What the rasclat? This is a jail cell—I've been ready.

Kwae jumped off the bed, reeling from his angry thoughts. Keys clanked as the guard opened his cell. Kwae smoothed his wavy black curls, cleaned the yampi from his big round eyes, and licked his semi-full lips. He'd definitely have to thank his Afro mother for those lips and his Indo father for his eyes, 'cause he could enchant almost anyone with them.

"Yeah, Mr. Kwaesi Ramlogan, yuh better get yuh pretty-boy act together," the Indian guard repeated. Kwae allowed himself to be handcuffed. Stupid Indian officer always following stupid African officer. What a bunch of monkeys. Wait—I guess I'm a monkey too, or else I wouldn't have ended up in all this cow dung.

They left his cell and started down the hall. Kwae's flared nostrils caught the stale pissy stench that filtered through the air from the uncleaned cells. Twice a week the cells were cleaned. They probably kept it like that so the stench would punish the inmates. Worse yet, when the cells were washed out, they never fully dried the place, so sometimes it was damp for two days straight, especially now in the rainy season. Worse yet, his cell had been previously occupied by an inmate who had died of pneumonia. That would be just Kwae's luck—he'd probably die before the case was over.

It had been one month already without closure. Damned bloodclat stinking jury. I already told them I was guilty of trafficking marijuana. Couldn't they believe I was innocent when I said I *didn't kill Redman? Sure, I used to sell him some good herb, but I had no reason to kill him. After all, he paid up well.*

By the time Kwae reached the courtyard to board the waiting van, he was angry again. Being hot-blooded was a side effect of being mixed, and even though he didn't like the emotion, it felt good to be angry. What made him even madder were the potholes that the van hit on the way from the Port-of-Spain jail to the Hall of Justice. He felt that they could have walked him to the hall. It was just three streets from the sick, mustard-colored walls of the jail. He would have been able to walk down the street like everyone else and get some air, even if it was more polluted than his country air in Couva.

"Hey, drive," Kwae called as the van bumped along.

"Yeah, Mr. Ramlogan. What tune you have for us today?" the driver asked, while the two monkey officers with Kwae in the back laughed.

"Let we go straight down Frederick Street and turn across the park nah, insteada goin' on to St. Vincent Street. They got them sweet girls lined up outside their work places this morning 'cause it's Friday, so you know is only tight jeans and short skirts on parade," Kwae goaded.

"Yeah, Horse, let we take Frederick," the dougla officer in front by the driver piped up. "St. Vincent Street only have a bunch of ministry workers that not as hot as the girls in the private businesses."

Kwae smiled. *One can always count on one's own kind to feel pity. One can never count on the African or Indian Trinidadians, as they hate douglas for having the best of both gene pools. The only time they like you is around voting time. The Africans will say, "Boy, yuh have African in yuh. Be proud. The Indian doh like yuh." The Indians will say, "Beta, yuh have Ganges blood flowing through yuh, doh yours is only half." Fuck 'em. They can all go back to their motherland for all I care. Both races are the same—a bunch of persecutors.*

As the driver continued down Frederick Street, having been persuaded at the thought of hot mamacitas in tight pants, Kwae was looking out for one particular place. He did not care about seeing the girls. He just wanted to pass round by Woodford Square. Somehow this park reminded him of a place that was special to him and Vish. The square was like a breath of fresh air in the polluted city, its tall trees and grassy areas a refuge for many who wanted to sit on the park benches and enjoy nature.

As the van came up to the square, Kwae saw a vagrant taking an early-morning bath in the mermaid fountain at the center. The vagrant reminded him that the country's deprived and poor were growing in number. *Maybe that's why some have to depend on so-called criminal avenues—to avoid these depths of depravity.* Water splashed onto the ground startling some pigeons. As they glided off together to find the perfect spot, they suddenly turned into scarlet ibis as Kwae's thoughts turned to Caroni Swamp.

Kwae liked the swamp. Both he and Vish enjoyed watching the sun dip behind the mangrove trees and sink into the Gulf of Paria. Even though the mangrove concealed snakes and the dark waters contained caimans, Vish liked to motor quietly with him to see the scarlet ibis around this time of evening. As for Kwae, he had one thought in mind—to make sure he wrapped up his deals on time, and swiftly. The swamp was one of the best places to make his pick-ups. Even though it had waterways reserved for tourists to explore the mangrove, many were not open to the public. However, those with local knowledge could venture along these wide waterways and meet other boats for quick exchanges of all kinds—not only narcotics but even human cargo. Maybe that's why there were so many South Americans in the country. The funny part was that they all claimed to be here because they wanted to learn English. Sure, there were some who came to learn the language legitimately, but others were here to feed the appetites of the big-belly men of the country. No wonder the government had a hard time putting them out.

Kwae liked to think of the swamp as a miniature Amazon River. It could lead to the sea or carry you to different landing spots in the center of the island. Of course, one had to know these routes well or the place would seem to have only dead ends. Fortunately, the police had no knowledge of the secret passageways that had been created since the time of the Amerindians. One of these waterways led to the back of a car parts dealer. Kwae used to tell Vish that he was going to pick up some parts for his brother. He hated to lie to his love, but he needed the money. If Vish began to look skeptical when he would go to make his deals and collect his goods, Kwae would fire up the engine and speed through the waterways. Vish's beautiful Egyptian eyes would immediately light up and his wavy curls would blow and Kwae would rejoice in the fact that he had found a dougla of his own.

The only problem was Vish's bitch Indian mother. Like the typical mother, she didn't want Vish getting mixed up with him cause of his odd-job attitude and adventurous ways. *If she only knew we're more than just friends, that ours is a love as hot as mother-in-law pepper sauce! We're destined to be together. So what if we can't make little pickney. There are enough crackheads in the world today . . .*

Kwae jolted back to reality when the van slammed into a pothole just before stopping in front of the Hall of Justice. "Oh shit, man! Drive!" Kwae shouted. "Like yuh toutoulebay after seeing all that bottom in the road!" He felt a slap on his head for the rude remark and was hurried out of the van. Cuboid walls loomed as the guards walked Kwae up the long red-stoned flight—the Hall of Justice, where many tears had flowed and criminals had been sentenced or set free. Midway he caught sight of a familiar form at the top. "Vish," he whispered softly.

The Afro guard heard him and started laughing. "Ah, man. I see yuh lover boy here."

"Wait a minute," the Indo guard said. "This one is a buller man? No wonder the boys didn't want to touch yuh." The guards laughed and talked about Kwae all the way to the courtroom.

He didn't mind. *Vish looks so beautiful with clean shoes and all, but his hair is cut short to the point that he looks almost Indian. Too bad,* Kwae thought. He liked to stroke the dougla waves. *I wonder if his mother made him cut it.* Although Vish did not appear to see him, Kwae would definitely catch his eye inside the courtroom.

*All that matters is that Vish is here to defend me. He will tell the jury that we were together the day of the murder, at least most of the day—after all, didn't the boys in blue catch me at home? So I could never have done the dirty deed of chopping off Redman's phallus and then burying him at the shores of the swamp. That would have taken a lot of time. The bastard who did it deserves to suffer in Hell's fire for eternity and to be haunted by La Diablesse and the douennes.*

The case mulled on during the day as ethnic fatigue settled into the judge, jury, and lawyers. Finally, Mr. Vishlal Thomas was called to make his oath. *This is the moment of truth,* Kwae thought excitedly. Vish made his oath staring straight ahead with a stone face.

The defending lawyer began to pound out his questions. The questions seemed endless. Kwae felt sorry for having to put Vish through this. *Why doesn't Vish look at me for support?* he wondered. Then he realized that Vish's mother was there, her face looking like frozen baigan choka. Gasps of shock from the jury interrupted his reverie. Vish was repeating the word, "GUILTY!" Everyone was silent. *What kind of sick joke? Is this for real?* Kwae felt his palms moisten. Vish didn't look his way.

"Doh chain my head up!" Kwae yelled. He rose screaming and rushed toward Vish. Instantly the guards floored him and stabbed him with a tranquilizer. As the drug settled in, Kwae lay motionless, unable to accept that his dougla had done this to him.

When Kwae opened his eyes, he felt the coldness of the floor seeping through his back. He was in his cell. He could barely move as the tranquilizer had only partly worn off. He began to think. *How could Vish carry me on this merry-go-round? Is he part of the Scare-'em Crew?* Just the thought of it made his stomach churn, and he had to turn on his side to throw up. As he rolled back, turning his face away from the puke, he heard keys clanking and officers jabbering loudly. The Afro officer didn't have his usual silly smirk. The Indo one had a container in his hand which he upended, drenching Kwae in cold water. Kwae had barely uttered a few words when he was cut short by the sneering tone in the Afro officer's voice.

"Time to get ready for the hard life of jail, yuh buller criminal."

"Yeah, no more pretty-boy treatment," the Indo sneered. Kwae shivered as they handcuffed him and dragged him through the pissy walkway. This treatment was far harsher than that which he had received earlier. Now he was a convicted criminal and as good as dead. He didn't care. He felt dead already remembering Vish's betrayal. His soul seemed to have left his body, and he didn't have the fight in him to protest or even to try to walk.

As the stench stung his nostrils, he remembered Redman's murder scene. He had just walked into the car parts place at the swamp that day when he saw the big burly body lying facedown in a puddle of blood. He had been so stunned at the sight that his eyes began to blur. His mind became so cloudy that it took him awhile to realize that the scene was actually real. Unfortunately, instead of running out the back entrance, he headed through the front and tripped over a cutlass. As a reflex he picked up the bloody cutlass and then dropped it and continued running. His fingerprints on the cutlass led the police straight to him. *Of course those were the only prints the lazy morons decided to take.*

Kwae's mind shifted back to the present. His underarms began to hurt as the guards dragged him to the visiting room where they had fun taunting him, tapping him up, and threatening to do all kinds of strange things with his rear end. *They can't scare me—I'm as good as dead. I just can't believe these bastards are so sick.* They left him sitting in the visiting room listening to the hum of a radio down the hall. *Who could be coming to see me? Maybe this is part of the new treatment—how wonderfully torturous.* His thoughts drifted back to the courtroom and Vish's testimony . . .

Kwae's vision was still blurry from the tranquilizer when a figure appeared in the doorway. *My mother? Vish? Wouldn't it be a laugh if it was Vish's mother?* He could make out a buff shape and a big head. "Doh tief my head," Kwae choked out. His blood pumped faster as the blur turned into a man pulling up a chair next to him.

"Yuh know what your problem is, dougla?" the man began. "You think too much about the wrong things."

"You jagabat!" Was it really Redman? "You and my Judas man, eh?" Kwae's voice rose as he tried to get up from the chair.

"Actually, you little cynic, your mother and I," Redman replied coolly. Kwae stopped short as the words registered. "Your mother was right. You do have a short fuse."

"Don't even try to bring my mother into this," Kwae growled. "I won't fall for that piece of la."

"You don't have to." Redman placed an envelope within Kwae's reach. Kwae stared at it, then picked it up and spilled the contents onto the table—a badge, an ID card, and a tape recorder. He read the name on the badge—*Simon Redman James*.

"So you were an undercover, huh?"

"And still am."

"And the tape recorder?"

"Play it." Redman leaned back in his chair, a smile curling the corner of his mouth.

*Is this all part of his extended torture?* Kwae wondered. *If it is, I'll have to give the local boys credit for going so far.* He reached out and pressed play.

It was a conversation between Redman and his mother. She was crying and going on about how she had to find a way to keep Kwae out of trouble so he would not end up in jail. He needed a strong lesson to make him quit his life of crime.

Kwae stopped the tape. "So why did you decide to help my mother?" he asked softly.

"You see, kid," Redman's voice boomed, "I realized that you were different. I thought since your mother knew what you were into, she coulda talk you out of it. But she's a smart woman, and she knew you would not change your ways just through her talking to you."

"So you all decided to shake me up a bit, huh?"

"Yup. And your boyfriend was pretty keen on being the one to declare you guilty. He was upset at being drenched in your lies."

"So what now?"

"You're free to go." Redman got up and left.

Kwae sat, the words *free to go* resounding in his head. He still felt as though something was weighing him down. Two new mixed recruits appeared and escorted him to the showers.

While the refreshing water sprayed over him, he thought that maybe working with his brother wouldn't be so bad. *Maybe I could even get a car of my own and join the Indo boys on the track. Yeah.* His weight was washing down the drain with the dirt from his body. *And as for Vish, well, I hope he can forgive me. We'll just have to find a new lovers' retreat and stay away from the swamp. Who knows? Maybe we could explore Asa Wright—after all, they have caves and lots of birds up there in the forests of the Northern Range.*

Kwae dressed and gathered his belongings. He walked across the building and passed through the moss-green iron gate of the prison. Outside he took a deep breath—*Ah, the fishy smell of canal water!* And in the car park across from the jail, he heard the putt-putting of a car engine. It definitely needed a new transmission.

# NOWARIAN BLUES

BY RAMABAI ESPINET

*Santa Cruz*

I was at a midlife crisis, though I had only just hit thirty—a
fool, a failed musician/songwriter—and my question
those days was always the same, *Where to live?* A migrant's
question, the first uprooting all it takes to turn you into a rolling stone forever. The song in my head had a title, "Migration Blues." It had two or three unfinished lyrics too, what I
thought of as the bluesy half-tones of my own makeshift life:
*Moving south / ocean waves / a backyard / mango trees, plum, and
zaboca / ackee trees in sunlight / the sea at my back / would I still
cry / I, and I and I / would I be happy / would I be sad / moving
south again . . .*

I had not been a successful migrant. This I will admit freely.
Not that too many migrants make it anyway by dint of their
own resource, especially taking into account the color scheme
of these northern climes. No, it takes *backative* to make it: the
sale of family land back home, the hitching of your wagon to
a well-established husband, of the appropriate hue, maybe, a
disconnected act of whoring or kissing ass, growing a thick
hide where once there was skin.

Sometimes the need for a change of gears overpowered
me, although at the time I was working in relative comfort
and autonomy for a modest worker's wage as a counselor in
a shelter for battered women. I took offense one day when
a lunchroom argument erupted about rough sex, which was

fine, they all agreed, as long as the controls, put in place beforehand, remained intact. This got me irate. "How can anyone guarantee this?"

"Well," and they spoke as one, their patronizing, indul-
gent tone setting me off further, "we discuss it before, agree on
the limits, and then proceed. We are reasonable people and
besides, who would risk a relationship for some excessive pleasure?" A relationship. The very word put my teeth on edge. A
roughness that was smooth, smooth.

I couldn't stop myself: "But how allyuh could program
everything so? Yuh discuss everything beforehand? Sex too?
Next thing dey go be setting up guidelines for 'managing dangerous sexual adventures' or some stupidness like dat . . ."

One of them spoke. Her voice was dangerously kind as she
murmured, "And what would you know about it, you? Sexual
adventures? Come on, now . . ."

The Trini in me was crazy, my anger too alien and *damn
ignorant* altogether in that charnel house of political correct-
ness. My rage let them off the hook. It left me sitting there
perplexed and wondering about my own freakish take on everything. I would, if I wanted rough sex, have plunged into a
maelstrom with my lover, his every move and mine unpredictable, dangerous, taking both of us into uncharted territory—or
else why bother?

It hit me that I had to leave this city soon. I had worked at
Carrie's Place for two years, and its vibe was now claustropho-
bic. I was bred in such an ordered space—missionary zeal, appropriate codes of conduct, common sense—and the demon
inside me busted off its fragile tapia roof as soon as it could. I
left home alone, estranged from my family who migrated after
I did and settled out west. I ended up here, in Toronto—one
more immigrant, a visible minority worker counseling bat-

tered women and children. Their fright in the face of life's blows, the cavernous wasteland of despair my job revealed, pushed my own unease into the background and helped in postponing my own reckoning.

I felt useful there. And I liked feeling useful. But I was lonely, no lover, no real friend except Ella from back home, she who had migrated too and married instantly and well to a prof in the university where she first landed a clerical job. Now she was the manager of the institution's Office for Racial Equity, almost an ombudsman's (-woman's) position, she would brag, poking fun at my own lean and hungry ways.

"You need a good professional man who adores you and who you can grow to love, sweetie." She would chuck my chin and threaten to introduce me to yet another engineering type from her husband's department. "They come in all stripes these days, sweetie," she would go on, until I collapsed, giggling at the thought of a procession of would-be suitors inspected by her, surreptitiously or otherwise, and all for my benefit, though a couple of times she did let slip that a meeting had gone on too long or a setup for me had, alas, boomeranged in her direction.

Ella would cheer me up but it would not last, the doom of the years ahead slamming into my lone wolf ruminations. It wasn't another person so much as another beat that I yearned for, one not overcome by the ease of propriety, one with a cussed, impossible sense of style. It was Trinidad that I longed for—that crazy, maverick place, the strange logic of its illogic, its contradictions, that walk and talk that haunted me day and night, which would not, could not, leave me alone.

In this mood I telephoned Micah, not my lover really, although we had been lovers and friends for the last two years in what we saw as a thoroughly modern, noncommittal sort of way, separated by the wide Atlantic. I wailed and ranted about my sorry lot and in the end accepted an invitation to stay at his house while I sorted out the misery of my untidy life.

Flying low over the Northern Range, picking out the Rasta huts in small clearings, wondering who lived there and how they managed for everyday things—no road, no waterway even, just a hut, a vegetable patch maybe and then deep forest, the symmetry of valleys and mountains undisturbed for centuries. I could hardly contain my anticipation as the contours of my early island home defined itself, its odd shape, its forest, swampland, and undulating plains set out in such clear geographical alignment that surely, only a deliberate hand, the hand of an ancient god, could have achieved it.

Arriving at Piarco airport, the air washed clean after the rain, my heartbeat quickened as I spotted Micah waiting, exuding his usual restraint, looking older than our meeting last year, his beard now beginning to gray slightly. I felt tender toward him, his unconcerned elegance, his long tapering fingers, his deep sincerity. This is a man I could love, I thought, unlike Ella's fix-ups. Micah held me close, his warmth a welcome relief from emptiness, and I thought how fine it would be to have a shoulder like his to lean on. The talk was light on the way to his house—the latest scandals in the country, corruption, crime, calypso, the IMF and World Bank antics, the dependency of the so-called Third World. I asked about his own assiduous grassroots work.

"The revolution ent happen yet?" I said it as a joke and he grinned wryly.

"Well, no," he joined my mood, "but we still trying. It go happen soon, don't fool yuh fat about that."

We drove along the Eastern Main Road, ducking into the

drive-thru market at the Croisee in San Juan, then continuing
on the Saddle Road running deep into the Santa Cruz Valley, to his house secreted inside the mountains. The forested
peaks lay serene, unmoved by the suburban elements cutting
into their sides, the poor people at the bottom, still scrabbling
in the dirt, the professionals at the top, their homes cut into
terraced rock faces, the whole purple mountain range tumbling behind these architectural wonders perched on rocky
promontories like wary gabilans, their claws and beaks at the
ready, waiting to swoop down on prey as the opportunity arose.
I shuddered at the thought and Micah put a protective arm
around my shoulders. A kind man, a good man, but a gabilan
all the same, poised for swooping.

We arrived at his house. And the preceding months
gave way to a deep and eloquent exhaustion. I slept at once.
Whenever I awoke he was there, teasing and playful. My love,
I thought hazily, through our meandering bouts of lovemaking and sleeping. Home. I was lying deep in a mountain cre-
vasse, in a pitch-black night, no moon, no stars, only smooth
touches from his hands, the air thick as velvet, cool as velvet,
wet and dry in turn, the nightbirds' great wings holding the
darkness intact, pedaling the night air into an early dawn,
a dawn full of rosy promise, promises as vast as the distant
savannah rolling out from the edges of these northern hills.
Dawns and sunsets merged into the steady rhythm of insects,
birds, and frogs—cigales and flying crapauds, cocks crowing
and dogs barking—old noises that settled me back into that
time when the world began.

Then I awoke. I discovered that it was three days after
my arrival. The house was washed over with the last late gold
of daylight, that hour just before a sinking feeling of tasks
left undone overpowers you and night flattens the land. On

the bank at the top of the hill, adjacent to the driveway, Micah had planted an herb garden and the fragrance of thyme, chives, parsley, and tulsi bushes rounded out the evening air. I was touched by this; it had been my suggestion on a flying visit two years ago when I first saw the house with its unused stretch of paragrass running wild, a clean sweep from top to bottom.

I walked slowly back into the vast room with the bed, a great flat throne, in the middle of it. Night was falling now, and fast; I had forgotten how rapidly twilight turned into darkness here. The bed floated serenely in space, the undefined room lapping at its vulnerable edges. A wide veranda surrounded the room, forming an L-shape, ornamented with intricately carved wrought-iron fretwork. The sliding glass doors on both angles of the "L" were open but protected from mosquitoes by screen doors and barricaded against the night with burglar bars. I sat on the bed staring through these bars. The night had turned again, whispering and sighing and heaving great petticoats to hide or show women's wares, shifting itself onto the flattened marriage pallet. I had no responsibilities, nothing to live up to. Yet the ominous sense of things left undone weighed heavily on me, that and the unrelieved darkness of the outside.

I got up, moving further inside the vastness of the room. Off the main area there lay an open dressing room leading into a bathroom, both immensely spacious. In the bathroom the toilet and bath faced each other squarely. The dressing room was lavish. Cupboards everywhere, mirrors, folding doors, sock drawers, shoe racks, suit closets, shorter blouse-hanging areas. An elaborately crafted his-and-hers affair. His into hers, his everywhere, hers intertwined into his.

The next morning I struggled through the open doorway

to the bathroom. He was already there and called cheerfully to me from the shower. The smell of my offal mixed unhappily with the steam from his bath. The steam was oppressive, and anyhow, I didn't like sharing my bowels so early in the morning. No coffee yet or anything. He remained cheerful, not the least bit bothered by the smell. He soaped and sang, loud and off-key, and came out toweling himself, his workmanlike attitude readying his body for the day.

I left the bathroom in his wake. In the large his-and-hers, he was now dressing. I had flung my makeup case and moisturizer on the dressing table the night before. In the few minutes between the end of his bath and my lingering moments in the toilet, alone, he had given it its appointed place on the left side, cutting the surface into two uneven divisions. His joke was lame. "One-third for female paraphernalia, two-thirds for male needs." My hurried flight to the kitchen on the other side of the house, groping for coffee, did not miss the reality behind the joke nor the inexplicable sense of desperation that descended upon me.

Stumbled upon by the merest of chances, my connection with Micah had moved from astonishingly large bedroom antics during our occasional trysts, into this more domestic visit. Until now, I had let it drift, no problem, but my coming here for a longer stay meant that maybe I too was wondering about the possibility of permanence. He, I was beginning to understand, had always had it in mind, partly because of a mad desire to hold onto passion, to go to sleep with it and wake up with it, but also, his needs ran to more careful arrangements which included assets, earning power, social status, and housewifery. What he called desire also held the underpinnings of marriage, all of the parts finding their appropriate places. I knew the signs; I had run out of an earlier life that contained all of these expectations. But my discomfort was hard to explain, even to myself, and muddled was what I ended up feeling.

Micah was a mixture of several different races, too many to count, he would say. He was hard to pin down, and easy in his careless *nowarian* identity. In Canada, where these mixings are now being taken so seriously and theorized upon at length, he would be indisputably *mixed-race*, *biracial*, or simply *black*. He cared nothing for these labels, though, he moved through a world unimpeded by these divides, embodying all of them, as it were. Micah—a man to long for, coppery skin, greenish-brown eyes, curling hair and eyelashes, his body taut, his step light, his voice constantly teasing.

In Canada I am *South Asian*, the name Geeta signaling my arrival long before I appear, circumscribed by every element of that detail. I marveled at Micah's indifference to race. I also wondered if I really liked him so much mostly because he was not part of my fixed prescription for existence. But I shrugged off these prying questions and relaxed with him over the extravagant dinner of home-grown blackstick cassava and stewed red fish, shrimp, and pumpkin that he had cooked, becoming more mellow after the old-fashioned rum cocktails, the *c'est quittes* he made with such finesse.

That first week after I awoke, I tried to find my space inside his big, quaintly designed house. Micah had made himself a cozy office in an antechamber just outside the bedroom. He had thought too about my needs. In one corner of the bedroom he had placed a small desk for me, where it was open and airy. But alas, from every direction my back was exposed—to a door, a doorless doorway, and the open grillwork of the burglar bars with the veranda running alongside the entire perimeter of the bedroom. There was no clutter on the desk, only a small lamp and a small bookshelf above it. No computers, printers, faxes, no buzz. A clean space, well-intentioned but so exposed.

The first night that I sat at the desk with my notebook, though, I was in heaven. I had found ways of blocking myself off from the elements by draping a shawl over the chair, and another over my shoulders. Tropical nights get cool in the later months of the year, especially up in the Santa Cruz hills. I put my hands under my chin and stared at the wall, happy, quiet at last, simple.

He came in, stole up to my chair, pulled back the shawl, and kissed, then licked the nape of my neck, "Geeta," he murmured, "Geeta, my love." I closed my eyes, enjoying the hardness of his body, his smell of musk and a promise of sex. Then, unexpectedly, he said, "Oh God, I really like it when we work together like this." He slipped into his office, left the door open, and began to work noisily, shuffling papers and announcing his activity: "Right! Now this one is for tomorrow, ay ay, how Sonnylal file get left back here, hmm . . . Tomorrow ah should try and meet him, and Sheila de day after, uh hmm . . . They need the appointment with the Housing Authority soon, the development in Matura filling up fast fast . . ."

He was happy, humming as he shifted paper or filed this and that, opening and closing the file drawers.

"Aha!" he exclaimed, ruffling through a pile of newspaper clippings. "Hear nah." (Throughout this he was obviously assuming that my listening was a settled part of his sorting and whiffling through the paper pile.) "Listen to this joke. A letter to the editor:

*Dear Sir:*
*If a Tobagonian is prime minister this time around, can*

*we, as an enlightened population, entertain the possibility that next time around it can as easily be a man from Debe or Penal? An Indian prime minister, if you please! Can we entertain the possibility that it might equally be a woman from the Indian heartland—from Caroni or Chaguanas? Can every creed and race find an equal place here? What is equality?*

"Question, mih dear, question!" He chuckled dryly, waiting for a response, and when there was none, continuing his chatter nonetheless, failing to notice when I stole out to sit in the sunken living room, deep inside one of the big couches.

The stupid letter had filled me with questions—unspoken and unanswered between us. And where to start? My depression was not helped by the setting. The raw glass front let the night in, gaping and gawking, while I sat framed in the low halo of light, which from the outside would surely eviscerate the room and its contents. My sense of exposure was enormous, yet pulling his deep drapes shut seemed completely out of the question. I let the nasty dark overwhelm me and was in tears by the time he found me. He said nothing, only moved to the couch to sit quietly with me and look through glass at the outside, while the outside observed.

Later, the moonlight made lined patterns on the floor of the bedroom. It was then that I noticed the carambola tree, stretching and arching toward the bedroom, its tessellated black trunk clean of vines and stray leaves, but studded with golden budlike growths. Little golden warts on a tree trunk under the moon, a cold moon.

More doubt crept into my heart in bed, during an act of love. His lovemaking was slow, deliberate, a desire to sample and ponder mixed with the earlier, carefree excitement. He ranged over my body, I couldn't help thinking with some displeasure, calculating its assets, quantifying, almost, the degree to which the effort was worth the price. What price? What was he spending? My ungenerous self took over. I resented being pored over as his particular object of desire. But my sensual self remained present too, loving his possessiveness, wanting it, watching him pore over my breasts and buttocks, evaluating their heft before letting himself go.

Some peculiar anxiety had been invading me for the past week even as he had aided in my recuperation. Now, exhaustion gone, I came alive in sex and knew at once. It was when he turned me over and deliberated on his next move while pulling the hair back from the nape of my neck. He kissed and slurped at my neck but the act was different somehow. My body intuited that it was my hair that was alien: He had been expecting a different head of hair. My hair is straight, dropping clear past my shoulders in an uncomplicated, clean cut. His hands were too inexact somehow, grabbing for something else, maybe more hair, or maybe none, a shorn head perhaps, shaved clean. Not a woman's head, I thought irrationally, even though many women wear shaven or short, cropped hairstyles. But the thought that had come to me unbidden could not be dismissed: He was fresh from another lover. I realized that I had never claimed him before, nor cared to own him, yet this dynamic was different and strange.

We had always been flexible in bed, not caring who took the lead, so perfectly did our moves synchronize themselves. From the start he had described it as not caring who was *man* or who was *woman*. But tonight something had changed. He was being *man* but he wanted me to be a man too. The intruding lover had been a man. Of this I felt sure. Sure too that this could not have been the first time. He would continue to protest his fidelity to me. No doubt it was true, insofar as he had not taken another woman. I loved him back with a vengeance, hungrily, greedily even—"Oh my God, Micah, Mikey, Mikey, sweetheart, Mikey honey . . ."—while wondering what to do with this certainty, until a great wave left me alone on the farthest shore.

It was immediately afterwards that the feeling of panic and terror rose up in my throat. It was unyielding in its grip upon my consciousness. Nothing as ordinary as a fear of abandonment. No, it was the opening of a great bottomless cave of emptiness stretching interminably forward, a vacancy that would not be filled by the everyday, that yearned for dissolution into another's consciousness, that knew the impossibility of that longing for annihilation into death, the little death.

I awoke much later to hear sounds outside, whispering, rustling, a feeling of menace in the air. I opened my eyes but did not move, rigid with fear. I turned toward Micah but an iron hand held me down. I lay still and waited. His hand left mine and all in one motion he turned on his belly toward the doorway; it was then I noticed the gun in his hand. The rustling lasted a few seconds longer and then stopped abruptly. The doorway beyond the burglar bars was wide open to the night. Why, in a country where sudden wealth had brought an avalanche of crime, would he leave himself so exposed? I was afraid beyond all reason, but instinctively I knew that no sound was to be made. He crouched, motionless, for several more minutes, the gun still pointing into the darkness, then he rose decisively, pulled the doors shut, and drew the heavy drapes together. *They* (who? who? I asked, but no answer came) *are gone*, he said. *It's all right*. He pulled me close and stroked my back, my hair. In comforting me he was relaxing, becoming the master of the situation again. I wanted his touch, I closed my eyes and tried to feel safe in his arms, but just as unerringly as before I knew that these were not burglars and all was not as simple as he wished it to appear.

The next morning it rained and rained. From inside the burglar bars I saw that overnight the carambolas had invaded the tree's black trunk. Carambolas are strange fruit, alien sojourners from another dimension. Star fruit, five-fingers, carambolas. They lined themselves along trunk and branches like sentries, short, green, and golden, thick and phallic, impervious to rain, thrusting forward dumbly, held securely by their short black stalks. Carambolas resemble cocoa pods in shape, but their surface is succulent crisp, not hard. Cocoa pods, though, hang in some kind of collaborative truce between gravity, the tree trunk, and the leafy earth underneath, eventually ripening and bursting at the seams, the beans leaking out of their sweet cotton wrapping, the collaboration extending to squirrels, manicous, and even the occasional manicou crab. Not carambolas. Carambolas float arrogantly, gold on black, each alone, separate, breaking the even back of the trunk, gloriously wet. I looked at them wonderingly. Life can be this simple; this brutal.

I decided against questioning and accusing and, inevitably, threw myself on his mercy. My questions were now more complex and I hardly knew where to begin. Still I desired him more, even as the vacant days and nights loomed ahead, even as I knew that the maelstrom I sought would come to an abrupt end and I would be disconsolate for days, maybe months afterwards. Any idea of sharing would torture me beyond sanity. The bisexual connection (if it was true, and I would never ask) would be a greater torture. Its secrecy would fill me with contempt, yet if he told me, it would be the end.

And my suspicions would not be allayed. The space that I was groping for at the beginning made sense only as I calculated its loss, but the realization left me nowhere. The futility of my needs hit me in the face—mine, his, Ella's, even the folks at Carrie's Place—and despair too at my own contempt for people's struggles. Yet, no way could I have apprehended Micah's impact on the rest of my life. Not then.

Early the next day he went into Port-of-Spain to take care of urgent matters, he said. The house was busy, filled with people about their daily duties—the maid, the gardener, the workers for the vegetables and orchard crops at the back. "Don't worry," he said, kissing me absently and moving to the door without a pause, "nobody will come here in the daylight. And I'll be back in three hours."

I hung around all day, listening to his jazz collection, working in my song book, chatting with the maid who showed me her secret ingredient for oil-down, a breadfruit dish I had only heard about but never tasted before, growing up in the southland where Indian food ruled. I felt uneasy in the house as evening drew nearer and the precision of his three hours stretched into the whole day. I locked the back door and went for a walk along the ridge, along a path beaten through the bush so thoroughly that it looked like a clear road, one that I felt had been there for hundreds of years, a natural pass through the impenetrable mountains of the Northern Range down to the sea's edge. At the top of the ridge I could see the ocean in the distance. The symmetry of the land's contours was perfect, its equilibrium hammered out over eons of time, and once more I felt a pang of misgiving about the life I had chosen so far from here. I was home again, unafraid of the hidden perils of the place, of Micah's mysterious expeditions, the whispers in the darkness outside, that outside peering menacingly into the wide-open house.

I struck out through the underbrush on my return, finding another more secret path that was entirely camouflaged from house and ridge and feeling sure that last night's visitors had come this way. Rounding a curve in the path, I sighted the broken-down gazebo before they could see me, and I stopped in my tracks. Their voices were low, murmuring, and as their figures came into view I saw that they were saying goodbye. The man reached out and his hand ran directly down the length of Micah's thigh, on the inside, right down the inside from crotch to mid-thigh, and then he half-turned to go. I stepped out sharply. Seeing me midway down the path, Micah waved and called gaily, "Geeta, come and meet Legano."

Legano shook hands with me gravely, politely, and then said he must go.

"Legano came to help me plan the revolution." Micah was laughing now, hamming it up too much, I thought. And had I actually seen what I thought I had, from the hand of this man, small, well-built, with a dapper look, a shaved head, an absolutely neutral countenance underneath the striking pallor of his gaunt face?

Legano left and Micah gathered me close as we walked toward the back door of the house. He mentioned that Legano had brought him some papers to be signed but I couldn't buy that and listened in silence, wondering what the real story was. It was more than paperwork and more than the physical intimacy I thought I had witnessed, my instincts leading me into a cul-de-sac once more, questions and more questions that I knew I should never ask.

The carambolas remained intact and beautiful, stalk and fruit in perfect symmetry, while we continued our holiday antics in between his unpredictable forays to town, always urgent and unplanned. Our lovemaking retained its tacit delicacy, but as we approached the end of my stay, the sex itself got more wild and hectic, frantic even. I forgot all my earlier reservations. It was a roughness as smooth as silk, and savage as waves crashing into the rocks on the north coast. I could ask for nothing more. We had found our own spaces in each other and the simple pleasures of love had changed everything between us.

We drove to the northern beaches, up to Yarra, went by boat to Paria, climbed the hills of Platanal, battled at the mouth of Shark River just where it flowed into the sea at Toco, and lay together on a flat rock at the eastern edge of the island, near the lighthouse where two seas lashed and embraced ceaselessly, throwing up a barricade of cliffs and waves and whirlpools, with tiny cairns of polished stones anchored in coves along the shoreline, amidst the treacherous surf.

I had regained my strength fully. I laughed at his silly jokes, drank his rum swizzles, cuddled with him on mornings. The gaiety in the air was hurried, and almost palpable in its intensity; all the earlier doubts had dissolved into a hoarding of this time, a time I wanted to last forever. My earlier picky attitude to his house, the arrangement of space, his rambling work habits, and my own solitary needs made me more than a little embarrassed and I found the heart to wonder, too, about his irritation at some of my own ingrained habits. I thought a lot about the song, which had turned into "Nowarian Blues," and even began to hum the melody, but I felt strangely shy about confiding to Micah my desire for mango and zaboca and ackee trees, for a backyard filled with wide arches of drooping branches that you could swing on in perfect safety.

\* \* \*

The island was rocked by a coup two months after I left and Micah was involved in the storming of the ——— buildings. He was blasted on the front steps and I heard afterwards that he lay there in the sun for two whole days while plotters and hostages dueled it out. His quick note, written in pencil on brown shop paper, arrived ten days after news of the coup reached me.

> *A coup inside a coup. Not what I risked everything fight-*
> *ing for.*
>    *I won't make it. Trying to leave but I'm in too deep.*
> *No hope, Geeta, my love. Another day for the wicked and*
> *one more for advantage that could never done.*
>    *I love you, you know. We might have made it.*

(Mikey)

I found myself writing and rewriting the song the day I got his note. "Nowarian Blues," its grief deep inside the catchy rhythm of its lilting melody, is still a much-played jazz note twenty years later. Maybe we could have made it, through his ambiguous sexual inclinations, his ordinary human sexuality that threw me into such doubts. Maybe we could have made it if he had not been betrayed. The rustling in the bushes early in my visit—was he already marked? Did Legano, who disap-peared from the face of the earth right after, I was told, did that snake do him in? The note had been mailed by Legano, though. His scrawled comment, stuffed in the envelope, was brief. *Found this on Mikey. Sorry. Legano.* I was grateful that he had sent it and also nervous that he had my address. He must have gone back to the house to find it. A survivor. Like me. Was I, God forbid, a factor in the equation surrounding Mikey's death? Jealousy, maybe? The cold hand struck at my heart again. Mikey. Everyone I met during my stay in Trinidad had addressed my lover as Micah. Everyone except me and, I now realized, Legano. Maybe we would have made it because of our true connection—Mikey and Geeta, primal, uncomplicated, clean. But who knows, perhaps not even that could have saved us.

The day I left, we had lain in bed together for a long time. He had shifted between hugging me tightly and holding me at arm's length, staring into my face. I grew uncomfortable. "Like if yuh trying to memorize my face," I joked.

And he had nodded seriously. "Yes," he whispered. It seemed to me then that we had reached an agreement beyond words, but I couldn't tell if it was for all or for nothing at all, the silly words of that love song still ricocheting through my brain on the flight back, a flight I thought would never end. It wasn't anxiety that I felt, just an inexplicable sense of belonging, though no such words had been spoken between us. No words; something else had taken care of that. Call it carambolas, gold-black nowarians, all-knowing, alien fruit standing in the rain.

# BETRAYAL

BY WILLI CHEN

*Godineau*

A t Godineau, the sleek little boat shot out from under the canopy of mangrove branches like an arrow pointing toward open sea. The only glints in the moonlit ocean were the helmets that crowned the two men seated like robots in the narrow cabin of the speedboat. Painted black, equipped with two powerful 100HP Johnson engines specially assembled and mechanically assisted with turbo jets, the vessel was fast and undetectable as it roared to a destination only eighty miles away—a secret bay of the mainland where, unseen and with engines muffled, the men would pilot the craft upriver along banks whose trees cast an aura of gloom over the compound on the Venezuelan coast.

Balbosa, Manickchand, another Spaniard, Vasquez—who was as cunning as a forest quenk—and a Trini Indian of skill and courage had made countless trips into this dark camouflaged cave within the interior of the compound. Tonight they removed the lids that concealed the boat's cabin cupboards and lifted plastic bags tied with red ribbons, then hoisted the cargo onto the trays of one-ton four-wheel drive Mazdas equipped with tools, hooded lamps, and extra tanks of gas necessary for perilous journeys through the jungle.

Expeditions from Trinidad by speedboat to the mainland took place at night. It was the cloth king of indisputable wealth and authority, Sabagal, who commanded this unlawful business that had made him a kingpin operator of devious courage, a figure of charm and power.

The strength of Sabagal's dominion was in his dexterous voyages and skills deemed inherited from his father who had peddled blue dock jeans, colorful scarves, and head ties across the country roads in bygone days. His father had never worried that villagers were slow to pay for goods, or cared about the pain he experienced as ferocious pot hounds gnawed at his heels when he entered the yards through the mud traces of the country villages. His frequent visits had paid off over the years until he was able to purchase an Austin 8 that took him further inland, into secluded districts where he clothed the people with his cheap, colorful fabric.

Like his father, Sabagal also sold haberdashery of pots and pans, window curtains, miscellaneous kitchen implements, brass bowls, small mirrors, lamps—anything that attracted naïve housewives who spent time talking, laughing, touching, then eventually buying Sabagal's goods. Sabagal would check his money, using rubber bands to hold his notes together. There would be a song in his heart.

Eventually Sabagal hired salesmen, bought two more vans, and as his business prospered, his wealth increased. He acquired properties in the city, at Bay Shore, Otaheite, along Trinidad's central coast, and at Maracaibo, El Tigre, Santano, and Margarita. He sold a larger variety of clothes and other silken fineries which yielded immense profits. His name became well-known across the land, but his lust for power and wealth overcame him. Greed thickened his blood to craftier ventures, which became devilishly uncontrollable and all-consuming.

Lured by mainland drug dealers into the high woods of that vast countryside that bordered the shores of roaring waves, Sabagal found himself surrounded by hefty men, bearded like ancient prophets. Unsmiling and grave, they emerged from a cave where bats whirred with grievous squeals and over-flapping wings. On skids on the higher terraces of the grotto were bags and boxes of cocaine and other drug-related pouches and vials of liquids. Here in this secret lair was the stored bank of wealth, guarded by thieves and hoodlums.

Further into the cold dark corners of the cave were boxes of loot from vessels traversing the ocean—cartons loaded with electronic equipment, whiskey, radios, stoves, refrigerators, and heaps of massive bundles stamped with foreign markings in foreign languages. Sabagal was stunned by the vastness of this store of contraband that amounted to a countless sum. He stood between four men armed with Uzi machine guns who also carried radios and cell phones. He had come to see the evidence. He was satisfied. He opened his carry-on case and Vasquez brought the papers to be signed.

Sabagal realized that more lucrative drug deals involved higher risks. He was soon entangled in liaisons with unknown men of extraordinary wealth. He took his chances.

But tonight he was surrounded by his own men—Balbosa, Manickchand, and Teemul the Trini Indian—who had quietly entered the inner cavern with Vasquez, along with a band of haughty figures, their weapons hoisted overhead, their foreheads banded, their eyes clouded by the dark undertones of evil. The unsmiling strangers, together with his own men, seized Sabagal. The ruffians' coarse calloused hands were too abusive for Sabagal, who stood surprised at the sudden violence.

"What wrong with you?" Wordlessly, they grabbed his shoulders and tied his hands behind his back. "Aye, what you doing?" he protested.

A hand slapped his face. He felt a stunning blow on his neck and his eyes dimmed. He pushed and twisted, stumbled over rocks, but they kept him pinned. They seized him around his waist and grabbed his collar. Each time he resisted, they punched his stomach, slapped his face and ears. His heart beat rapidly. Balbosa had betrayed him. He had tricked him into coming to this mainland cave. He had promised new deals with strange underworld figures, these Spaniards with warahoon guards who stood with their sharpened blades of steel pinned on their waistbands. Sabagal had been kidnapped.

Despite his outcries and struggling, they ignored him and dragged him to a wall of unhewn rock. They lashed his wrists together and tied him to the wall, hands high overhead. They removed his boots, dropped his pants, and Sabagal stood on cold ground, a figure of desolate hope. They brought him papers to sign, promissory notes, pages of information quantifying his enormous wealth in cash and real estate which they had scrawled on his notepad. They twisted his thumbs, lowered his hand, and proffered him a pen to sign, but he refused. Slaps rained on his head, and they struck his shins with a steel rod. He resisted, prayed and yelled, cursed in the darkness as the men continued to torture him. The lashes on his feet brought more pain. He screamed in agony as they bent his fingers back. Then a finger snapped. He began to breathe heavily, then he became unconscious. He hung limp and wet, eyes closed.

Suddenly terrifying growls, painful groans erupted around him and he awoke. Primordial beasts with red unblinking almond eyes surrounded him. Gray monstrous animals—bears? wolves? mountain beasts? or denizens of the cave? He cringed at the long white fangs and the slabbering tongues of blood. But where were his enemies, the mute band of terrorists who had tortured him? Confronted by this disastrous sight, body and mind once more collapsed to nothingness.

\* \* \*

Hours later, days, or was it a week? He had lost all sense of time. He remembered people from whom he had taken money and not delivered garments and household articles. What about the old woman whose cash he had confiscated? Bundled one-hundred-dollar bills tied with vines. The couple who had saved all their cane-cutting money accumulated for years. And the papers, the land transaction deeds he had secretly convinced illiterate people to sign. The stolen jewelry, the numerous frauds and crooked deals all flashed before him. Until now he had not realized to how much his evil deeds had amounted.

He was hungry and thirsty. The men were prodding him. He opened his eyes and snapped to his senses—they were unshackling him. He crumpled before them. The proffered bowl of food and frosty drink was tempting. Mumbling, pleading, he stretched out his hand, but each time he reached for the bowl, Vasquez presented the pen. "Sign and you will get all you want to eat."

"Quick or you go dead right here, minute by minute," Balbosa threatened. "Snake go crawl all over you."

Sabagal saw it then—the huge reptile unwinding itself in the bamboo cage. Python or macajuel? He trembled, then reluctantly grasped the papers and signed where he was told. Balbosa placed the pages in a black leather bag and zipped it. Sabagal was raised up. Several hands grasped his feeble body and dragged him out of the cave.

It was night. A palpable calm hovered over the still sea. Only the glittering stars gave the scene a sign of life. The black racer was tied under the jetty. But the men lowered Sabagal's beaten body onto the floor of another power craft specially constructed and outfitted for the high seas.

Across the bay the stuttering engines came to life. Salty

sprays flew over the heads of the crew as the boat sped over the water, the shoreline lost in the darkness as the ocean opened up before them. No one tended to the prisoner lying on his back, groaning at the bottom of the boat. Minutes later a light appeared in the east, a dazzling beam that grew brighter. Then they heard the unmistakable drone of a powerboat.

The vessel grew in size, a double hull with intense search beams. Twelve men stood on deck, strapped on the bow. The craft drew alongside, cautioning them to stop. Sabagal wondered if his men were involved with the crew of the other boat. On that watery stage of the ocean theater, the two boats floated against an inky sky, their crews facing each other silently. *Ra tatta tatta ta!* The marine stillness was shattered by rapid explosions of machine guns erupting into smoke, flames, and splattered blood, shots ringing out as bodies heaved and fell.

Sabagal remained motionless as the men dropped around him, his attackers who moments earlier were full of energy. Total massacre onboard—except for Sabagal, lying motionless on the bottom of the boat. Then, from the invading craft, a long pole loomed and lifted the black bag out of the gore, plucking the treasured documents with Sabagal's signature scrawled by his cramped hand only moments before. The double-hulled craft awakened to new life and headed toward a horizon tinged with a hint of dawn on rose-pink clouds, leaving a trail of frothing foam gradually dissipating to nothingness.

White herons suddenly lifted off from the mangrove, its branches relieved from the weight of the birds as the cargo of the dead floated past. The spectral sight of death was disturbingly macabre even to the birds perched in clusters. Soon the sky was alive with whirring white wings and chattering herons, as if their cries protested the invasion of their roost.

Below, the floating vessel grimly displayed ruptured bodies strewn across the bow, blood-soaked and exposed, as water seeped through the holes of the bullet-punctured boat.

A lone fisherman, casting his net in the bay from a rock, was curious when the noisy gulls hovered over him. Then he saw the boat, drifting listlessly. He assumed there was no one in it until he waded out and discovered the gruesome cargo. Two bodies, shattered by powerful machine-gun fire, were without limbs. A third had its chest ripped open. The others, lying lopsided across the cockpit, were unrecognizable. The horror was too much for the fisherman. He splashed ashore and, leaving his fish and cast net behind, ran to the road yelling like a madman. At the center of the road he waved his hands until he was picked up by a passing motorist. The driver was stunned, thought the fisherman was insane, could not understand why he was behaving in such a manner. But when he looked in the direction of the mangrove where the frantic man was pointing, he saw the place coming alive with a growing crowd.

At the St. Christopher Nursing Home, Sabagal lay still like a white log. Shaven, wrapped like a mummy, he hovered between life and death. Because painful wounds all over made eating or drinking impossible, plastic tubing harnessed his body—protruding from his mouth and nostrils, drips slowly entering his veins, his eyes closed. His family gazed at him and wished he would open his eyes, bring some hope to their yearning to see him live.

His wife Nicola was thankful to the inspectors for hiding her husband from public scrutiny when they escorted the bodies from the boat at the Godineau mangrove. Sabagal had not been identified in that mass of human remains because policemen had kept the crowd away from the bodies.

Still, Scobie and Habib, his home-based trusted men, feared that Sabagal's enemies might return to kill him. Overcome with the horror of Sabagal's suffering, they pleaded with the doctors to let them stay late nights in the ward and keep watch, their firearms concealed under their coats. Always on the alert, the two men guarded the steps, watched the elevators open and close, even scrutinized the nurses and maids in their starched white uniforms as they came with their trolleys and trays. Scobie and Habib took no chances. In the past, men had disguised themselves as women and killed patients who had survived prepared executions. The drug-and-gun game of power and death had become a dangerous calamity in districts where the youth were daring and careless. Automatic weapons and more sophisticated rapid-fire Lugers and Smith & Wesson handguns were available, smuggled in in plastic kegs strapped under the hulls of fishing boats and even in the bellies of groupers and sharks.

For weeks, Sabagal remained unresponsive, and except for a faint heartbeat, became an unknown casualty since, fearing his attackers, his family had kept his identity secret. A specialist was brought in from overseas, and later a team of experts. Sabagal's broken ribs had healed, but the blow to the back of his head still caused a severe throb. He constantly envisioned horrific monsters tormenting him as he drifted between dream and total unconsciousness. Those at his bedside felt despair but prayed the rosary as Father Ignatius repeatedly crossed Sabagal's forehead with holy oil, invoking the spirits and holding his hand as if to lift him out of the throes of Hell.

On a Saturday, six weeks later, Sabagal's eyelids fluttered. Nicola was seized with happiness. She laughed and shouted, "Sabi opened he eyes! He is alive. Gosh—he eyes open."

She had been rooted at his side, only moving to whisper in

his ear, wipe his forehead, or kiss his pale cheeks. Now Nicola only cared about the new life given to her dead husband.

During the six weeks Sabagal had been a patient at the prestigious nursing home, the underworld believed that he had been kidnapped and taken to some remote village in Venezuela. And then the secret came to light as the story unfolded in the dailies. Journalists arrived with popping cameras and wrote their front-page blasts in heavy print. *Sabagal—the Cloth Merchant, Entrepreneur, Drug Lord—Has Survived His Ordeal.*

So Sabagal was removed to a safe house far from his own mansion, perched high atop the hills overlooking the city, where he peered down at the numerous properties he owned and the lands that stretched to the coastline. A sense of belonging was impinged upon by a feeling of lost hope and uselessness creeping over him. His arms, his whole body was still sore and he could not breathe properly. The neck brace kept him uncomfortably immobile as he sat in his special chair. His head kept shaking, and the fever kept his teeth chattering. He was alive, but hopelessly drained of strength and deprived of the will to live.

Memories filled him with remorse or angered him. Balbosa, Teemul, and Manickchand were never dead in his mind. Their falling and covering him on the floor of the boat had saved him the night they were mowed down by the marauders in the double-hulled craft, but he could still hear their voices in the cave when he hung like beef against the rocks, tortured and despised.

Only Nicola's patient understanding brought him hope. She encouraged him to pray for his wrongdoings, to be grateful for new life. The beatings he had suffered were lessons, though painful, that should bring him back to his senses.

She fed him pablum, crackers, and fruit juices, changed his clothes, and powdered his face. She untied the pit bulls in the yard, and added locks throughout the premises.

Slowly Sabagal regained his strength and began to walk unassisted. He assessed his position with his dear wife Nicola, who was consistently at his side, a devoted caring nurse bringing him comfort. She cooked his favorite meals which he still had trouble eating, washed his clothes, answered his calls, and read him the daily newspapers. Both maids were sent home temporarily because she wanted absolute privacy for him. But she kept the two armed guards, dependent and loyal Scobie and Habib.

One afternoon while Nicola was in the kitchen, Sabagal called both guards. He briefed them about the documents he had signed in the black pouch which had been taken by the men in the black double-hulled boat.

Scobie and Habib began their investigation, which eventually led to a boat at Carenage. Assuming the roles of repairmen in the gulf, they rowed their pirogue between the yachts anchored in the shallow bay. They tied the pirogue to an empty yacht, swam to the boat, and climbed aboard. At once they were confronted by a man who emerged from the cabin. He was tall and naked to the waist. He rushed at the trespassers with a piece of pipe. But Scobie was prepared. He swung the heavy chain that lay on the bow, knocking the man flat on his back. At first he seemed unconscious, but then he rose and fought like a beast. Muscles swelling, he grabbed Scobie's arms, but Habib struck him again with the swinging chain. Finally, they subdued him and taped his mouth and eyes, the deep gash on his forehead splattering blood. Habib searched the boat while Scobie nursed a sore hand which he suspected was broken.

* * *

Sabagal was impressed with his two men. They had recovered the urgent documents. He did not question his men about the details—the return of the precious documents was heartwarming enough. But Nicola was perplexed that her husband did not ask for details.

"We had a hard time, boss," Habib said. "That man in the boat gave us hell. Lucky Scobie was with me."

"My hand and shoulder in pain, boss," Scobie said. "If that man had a knife we woulda be dead."

"You did a good job, men. Thanks. I get plenty licks in the cave too. I passed out. My own men, Balbosa and Teemul, nearly killed me. Imagine that your own friends are your worst enemies. But I don't want to think about that. I have to thank God that I did not die."

When Scobie and Habib left, Sabagal sat in his rocker gazing down at the bustling city of Port-of-Spain, deep in thought. Nicola brought him a drink and sat next to her husband. "Drink the juice, medicine after," she said. She wondered why he kept so quiet, so thoughtful. "Well, things work out nice. Those murderers don't have no hold on you again."

Sabagal said quietly, "Call Father Ignatius. I want to see him."

"You still not well . . ."

"Call Father," he insisted. Nicola felt his forehead and pulse, then handed him his drink, but he refused.

Father Ignatius, a tall spectacled man, white-gowned, his crucifix displayed on his chest, arrived the next day. It was drizzling and the winds were strong. Nicola was saying, "You not eating anything. I had to dump all the food yesterday. You not even drinking. Don't you want a sandwich?"

"No. Look, Father coming up the stairway."

Sabagal attempted to stand as he greeted Father Ignatius, but the priest pushed him down gently.

"Father, I am happy that you have come. Look, Nicola. We have to pass these properties to Father. If they don't sell, Father, you can auction them. The money coming from the sales I want you to keep it. So many people in the parish are poor. You have organizations, do what you like. All my life I have been a wretched soul, and I want to be relieved of the burden. I thought money would bring happiness. Now I realize that material things are temporary. I feel happy to give to charity."

Father Ignatius sat amazed as Sabagal handed him the papers. Slowly he smiled and said in his Dutch accent, "God will bless you. Immensely. But you look pale and so thin. Have plenty rest now. Nicola will tend to you. You are lucky—she is good to you." He stood to leave and thanked Sabagal. Sabagal remained motionless in his chair, his eyes riveted on the scene below.

"He not eating and drinking at all," Nicola worried, walking with the priest toward the door. "He was only asking for you. Nothing was on his mind but you."

Father Ignatius patted her shoulder. "I'll see you at Sunday Mass," he said and blessed her.

She locked the front door and returned to her husband. His head was down over his chest, his hands tightly clamped onto the chair. Nervously she felt for his pulse. She frantically placed her hand over his breast. She threw her head heavenward and bawled out, "OH, GOD!"

# BURY YOUR MOTHER

BY JAIME LEE LOY

*Palmiste*

When a holy person dies, black butterflies float like ash to tell the heavens of their coming. When someone like you dies, my mother confides, gray vultures dig to their death in the soil. You will never make it to God, she hisses. Children pay for the sins of their fathers.

Unearthing years of rubbish from my mother's cupboard, we find a rotting crib, my father's wedding tie, his *Playboy* magazines, his underwear. After nineteen years the widow shows me her wares.

"What de ass I keeping all this here for? Dead and gone." She speaks of things I will never have. She insists he never loved me. "If I didn't have you," she mutters, "Parker woulda marry me long time. And to think I was the one who wanted a girl." Distracted, she thumbs the pants my father wore the evening of his death.

*Sudden and violent, crashing to the bedroom floor.*

*Aneurysm.*

"Stop it!" a little girl screams. She is sitting on a chair, her fingers scissoring the ears of her stuffed rabbit, needling at its fur with her nails. Like a tree being felled, a big man died, leaving his little girl screaming. Everyone else on the porch having a Carib, telling stories of strongman Dennis pulling up a devious kingfish with ease. Everyone beginning to ask, "But where Dennis gone, man?" "Dennis man! But where he gone?" When they find her she is turning purple, hitting her head methodically, her mouth opening and closing like a choking fish. Her mother appears, moaning like a wounded dog, scraping at his clothes. At the funeral they have to hold May back. She is bawling like someone is cutting her open.

Unlike the fuzzy-rimmed nature of dreams, distinct memories of my father resurface in the corners of late evening. I remember fussing from my crib and his insistence that she deal with the problem. I remember him beating me and my fragile, then soft-spoken mother sweeping me away to their room. I remember her crying, the sound of the rocking, and the colors on her dress. I remember what she has told me to remember.

Yet when people speak of him, their voices break. They recount their version of strongman Dennis with the gentle heart . . . *You can think you know a man when he doesn't live in your house or share your bed. Women are more transparent. May can smile through cracked lips and caking lipstick, squint joyfully through scraggly eyeliner, but people see the scowl.*

"The man dead and leave me here to mind you." May continues unearthing her hoard. "Why you think Parker won't marry me? Who want a woman with another man child?" Parker. Parker, who has a habit of looking at my friends. Measuring them with his eyes and saying they are growing up nicely. He used to ask me to call him Daddy. I think back to the first time . . .

*I am in my mother's room. He turns the handle on the door, then leans back against the wall, perusing me from head to toe. I'm caught between him and my reflection, and he watches me lasciviously from both sides. I do not yet have hair between my legs. I am still a girl, uncomfortable in my flesh. Water dripping onto the floor; Parker is blocking my path to the cupboard. His mustache twitches as he funnels his fingers through his hair, his slanted eyes smug beneath bushy eyebrows. I scream out for May, who is putting on her makeup. "You should stop leaving your towel in this room," she says without turning. Minutes pass. I am crying as I stand between them, one seated by the dresser, one standing by the cupboard smiling casually.*

*Half-Chinese, half-black, a drizzle of Indian. More than a drizzle of pervert and five years younger than my mother. It is the playful giggle he lets escape that irritates her. My mother steupses loudly, her half-Trinidadian, half-Chinese accent crashing together. "Why you always trying to make me jealous, boy?" She shakes her head and turns to me. "As if you are anything compared to me. Next time, bring a damn towel with you. You know the man have keys. He could come at anytime and you wouldn't know." My stomach turns.*

*She turns to him. "Parker, is this little girl you watching? Don't let her get to you." And just like that he slips outside. No spectacle.*

*He just oh-so-slowly disappears behind the door, saying, "You getting big fast." Making a subtle sucking noise, "Aye, Marie?"*

May's mention of Parker is purposeful. She sucks the curve of her teeth. It is Friday, her night for cooking and washing his clothes. Parker will leave his mother's house in Debe seeking the services of our home in Palmiste. He craves a house away from the main road, away from the greasy air of the doubles stands. Away from the restlessness. He will come bearing baskets of laundry, then perch proudly like an overstuffed pigeon at our dining table. As if by magic, bowls of Chinese noodles, lemon chicken, and fish in black bean sauce will appear. When the pigeon is full to tipping, May will usher him to her room.

When they have gone, I will sneak into the kitchen with my plastic containers and metal spoons. I will hide the food I have stolen and then leave the house to eat with my neighbors. Swapping the roofs of these friends each evening, I leave no chance for them to tire of me too quickly. They shake their heads and gossip about *strange Chinese people*, pitying me my *shop Chinee mother* who, they whisper, keeps both money and man in her underwear.

Until the next Friday, dishes will sit in the sink, recline on countertops, and stink behind cupboards. Mounds of pots filled with water, week-old food floating in its sour. The air is stained with a stench of unclean habits.

"This blasted waste-a-time child I have! No cooperation. None, none!" I am evading her eye, watching movement behind her. A solitary cockroach slips behind the door. I think of all the roaches and mice I have seen in this room, this room that smells like the kitchen sink. I should be happy we are selling this house. But a tiny insect burrows deeper into my heart, ripping away at flesh and chewing through soil. It scurries through my veins, leaving dust inside my blood. Flattening itself at the corners of my mouth, turning the red in my lips to purple.

I do not tell her I am pregnant. The scandal would crumble her standing at church, my eighteen years proving me a middle-class slut. Four months and a flat stomach. *Thank God.* I want badly for it to be my boyfriend's child. He is my first lover. The uncertainty is worrying.

Getting pregnant was rough. One day I was his girlfriend, the next a knocked-up bitch. After years of waiting to have sex, he was disappointed this could have happened on the first try. He was even more disappointed I didn't bleed.

My boyfriend sees our new burden as something I have caused. Yet he is willing to afford me the comforts of air-con-

ditioning and sterilized instruments. He says that I will escape
the back-room experience and the refusal at the public hos-
pitals. And that I owe him for this proof that he really does
love me. "You won't have to go San Fernando General," he
declares, "or alone to St. Clair Medical or Westshore." He says
that terminations are on Thursdays only. Awed at his own
generosity, he watches me and smiles.

I dream of a baby with the face of my mother. I want to kill
the unwanted. Using a metal hook, the large type they use for
kingfish, I pierce my belly, round like a balloon and slippery
like jelly. Slipping through easily like a pin into Jell-O, I wiggle
the hook around to snag her. She slips away from me, digging her elbows into the inside of my skin. She is fully grown
and heavy. Laughing, she sings, *I am here inside you. And I will
always be your mother.* When I awake screaming, soaking in
sweat, my boyfriend cuddles me to his chest. He cuddles me
until he finds out that I am weak. That I was scared and can-
celed our Thursday appointment.

"And you call yourself an independent woman! A liberal
woman! Suddenly you playing virtuous and want to go fuck
up our life?" My sky is falling, and he insists that his will fall
harder. I wish I could rip him from within me. But I have begun to love the hardening jelly, the eyeless, legless, squirming
thing. Finally my boyfriend leaves. He does not know I have
already said goodbye.

"You think I stupid ah what?" May asks suspiciously, as I sur-
vey the mess around us. "I know you want these things. But
is mine."

I think about Ma Sheila, my father's grandmother, whom
May cared for when she went senile. Fed her daily and washed
her face, all the while moving out her antique dressers and

heirlooms. Our house became storage for stolen objects of love which May will not let his family have, not even her own sister Carol, whose children came all the way from Rio Claro to board with Aunty May to go to school. Paying one day late, Carol found her children with their empty lunch kits standing in the hot sun outside our house.

People say my mother went crazy after her husband died, but Aunt Carol says she showed signs before that. When she was in her teens, she ran after her mother with a knife. When I was born, she started talking to herself. May has no friends. No family left. But Carol lingers. She says she does it for me.

I have abandoned our cleaning. Sidling toward my bedroom, I slip inside and lock the door. The erratic pulsing begins, beating against my temples with water forming and slipping beneath my chin. My eyes get dry, then misty. Heat like anger, like passion on the verge of unmanageable, rises within. But outwardly there is only a slight twitching of the lips and a dimming of the eyes. A fleeting image of what grows inside me leaves slime in its squirming, with feelers for eyes . . .

"Maria, what the hell you doing in there?" May screams.

A poster with *Keep Out* crayoned against intruders grazes her face. I know she's pissed, cheek pressed against the wood. I can lock her out, hide the tins of corned beef I have stolen from her bedroom, and clean my room till it looks like someplace else.

"Maria! What the ass you doing, you stupid little bitch?"

I ignore her. Scribbling lines on photographs I keep hidden under my bed, I leave the father, the two smirking children eating tamarind and standing aside. I blot out the pregnant woman, gouging her face with crayon and marker, darkening the belly where I once was.

"I was happy before you came," I hear. "I should have gotten rid of you. But *I* was the one who wanted you. A girl. A girl!"

I picture her tears that do not slip from their pockets.

"He told me he didn't want any children. He probably didn't want you so he could go fuck Alyssa! Get some other woman pregnant."

Alyssa was once my mother's best friend. Alyssa would not have wanted to fuck anyone. She joined the convent when she and May stopped speaking. A slap in the face to my mother. To walk with the Virgin and turn her back on the Pentecostal faith—

"I want to go back! To undo you. You remember him after you were born, but *I* remember what he was before that! Too late! You hear me? He loved you too late!" Mother is still trying to convince me. But once is enough to convince. Anything more is for her personal pleasure.

I remember how I used to love her, dragging behind her, clutching at her dress. When I was a little girl, she used to try to want me. Now she thinks that I am possessed. That my rudeness and unwillingness to do as she says is a mark of the devil. *You were born this way, just like your father, and no matter how much I try to beat it out of you, you remain the same.* I feel the stinging from week-old beatings, and I smell his burning pictures from last month when she *purged the house of the devil.*

I keep scribbling. The lines move to my arms and my thighs. I use permanent marker now, not the cheap ones I used as a child. I zigzag onto my skin, pressing hard so the pain numbs my thinking. She will try to embrace me in the morning, try to rub my skin clean of yesterday's pain. I dig another line into the door with metal scissors and color it purple. She will ask me to say, *I love you.* I promise myself that these lines will prevent me. After years of forcing myself to forget, I vow to remember.

Nothing eases me. He will still be dead. And he will still no longer want me.

I first asked Aunt Carol what *abortion* meant. Four years old and I was asking the whole family. I hadn't yet learned about secrecy. That some things paraded openly through the doors of people's homes, and that others were meant to hide behind them . . .

I wear black eyeliner now, thick and smudged. *Don't cry, bitch,* I tell myself. I have entered a new phase of training. To bury my mother. I thumb my belly and poke at my navel. There is a small bulge now. The pounding on the door is replaced by a buzzing behind my eyes. I add to the list I have started on my wall in pencil:

1) *She grew up in the country and thought her husband was Prince Charming, frolicking his horse into the affluent suburb of Palmiste. He would place her in a pretty house and pay her to raise babies.*
2) *Born into a family of nine, she was neglected by her parents, who preferred their younger English-speaking Chinese children who did not remind them that, with their slanted eyes and jarring accents, they would never fit in—*"May, yuh want ah rice and ah char sue pok to tek friend in school?"
3) *Prince Charming was never home, always escaping, then he died—escaping blame.*

My pencil point snaps. *So what, May? Your man died and mine ran. You remember my boyfriend. You sat on his lap asking why he was with a girl like me. Giving him the eye, dressed in your bra and shorts. The one who loved me till he met you—the famous crazy May. Like you say, all men are assholes that leave us fat and bitter. They eventually realize our biggest fear—they leave us to ourselves.*

"When I sell this house, if I have my way, you will get absolutely nothing," May taunts on the other side of the door. Her voice simmers again and she makes a clicking noise through pursed lips. "Parker wants to move in with me," she says dreamily, "but I have to watch him, you know. He might be after my money. Once I sell this house—is plenty money it selling for." May's distrust for Parker cowers next to the seething of my own. My distaste for him resembles disgust between lovers, bubbling beneath the skin, heating the blood and sharpening the eye. It resembles in its intensity and its inability to resolve. It is not love but its opposite.

After my father died, university funds and insurance were transferred into her accounts. May enrolled me in the government school-feeding program. At night, hungry, I went to neighbors, palms outstretched, learning how to beg. All those years fed by neighbors, scantily clad and denied shelter, locked out at two in the morning, barefoot, in nightclothes, watching the wealth my father left me buy her fancy dresses, cars, jewelry . . .

I want to forgive her. *But to forgive, you must first love.*

I dreamt last night that there were earthworms in my belly. They shuddered and rumbled beneath my skin. Their bodies caressed, gnawing in darkness like creaking doors and loosening hinges. All the while they ate of themselves. I am making a plan to move quickly, to move before they travel the length of my throat and slide through my mouth.

I think of Ma, May's mother, who lives in Mayaro selling her preserves—red mango, salt prunes, and cherries—from her seaside shed. She does not interact with outsiders, especially since Pa died, except for one neighbor who taught her local folklore. Douens haunt her dreams—those unbaptized souls of dead children, their heels on feet that face backwards, racing toward unsuspecting children, enticing them away.

Ma also invents her own folklore about the dead and the living. Dark nights with a full-bellied moon and barefoot walks on fish-stained sand have given her insight. *When unwanted souls are born, they are born into suffering.* Ma says they know their own anguish before their real misery begins. *In the belly they writhe with resentment, and in the cradle they ponder vengeance. An unwanted soul will grow to destroy the hand that feeds it.* She once told my mother to send me away. Three of her own children had been raised by a cousin. She warned May about my unwillingness to stop crying when my father died. She warned her about my seeming insensitivity to beatings and my stubborn resolve to grow distant.

May once nurtured my physical likeness to her, but it became clear that I had been born with *his* eyes and *his* manner. My only likeness to her was in my growing inability to be consoled. When he died I screamed for months. Now I scratch photos, dig lines into doors, and devise a plan—a plan to *purge this house of the devil.*

At the back of the house is an unfinished addition. Two hundred thousand dollars' worth of concrete and wood, and an upstairs landing with no enclosing walls. May likes to climb those stairs to talk to God at night. She senses my father walking behind her, scurrying like a mouse in a box. No matter how much he hurries, he does not leave the house. I think he does it for me. May does not believe she has seen her husband. She says the devil wears many faces.

"Honey, you know I love you, baby," May coaxes from the hall, spit moistening the crease of her lips. "Come and help Mommy, nah? If you help me I will give you something special." When bartering, she switches with ease from scorn to affection. "Mariiiiaaa," she coos through the cracks in the door, "you know you need to help me or you may end up with nothing, sweetie. Come on now."

I exhale loudly and continue to scribble, continue to relish the sound of my markings.

"Maria, you fucking little ingrate! Yuh better get yuh ass out here now before I break down this door. Parker coming this evening and I have to get this place cleared up."

It is Friday, the night before we are to surrender the house. Tomorrow morning the pudgy Indian man will arrive with his piece of paper, although unsorted boxes still line the doorway. The moment he saw the house, he said, "I'll take it." Crammed at the end of a flowing row of tall-stemmed houses, the oldest one, though that could be altered, it is nevertheless positioned in prestigious Palmiste.

*Doesn't he live in Port-of-Spain? Your man will mind you. And you have man?* May had snorted. *Why you don't ask his parents if they will let you live there?* I know where she will live. She has already purchased a three-bedroom house by the sea in Westmoorings . . .

I am digging in her cupboard while she is at her choir meeting. I pass my hands melancholically along the doors' wooden panels, grieving the house . . . Gruesome were its stories, lonely were its nights . . . I imagine toppling Parker from atop the San Fernando Hill, watching him tumbling, tumbling into the city, where he becomes a barely visible dot crashing soundlessly amongst the buildings, disappearing forever.

Parker likes to roost on the unfinished upstairs landing, his face to the moon, his back to the stairs. When overstuffed, when sitting with his legs dangling over the edge, I will approach him. While he gazes at the sky, I will show him what it feels like—what it looks like when the sky is falling. He speaks to God here too, while she prepares the room.

I need to build the courage. Enough force to push him over and enough liquor to ease my fear. If he does not die, he will break his legs. Creaking doors will be replaced by creaking bones. He will only have a glimpse before he falls—the colors of her dress and the scent of her perfume.

These things I have already stolen. They sit beside the tins of tuna in my bedroom closet. She will probably blame the spirits. Insist it was the man on the stairs with the face of the devil.

My palms sweat as I begin to doubt myself. He will be arriving soon. And I will be waiting in the darkness like the many times he has waited for me. I picture him falling like a stone to the earth, the worms chewing through his ears and wriggling in his pockets.

I continue digging through her cupboard and its mess, throwing aside plastic bags and toilet paper rolls. May throws away nothing. *Saving for a rainy day, that's all.* I am looking for the Coca-Cola among the groceries May hides in her bedroom. She developed this habit when I was five years old. If I did not do as she said or as well as she expected, I was left without food and given tap water to drink. Sometimes she sold me her wares at half-price—a tin of sausages for two dollars, a pack of maxi-pads for four.

I find a letter to God on her dresser. She writes messages to Him on pieces of paper and drops them into the collection pan circling the pews. While others drop money to purchase a spot in heaven, May tries for free advice. Perusing this letter, I nearly choke on the crumbs at the back of my throat. It is not a letter to God but a letter to Carol, begging her for advice. My mother knows.

She tells Carol I am pregnant, that Parker found my secret writings on pieces of paper inside the box below my bed. She says that I have always been a whore, I have always been unworthy, always been beyond the assistance she has offered me. That Parker spoke to my boyfriend about my scribbled confessions. That my boyfriend left because I had been with someone else. I realize now that May has taken Parker to see the pastor, to cleanse his unapologetic soul of what he has confessed. But May does not write this in her letter. Parker will blame it on the liquor. I will be blamed for leaving doors open.

I am nauseous. The worms are stirring.

I should have known. I have been careless. I should have settled this before it had a chance to grow. I should have settled him before he had a chance to make it happen.

*I thought I was dreaming. I stirred slightly to the smell of rum on my lips and a firm grip on my wrists. Then she was there. Had come home early and found us. She beat me till I woke fully. Then she cradled his crying blubber in her steel arms, his jelly skin, his cries for help. Her victim of evil. I was left to clean my own blood. That was the day I began to see roaches, began to smell rum in corners of the house. I thought that I was crazy. That I was just like her . . .*

May used to say that two man-rat can't live in the same hole. She used to say the same for two women. She fears me now. That I have something inside me she could never give him.

I want to leave her. I no longer want to carry her with me, nestled in my underbelly, festering below my skin.

They have returned.

May is in the kitchen singing about Jesus, and the pigeon is upstairs looking at the moon. Creeping in the shadows, I can hear him breathing, murmuring songs from choir practice, and snapping his fingers. The light from the sky glimmers on his forehead and the dust from the walls crawls onto his clothes. May's dress itches my legs, her perfume smells like stale flowers. I am barefoot and I am armed. Clutching a razor, I hope to hurt him with one swipe.

*May says the taller the building, the closer to God. The landing is high enough. If I can catch Parker off-guard and squirming, I can push him without resistance. I hope he topples with his face to the soil. The rum is settling. I feel the dirt between my toes, underneath my nails. Between my fingers. Buried in the ground beneath his swinging feet are shards of glass and bits of galvanized steel. Hidden amongst the splintered wood and bits of concrete scattered in the backyard.*

Wisps of melody float from the kitchen window below. "Jesus reigns, Jesus saves . . . Jesus is there for you always."

I sneak behind his silhouette propped upright by bulky arms and coarse fingers. My hands shake as I get closer. Doubts swim through my mind. *I can't do this. What if he hears me? What if he grabs me?* The wishy-washy feeling of seasickness, the buzzing of rum fluttering through my eyelids is dragging downwards in my throat. *If I can do this, I can mute the voice pacing the stairs of my mind at night. I can bury her forever.* I hover over the unmoving figure; he does not sense me.

In a flash, I drop forward. I slice his right arm. He jolts upright, gurgling and slobbering. Before he can scream, I kick the back of his neck. There is blood on May's dress now, red spilling onto yellow printed flowers. Falling to my knees, I slam my body against his back and push, push. He squawks frantically, arms flapping, "Maaaaay! M-m-maaaaaaaaaay."

"What de ass you making so much noise for, man?" Then, "Jesus Christ, ah coming up now."

I grow hysterical, my shins grazing the floor until they sting. Only seconds have passed. He turns and is somehow on his feet. He smiles with sick certainty and swings to kick me in the stomach. I skirt backwards on my bottom, wooden splinters scraping my thighs.

"Marie, what you really think you doing?" he asks calmly. Edging closer, he staggers. Enough for me to spring forward. I hear footsteps. Elbows to chest—"What the fuck?" hurling from May's throat—I push and push. He falls backwards, his head hitting the floor.

May lunges at me. She claws like someone drowning just beneath the surface. Nails scrape through flesh. She draws blood. I feel teeth. And just like that, I fall.

The sky turns for a long time, and I feel a frenzied kicking inside me. Then I lie watching the sky, the frenzy subsiding to a fluttery squirming. I close my eyes as blood fills my mouth, remembering when I called her Mommy, the times I loved her as a child . . .

Something heavy thuds against my chest. Parker, coughing blood. Everything blurs.

I sense her beside me, hugging his trembling blubber in her plastic arms. I can barely hear her, vaguely bawling, tearing at the flimsy dress with bloodied flowers, a hovering shadow as the black of the night fades to gray. I think she says she loves me.

# STANDING ON THIN SKIN

BY OONYA KEMPADOO

*Maracas*

T rinidad never promised me anything. And I never trusted the confused strutting. From the time I came to visit as a shy child and them lovely Maracas waves chewed me up and spat me out—when I saw teenagers dressing like big people, rich homes flashing TV-style; everybody rushing, buying food, driving and eating and drinking, talk flying, pecong—I told myself, *Is a place for adults*. I promised I would come back. But it never invited me. No, not once. No matter how many times I came. That's because it's always busy keeping up with itself, getting on, carrying on at a rate. Horrendous rates. From Piarco Airport to Port-of-Spain, every time, I could see the mess'a the place right there. All along the road, without shame or design. Ignoring my arrival.

The Customs man looks at my mixed race and says casually, "Yuh come back home?" after Immigration just finished giving me hell. And then the Indian taxi driver is asking if where I'm going is up a hill. "Because my car does cut out on steep hill, like it have something wrong with it, but I don't like aksing my customer too much'a question before they get in my car." Business as usual. Down the highway. Shopping malls and disaster housing schemes stretching, factories, fast food chains, mosques, and the Hindu Girls School. It's always a bad time for traffic. Island of oil, pothole roads packed with cars crawling like lice, under an asphalt sun. At the junction by Nestlé's compound, diesel dark–skinned vendors comb through heat waves of glittering cars, dripping red pommeracs. Air-conditioned windows roll down, hands exchange cool bills for hot fruit. None for the limping polio beggar, or his black cracked palm. A neutral radio voice offers, *"Four victims were murdered in the country's latest fatality . . . A seven-year-old who survived by hiding under a bed reports that his father and brother were tied up, while his mother and sister were brutally raped by three men and chopped with cutlasses in front of them. All were then shot several times . . . Police say . . ."*

The big Indian-style homes with concrete balustrades, lots of sliding doors, fancy wrought-iron and designer "features," keep their eyes on the road, untrusting. And the patches of farmlands, bordered by Gramoxone-dead grass, lie low. While the white-teeth smiling billboards want to chat. But I never like talking with them—too fake and clever with themselves. To fool them sometimes, I might wave back at Miss World, dressed in her airline uniform welcoming me; cheers with the multirace bunch'a happy people drinking Orchard juice. The rest of it though—from the La Basse dump, leaking human scavengers and smoldering black clouds of corbeau vultures, the shantytown stretching up to Laventille, the marketplace in Sea Lots, to the ex–railway terminal—the place doesn't give a shit. But, you see the hills behind all of this? Ranging along the north, behind Barataria, Tunapuna, Arima—they are the ones you have to watch. Blue-gray soft in the rainy season, hard and fire-scarred in the dry season, they talk to you. Fanning, waving, calling you. They laugh, spread out, and mock the radio, echoing whatever they hear. They are part of it. The plumage. Trinidad.

"What's the use of it?" my sister asked.

"What's the use of it?" the hills laughed.

After all the bacchanal done, the mating season. After the Carnival flu run down your body and left you with a hollow cough. Mas camps collapsed, not a soca on the airwaves. Port-of-Spain is back to its normal self, going about doing the same things again. Post-Carnival sales for shoppers now. Headlines return to the killings and scandal after the feast of colorful, fleshy photos and aphrodisiac ads. Bank workers finished talking about who they saw in what costume, in what condition—gone back to comparing their children's school passes.

Port-of-Spain is trying to tell me now—anything you want you can find here. Selling itself. This is the New York of the Caribbean, or at least a Miami. Look, there's arts and entertainment, nightlife and a whole range of people—cosmopolitan. Get a job or something. Work to buy a car to go to the mall is what you should do. But the Savannah trees and the hills know more about me than that. "You can't stay," they say. "You can't take it in town. Go. But you will come back. Go and learn how your heart walks and the earth talks. But we will see you again. Closer."

"Don't worry," my sister said.

I am back with my child.

"Sheba! Sheba!" The Alsatian doesn't stop. Play-wrestling with my baby boy, a paw across his chest and his whole little arm in her mouth. But Oliver is laughing and dribbling, pulling one ear. Fur stuck all over his sweaty skin, dog saliva pasting down a patch of hair. A big tongue licks his cheek, slathering. He squeals, little hands fly up to his squeezed-shut laughing face. He grabs Sheba's mouth and pries it open, trying to shove his whole head inside.

"Ria, your dog's eating my child!" But it's okay. Play. The two of them in love with each other as soon as we arrived—a puppy for her, a bear for him. The two of them, sprawling round on the floor of my sister's house.

"Cheryl's coming up the hill!" my sister shouts.

Dog saliva's sliding into Oliver's mouth, will get in his eyes too. He's fumbling, pulling big black leathery nipples, sitting up. "Tot-tots!"

The car sounds, scrambles Sheba up and away. I grab Oliver and wipe his face on my skirt, before he tugs off after the dog, running to the gate.

Cheryl had had her baby too. Anika, a cuddly chunksie little girl, almost the same toddler age as Oliver.

"Bella, girl!" Big and warm as ever, "Long time no see! And this is yours?" Anika's legs try to clamp round Cheryl's large waist as the dog comes for a pat. "Look at his state!"

And we're laughing. Oliver laughing, trying to catch the wagging tail, all his hair plastered down, slick with saliva. "Is a real little Indian you have here, girl!"

Filing in together. In the open veranda–living room of Ria's home. Laughing but keeping an eye on Sheba and Oliver on the floor. Anika stuck in horror to Cheryl's chest. Filling in the last three years between us. Ria never preached to me yet about I told you so, or what do you expect from a Caribbean black man. But she held the reproach in her neat, pretty features, in sentences stopped just short of it. Never believed me when I said he didn't hit me. Suspected the violence that I had to save my baby from. Suspected the shouting, cussing abuse.

"What you expec'?" Broad-smile Cheryl must tease. "They only good for one thing. And even dat, sometimes, huh!"

"Just come," my sister had said. "You know we're here."

Maracas Beach we're heading to in the middle of the week. Just us and the babies and our lucky, good-to-be-women selves. Including my reeling, recovery, begin-again self too.

Now the hills, the hills. Beach. North coast. The road curving, curving. They have you, in controlling heights. Up through the saddle mouth, climbing. Green leaves close in then drop away, swooping back down to the valley. Closing in and carrying us on. Now Trinidad is flaunting, flirting slips of exotic dress. Lipstick-red slivers of chaconia and balisier between wet green. Orange immortelle lace canopy, flickering. Scanty. In the dark shade, pale heliconias bud peach, white lily tongues are wagging. Twisting and winding, the hills rolling a bellè dance. Fertility. Sliding you down a spine, they fling you, catch you breathless in the dip of a waist, hold you close. Clinging to moist, mossy skin. And suddenly, way below, the shiny silver-sea edge of a petticoat flashes, dazzling. Keep crawling along the bank of a neck, tree ferns dripping rain dew, pulling you secretly into intimate island plumage. Driving, slipping through bamboo, between quills, against the skin of a peacock. Sloping along the coast. Further. Drugged with mountain-soft damp breath, the lingering pungence of a cedar tree, we slow to a stop. And taste fresh cocoa flesh again. The jewel pods have been catching the sun. Sweet white pulp, in thick autumn-colored cups. Warm as blood.

A hip of the land lazes against sea—La Vache. And the beaches start pounding the names Maracas, Las Cuevas, Blanchiseusse, marching sleepy villages on and on. Deaf vultures soar high above river mouths, looking for scraps through hazy surf light.

"We reach, Mommy! Beach!" Oliver said.

"We know you had to come back," the hills said. And they laughed soft. "You see, we accustom. You might as well had eat the cascadura, because you keep coming back. Is okay. Go ahead." They waved us down the road past the police station, past the food stalls, flagged us into the old public-beach car park. And them hills stayed behind there looking, the whole time we spent on that beach.

An empty day for Maracas though. No weekend piles of cars and picnics, bellies and bikinis parading all shapes and sizes. No vanload of country coolies, with Auntie, Uncle, beti, and fine-fine pickney hiding to eat curry and roti. No fat "Putt'a Spain" people talking loud and stuffing chicken pelau. No hot chicks suntanning, rubbing lotion on their buttocks, pretending to ignore the gold-chain black guys pumping music close by, waving hi to the bleachy surfer boys passing. Not even a beefy bodybuilder in a Speedo or a hairy Syrian, carpet-world on his chest, passing today. The whole long beach almost empty, only the sleeping lifeguards, the red warning flags, and a couple of other people scattered further down.

The hills stayed. And they watched how we went to buy bake-and-shark with chadon-beni sauce and pepper. How we handled the children, trying not to get pepper on them, keeping sand from their mouths. My sister Ria could have fed them much neater if they were hers, but she helped anyway. Cheryl spread out, comfortable with her big size, red skin, and glasses, eating, feeding Anika double. In Ria's bikini and wrap, I tried to keep Oliver still for a few minutes to eat, to stop him from running off to the water or throwing sand. Feeling a little more breastful cause the bikini fitting good, proud of my flat belly but clumsy still, not sure where to put my legs on the rug. Or how preoccupied with mothering I'm supposed to be. Ria noticed. And the hills. And Cheryl said let's take the children for a splash cause Oliver won't stay. So we headed for the greedy rolling water. Anika not so sure. My boy squeaking and hopping, charging straight into the fizzing foam. While further out, in the big bay, the waves never stopped chanting, pounding blue drums and spume. White foam surging and coasting in, tickling and floating us shallow.

"Jump, Mommy, now!"

The dark hills watched how we held our babies' slippery limbs, how we coaxed Anika off her mother's chest over to me, how we let Oliver bump-along tumble onto the beach. Bobbing. Dipping. Little head bouncing, gulping salt. Shrill shrieking, more waves coming noisy and fast. Till we were all shivering and fidgety as the water. *"The body of a nine-year-old girl was found this morning among the cocoa trees in . . ."*

Currents kept nipping, tugging at my feet, digging ambush holes in the sand, pulling, "Come deeper. Bring your child out here."

"Let's get back to the beach," I told Cheryl. "The kids are getting cold."

Ria agreed.

And soon as we came out, that treacherous sea calmed down. I damned sure. Drummed smooth, peaceful, with a steady breeze till the sun joined in, slowed down to meet it. Slow afternoon heat. Then we dusted dry sand off sleeping fat cheeks, pulled on warm T-shirts and unhooked bra tops, packed ourselves into the car, and climbed back up into the hills' bosom again.

PMS day in the art department. Angelica Diaz is the madam of her girls.

"Seven women. Who needs men?" she laughed, gold tooth glinting, crashing bracelet arms and ring-heavy hands onto her desk. "You know what I mean? We manage quite well. Have a seat. And you, Carla, stop passing up and down outside my door! Where is your PMS badge?"

Her desk, like I imagined the inside of her car—a box of tissues, fresh-scent potpourri, a little dog with his head on a spring sitting on a doily. Her office, like the inside of her house—slim gilt-framed cheap prints of stylized flowers; a pink curly vase with an artificial bouquet and two proud photos of perfectly handsome children, of course in graduation hat and gown.

"Your portfolio is unusual," she said. "I mean, is good." Closed it and jangled her hands up, puffed her cleavage up and down above the desk. "But what you have here has nothing to do with what we need. I mean, you talented, I could see that. You's a artiste!" She puckered her orange lipstick, raised plucked eyebrows, and blinked mascara-heavy lashes at me. She is one of these women who must sleep fully made up, with foundation, blush, and all. Would wear a frilly negligee over her full-body Spanish-woman shape. Be born with long lacquered nails and take her first steps on stilettos. These kinds of women were born to rule. Right away, they run things.

She looked at me trying to sit up straight like her, put on some of the confidence.

"But you know what? I think you could do the graphics we need, even though you never done these kind of things. What we need most is flip cards. They're easy, you could pick it up quick. I like how you trying something. Different. You have yuh own kind'a style. And I would give anybody trying a chance . . . Yes, Carla! Yuh still up and down. I said I would give she a chance!" she shouted at the open door.

"You called for me, Angelica?" The tall smiley secretary appeared.

"No, I didn't call for you. This is Bella. She'll be joining us soon, part-time."

The girl smiled welcome. "Another female for the department."

"Yes, Carla, I wasn't looking for a man, I had enough'a them and I have a husband now, yuh forget?" Shook her head at me, laughing rich and throaty, patting her piled-up hair vigorously.

I liked this lady, how she so vulgar and full of herself. She liked me too. Looked me square on then said, "And you have a little baby. Well, I giving you a chance."

When I started thanking her—

"But is only part-time. And then you might get some freelance work cause sometimes clients need their own artwork done." Still looking me square, hard as a business deal. "You brave, girl. You going to live on your own here? You can't stay with yuh family? Trinidad rough, you know, it rough. It only looking so."

"Girl, you born with a gold spoon in yuh ass!" my friend shouted at me, pelting out the gate of my new home. "Come let's go round by me, I have some things for you. Look just so, you get this wonderful place to live. How long I had me eye on it but the stingy lady always saying she not renting. Now a job too. Yuh blessed, child . . ."

We swing round the corner into Picton Street, a few doors down to Francisco's grandmother's house, where he lived.

"Shh. She might be sleeping."

I followed him up the red painted steps to the small front porch. A real granny house, crowded with chests, wicker chairs, and plants everywhere. Francisco's clutter added more bric-a-brac—shells and pebbles collected on the banister, driftwood in a corner. He pried open the skinny front doors and let us into the gingerbread house. Cool dusky air inside and a swirl of bright speckles followed us in. In the tiny antique living room, the bent-wood furniture and radiogram are intact. A light, neat, and soft kitchen, treasured square tins in a row, tea towels folded clean. The snore of an old white fridge breathed gently too. These houses, and their insides, are the hidden pride of Port-of-Spain. Secrets, disappearing. Sometimes plucked out overnight.

"I have a pot here for you, come," Francisco mumbled, digging in the kitchen safe, a traditional wood and wire-mesh food locker. He pulled out a dinky little aluminium kettle, almost dolly-house size. "It cute, eh? You could have it. And something else . . . It's in the bedroom," whispering, "fabric. Luvely white cheese cloth, mmn."

When he pushed open his bedroom door, the paint held the top stuck for a second, then it sprang open, shaking the thin wall and fretwork. Piles and heaps, stuffed bags, hats, belts, and wraps filled the small space round the bed, his nest. Grabbing bags, checking, moving them aside, digging, he crinkled a noisy plastic one, a harsh loud sound in the small house.

"Shh, oh shit!"

"Francisco?" came from the sleeping room next door.

"Yes, it's me, Gran. Is okay."

We found the fabric, two big loads of it, and bundled back out into the bright. Back round the corner to my home-to-be.

Bursting through the narrow front doors—a scramble shook the house. Shook my heart to the core. The back door.

"Tief!"

A man running, dashing past the windows at the side, fly-

ing down the street, gone. With the gas tank. With my courage and bravery. Leaving me shaking, shamed of the fear I
carry.

"The gas tank, Bella! He tief it!" And Francisco starts
flapping.

We checked to see what else was gone, round the near-
empty rooms—nothing else troubled except us. We closed
the front door and went back to the tiefing spot, like it could
give us a clue. Eyes followed the tief's smudges on the wall,
to where his feet must have sprung and jumped into the little driveway and out to the free road. A little twenty-pound
cooking-gas cylinder. Francisco fuming more than me.

"We just turn our back for a minute, wasn't long we were
gone for, eh? And these things hard-hard to get. He gone and
sell that for crack, yuh know. Ass! The last time my aunt had
to get a gas tank was endless stress—up and down, going and
coming, checking Tom, Dick, and Harrilal, cause Texgas and
Shell never have any. The ass!"

"At least it was empty," I said lamely, and started checking the heaps in the rooms again. "What a welcome, eh? It's a
good thing nothing else is gone."

Francisco stood, glaring his googly eyes all round the
house, bristling and fiery as a ruffian terrier.

This couldn't break my luck though. No. This old house
was a piece'a charm come true. From the time I saw it, to
when Francisco took me to the owner—agreement and key.
Magic. A wooden white fretwork dream. Ramshackle iced
cake with a pointy tin roof. Shelter for me and my boy. Right
here in town, round the corner from work, from Francisco and
the Savannah. Tall narrow doors graced the dusty front steps,
banana trees colored the yard. Original cast-iron fence in its
concrete base, gate bent but freshly painted black. And as

fragile as an antique it looked from the outside, it was elegance inside, to me. Palace. High ceilings and doorways lengthened my spine, white everywhere dressed me regal. Wooden lace partitions, the layers of gloss paint, the care taken to cut each curl and detail so long ago—curved a delicate eggshell womb for us, pinpricked with sunlight patterns. At night, streetlights lit inside-out effects. Silhouettes of lace. Jalousie panels glowing like pleated rice paper.

It didn't need much more than the few things I had for furnishing. Cushions and a mattress on the floor, worktable, and plants. Some black-and-white clean checkered lino for Oliver's room so the splinters and dusty cracks wouldn't bother him. Now Francisco's gauzy white crepe to drape the front sunroom. I spread old cotton curtains to cover the holes in the floor there. Cozied it into a heavenly nest, weighted with round river stones, scented with vetiver. Haven. Our shelter. Shaken but not crushed.

"The tiefing is the problem though," my friend reminded me, shaking the louvered door in Oliver's room. "We have to board this up too." He checked the tiny window in the bathroom.

"No one can pass through that," I figured.

"Dat is what you think! Them jumbies round here will pass through a keyhole. They push children through. Is them boys selling they nastiness round the corner. Since they come round, the whole neighborhood change. You know they tief Gran clothes off she line last week? Imagine." He was still strolling around. Inspecting. "Thank God these windows have proper burglar proofing." Pushing his foot at a soft corner of the floor, pulling back when it crackled. "Look how rotten, Bella. Wood ants feasting like hell." Staring all up to the attic. "And you could imagine what going on up there! The other day, right in that office over so, they came in through the roof. And tief out all the computers."

"If they look in here first, they mightn't bother."

"Well. Don't mind. Anyway, at least they painted up the place before you came in . . ." He went on, the whole time. While we nailed up the weak door and put a new bolt on the front door. Going on, then gently urging me to be careful, always look out, especially when I coming in at night, to look out for them sprangers because they like rats round here.

I looked out for them. And the hills. And Trinidad. Eyes peeled. Listening to gruesome news, daily. Tucked close under the feathery, shifting beauty. Standing on thin skin, feeling bones moving under the soles of my feet. Watching the rainbow colors of oil on dark water.

# PART II

*TOWN*

# WOMAN IS BOSS

BY ELISHA EFUA BARTELS

*Diego Martin*

J ump high, jump low, somebody dead.
   Afternoons in July, it comes down bucket-a-drop in Diego Martin. This particular day the sky opened up over the Northern Range right on time and the expected convectional rainfall was beating its usual rhythms on galvanize. It would be another hour or so until the rainbow fighting through the clouds won and sun kissed us again and life could continue, squeaky clean after the afternoon wash.

As I rolled over on my mattress, my eye caught #1's work-in-progress, making me roll back over and shove my head under the pillow, hopefully blocking out art and light, at least until the latter was over for the day. I had to fall out soon to be rested enough to surpass #2's three-day cumulative anticipation, and staring at myself was too disturbing. I wanted to take advantage of that lithe young body enough that I'd worked from yesterday, straight through the night and this morning, sending multiple stories with sidebars to keep my editor busy. I was doing for me tonight, so the knowledge that surely somebody somewhere was dead had to take a backseat.

Hours later, as Jon Stewart's outstanding opening monologue made me gleefully imagine doing to him what I'd been planning for #2, the latter rang.

"Aye, babes. You home?"

"Yes. You coming?"

"Up the road. Waiting for your go and I there . . ."

"Come." Enough time to shut down laptop, find keys, finish spliff, out incense, and stick notebook and phone in my pocket as my song pulled up outside—he always thought of shit like that, knew exactly what I needed a moment before I did, ever-ready with the blanket, water, ice cream, right tune. Being the center of someone's universe was amazing and I couldn't possibly be giving enough in return. His being completely in love helped cover my debt, but even so, could this level of devotion be long-term sustainable? I tried not to think too hard, reaching instead into Billie's voice: *Filled with despair / There's no one could be so sad / With gloom everywhere / I sit and I stare / I know that I'll soon go mad / In my solitude.*

I opened the door as he reached out to knock, pleasant surprise interrupted as my phone emitted its low, discreet, single tone. I ignored it for the moment, heading for the car where I knew he'd open the door, hold it while I got in, then gently tuck it closed behind me once both legs were safely inside, knees almost caressing the dash.

People calling at that hour knew it wasn't their turn and should expect to wait. Still, such off-night calls were rare enough that once en route, I played the message, face wringing involuntarily as I snapped the phone shut.

"Babes?"

"Nada." I rearranged my expression. "So. Where we going?" We were always going—I didn't entertain in #1's space. #2 waited for my go to pull up to the house, given only when I was ready to walk out the door.

"Surprise."

"I hate surprises." He took me to Martin's via the scenic route (my designation for going all the way around the Savannah with a small run up Lady Chancellor) to Cipriani

Boulevard. The Savannah's circular nature despite a lack of roundness was irresistible, populated by flowering trees, joggers, and coconut and pholourie vendors, supplemented at varying times with corn soup or snow cone vendors mobbed by Bishop's and QRC uniforms, fellas kicking ball, parents and siblings pushing garrulous babies in strollers—the cacophonous charm of the world's largest roundabout made it my automatic route for anywhere it could take me.

He opened my door with a spliff in the palm of the hand offered to help me out. I took both, the question still lurking behind lowered lids—could anybody remain so attentive?

At a table under the big tree in the backyard, I waved at Martin, ordering a red rum and tamarind juice as we sat. We got lifted while endnotes of another delicious night in Ruthmin's kitchen teased my nostrils, my stomach commiserating with Tanker's wail of longing for Lena from the speakers. I allowed one hand to drift under the table, masking the action with my legs as I reached into his lap. The phone rang again.

Same caller, no message this time.

Across the table, the other eyebrow raised. "Somebody anxious, forget what night it is?"

"Sorry, babes."

"We good."

I felt bad anyway.

Shortly, sliding back into the passenger seat, I looked up at him and tried to smile. "Sorry, lovin'." I found myself saying the word twice as often lately, meaning it about half the time.

#2 took me back home, Billie's voice slicing deeper into my mind. I hesitated at the door, hunting for a reason to turn the key—not a fitting end to my night, especially since there'd probably be little appreciation for my cutting it short to grant this request—of course I'd cancel my plans and come home to "talk" since he thought it was important enough to call, knowing full well he shouldn't have.

The latch plunked reluctantly back from the well and I pushed, then pushed again, annoyance rising. The door was still sticking—the last flood seemed to have swelled the wood and no amount of hot sun would shrink it.

"I'm here."

He paced the big room, all but pawing and snorting. "I hear this one might be serious."

"What?"

"I want it to done."

"Want what to done?" For dragging me away from a previous engagement, the least he could do was make sense.

"Him. Stop seeing him."

"I'm sorry . . ." Again. Maybe I meant it.

"No. I sorry. But I can't help it. This one different and I just . . . not handling it. I not trying to cramp your style, babes, but just . . . not this one . . ."

"Hear what—I need a cup of tea. I coming." I prepped my favorite mug with Lipton Yellow Label and two teaspoons of brown sugar, turned on the fire under the kettle, and returned to the big room, dropping into the couch and silently thanking it for being the most forgiving thing in my life these days. "So, why?"

"I don't know, and I feel shitty asking you, but I not dealing, and I don't want this to mash us up, so I asking you to let this one go."

"You asking plenty, wanting me to throw away a relationship because of some vague, undefined . . . unease. You better come better than that. I don't know if I can agree, on principle. I mean, if I give up this, then what? What else after that?"

"You know is not like that. Come on. You trying to tell

me you can't do this one thing for us? This small sacrifice to maintain something more important?"

"And what about me? Why I have to be the one to fucking sacrifice? Why you can't just fucking deal?" I was defensive, happy equilibrium threatened.

Everyone in the equation fulfilled a function. I got everything I wanted. #1 got the live-in and accompanying perks without a permanent mosquito in his ear. #2 got as much as or more than he expected since he knew when he got involved that he wasn't #1. And Kaya got the relationship with accompanying perks and protections, without the worry of some jealous man showing up at the club four out of five nights, making trouble and cutting into her customer time and tips. Each person effectively purposed.

"I was hoping I wouldn't have to bring this up cause I know you'd get vex. I was hoping you'd get bored with him."

"Sorry." Again.

"No, *I'm* sorry."

Conversation shifted into silence. I went back to the kitchen to make tea, confused. I'd never expected the #1 beneficiary to have a problem with the arrangement.

By the time I got back to the big room, in-hand liquid warmth spreading, the door was thudding closed, Post-it fluttering: *end it tonight. never see him again. please.*

I gulped my tea, grabbed keys, phone, and notebook, and left Diego with such haste that I nearly killed a pedestrian too stupid to realize the Cocorite walkover exists because the maxi-ride there tempts fate enough. 3canal didn't make it through "Watch Dem" the third time—*we ent takin' dey lies / propaganda tearing de place asunder / we want a new agenda*—before I parked in Charford Court.

I gestured to Face's shadowy outline by the stairwell that

I'd be back soon and immediately cut across from Charlotte Street along Oxford onto Henry, blowing a kiss over my shoulder at Renegades' panyard to make up for bypassing my usual melodious route. The job made me a regular in Port-of-Spain at night even if average citizens weren't, and the panyard knew me too well for me to pass without stopping in.

Two-thirds of the way to the Promenade, "Watch Dem" still in my inner ear, I stepped up from Henry Street into the dark, narrow stairwell, each foot automatically falling into the next worn spot, bass thump reverberating Gregory Isaacs's "Cool Down the Pace" through my pelvis, then cut through skanking pipers and rootsmen and women only to pull up short, sense of purpose deflated. If not here, I didn't know where else to look for #1.

As I turned mindlessly, a skinny man in a Rasta-colors mesh vest, matching hat bulging, center-stitch Clarks, obligatory black bottle and spliff in one hand slid up and grabbed my elbow with the other. Flashing gold with every word: "Sistren, you hadda leave here now."

"Excuse me?"

"You hadda ride."

Confused, I allowed the pressure on my elbow to lead me back to the street that only seemed refreshing after the stifling dive I'd just been ushered out of.

"I know who you come for, but you hadda wait home." Urgently hissing this instruction in my ear, he hustled me into a light blue pH car idling empty, off-route as if its driver didn't need fares. "Fidel, take this lady for me, nah." He rattled off what I belatedly recognized through mental earmuffs as my address, and the car peeled out before I could collect myself.

By the third red light run, I managed to squeeze out, "Drive, I'll take it here."

"But miss lady, Ras say take you Diego."

"Thanks, Fidel, but I can't make any promises about the length of your life if you don't stop this damn car so I can get out right fucking now." Fidel acquiesced. But as I memorized his face, suspicious and fearful eyes followed me out onto Green Corner, sticking, worried that I was leaving them ransomed.

A few blocks later, Face emerged from the stairwell as I reached my car. Unusual. We rarely spoke in public. He peered up at the fifth-floor railing behind which his daughter was trying to wriggle out of her mother's arms. A shrill voice descended, fighting to cut through Port-of-Spain smog, the panyard's loose, jangling harmony and the nearly tangible smell of the dumpster at the end of the yard.

"Face, go, nah. She don't settle if she could still see you."

He steupsed, short but eloquent. "Damn child have no right to be awake this hour, far less on the gallery. Aye, Star, plenty people mark your ride, eyeing up your plate number."

"Anybody we know?"

"Don't know yet. I go call, nah."

"Safe."

"Yeah, Star."

I drove not homeward but back around the Savannah and up Lady Chancellor for the second time that night and pulled over at the lookout, ignoring the other two vehicles parked as far as possible from each other to further identical purposes. Sitting on the warm bonnet, gazing at town spreading westward into the inky Gulf of Paria, I mulled over the night's events and reminded myself to call #2. He didn't know yet he could live without me.

Overlooking my turf was calming. The island never failed me. I strolled back to my door, pausing to take a mental snapshot for the road before ducking into the driver's seat.

Speeding down the foreshore with one eye running along the edge of the island instead of the road, I switched out the Canals for my 12 bootleg, "answer when it call" blaring through open windows, anticipating my imminent opportunity to do so . . . *feel the change coming in, it's overcoming you, answer when it call . . .*

I stopped by Peake's for a Royal Castle Neptune's Catch and post-smoke Tunnocks, finished the sandwich before I crossed Majuba, was licking the chewy, chocolatey wafer from my teeth by Diamond Boulevard, and could taste the coconut water calling from the fridge before I had my key out the ignition. Hopefully, the preemptive strike against the munchies would hold me until morning and I wouldn't remember the Guinness ice cream tucked away in the freezer behind the rainy-day sorrel, pastelles, and pelau.

He wasn't back. I wasn't surprised.

I poured coconut water into my proudly stolen BWee glass and put on the kettle, knowing the glass would empty quickly. I prepped my mug and scribbled *tea* on the list on the fridge, lifted the latch and lid of my wooden box just enough to slide out a skinny spliff and fire, threw an eye back at the kettle, and went to deposit clothes in the bedroom.

I shrugged out of my dress, letting it puddle around my feet, then lit the spliff as I stepped out of my wedges and over the puddle to catch the boil and whistle of the almost-empty kettle. I turned the fire off, filled my mug, lit incense, and hit play on *Plantation Lullabies* with an already heavy-lidded nod to Me'Shell for being so right, the sandalwood scent wrapping around my smoke, hot tea in the works.

It was 4:32 a.m.

Morning proper found me on the couch, sun shouting me

awake through too-thin curtains. My bedroom was protected against this onslaught. Why hadn't I made it there? Based on the stillness of my surroundings, neither had he.

It was already a slightly sweaty, but otherwise perfect beach day, and the stickiness was nothing that couldn't be justifiably alleviated with a bikini. I jump-started myself by flinging open the traitorous curtains, then dug out a bathing suit and complimentary wrap and rolled one for the road. A morning at Hundred Steps would help clear the funk so my mind could track the story.

I took St. Lucien to Majuba Cross Road and over the hill toward Maraval, past the maxi-taxis turning around at the wider but still too small bend in the shaded road, twisting and climbing between the wall of vegetation broken by impossible-to-reach houses on one side and the immediate drop into the valley on the other. Burning it on this hill with Manu Chao bubbling in my speakers was the perfect precursor to driving up Moka, Maracas Bay, and beyond. This morning I caught myself singing along, substituting home for Tijuana, *Welcome to Trinidad, tequila, sex, or marijuana* . . .

I didn't pay much mind to the car behind me until almost Maracas. Truthfully, even if I'd noticed the car before, coming over the hill with one lane in either direction and too many bends to overtake safely, I wouldn't have thought anything of it. And since Moka, I'd been lost in my favorite view, again with one eye on the road while the other ingested the edge of civilization, quick peeks accumulating to slow discovery of coastline all the way to the bay. I loved rounding a bend to catch a glimpse of mist hanging low over the sea, the Green Hut coming up on the left for my required dietary supplement of red mango, chow, and tamarind balls. I dropped at least twenty dollars there every time and made a second stop for bake-and-shark at Maracas, regardless of which beach I spent my day on. For now, I pretended to ignore the warm smells emanating from Richard's and Natalie's that almost made me wish I were already on my way back to make that second stop.

Did I vaguely remember this pale blue Sunny behind me since Diego? If so, it didn't pass by while I was pulled over at the Hut and was now up my backside again. I tried to recall if the license plate in my rearview was the same, because the car was on the nondescript side of familiar, one of thousands on the road in that make and color, but something about it tickled the back of my brain. Was it following me? The job wasn't high-profile—nobody reads bylines except media people—but I couldn't think of any other reason I'd be a target. One look should assure would-be bandits or kidnappers I wasn't worth their time.

After the last ten minutes of more-pothole-than-road to Hundred Steps, I made the hard left onto Phillips Trace slowly, trying not to fuck up my ride, coasted to the dead end of unevenly packed dirt and parked, the sole car. I'd never seen more than three cars at Hundred Steps, so on a random weekday if I were one, chances were slim the Sunny'd be another. It had to be going on to Blanchisseuse.

I grabbed my bag off the passenger seat and got out just in time to hear muffler and undercarriage bang and scrape off the bumpy and potholed ground, hardness belied by the weedy cushioning sprouting everywhere. Pale blue Sunny. And it was impossible to squeeze back out past someone driving in.

Lacking the hasty-exit option, I debated fiddling around in the car until they had trekked the 136 steps down to the beach versus pelting down there and picking a cave where I might remain undiscovered and unbothered. Assuming the tide was out enough, the beach was just big enough for a full Sunny and me.

The blue Sunny pulled uncomfortably close, its heavily tinted passenger window slid partway down. A pair of fake jewel–encrusted darkers hissed, "We watchin' . . ." The intimidation attempt suffered from the obvious difficulty of projecting the evil eye from behind fancy darkers with one's driver-slash-backup also obscured, even if his darkers weren't also distractingly bejewelled. Thus dismissing the encounter as stalled small talk with overly accessorized strangers, I spun out from between our cars, hit the lock button on my key ring, and skipped down every other step, more buoyant with each one. The beach jumped up to meet my increasingly jubilant feet, and none followed.

I dropped my bag on the deserted swath of sand, flung keys and wrap inside, and ran to the water. It licked my toes, dragging tongues of waterlogged sand over them on its retreat. I waded out till I was chest deep, bobbing gently in water calmer and warmer than any man-made and maintained pool.

Having navigated the steps and the first splash of water on inner thighs and lower belly with that slight chill of sea breeze, I flashed back to the mystery lady in the blue Sunny. Why follow me all the way out here behind god back to accost me with some cryptic bullshit? Who was that masked woman? She didn't look like #1's type. Or #2's. Something about the pale blue Sunny faintly rang a bell, but I still couldn't quite pull it into focus.

I shook my brain for loose change. Any recollection of a pale blue Sunny—had #1 ever driven one? gotten picked up in or gotten out of one? mentioned somebody driving one? #2, maybe? Kaya? Pale blue Sunny . . . and there it was. The memory popped so clearly into my mind—being pushed into it outside the Henry Street hawk and spit, looking up at gold-teeth Rasta in confusion, marking Fidel's face. No wonder the

driver hid behind darkers, too, just now. He knew I'd make
him out.

Waterlogged and pruny now, lingering feet dragged me back
up the beach. It was hard to leave the water, but lunch with Kaya
was the reason today's bake-and-shark would be going home for
dinner. The wrap was just enough clothing for Frankie's.

Inside an hour later we were carrying curry goat and buss-up-
shut to an outside table to watch the avenue mêlée while I
gave Kaya the rundown on everything since we'd spoken the
previous day. She smiled slyly, dropping her eyelids and her
voice into its lower register. "Look you," sucking thick brown
sauce from articulate fingers, "you didn't even want a boyfriend. Now you have live-in man and outside man, plus me.
Should I be worried about my shrinking time slot in your busy
schedule, my *Social Dora?*"

"I am not a Dora. God, my mother says that shit."

"Mother know what she talking 'bout."

"You don't know that woman. And lemme tell you, she
wouldn't like you if she knew the sexual deviancy you engage
in, encouraging me—her one girl-child who she hoping will
provide her with some picky head grandchildren. That woman
would cut your tail. Anyway, what the ass going on with #1?
Tell me stop seeing #2, ride out in super-stealth mode, can't
reach home or answer phone since. I gone looking for him,
and his goldteeth Rasta partner take me for some obedient little wifey to just hustle out the bar talking 'bout I shouldn't be
there, boldfaced enough to try and send me home, and know
my address to boot. You said #1 could handle my stories, and
he say the same thing when we put down ground rules, so
wha' he acting up for now?"

"Dread. I don't know. All I saying is he fine, paying the

bills, he have goals, he love you, you already living together in the house you own, so just fucking commit to your life already. You don't even have to give me up. He'll find it hot if we just let him watch, and you know I don't business."

"But #2 think the sun rises and sets in my eyes."

"Yes, yes. I get all that Roberta Flack shit, but look. He's a child, can't do nothing for you, and when you get older faster than him, he'll stray anyway. Plus, you only act a little interested in monogamy, #1 might think the sun rising and setting in your damn eye, too."

I trailed Kaya home, tormented both by the now pervasive aroma of bake-and-shark (even with a bellyful of goat) and knowing her beautiful body would have to wait while I made some considerably less enticing calls. Since Face was tracking those tracking my car, I wanted him on Fidel, goldteeth Rasta, and darkers-wearing mystery lady one time. At least we'd find #1. Who still didn't answer his phone.

I finally sat on the bed, reexamining the details with Kaya's naked bottom. "And why Fidel and fancy-darkers follow me from quite Diego to accost me by Hundred Steps just to say they watching me, no particular reason? They reporting to #1 if I see #2, or wha'?"

The bottom I was admiring dimpled attractively as Kaya lifted her head just enough to speak. "Obviously goldteeth Rasta in something with #1, and whatever it is deep enough that he know 'bout you. So his people musta recognize your car from when you park in Charford—or maybe they following you since you leave home, or regular, since he clearly know where you living—and they tell him you coming before you reach the bar. They know you only know one place to look for #1. But hear what—I really don't care. What I care about is why you still wasting time wearing so much clothes."

"Sorry, babes. I coming."

"You better be. And then you will."

I quickly unwrapped myself for her. No further thought of men, mothers, or their mysteries distracted us as she undid the strings around my neck, back, and hips.

Hours later, watching the sun drop below the window frame as the coquis' evening refrain built harmonies, I tried his phone again. No answer. I buried my face in Kaya's armpit and allowed myself to sleep a little as the evening expanded.

My mobile woke me. Two messages. I hadn't called #2. He was worried. Nothing from #1.

I called Face back first, creeping out of bed without stirring Kaya, to pace through his questioning, for the first time in years of surreptitious encounters, whether my relationship with #1 was other than idyllic. I liked the interrogation flip even less when he interrupted my hesitantly edited account of our status.

"Hear what, Star. I not minding your business. Just trying to make out the big picture. If you don't tell me everything, info don't link. No context."

I didn't tell Face about #2. Divulging my arrangement wasn't an option. I couldn't have informants passing judgment (or information) on my personal life. Knowledge is power, and my working relationship with Face depended on his lack of power over me.

I turned to my notebook. Things always made more sense on paper:

—*#1 told me to end it with #2, then left.*

—*same car outside hawk and spit and Hundred Steps.*

*Fidel just happen to be idling on Henry Street night before,*

*or is darkers-wearing mystery lady goldteeth Rasta's ac-*
*cessory as well as #1's?*
*—thus, who's included in "we" watching me? they watch-*
*ing me for someone specific?*

Too many questions. I stared at the page, willing the words
to morph into a graphic explanation of what the fuck was going on. Appended: *or am I being watched for reasons uncon-*
*nected to relationships/arrangement and #1's demands?*

Tried #1 again. Still no answer.

Time to reassure #2. I told him I'd see him as soon as I
could without making hard plans. He was happy just to hear
my voice and knew better than to expect more. He loved
me, wanted to be with me, was worried about me. With his
chatter in one ear and Kaya's breathing in the other, I realized I might as well be entertained if I had to listen to the
whining. I sat on the edge of the bed again, reaching out
to touch Kaya's sweet spot. The naked body turned toward
my hand, eyelids cracked slowly, and a tiny smile formed.
I pointed at the phone pressed to my ear, then beckoned
closer and met her halfway. Kaya snuggled up, throwing an
arm across my lap. I took her extended hand and pushed it
between my thighs. The hand obliged, fingers instantly making the voice on the phone less bothersome. I relaxed, legs
falling further apart.

As the afterglow waned, I wrapped the conversation. He'd
deal. He was #2.

Ordinarily, there was a constant, nearly relentless demand
on my attention. I needed to get home where I could be alone
with my thoughts—a too-rare occurrence. I gently pushed
Kaya off my lap. "I hadda ride, babes."

"What?"

"Sorry. I have to figure out what going on with #1, and if I stay here I'll be completely distracted by you." Silently self-congratulatory over the quick cover.

"I'll leave you alone. You don't have to go."

"I do." Breathe. "You'll see me soon."

"You coming to the club tomorrow night?"

"You know I will unless I can't. How many times have I not been there?"

"I just know you have other priorities right now."

"I promised I would, right?"

For the 2:00 a.m. ride, I pulled the emergency smoke from my hidden compartment. Mellowed to the strains of 12, now turned down low: *stop living your life like you born to dead . . .*

With temporary peace of mind, I relented and redialed #2 to take advantage of the situation under the pretext of making up. His unprecedented hesitation made him suddenly sexier than he'd ever been. As I pulled up to my house, I breathlessly informed him that in exactly half an hour my front door would be unlocked, inviting him inside for the first time, where I'd be naked, glistening, smelling of chocolate and mangos.

I leaned back in the driver's seat finishing the spliff, my spinning mind casting a loose net for relevance: brooding over #1's sudden unexplained resistance to one of my boys; considering #2's limitless adoration, manifested in zero-notice availability and loving gifts that transported me back to college relationships; wondering what business interest #1 shared with goldteeth Rasta to fund his art . . . and as the last of the smoke dissipated, I saw. I'd been looking at the wrong lover.

Over goldteeth Rasta's shoulder in the dim corner under the hawk and spit's darkened windows, #2—poorly lit, out of context, thus unrecognized. Bossman ordering minions. Déjà vu—hesitation before my wrist swiveled and I pushed the door hard, then pushed it again. "I'm here."

No answer. No surprise.

He was lying on the mattress we'd shared, in fresh clothes and what appeared to be a pool of his own blood—the stain would never come out. Or the smell. I'd loved that bed. The last time I lay on it still felt like the day I bounced on it at the store. Now I wished I'd made it there the last time I'd slept at home.

Mentally I recapped my entrance. What had I done, touched, moved? Or did the fact that I lived here make all that moot? Up close, it hit me. I was the last to see him alive, and the first to see him like this.

I called Kaya instinctively as I found myself in the car, winding my way back up Terre Brûlée, needing her inside me with the panorama of St. James calling from the window that so often framed me with the previous tenant's mural. As soon as I reached her, my mobile interrupted. I simultaneously remembered—#2 was on his way to my house.

"Fuck. Sorry. I have to answer."

"What?"

"Sorry." It never stopped. What else could I say?

"Hello. Look. I'm sorry." I explained somebody was dead and I was at Kaya's, apologized again for the wasted run, and promised to call. I rushed off the phone, needing to talk fast and refrain from admitting I had called him for makeup sex after leaving her. Instead, I said that after finding #1, I needed to make sure #2 was okay, and couldn't not answer because he was already worried about me.

Leaning on the windowsill again, thinking how lucky the neighbors were that I wasn't shy, as her writhing tongue flicked over me, I had another brief flicker of recognition. I assumed it was the result of anticipation now twice fulfilled, until thirty seconds later, when the thrill arching my spine ceased, leaving me cursing whatever had quenched the rising, swirling heat. As I turned away from the window the flicker of recognition returned, but before I could turn back to confirm the pale blue Sunny parked in the street below, #2 was in the room.

"I knew what you'd need—when I called I was almost here." Out of context again, blue Sunny waiting outside, but unmistakable this time.

"But, how you know where—?" Before I could get the words out, she provided the answer to all my questions, even #2's uncanny ability to provide for desires not yet voiced.

"Babes. I knew you'd need my support to get over this loss. I included him because I know he loves you and wants to be here for you. Who you think taught him to take such good care of you? I knew you'd need us. I'm sorry about #1, but he was getting greedy about too many things that weren't his to control."

Wrong lover again.

I thought back to meeting #1 at an art opening she had dragged me to, and #2 at the club that I slowly realized I'd never actually seen her dance in. My perfect arrangement, all her creation. Denyse Plummer sang it: *Woman is boss.*

# PROPHET

BY Lawrence Scott

*Maraval*

> *This is the dark time, my love . . .*
> —Martin Carter

I had come back to write about a nineteenth-century painter, an ancestor of the old family, and ended up reporting on something quite different. Sasha called from London a week after I had arrived back. "Patrice, can you do the story?" I could barely hear him through the drifts of snow I had just seen on the news.

"Which story?"

"Come on, man, where are you? I know you. You're living in your head."

"No, I'm living on the Saddle Road, Maraval."

"What!" he screamed down the phone. I didn't even have to lower the air conditioner or the cable—strictly tennis—both of which I keep at high decibels to block out the roar of traffic: a tropical blizzard.

"Take it easy, Sasha."

"You know what you just said?" he screamed.

"What?"

"It's where it's happening."

"What? What's happening?" Then I lost him to the airwaves and the snow.

I e-mailed him. Speaking to Sasha on the phone is like being bludgeoned. This is what I told him, trying out my landscape pieces:

*In the morning, I begin my walk in darkness and finish it just as the first light of dawn bleeds into the gray foreday morning. The ridges above me are the first to be lit where I walk among the villas of the rich in the valley of Maraval, an old suburb of Port-of-Spain. I've kept this up since my arrival. It's the one certain thing which I do at the moment. So much else is guessing. What are you telling me?*
*P*

*Beautiful, beautiful! And this guy, your artist, he did watercolors? I can see it in your language. But Patrice, read the papers. Look at the news. This is something for you. I know you can write about this. I know you'll want to write about this.*
*Sas*

Funny, I' thought. Why doesn't Sasha just tell me what he's talking about?

I read the papers the following day. First day I bought the papers since my arrival; usually, by the time I leave the apartment and the nineteenth century, they are all sold out. I would never buy a paper just before or after my walk, spoil my fraction of the dawn when I can hear myself think.

I read the articles on last year's missing children and an editorial. There were no leads on the children. I felt I was going to be sick. Then I went down to the main police station. "Who are you? You have a press card?" I overheard the talk: They were busy dealing this morning with the case of two stray police bullets injuring two infants in Carenage last night during a shootout. Nothing to do with the children I was seeking a lead on.

*This is a small island, Sas, that last year had a murder each day. The chief justice is on bail and under some kind of house arrest for alleged corruption. The leader of the opposition in the parliament is on bail also for alleged corruption. Everyone says, "He tief man!" There is a connection somewhere, they say. All of this I have just learned.*
    *P*

*Fascinating. But keep to the story.*
    *Sas*

I pass the police each morning on my walk coming up to the chief justice's villa behind high walls and slavering dogs. They put their lights on bright and catch me in the full beam. They slow down and take a good look. I can't believe it's my jogging shorts. I get cold sweats with police, a hangover from the '60s and '70s in a homophobic metropole.

I'm beginning to feel at home, but still missing the old, deserted estate house at Versailles in the Montserrat hills. Don't miss that narrow life though. I try out a next piece on Sasha:

*The clouds in the nineteenth century must have been the same over Saut d'Eau and the lit ridges of Paramin, the same gentle hills which welcome the seraphic flight of white egrets, the first birds to bless the valley as I begin*

*my walk along Collens Road. And the nineteenth century,*
*think what happened then!*
       *P*
*p.s. I went to the police station—no luck.*


*Keep digging. Keep writing.*
     *Sas*


As Sasha had first said, I was lucky with the apartment
on Saddle Road—with the position, that is. The block was
built in the late '50s, early '60s, and the old fella from whom
I bought it had changed nothing over the years. So the best
which can be said about the interior decor is that it has a dis-
tinctly retro look. I won't ever change the lampshades. "Right
at the center of things," the agent had said. I don't think she
understood her own irony.


*I'm definitely doing the story. How can I not?*
     *P*


Sasha would know what I meant without asking me to go
there.


Opposite the school from which the children have allegedly
been abducted. What a coincidence! Now I saw my luck.
Somehow I can't imagine it. Not here, not from Miss Beaubrun's School. "That won't do!" I can hear her at prayers in assembly every morning as she shrieks out the national anthem
and the children scream it out after her, echoing: *"Islands of*
*the blue Caribbean sea . . . where every creed and race find an*
*equal place!"* Hmm! *"God bless our nation!"* Hmm!
     Some of those mites, gone? Their voices fade when I shut

the door to the veranda. I find myself standing in the middle of the lounge looking through the glass doors with tears in my eyes. I know what I'm crying about, but I'll write the story. Is why I'm writing the story.

I try to get back from my walk in the mornings before the traffic blocks up Saddle Road, or rather, before the short-cutters start slicing their way off the Saddle Road higher up the valley and come through Fairways and fucking hinder my solitude and disturb the late sleeping chief justice on Golf Course View. Each morning now, I've noticed that a black car with tinted windows is parked at the exit to his road. Took no notice the first two times, but now I've come to look out for it. Suspicious? They're an East Indian couple, middle-aged. One day, from the corner of my eye I see that he has his head in her lap. Parking at this hour? Tender: He was like a baby wanting to suckle at her breast the way she held his head and looked down at him. The way he looked up at her. I wondered if they had just lost a child. Just a stray thought. What were they hiding?

T&T to the bone. Hug up me island. Rudder soca so sweet! Hug up me island!

*Bear with me, Sas. You know it's fascinating how the se-curity business has become real big business in such an unsafe place. Or so the talk is—because as I told these friends last night, you know, I'm a slow cruiser through the darkness of the darkest streets and all I can say is they are two fucking empty. Bravado, after two Merlots. Fear and dread eats the soul and everyone is behind their burglar proofing. Not the couple at dawn, easy to display their amorous rendezvous to me and the police, who take no*

*notice of them when they pass as dawn breaks and the*
*white clouds turn to dun.*
    P

Sasha is online. He replies right away:

*What's dun, Pat?*

*Sas, it's pinkish brown. What's dun is done. Oh gawd!*
*Bad eh?*
    P

*Sas, nothing is like the '70s, when the boys hung out on*
*the railings of Victoria Square and begged you to pick them*
*up and life was civilized and poor and we weren't dying,*
*being shot, or kidnapped. Well, just so, say friends whom I*
*can increasingly tell about my nightly sojourns—everyone is*
*home because you can no longer walk the streets at night.*
*And some PC jerk at More Vino, trendy wine bar on*
*Ariapita Avenue, butts in with, "Anyway, you'll fucking*
*get HIV." "What?!" I scream and question. From driving*
*around slowly at night, because that is where I feel most*
*comfortable, rather than being locked up in my cage of*
*an apartment, wondering what those poor kids are going*
*through. Odd, and always interesting, how homophobia*
*manifests itself—often through guilt and self-loathing dis-*
*guised as social responsibility.*
    P

*Pat, don't become too moralizing, and watch yourself. I*
*know this stuff is raw for you.*
    S

*The kids are all boys. Another one gone today. And none as yet found. The press keeps telling us the lurid stories of yesteryear because they don't have fresh blood. It isn't that I expect to find them out on empty streets playing or abandoned, or walking hand in hand with their abductor. I feel I need to have my finger on the pulse of this city, my beautiful belle d'Antilles. She, the city, is my femme fatale, my la diablesse, luring me into her darkness . . .*

*I fade out.*

*Take it easy, Pat. If you use too much of that kind of purple blood, you'll lose your readers and yourself.*
   *Sas*

*What? Not too dark, Sas? Well, what can I do with an insufferably romantic turn of mind and a burning anger for the things I love? Cynic, no, can't do cynic. What, like that fucker in More Vino? What does he understand about my desires?*
   *P*

*Cool it, Pat. Write your story, sweetheart. I love your romantic side.*
   *Sas*

*Are you worried about me, love? Condomize, as they say here. No bareback. The latest attack is on bi—big headlines about low-down and stealing a beautiful tender frame from Brokeback Mountain for their bigotry. Do people understand desire?*
   *Luv, P*

I get the paper now after my walk from the fella outside Hi-Lo. And it's the usual thing, looking for the monster in a stranger when the statistics tell us that the monster is probably the big bad wolf in your parent's bed or your priest in the confessional.

There're security guards and three policemen at the school gates. I tried to get past them the other morning in an attempt to set up an interview with the headmistress. No dice. "Miss Beaubrun just step out." Keeping her head down. And the guards? Look what happened again the other day! Who is slipping through and how do they steal these boys?

I feed birds and I watch birds. Binoculars are wonderful! And I must admit that when I'm watching the palm tanagers and my friend the one-legged tropical mockingbird, I'm taking in the arrivals and departures of the little boys in their khaki shorts and blue cotton shirts and their school bags bulging with libraries and sports kits. The national flag unfurls itself in the wind from the schoolyard pole and the children pledge their pledge. Education! Was all part of a dream once in '62. I feel sick. Independence!

Doorbell. No one visits me. No one knows me. Is it a welcoming party? Callaloo and crab? Trinidad does not do welcoming parties. All of we is one! You know what I mean?

"I just wanted to say if you could mind how you feeding the birds because they does shit the pawpaw on my planter underneath."

"Oh, sorry. I'm Patrice." I put out my hand through the burglar proofing to shake the small hand of the delicate Indian lady from downstairs. "I'm sorry. I'll stop feeding . . ."

"I'm Savi. And the water dripping from your air conditioner onto my louvers."

"Oh dear, well . . ."

"I go get the fella in the yard to fix it. Run a PVC pipe . . ."

"Yes, anything. I'll pay."

"Good. Have a nice day."

"You too. Excuse me. It's terrible, isn't it . . ." But she had slipped down the stairs in the shadow of the palms on the landing. Then she called up, sticking her head around the pillar.

"You like using your binoculars?" Then, like an afterthought as she flew, "You shirt pretty, eh?"

"Yes, you know . . ." But she was gone again, as swift as a hummingbird. I wondered what she thought of the disappearing little boys. I wanted to talk to people in the apartments. Someone must've noticed something. She's been keeping an eye on me.

I've forgotten with all the frantic e-mailing to mention Carmella, my neighbor opposite on the same landing who amounted to a welcoming party—Chinese delicacies passed through a crack in my door the first morning. "Thought you would like these." Steamed wontons! Why not fried? I leave them for my lunch. Never saw her again for days, except I notice that every time I park my car under her window, she parts her curtains and looks out. Always at the window, peeping. I wonder what she's seen.

It's this one boy! He disappeared the day after I arrived in the apartment. Odd that the school has not been shut down. That would give me some peace but it might make it more difficult for me to learn anything. I still feel I will discover something as I sit here on mornings like James Stewart in *Rear Window* with Grace Kelly. Love those oldies with the stars. There's no Grace Kelly here. I wanted to be Grace Kelly once.

I sit with my binoculars, not lame like James Stewart. I stare into the assembly hall, keeping a watch on the main gate and playground. I train my binoculars on the tiptop flowering of the palmiste where the blue-gray tanagers and keskidees love to feed on the berries of the flowering royal palm.

I had been doing this the morning after my arrival, when I saw him being picked up by a respectable-looking gentleman in a smart Rover. Not the most common car here, I thought, Japanese dominate with a variety of Nissans. The boy was black and also the gentleman, what I called old-fashioned political type, like the first crooks who stole all the oil money in the '80s. Of course, then I thought nothing of anything. It is only now, piecing together the stories, that I realize that I was probably the last to have seen him.

I phone Sasha: "I think I was the last to see one of the little boys." Then, I can't help myself.

"Take it easy, Pat. Come, come . . ."

"I keep going over the moments and wondering what was in the frame which could tell me now that the man was or was not his father and if the little boy was at all anxious, resisting, being forced, some clue. I wish now it was not just the binoculars but the digital which I could have clicked away on and had the whole scene over and over to examine." Sasha had given me the digital, bless him. "But as you know, not like me to have any of that ready. Not like me at all. I have just bought my first mobile, cell. As I said, I'm stuck in the middle of the nineteenth century."

*Patrice, it's been days! Where's my story?*
   S

*Sasha, as soon as I've got something you'll be the first to know.*
   P

I lie.

*p.s. I'm very close now.*
   P

He doesn't reply. He's getting impatient.

I was entertaining myself with the daily opera, Australian Open over, and checking the gate and the playground when the doorbell went. Wontons? I could do with a Carmella visit. Shitting birds? Leaking air conditioner? Not Savi, please. I turned the lock, slid back the emergency chain, opened the door. "Oh my god!" The man in front of me carried what seemed like an enormous machine gun pointed almost straight at me, but a little down to the ground when I looked again, catching my senses. I quickly wondered how he had gotten into the foyer. Then that thought slipped away.

"Good morning, sir," he said.

"Morning, officers?" I presumed that was what they were. There were two of them, standing one behind the other outside the padlocked burglar proofing. They looked like commando fighters, not police officers. This could have been a scene in Gaza.

"We would like to come in," the front one said.

"What's this about?" I asked, reaching for the keys on the

TV table, thinking this is quite extraordinary. And from some-where, outrage, a feeling for my civil rights entered my head. I stopped reaching for the keys. "Have you got a warrant?"

"We don't need a warrant, sir. We just want to talk to you. If you refuse we'll go away and come back with a warrant and then it might be worse, you know." He was losing his formality.

"You threatening me?"

"It won't be threats, sir, if we have to go and get a warrant, but we probably won't choose to do that. We can get through here quite easily, you know. Obstructing a police investigation does not improve your case."

"Case? Which case? Is there a case? Talk to me from where you are, you don't have to come in."

"Hiding something?" Then this first police officer stand-ing closer to the gate turned to his partner and said, "I won-der what they does have to hide. You have something you don't want we to see? We not going to interfere with you, you know." *You know, you know,* it was like a nervous tic with this one, and the other one was smiling constantly, leveling his gun at me from time to time, till he noticed, and then pointing it at the ground again.

"Maybe he want us to interfere with him." The one at the back laughed and they both laughed now. "Look, open the focking gate, eh! Sir. Or is it *madam?*"

I was terrified. The first one rattled the gate with the bar-rel of his gun.

"Open the focking gate, you buller man!"

I don't know where I got the strength or the nerve. I slammed the front door shut, bolted it, and ran into my bed-room and shut that door too, imagining that I would have to lunge under the bed to escape the bullets ricocheting around the room. I had left the air conditioner on high and the room was as freezing cold as a morgue. I was terrified. I was sure they would blast themselves in. When that did not happen, I knew they would be back with the warrant. What could I do?

There was a gentle knock at the door after what seemed like an eternity of silence and the muffled passing of traffic on Saddle Road. I thought if I looked outside I would see that it was snowing. I was that dislocated. I felt lonely, realized how isolated I was without any family here now. How had those brutes gotten into the compound and then into the foyer? And why me? And my address? I squinted through the glass peephole and saw a distorted Carmella with a plate of steamed wontons. I opened up.

"What going on?" She was a ministering angel.

"I don't know."

She came inside and sat on the sofa, placing the plate of wontons on the coffee table. She was like a long lost friend. The smell of the wontons pervaded the room. They looked like slabs of white flesh.

"Here, have a shot of brandy." Carmella extracted from nowhere a small silver flask. It was metallic cold. I unscrewed the top and tipped the flask to my lips. I noticed that she was wearing a beautiful red silk kimono dressing gown. I was revived by the medicinal brandy. Carmella must've been very beautiful in her youth, she was ageless. She still dyed her hair jet-black. She could've been fifty-five or eighty. Then she said gently, without alarm, "Now you see what the police are like here. Them is part of the problem. How them could catch bandits and kidnappers? Drink some more brandy. Eat a wonton."

The brandy I sipped again, but the slabs of white flesh revolted me. Their spicy smell going quickly stale, the soya sauce sickly sweet.

"You have family, Patrice?"

"No, yes, all gone away. You know how it was? Black Power 1970. Parents bury in Lapeyrouse. Anyway . . . you know . . ."

"What you doing here then?"

"Love. Hug me island, hug me island." I laughed.

"I see. You need somebody to help you, you know."

Carmella advised me to call a lawyer. She got the phone number of one she had once used. "Her name is Jackie Sealy. And don't worry with what them fellas tell you, eh, don't worry with them, their mind sick, *oui*." She must've been lovely as a young woman. I was reminded of *The World of Suzie Wong*.

When I asked her if she had noticed anything unusual, she just said she didn't see too good. I didn't want to quiz her, at least not at this moment. I was terrified. The police could return at any moment. I called Jackie Sealy. She said I should insist on a warrant and call her the moment they arrived and she would be over for the interview. "The way they threatened and insulted you is not on," she said. There is goodness in the country, I thought.

As I waited for the police to arrive, it occurred to me that if someone had seen me looking through the binoculars at the school, they might well have reported me as a suspect. That thought made me sink deeper into the hammock. It was just that way the morning after I got here, when I had seen him arrive and depart and not thought anything of it—a little boy of ten or thereabouts getting into that Rover with a well-dressed gentleman who I thought must be his dad, or even a minister of government. No, they're too smooth, dressed up in their big suits as if against the cold, and they go off in tinted cars which break the vehicle regulations. Anyway, black on black?

"What does that mean?" Sasha asked when he phoned. Trying not to worry him, I explained that people had theories that crime here was committed by black people on Indians. I told him I had no evidence of that. Did anyone? Evidence was not what people needed to believe something like that here, just a racist mind.

"Watch how you put any of that."

When the police returned, they were quite different in manner. They had their warrant to search and interview. I told them I was instructed to call my lawyer and they accepted. My suspicion was that they were doing everything by the book because they really thought they were onto something, a serial pedophile, and if they messed up because of procedure they would have no case.

The crunch came after the formalities and in the middle part of the interview. Jackie scrutinized them and examined every phrase in their questions. I felt so safe with her there. This would be such a good bit for my story. I had a small tape recorder with an omni mic running that I used for my research. I might not get everything but it would be wonderful to get even the scraps of this interview and the noises as they opened and closed cupboards and doors. I knew that if Jackie weren't here there would have been obscenities. I had flicked on the tape just before they arrived. They missed it in their cursory search of the lounge, they were so obsessed with my bedroom and my dresser where I kept my underwear and socks. I watched them snigger over my jocks and briefs. Don't think the tape got that, more raising of their eyebrows and nasty smirks. Jackie, for a moment, was on her cell. They were even in the dirty clothes basket. They had those white gloves which they slipped on. I thought of condoms as they inserted

186 // Trinidad Noir

their large black fingers. An erotic thought allowed me to escape my fear. One of the guys was very good-looking and sexy in his uniform with all the gadgetry of arrest and constriction hanging off him. If I were going to write sado, this would be where I would have to begin.

"Do you have a pair of binoculars?"

"Yes." They had picked them up in the search, so I don't know why they were asking me. Jackie whispered that they had to do their job this way. That was fine. She was almost holding my hand.

"Do you use them?"

"Yes."

"Did you use them this morning?"

"Yes."

"For what purpose?"

"Bird watching."

"There is a witness ready to testify that you were seen training your binoculars on the school opposite."

"Yes, I do look at the school opposite."

"For what purpose?"

"It's unavoidable, really. Birds fly where they will." I said this with a flourish of my hand.

"This is a criminal investigation, sir. We expect you to take our questions seriously."

"My client is taking your questions seriously," Jackie interjected. She smiled at me encouragingly. "You can put the question again, officer."

"Very well. For what purpose did you have your binoculars trained on the school and the schoolchildren?"

"Well, seriously, it is unavoidable when looking at birds, as you can imagine, but yes, I thought I would do a bit of detection. We're all aware of what's happening. There doesn't seem to be too much detection going on in this country." I could hear my voice getting excitable. Jackie was warning me with her eyes.

"I would caution you, sir, to answer the questions appropriately, otherwise we will have no choice but to charge you with obstructing our legitimate police investigation into the abduction of a number of children from Miss Beaubrun's School."

"You might make better use of your time trying to find the abductors and the children and that little boy, rather than wasting your time interviewing me."

"Sir, I caution you."

"My client apologizes, officer. It won't happen again." I could see that Jackie was saying this to me. Jackie was a smart young black woman trained at the local law school. Carmella said she was the best in town.

"What do you mean, *that little boy?*" the officer asked. The room was as silent as a tomb. The glass doors to the veranda were closed, but at that moment you could hear the cries of children drifting over from the school. It was recess. Jackie looked at me. I looked back at her and we both turned to the officers sitting opposite. It was fear. It was some intractable part of my unconscious, some memory I could never remember. My memory expressed itself as tears that welled up in my eyes and ran down my cheeks. I expect the officers thought, *He's cracking up, we'll get a confession any moment.* Jackie seemed pretty apprehensive, as if saying, *What haven't you told me?* She got me a glass of water and a tissue from her bag. It smelled of some kind of Chanel. Gradually, I pulled myself together and spoke.

"One of them. The day after I first came back, I was doing what I told you, bird watching. I saw that little boy, the one who disappeared on the twentieth of November. I've been reading the reports. I feel sure it was he that I saw get into a Rover with a well-dressed gentleman. It was mid-morning when I have a break and I thought it odd that the boy was leaving school then, but other than that I did not think anything, because at that time I did not know about the abductions, having just come back into the country. But piecing together the stories in the papers, I feel pretty sure."

"Why all the interest?" This question was spontaneous and not one of their prepared ones.

"I write. I'm writing a story about the disappearing children for a journal in London."

"But you've been withholding information in a criminal investigation. Why didn't you report this?"

Jackie was looking intently at me. I had not told her this.

"When I first saw him, I was unaware of the abductions. When I found out, my visit to the police station did not inspire confidence. You fellas don't get good press."

"I would not play detective, sir. And now, to clear you from our list of suspects, we will require you to come down to the St. Claire Police Station and give us your fingerprints and other particulars."

Jackie nodded. This was appropriate formality.

"Yes, certainly. But you know, when you came earlier, even today when you were going through my private things—"

"If you or your lawyer has any complaints, sir, you can put them in writing to the Commissioner of Police. You understand? You know."

There it was again, *you know*. That nervous tic. This told me that they had reached their limit of good behavior. The fuckers. They were going to get away with their obscenity and brutality.

"One thing, sir. We would like an item of clothing from your soiled clothes to match a stain there with other evidence."

"You what?" It was all in his eyes: the hate, the brutality which he had not been able to administer.

Jackie was utterly professional. "I trust that the item of clothing will be returned to my client in the proper manner." They did not bother to reply, so Jackie repeated the question.

"Yeah, man," the officer replied.

"Officer, I will repeat my question a third time and I will expect you to take the matter of a criminal investigation seriously. I trust that the item of clothing will be returned to my client in the proper manner."

"Yes, madam."

Jackie went down to the police station with me and the officer on duty did the required.

Weeks have gone and I've not made any headway with my little boy or with my weight, despite the fact that I am walking each day. Walk faster, eat less. How will I make the road on *j'ouvert* morning?

I get these ideas into my head on my walks. I have been noticing this house, cute little bungalow, just around the corner, really, with petrias that have just burst into bloom, bluey-purple; gorgeous color, and I love that I know the names of trees. The house is empty, or looks like it is. I wonder about that each morning as I pass and dream. I have been building a fantasy to give up my cage and move into this bungalow. I can see that there is a garden behind. The porch has been closed in, pity, fear!

I'm still shaken by my visit from the police. I keep my focus. No, not on my childhood, my stolen childhood, but the stolen childhoods which are at the moment plaguing this city.

* * *

I think the teachers are having a meeting today. No kids have arrived. That's ominous. I hope now that they are not going to close the school, though I will completely understand why if they do. What have I got? Absolutely nothing. We need detection. Do you know that DNA is not allowed as evidence in the attempt to prosecute in this country? What are they going to do with my soiled briefs?

There he is. I can see him. He's running along the pavement opposite: khaki pants, blue shirt, satchel for a mountain climber on his back, a mite stacked with education books. Remember what Prime Minister Williams said back in '62: Your future is in your school bag. I feel to be sick. He lifts his head with his mum and dad's hopes and ambitions, not to mention Miss Beaubrun's injunctions based on the national anthem, where every creed and race find an equal place, and as it was just Christmastime when I came, the carols of the story of Bethlehem. What I think is that every creed and race does have an equal place and that any of them could be the abductor of the children, of my little boy. He has a name. His name is Elijah.

> Sas, Can you imagine the weight of that name in a country that not only needs a prophet but a promised land to go to? No, fucking hell no! Not any more of those. Can't we just stay here and clean up the shit we've got? Sas, how cynical can I get?
> P

There he is, the smallest boy of ten that you can imagine. He is skipping alongside the gentleman. I take it to be his father. It's a dream. I'm that obsessed. It's just that he looks like I looked at ten in khaki pants and blue shirt. A disappeared childhood. I once said I loved my childhood.

> *The couple, each morning parked just below the chief justice's house in the ferny gulch with the bamboos, are there again today, Sas. They were having a row this morning. Where do they fit in? Still suspicious. Then I notice that the house, the cute bungalow, has two cars parked underneath. One is a Nissan Sunny, can't make out the other. Oh no, someone has bought my bungalow. There's a lot of garbage out this morning, stacks of old newspapers and several black plastic bags. They're moving in? Moving out?*
>
> *P*

"You feeling okay?" Carmella asks through the burglar proofing when she hands me her weekly delivery of steamed wantons.

"You want to come in?"

"You want company." She tells me, sitting on the sofa, that despite her bad eyesight she remembers that she did notice the Rover. "You know why?"

"No?"

"I had an old man friend who used to drive one and come and take me out. He died this year. I get accustom looking out of the window when I hear a car arrive to park under the window. Next to your place is my place, but I don't have a car. He used to park there."

"I'm sorry."

Odd light today. When this happens, everyone says it's Sahara dust. The Harmattan! A dusty wind across the Middle Passage.

When I come back down from the hills after my walk, pass the couple in their car, I notice that one of the cars from the cute bungalow is parked outside on the road. It's a Rover. My heart misses a beat. The windows and windscreens are caked with dirt and someone has scrawled something in Sahara dust at the bottom of the back right-hand side window. Because it's just by me, I stop to read, to decipher, because the dew, like tears, has smudged the message. It's just one word, two—*Elijah Help*.

I do my duty and call the police on my cell.

We're too late.

*Sas, this is a dark time, my love. The bodies of the boys have been found. A boy of twelve was drowned in a pond. The autopsy revealed sexual assault. Another boy was raped, rupturing his internal organs. Another two boys were found raped. The boy named Elijah was buggered, beaten, and tortured. The owner of the Rover was picked up, but without DNA will he be prosecuted? The Minister of National Security, speaking on crime in the country, said that free education had been given, unemployment was down, the economy was buoyant: Youth are not availing themselves of these opportunities and they have lost sight of God.*

*Well, how much darker can we get than this, Sas?*
*P*


*Phone me.*
*Sas*

# HOW TO MAKE PHOTOCOPIES IN THE TRINIDAD & TOBAGO NATIONAL ARCHIVES

BY ROBERT ANTONI
*Uptown Port-of-Spain*

*First Message*

dear mr robot:

now as i have lil chance 2 catch me breath & cool down some
after all dem boisterous carryings-ons of las night, of which
i can only admit shameful 2 have play my own part in dem,
my womanly desires catchin de best a me unawares much as
i fight dem down, cause lord only know dis pussy aint get a
good airing-out like dat in many a long day, & now it finish at
last wid all dat amount a pulsatin & twitchin-up so sweet & i
could collec meself little bit & sit down cool & calm & quiet
enough dis mornin 2 write u out dis email & put it all down
clear in b & w fa u 2 hear, so LISTEN GOOD what i tellin u,
eh: if u tink u could get u fockin hands pon dat machine easy
as dat, u mad like fockin toro!!! i aint oversee dese national
archives all dese amount a fockin years only 2 be ram-jam-
tank-u-mam quick & easy so, u unnastan? & i dont give a
FOCK if u is wealthy whiteman, or famous books writer from
amerika, or whoeverdeassitis, aint NOBODY does touch dat
xerox machine but me, u unnastan, & miss samlalsingh under
my own supervision, & u could fock me & miss samlalsingh 2

till BOTH WE PUSSIES SMOKING LIKE BUSHFIRE, but wouldn't get u no closer 2 dat machine, u unnastan?

good

now u unnastan

so mr robot i done check tru de card catalogue & fortunate for u in de c f stollmeyer esq collection is most a de numbers a dat journal u looking fa, DE MORNIN STAR, dating from 5 feb 1845 tru de following year approx, & i give dem a lil looksee meself & most is in pretty good shape & not 2 smudge & fade so u could read dem easy enough, & i check fa dem papers 2 a dis man u name, J A ETZLER, & in de stollmeyer esq collection u gots dem 2, 1 call PARADISE & nex call ME-CHANICAL SYSTEM & a turd i cant remember so good de name a-tall wid some longass fockin title bout MIGRATION 2 DE TROPICS & MATRIXULATION OF SOMEBODY OR SOMETING SO, & of course u got copies of all de local news from dat era 2, p o s gazette & guardian & standard & all de res

anyways, u gots dem all, mr robot, & me or miss samlalsingh will hol dem for u at de reserve frontdesk, but bear in mind mr robot what i tellin u, eh: rules is rules & laws is laws & u cannot remove NO documents from de premises a-tall a-tall, & as de sign post pon de wall behin de selfsame frontdesk read clear enough fa u & all to see in de queens own proper english & let me quote, UNDER NO CIRCUMSTANCES ARE PHO-TOCOPIES OF ARCHIVAL DOCUMENTS PERMITTED, AND ALL LAPTOPS, SCANNERS, OR OTHER ELEC-TRONIC DEVICES ARE STRICTLY FORBIDDEN ON

THE PREMISES, only PENCIL & PAPER mr robot 2 write
down what u want & take enough notes fa u research

cordial,
miss ramsol
director, t&tna

ps mr robot if u want 2 see me again 2night u could please
meet me at pelo roun 9

## Second Message

dear mr robot:

so u asks me las night when we did get tru wid all dat amount
a jookin-up & shoutin-down de place so sweet like dat mother
of jesus!!! & we was relaxin lil bit catchin a cool, & u wants
me to tell u lil someting bout my family here in t'dad & where
we comes from, & i dont mind 2 tell u since being a coolie aint
noting shameful fa me 2 feel embarrass bout a-tall, & even
dough in trut i aint know 2 much bout where we comes from
meself, only as i was sayin las night dat de furs of my ancestors 2 reach here in dis place come from calcutta pon de very
FURS ship a dem indenture coolies, de FATAL ROZAC, &
u sit up in de bed jus den wid you toetee still half-hard still
stannin-up like a stanpipe jus as i say dat exclaimin loud loud
HOW FOCKIN COOL IS DAT?! dat my ancestors arrive
here in port-of-spain de very same year as u family reach here
wid dat crazyass man ETZLER & he TROPICAL EMIGRA-
TION SOCIETY, de selfsame year of 1845

& i was tellin u how deepa, she was my great-great-great-gran-madoo, how she meet mahun, he was my great-great-great-gran-padoo, pon dat crossin from calcutta, but in fac i aint know if it was calcutta we comes from a-tall since de history a all dem indenture coolies in dis place reachback ONLY so far as de PORT dey disembark from, either calcutta or madras, wid all else before dat chop off & obliterate fagood faever, cause in trut my gran-madoo use 2 have a tiny lil sketchin dat she say pass down 2 she all de way from deepa, & even dough dat sketchin disappear long time i could remember it good good & it was a lil stream wid some rocks & lil bamboo bridge crossin over, & if u turn de paper it did write in handscript PUNJAUB 1822 pon de backside, & so me did start to tink from den DAT is where de family comes from in de northwes part of india, & we was probably punjaubi in trut, since where else would dat sketchin come from? & why else would deepa & my gran-madoo have it like dat? but nobody know fa sure

deepa was 20 when she make dat crossin from india & mahun only 18, & how dey meet was by coincidence 2 a dem wind up lyin side by side pon de pallet down below in de bowels a dat ship de fatal rozac as i was sayin, & deepa was sick sick & weak wid dysentery fa most a dat whole voyage, & even dough mahun scarce even know she, he did feed she grain-by-grain wid he own ration a daily rice & hers 2, fa she 2 gain back she strength like dat, & he give up most a he own 3 tincup a daily water, 2 keep she from dehydratin like dat, & when dey reach in t'dad at last after 96 days of voyage from calcutta & 41 days from de cape, & dey was BOTH near dead in trut, dey have de very good fortune 2 get hire out pon de selfsame cane estate in de south a de island near san fernando dat wasnt even much of a town yet in dem 1845 times, & so from de start a dat voyage cross de sea, mahun & deepa never did spend not even 1 single night separate

mahun & deepa was both de same sudra caste, & dat was good & bad 2 in different ways, furs it was bad since sudra was de servant-caste, de lowest a de 3 castes after brahman & kshatriya, but mahun was even LOWER den she as u will hear in a sec, de lowes a de low, only people lower den he is pariahs, but dat was GOOD 2 in de sense dat since mahun & deepa was de SAME sudra-caste dey could marry widout breakin de law, by which i means de CASTE LAW, & deepa & mahun DID marry 2 as u will hear, cause u might tink dat after dey reach in t'dad dose laws of fockin caste did no longer apply 2 de coolies, & dat crossin 2 a new land & life would put everybody pon de SELFSAME level, but u would be very wrong mr robot & dat is 1 ting de chupidee whitepeople didnt have NO FOCKIN IDEA, cause even dough everyting ELSE change fa dem indenture coolies, de separation of caste is 1 ting dey still maintain in dem ole days very stringent & rigid mongst deyselves

but mahun was even lower den just sudra, as i was sayin, he was a CHAMAR-sudra & dey was de leather-workers who mutilate de hide of de sacred ox, but dat was bad & good again as u will hear, cause dat skill of leather-workin 2 make de shoes & belts & bags & such, but mostly shoes, mahun had plenty skill in dat from a lil boy, even dough it was look down pon in india so bad dat even de SHADOW of a chamar pon de food of a holy fockin brahman would contaminate it & u got 2 trow it way & not even a mongrel dog could eat it, but dat was a GOOD ting fa mahun cause before long de overseer of dat estate find out bout he skills fa makin shoe, & nex ting u know

he take mahun off de canecrew & put he 2 make boot fa he &
shoe fa he wife & doux-doux & ALL de whitepeople, & soon
as mahun catch enough money from makin de shoe he marry
deepa in one bigass fancy MONSOON WEDDING PON DAT
ESTATE!!! & now de overseer take deepa off de canecrew 2 &
put she 2 assis mahun in de shoeshop, so listen here wha happen how de whole ting did catch like fockin bushfire

cause furs mahun was makin shoe fa de overseer & de res
of de whitepeople pon dat estate, & in trut he & deepa was
makin dey daily wage by law like all de res a dem indenture
coolies, ¢25/day each, & sometimes dey would get a lil ¢5 or
¢8 lagniappe from de overseer wife or he doux-doux or 1 of he
daughters when dey get a nice shoe, but nex ting u know all
dem COOLIES come 2 mahun & deepa 2 make DEY shoes 2,
at ¢18 fa man-boot & ¢15 fa woman-shoe & ¢9 fa child-shoe,
& mahun could buy a whole cowskin fa ¢50 from de butcher
dat he was trowin dem way anyway & sometimes if a cow dead
from disease dey didnt have 2 pay nuting fa dat hide a-tall, so
jus as u could imagine nex ting u know word spread round 2
all dem other estates 2, & mahun & deepa was makin plenty
shoe fa de whitepeople, & even MORE fockin shoe fa de coolies now, & before long plenty plenty money was wetting dey
palms in trut!!!

so nex ting u know de 10 years of contracture fa dey indenture labor was finish-up, so deepa & mahun was entitle 2 free
passage back 2 india now, or else according to de new law jus
institute den if dey elec to remain here, dey would receive a
parcel of 10 acres of land 2 put in agriculture fa deyself, but
deepa & mahun didnt want 2 go back 2 india not fa noting
cause dey was RICH RICH coolies livin like king and queen in

t'dad now, so dey choose 2 take de land dat was 5 acres each, or 10 acres 2gether, but since mahun & deepa didnt know nutin bout agriculture neither but only makin shoe shoe shoe & more shoe, dey didnt want dat lan in de country, & so dey sell it off & take dat money + what dey had save-up 2 buy a shop in san fernando on coffee street 2 make & sell de shoe, wit a floor on top where dey could live wid dey children dat was 3 now, 2 boys & 1 girl, & ALL a dem born trinis!!!

so now mr robot u have a lil bit bout where my family comes from & how we reach here in t'dad, dat i dont mine telling u as i was sayin, cause being a coolie aint noting fa me to feel shame fa, but i was just about 2 finish writin out dis email dis mornin 5 minutes ago when miss samlalsingh arrive fa work & she explain 2 me how yesterday thursday when i did had de afternoon off & she was in charge, u come in here in de archives sayin how MISS RAMSOL GIVE U PERMISSION 2 USE DE MACHINE & copy u copies of dat MORNING STAR journal or whateverdeass it is of dis crazy man ETZLER u say u writin u book about, & u tell miss samlalsingh how u & miss ramsol is tight tight now fockin down de place like wild tigercats mos every night, & miss samlalsingh know is tru 2, but mr robot she tell u jus as i instruct SHE enough times, dont matter if is de QUEEN A FOCKIN ENGLAN PUSSY U FOCKIN, dat dont give u access 2 dat xerox machine, & i aint know who de fock u yankees tink u is, just cause u skin white like u toetee make from gold-bar & u pums smell like french perfume, but miss samlalsingh is more savvy den dat & she see tru u boldface lies straightway & dont let u near dat machine, not fa fockin hell mr robot, so listen here mr robot what i telling u, eh: u best learn some fockin manners & behave youself & follow de rules jus like everybody else, unnastan? eh? cause laws is laws & rules is rules & aint no exceptions fa dat xerox, not fa u nor nobody else, unnastan?

good

so watch u fockin self mr robot, unnastan? eh?

cordial,
miss ramsol
director, t&tna

ps if u want u could please 2 meet me at pelo 2nght again roun 9
pss & me or miss samlalsingh will be holdin someting fa u at de reserve frontdesk from de p o s gazette of 1845 dat would be of interes 2 u i tink

### THE PORT OF SPAIN GAZETTE
30th November 1845

### FIRST LOT OF INDIAN IMMIGRANTS
We have much pleasure in announcing the arrival this afternoon of the long-looked-for coolie ship, the *Fatal Rozac*, 96 days from Calcutta and 41 days from the Cape of Good Hope, with 217 coolies on board, "all in good condition," as the bills of landing have it. There were five deaths on board during the passage, but the general appearance of the coolies is very healthy. When our people are informed that there are count-less thousands of these coolies, inured to a tropical cli-mate, starving in their own country, and most willing

to emigrate to the West Indies, it may be the means of opening their eyes a little to the necessity of working more steadily and giving greater satisfaction to their employers. Coolie provisions also arriving aboard the *Rozac* are available at Losh, Spiers & Co. at Richmond Street Wharf. The *Fatal Rozac* is a fine vessel of 445 tons, and is manned by a crew of lascars.

Coolie provisions (very *cheap*) include:
  *rice*
  *dholl*
  *ghee*
  *tumeric*
  *chillies*
  *tobacco &*
  *"Indian hemp"*


## THE PORT OF SPAIN GAZETTE
### 5th December 1845

## ARRIVAL OF THE ROSALIND

We have the pleasure of announcing this morning that the *Rosalind* arrived in port, 52 days out from London and 27 days from the Azores, bearing a number of passengers and discharging a good deal of long-awaited goods and produce. Included among the travelers were the first lot of "pioneers," 31 in number, of the "Tropical Emigration Society," a certain joint-stock association formed in London by Messrs. A.J. Etzler and C.F. Stollmeyer, who arrived also aboard the *Rosalind* amongst their enthusiastic followers. Mr. Etzler is apparently a self-styled inventor, scientist, and philanthropist. He is here in Trinidad not only as director and founder of the T.E.S., but also as Consulting Engineer for the construction of the Great Western Railway, Trinidad's first rail system, which will connect our capital with San Fernando and other locations in the south. Mr. Stollmeyer, secretary and agent of the T.E.S., has been a printer in London and Philadelphia (U.S.A.). The *Rosalind* is a fine vessel of 490 tons under the charge of Captain James Damphier. Goods and produce may be purchased at Losh, Spiers & Co. at Richmond Street Wharf, and include the following:

*fine linens*
*men's and women's shoes*
*female lingerie & hosiery*
*women's lipsticks & powders*
*sherry & wine*
*champagne*
*brandy*
*Spanish salted hams*
*Dutch Edam cheeses*
*medicines*
*writing paper & pens*

*Third Message*

dear mr robot:

i wish to broach a certain topic wid u mr robot & i hope 2 EJUCATE u lil bit bout how we feels here in t'dad, & what is de proper attitude & etiquette involve, & dat is de subjec of

PUMS, cause las night when we did finish up wid we TURD sweet jook fa de night mother of jesus!!! & we was lyin dere catching de cool relaxin lil bit & i was feelin so NICE mr robot, so comfortable & relax, & i jus let a good one fly, & stink good enough from all dem delicious curry crabbacks we enjoy so much from we dinner down by krishnahouse, & fresh seamoss drink, & in trut mr robot when i let dat pum go & stinkin up pretty good, straightway u pinch u nostrils & look at me all squeezeface & disgust like i is bushmonkey wid no manners, but dat only go to show mr robot how u dont understand nuttin bout how we feel in t'dad & what is de important HEALTH ISSUES involve in de subject of PUMS, same as BELCHES as a matter of fac

cause here in t'dad nobody would never make such a fuss and make u feel bad and look pon u all squeezeface and disgust when u let a good pum lose like dat, jus de OPPOSITE mr robot, people here in t'dad understan how pums is a natural organic process & nuttin to feel shame a-tall but only a tru expression & celebration of de goodness of life & mr robot why u want to hol DAT back? & not let it show how u feel happy & content in de moment & SHARE dat happiness wid other people? cause lord only know, human beins come out de womb pummin, & we all go 2 we grave pummin 2, so why u want to hide it way? & in trut mr robot de bes ting dat could ever happen to u in my opinion, & de bes ting dat we trinis could teach all a u fockin yankees, is to let youself loose lil bit, & free-up & let down u guard, & learn how 2 ENJOY DE SIMPLE PLEASURES OF A SWEET SWEET PUM

dat is my hope fa u in dis life mr robot

cordial,
miss ramsol
director, t&tna

ps see u at pelo round 9
pss me or miss samlalsingh would be holdin an article from out
de guardian weekly health advise column of dr brito salizar,
dat would be very informative & prove 2 u what i sayin

## LISTEN TO YOUR BODY
## 'CAUSE IT KNOWS BEST
### the GUARDIAN'S Weekly Health Advice Column
### Brito Salizar, M.D., O.B.E.

Today, in response to a number of inquiries expressing
deep and understandable concern to arrive of late at
this P.O. Box, December being the official opening of
*châtiaigne* season (♫ *châtiaigne châtiaigne, the musical
fruit, the more you eat, the more you toot!* ♫), we shall
consider, in some detail, the proper and healthy attitude toward "flatulence," or, as it is called here in Trinidad in the local parley, *pumming*. Now: In a number of
so called "advanced" societies, historically speaking, it
is known that the unguarded and boldfaced expression of flatulence is widely frowned upon. This may
be so. What must be understood clearly in the first
instance is that these particular *morés* have never held
any sway whatsoever for the health profession, and
absolutely no subscribing to by medical science and/
or practitioners of the same. They are purely *societal
conventions*, inconvenient at worst and misleading at

best, and should be dispensed with immediately.

How can we say this, and with what surety? Well, do the beasts of the field, the fowls of the air, or the fishes of the sea strain so inexplicably to hold up their flatulence? This could and should never have been for the history of human civilization, and sad that it has ever come to pass! In fact, the restrained or incomplete expulsion of gasses from the body is known to cause a number of health issues, physiological and psychical, e.g., premature aging and mental blindness. It plays havoc with the entire circulatory system, including the blood. Where the gasses collect, joint pains are frequently encountered. There is occasional osteopathy.

Let me end on a personal note: Myna, my old Venezuelan grandmother, was in her later years confined to a wheelchair. This did not deter her. When the need arose, she would shift her weight in her chair as best she could and lift up the appropriate buttock manually, even in mixed company. *Fait accompli*, and smiling blissfully, she would tell us, "*El culo está contento!*" ("My pumsee is happy!") She lived to 98.

### Fourth Message

dear mr robot:

you is a fockin shitong mr robot is what you is!!! all night long, 2 a we jookin down de place like no 2morrow, & u playin so fockin innocent, never mind dat jookin was so sweet & i can only admit shameful how much i was lovin it 2, my pussy still pulsatin & twitchin & smokin-up lil bit so nice dis mornin

sweet jesus when i reach in the archives, & miss samlalsingh
come runnin 2 tell me furs ting what take place yesterday
thurs afternoon during my half-day off, how you did come inside here totin U OWN PERSONAL XEROX MACHINE,
wherever de ass u get it from, & u tells miss samlalsingh how
i give u EXPRESS PERMISSION to bring dis machine inside
de archives like dat, & u tells she how MISS RAMSOL SAY
u could copy out as much copies as u want to do u research
fa dis fockin crazyass man ETZLER & dis book u say u writin, even dough of course miss samlalsingh know straightway
dat was only another 1 of you boldface lies & SCHEME IS
SCHEME U SCHEMING she again to copy out u copies, &
she tells u NO FOCKIN WAY MR ROBOT!!! but u carry u
bigass machine inside de place regardless & plug de plug &
commence to copyin out all u fuckin copies

but miss samlalsingh tell me how before de furs 5 copies
come out from u machine, or maybe de furs 2 numbers of
dat MORNIN STAR, whilst she was bawling down de place
hysterical like i instruct she in perilous situations like dat, to
SHUT DOWN DAT FOCKIN MACHINE STRAIGHT-
WAY MR ROBOT!!! & miss samlalsingh tell me how furs
ting before u know it, ALL de visitors in de archives including
we famous local scholar & historian michael anthony, who
happen 2 be dere in de archives yesterday 2, commence to
queuing up straightway in a long long queue, all of dem fightin
down each other now 2 copy out DEY copies wid u machine,
& dey was all shouting dat if some fockin foreigner yankeeass-
whiteman could copy he copies den DEY COULD COPY
DEY COPIES 2, & before de furs 5 copies come out u didnt
have no choice a-tall but let miss roses copy she copy of recipe
fa guava duff out last saturday gazette, & mr hosien want 2

copy he copy of de sunday horseraces-paddocks-lineup from de standard, & michael anthony want to copy out a next article from some bigass old book he got bout french and spanish colonial architectural occupation in oldtown p o s or some shit so, and u had 2 let dem copy out dey copies 2, cause if not, u would have pon u hands a RACE RIOT FOR EQUAL & FAIR USE OF DE PHOTOCOPY MACHINE IN DE T&T NATIONAL ARCHIVES

so in trut mr robot i aint know how much of copies you manage to copy out yesterday afternoon, dat i can only suppose not much more den de furs few numbers a dat MORNIN STAR, cause u had to let all de rest 2 copy dey copies 2, & den miss samlalsingh say u had to put in more ink was so many copies dem people was copyin, and den dat xerox start to smoke from overheat-exhaustion jus like my pussy did wear out and break down las night from all de jookin, so before u know it was 5 oclock, time fa de archives to close, & u didnt scarce get tru 5 numbers a dat fockin STAR, & after longlast wid all she shoutin and bawlin miss samlalsingh could pull de plug pon u machine & shut it down, but i say it serve u fockin yankee-whiteass right

so mr robot u best listen good good to me here now what i tellin u, eh? & dont try dat one again, u hear? eh? cause laws is laws & rules is rules and NO PERSONAL PORTABLE FOCKIN PHOTOCOPY EQUIPMENT allow inside, & u know it good enough, even dough in trut according 2 miss samlalsingh dat machine u was totin wasnt so small a-tall a-tall, but she say it was BIG as a BARREL of BABASH BUSH-RUM wid you redface strainin hard 2 carry it, dat me & miss samlalsingh couldnt help weself from laughin lil bit at dat, & i hope it give u a fockin

HERNIA mr robot, jus so long as it dont ruin u jookin equipment, cause dat would be a shame in trut

cordial,
miss ramsol
director, t&tna

ps see u at pelo 2night round 9 same as usual

*Fifth Message*

dear mr robot:

i only gots 1 ting to tell u, so LISTEN GOOD: u best haul u
fockin ass & go home back to new york or whereverdeass is de
shit place in amerika u comes from, cause u say u cant take it no
more, u goin crazy, & all u wants to do is copy out a few copies
to make de research fa dis book u say u writin bout dis crazyass
man ETZLER and he TES, but u cant do it, u jus cant do it, u
done try everyting & every scheme is scheme u could tink of &
noting work, noting a-tall, 3 months now u tryin & STILL no
photocopies, & u say how dis place t'dad is de turd world & we
is all bushmonkeys livin here, dat we dont know noting bout
noting a-tall, but i could only tell u DIS mr robot: TENEGRITY
& IMPESTUOSITY is what we got aplenty here in t'dad, dat u
never bounce up de likes of noting like DAT before in amerika,
cause rules is rules & laws is laws & when i say NO photocopies
allow in de t&t national archives i means NONE, no matter
who u is & what pussy u fockin, even if it is de director MISS
RAMSOL OWN, & if u cant write out u notes wid pencil &
paper like everybody else, den 2 fockin bad fa u mr robot!!!

& in trut mr robot i could tell u someting else: i got a good mind to tell my brothers how u do, cause if raj and lil buddah only FIND OUT, would be proper hell to pay, i could assure u bout dat, how u did try & subjuice me only to gain access to dat machine, & how u succeed sure enough but ONLY in de subjuicing part, & not de machine part a-tall a-tall, & soon enough 2 of we was jookin down de place like no tomorrow, & i could only admit shameful how much i was lovin it 2, but den mr robot U FIND OUT sure enough how SWEET is coolie-t'dad-pussy in trut, & nex ting U CANT GET ENOUGH NEITHER, same as me, & u say 1 ting fa sure dey aint got NOTING like DAT in amerika!!! dat coolie-t'dad-pussy, & soon as we start to jookin down de place like dat u forget every scheme u was schemin to try to get u hands pon dat xerox machine, & all u wants is jook jook jook & nex jook again every night 2 of we screamin down de place like wild tigercats, & nex ting like u forget everyting else, book-writin & TES & ETZLER & all de rest, & only jook is jook u want to be jookin so sweet every night & me 2 mother of jesus!!! but now u say u done had enough, u oversaturate & cant take it no more, & if u cant copy out u copies u give up and goin back home 2 amerika, & i say in trut i dont give a fock mr robot, only ting i would miss de jookin, & i got a good mind 2 tell my brothers lil buddah and raj how u do

cordial,
miss ramsol
director, t&tna

ps u say u dont want to see me never again (less u could make u copies), but if u change u mind u could meet me at pelo round 9 same as usual

pss & i would make sure 2 be wearin dem dentalfloss panties u love 2

### Sixth Message

dear mr robot:

i so sorry!!! soon as raj and lil buddah tell me what happen i did feelin so bad, i rush fas as i could down to de hospital & still wearin my panties fa u from las night 2, but de nurse say u done get a discharge & leave de mergency room & only a little rattle wid no broken bones but only dem 2 blue-eye and buss-up nose, cause i was sittin dere in pelo waitin fa u so long & den i start to gettin vex 2, vex & sad both, so i call my brothers pon de cell & tell dem come carry me home, & nex ting my brothers lil buddah and raj come in pelo & dey see me sittin pon de bar & lookin so forlorn mos in tears, & dey asks me straightway what happen wid u lil sis? & nex ting u know i tell dem everyting, de whole long story come spillin out, bout how u did subjuice me jus to try & copy out u copies but still i stick by de rules no matter what, cause laws is laws & still i wouldnt give u de copies but take proper advantage of all dat sweet jookin sure enough, cause i aint no fool mr robot, but now u say u vex & cant take it no more & want to go back home in amerika, fock-&-run

raj say OH-HO!!! he say FOCK-&-RUN?! fockin yankeeass-whiteman want to FOCK-MY-LIL-SIS-&-RUN?! & right den lil buddah chime in behind he sayin sis, i didnt jus hear you say FOCK-&-RUN?! please dont tell me my ears didnt jus perceive u sayin FOCK-&-RUN?! not FOCK-&-RUN?! & nex ting u know lil buddah & raj bolt from inside pelo out de door & no way i could hol dem back neither, cause dey was in a rampage on de search fa u now in de hilton or wherever dey could find u mr robot, & i did know dat would only mean plenty plenty trouble 2, so onliest ting i could do is knockback de rest of my rumcocktail & hurry hail a maxitaxi & go home fas as i could to wait fa dem, & soon as my brothers reach home i ask dem U FIND MR ROBOT?! & raj say give he 2 blue-eye, & lil buddah say buss mr robot nose, & i say what u do dat fa? how u could buss poor mr robot nose and give he 2 blue-eye? & lil buddah say sis, u dont say FOCK-&-RUN & ask WHAT FA? not FOCK-&-RUN, so i ask well where mr robot is now? & raj say mus be de hospital

so mr robot i was feelin so bad when i hear bout this beatin raj and lil buddah give u, i rush furs ting down to dat mergency room & dont even tink to change from out my panties i was wearin special fa u, dem dentalfloss ones u love so much & say dey aint got noting like dat in amerika neither, dats how bad i was feelin mr robot, & den de nurse tell me u was only a little rattle & she give u de discharge & now in trut i was more distress den ever mr robot, cause u wasnt dere dat i could explain everyting, & say how sorry i feel, & i go back to pelo & u wasnt dere neither, & i check de hilton & u wasnt dere neither, & now i was goin mad, i jus dont know what i could do i did feel so terrible, & onliest ting i could promise u mr robot, if u come in de archives dis morning u could make a few, only a FEW photocopies mr robot, but i know dat few would be enough to make u heart feel glad

cordial,
miss ramsol
director, t&tna

ps plus mr robot we would be private back in my office where
de machine keep
pss & i would still be wearing dem fa u 2


*Seventh Message*

dear mr robot:

I say YES mr robot, YES YES YES cause i was so happy when
lil buddah & raj reach home las night & tell me how dey find
u in de hilton, where i say u was stayin & we did have so much
of sweet sweet jookin in dat hotel 2 mother of jesus, & raj and
lil buddah say u had all u bags pack & ready to go back home
in amerika, & so sad & forlorn dat all dis time u have dedicate
2 research u book & now u have 2 go home empty-handed,
except fa dem 5-6 photocopies u manage to copy out yesterday pon dat machine dat i give u permission, but u say dat aint
enough, u say dat aint noting a-tall, u need to make PLENTY
PLENTY more copies fa u research before u could write dis
book, but now u give up cause u cant fight it no more, & u
bags pack ready to go home empty-handed

so lil buddah & raj invite u fa drink downstairs in de hotel
bar, dat dey could discuss dis matter wid u men-to-man, & u
say ok, u would take a drink wid dem, & lil buddah say well
u know mr robot, de people got dey rules, & if de law say no
photocopies pon dat machine in de archives except what miss

ramsol make, cause she in charge, den u gots 2 abide by de
rules, & raj chime in 2 & he say yes, rules is rules & laws is
laws, but is not only de ARCHIVES got dey rules, & here in
t'dad WE got a NEX law dat say u dont FOCK-DEY-LIL-SIS-
&-RUN BACK HOME IN AMERIKA, not so easy as dat mr
robot, not dey lil sis, so raj say mr robot u got to do what is
right & proper according to de rules, & lil buddah say yes it is
mr robot, so let we cease from beatin round de bush & come
direc to de point here: lil buddah say he KNOW u would want
to follow de rules mr robot & do what is right & proper, cause
dat mash-up face & bust-nose & dem blue-eyes is only a lil
TASTE of what u would be tastin if u dont, & lil buddah say
look here mr robot, u want to copy out u photocopies in de
archives? u say is plenty plenty more photocopies u needs to
copy out in de archives? well we only offerin u a lil suggestion of
how u could do it, as much of photocopies as u want to copy, as
much of copies as u could ever WISH TO COPY, & lil buddah
say, & let me tell u someting else mr robot: u tink u could find
anyting so sweet as lil sis in amerika? all dem hard-back womens
dey got in amerika & so stingy 2? what u goin back dere fa? lil
buddah say mr robot, u could have dem BOTH, pussy & photocopies, as much as u could want, only ting is u got to do what
is right & proper by de rules, u got to follow de rules

well raj & lil buddah say u did start to SMILE lil bit now,
u was still sad & folorn but now u was smilin lil bit 2, now dat
dey plant dis idea in u head, & mr robot u say ok, u not going
back home in amerika, flight cancel, u stayin here in t'dad &
u doin what is right according to de rules, & u tell raj & lil
buddah please to tell miss ramsol u would be in de archives
bright & early tomorrow mornin to settle everyting good and
proper, & anyway u did always dream to settle down in t'dad,
& despite dat a trini wife & trini children was never part of

dat dream before, it is now, cause you doin what is right and proper according to de rules, and raj and lil buddah say dey was smilin now 2, & all 3 of u was smilin happy huggin up 2gether, 2 coolies & 1 yankee-whiteman, & raj stand up to he feet & raise-up he glass & say, let we drink a toast to mr robot, we new yankee brother-in-law!!!

cordial,
miss ramsol
director, t&tna

ps mr robot i would be waitin in de back room wearin my den-talfloss panties, & dat machine runnin waitin fa u 2
pss MONSOON WEDDING IN U TAIL!!!

# THE BEST LAID PLANS

BY DARBY MALONEY

*San Juan*

> *The best laid schemes o' mice an' men*
> *Gang aft a-gley,*
> *An' lea'e us nought but grief and pain,*
> *For promis'd joy.*
> —Robert Burns, "To a Mouse, on Turning Her
> Up in Her Nest with the Plough"

K a Pau was humming with gamblers. Coins clinking into machines echoed throughout the casino punctuated by winnings jangling in metal trays.

"Hey, Andre!" Honesto bounced his friend on the arm and leaned over his shoulder to peer at the images crossing the screen. "How yuh goin'?"

Andre looked up from his twenty-five-cent game and grinned. "Not bad. What's happenin'?"

"Nothing much," Honesto yawned. "Yuh winning?"

Like clockwork, Honesto showed up at the casino each Friday night looking for his friend. He and Andre had met a few months earlier when he had arrived in Trinidad from the Philippines. Twenty-nine-year-old Honesto been recruited to work in Trinidad as a pharmacist. Andre drove a taxi and was looking for a return fare from Piarco Airport when Honesto had emerged from Customs. Since then, they had become friends, with Andre providing taxi service for Honesto and his Filipino buddies.

"Win some, lose some," Andre shrugged. "But," he winked, reaching into the white plastic container for more coins, "mostly winning." They laughed as Andre pulled the lever, the screen blurring and whirring before abruptly stopping. Immediately coins rattled into the tray.

"Way to go!" Honesto slapped Andre on the back.

"If this keep up," Andre declared, "I go make my car payment this month. This machine hot. Before you came, I hit three lemons and made an easy hundred. This better than driving taxi."

"I hear yuh, man. Sometimes it's like that. Yuh get lucky and hit a good machine."

The cocktail waitress appeared with Andre's Carib. He reached into his pot and dropped some coins onto her tray. She turned to Honesto. "Yuh having the same as your brother?"

"Yeah, but he's not my brother," Honesto grinned. "He's not good-looking enough."

"You lucky to look even a little like me, boy." Andre scooped more coins, inserted them into the machine, and pulled the lever. Two cherries appeared as coins clanked below. Again Andre fed the machine. When the spinning stopped, there was silence. He deposited more coins. The reels whirled and twirled then stopped. Nothing.

"Hey, you're losing your touch." Honesto edged closer. "Let me try."

"Find your own machine," Andre replied. "Yuh may be my friend, but there's no way I'm sharing this cash cow with yuh!" He fed the machine again. The machine hummed like a blender, followed by clattering coins just as the waitress returned with Honesto's beer.

Honesto reached into the winnings for her tip. "Timing is everything!"

"I need another pot," Andre bragged. "Go get me another pot. This baby is set to pay." While Honesto went to the cashier's cage for the container, Andre dropped more coins into the slot. The reels raced, then stopped abruptly—three cherries on the pay line, more jangling in the tray.

"Thanks," Andre said, taking the plastic container from Honesto and scooping up the coins. "Stay here and keep my place. Whatever you do, don't give up my machine. I'll be right back." He drained his Carib.

"Hey, man, can I play with your money while you're gone?"

"Use yuh own money," Andre retorted, standing the empty bottle sentry-like behind the plastic pots.

"I'm broke."

"What the hell yuh mean yuh broke? Is payday!"

"You know I send my money home to the Philippines on Friday. Hey, you don't want to chance letting her get cold while you're gone, do you?"

"Okay," Andre laughed. "Just don't get too attached." He turned to leave and then stopped. "But what if yuh win with my money?"

"It's yours," Honesto said.

"No, no, that's not fair," Andre protested. "If yuh pull the arm and win, the money's part yours."

"But it's your money and your machine."

"Hear what. If yuh win, we go split it, 50-50. How that sounding?"

"You sure?" Honesto asked.

"Yeah. Keep she warm!" Andre grinned. He turned and headed for the washroom, maneuvering among throngs clus-

218 // Trinidad Noir

tered around the slots and tables, drinking beers while waiting for a machine.

"Good evening, good evening, Mr. Persad," beamed the manager. "How is everything tonight?"

"Real good," Andre grinned. "Just don't go resetting my machine before I come back!" They both laughed.

When Andre returned from the washroom, an annoying bell was clamoring like a car alarm. Then he realized that the flashing amber light was above his machine.

"Yes, yes! Honesto! We win!" he shouted, craning to see the face of the machine through the crowd that surrounded Honesto. He caught a glimpse of the manager conferring with Honesto. The manager straightened and worked his way through the crowd past Andre. "How much is the jackpot?" Andre asked.

"Twelve thousand dollars."

"All right, man!" Andre yelled. He shouldered his way to the machine. Three magenta sevens crossed the pay line. "Hey, Honesto!"

Honesto stopped scooping coins into the plastic container. He jumped up and hugged Andre. "Jackpot!" he beamed, pointing to the screen.

"I knew this machine was going to pay big!" Andre crowed. "Twelve thousand dollars! I calling Mary."

While Andre was on his mobile with his wife, the manager returned and handed Honesto a check. He shook Honesto's hand then left. Andre pressed off and shoved his cell in his pocket. He rubbed his hands in anticipation.

"Lemme see that beautiful piece of paper." Honesto handed him the check. "Hey," Andre stared. "This check is only in your name."

Honesto shrugged. "The manager said they only put one name on it."

"So let we change it now and split it," Andre said.

"They don't pay out that kind of cash," Honesto explained. "That's why he gave me the check. Monday on my lunch hour I'll go to my bank and cash it. I'll give you your half when you pick me up after work."

"Okay," Andre answered. "But I really wanted to go home and throw money all over Mary." They laughed and finished gathering up the coins. On their way to the cashier's cage, they passed their cocktail waitress. Andre tilted one of the brimming containers above her tray. "Is good luck to share the wealth," he grinned.

The cashier handed Andre over three hundred dollars for the coins. "We hafta celebrate, Honesto. Where yuh want to go?"

Honesto paused. "Now that's a tough one—seeing as we can go anywhere we want!"

On Monday, after collecting his boys from school, Andre headed for the San Juan SuperPharm to pick up Honesto. He hated traveling in Port-of-Spain at eight in the morning and three in the afternoon because that was when parents were delivering or retrieving their school-age children. Parents refused to risk possible kidnapping by letting their children travel. Soon the rainy season, with its intermittent downpours, would increase the congestion.

When he finally reached the pharmacy, it was after four. Honesto was not outside. He never waited in the tropical sun if Andre was late.

Andre turned to Brandon and Adam. "Allyuh wait here. Don't touch nothing. I'm coming back just now. After I drop off Honesto," he added, "I go carry allyuh to MovieTowne in the arcade and we go celebrate." He disappeared inside the pharmacy. Soon he and Honesto emerged.

"Hi, guys." Honesto nodded to the boys as he got into the front seat. They smiled back.

Andre slid behind the wheel and turned expectantly to Honesto. "So where my money, boy?" he asked with a smile.

Honesto looked down. "Sorry, Andre."

Andre stared. "What yuh mean, 'Sorry'?"

"We were really busy today, Monday and all. I didn't have time to go to the bank." Honesto looked up. "But I will tomorrow. I promise."

Andre was silent. He felt a sick churning in his stomach. "I hope yuh not lying to me."

"Of course not," Honesto said quickly.

Maybe too quickly, Andre thought. "Because I really counting on that money," he continued slowly. "Where Mary working, they closing down by the end of the month, and I have to keep up the installment on this car." He paused. "And yuh know long time we putting off Brandon operation."

"Don't worry. I was just busy," Honesto assured him. "I'll cash it tomorrow." They rode in silence for a while, and then exchanged small talk until they reached Honesto's apartment.

"So I go pick yuh up after work again tomorrow?" Andre asked.

Honesto handed him the fare. "Yeah. Four o'clock at the pharmacy."

But the next day Honesto was not there. The clerk told Andre it was Honesto's day off.

"He tell me to pick him up here this afternoon," Andre insisted.

"One of you must have made a mistake," the clerk shrugged.

Andre left. He sat in his car dumbfounded. Then he pulled out his cell and dialed Honesto's number. The phone rang and rang. No one answered, not even voice mail.

"Yuh sonofabitch," Andre said softly. His jaw set as he started up the car and headed for Honesto's. How he could stiff me like that? For months I chauffeur him and his friends wherever they want to go, give him priority over my other customers. I invite him to my house for Christmas, not just because he was alone and far from his own family, but because I like him. Mary and the boys and me, we even organize that birthday party for him and invite all the Filipinos. "That sonofabitch," Andre repeated as he swung onto Jerningham Avenue.

A few cars were parked outside Honesto's whitewashed, two-story apartment building. Andre pulled into visitor parking, got out, and strode to Honesto's door. He pounded on the painted metal, then stepped aside so he could not be seen through the peephole. He waited. There was no sound from within. Further down, someone was blasting Machel Montano's "One More Time." Andre banged on Honesto's door again. He in there, all right. He just too coward to face me. Angrily, Andre started back to his car. "He can't hide from me," he fumed. "He must go to work."

"Andre!" Honesto stood, head bowed, in his doorway, a cowering child called to the principal's office.

Andre turned. "Give me my money now," he demanded. "I want my money, boy."

"I don't have it."

"What the hell yuh mean you don't have it?" Andre shouted.

Honesto glanced around the complex nervously. "Please keep your voice down."

"I go keep my voice down when yuh give me my money."

"It's gone," Honesto said quietly. "I sent it home to my mother."

"No," Andre said. "Yuh send *your* money home for yuh mother, not mine. I want *my* money now."

"It's too late. I don't have it. Besides," Honesto added defensively, "it was my money. I won it, not you."

"But we agreed to split it." Andre's voice rose again. "Yuh used my machine and my money!"

"But I won. The money was my winnings, and now it's gone." Honesto stepped back and reached to close the door.

"Yuh lying sonofabitch!" Andre shouted, lunging at the door. The lock clicked.

That night as they lay in bed, Andre told Mary what had happened. "But he tief yuh money. How he could do yuh that?" she wailed.

"He just do it," Andre responded wearily.

"To me, all the money was yours," Mary declared. "It was your machine, and Honesto play with your money." She shook her head. "I just don't understand him. He's a pharmacist and he working for more money than you, and he won't even split it. And you was his friend."

"All he care about is the money," Andre sighed. "Money is the only reason he come to Trinidad."

"I still can't believe he could tief from us like that and get away with it."

Andre shrugged. "Tell it to the judge, I guess."

"Why not?" Mary demanded.

"Why not what?"

"Why not tell it to the judge? Sue Honesto for the money!"

"I thinking about doing that," Andre said glumly, "but there isn't enough money involved for that. After time off from work and legal expenses, it might cost me six thousand to get my six thousand."

"Six? Go for the whole twelve! Honesto obviously don't believe you have an agreement to split it."

"That is true," Andre agreed. "But it still risky to sue. There's no guarantee, and if we lose, we go be in more expense."

"There must be something we could do," Mary sighed, turning off the bedside lamp. "Even with all the crime in Trinidad, being victims like this is the last thing I would have thought."

Andre lay awake, his stomach churning. He tief my money. It was my machine and my money he sent home like clockwork to his mother. And I trusted him, that sonofabitch. My money, and now it's gone—he stopped. That's it! Why didn't I think of that before? Excited, he began to make a plan. Yes, it just might work. Life may not be fair, he thought grimly, but that don't mean I can't try to right the wrongs.

The next morning, after dropping Brandon and Adam at school, Andre drove directly to Honesto's complex. This time he parked outside on Jerningham Avenue. As he opened the car door, a pair of screeching keskidees flew from an overhead wire to a neighboring branch plumb-lined with ruddy mangos. He hastened to the nearest door on the first floor of the complex and glanced at the lock. Kwikset. Then he hurried back to his car and drove to the Priority Mall in San Juan.

In the locksmith shop, a middle-aged woman was seated behind the counter talking on her mobile. "Yuh think I pluck myself and get money? Yuh understand?" she was saying. She nodded at Andre and added, "Customer come. Call yuh later."

"Where Moony?" Andre demanded.

The woman slowly looked up from putting her mobile in her purse, rolled her eyes, and steupsed loudly. "What? Yuh don't even say hello? Where yuh manners gone, boy?"

"Sorry," Andre said sheepishly. "Good morning."

"That's more like it. I don't know what this country coming to," she continued, shaking her head. "First people don't have no time to talk with people, now they don't even say good morning! What you in such a rush for, boy?"

Great, Andre thought. A talker. "No rush. I just thinking 'bout all I have to do today, is all."

She shook her head. "Yuh going to have a heart attack, yuh keep up like that. This is Trinidad, boy. Nothing can't wait." To Andre's relief she turned and called out, "Moony!"

A stocky East Indian appeared from the back room. "Lightning Man!" Leo Moonsammy beamed, giving Andre a bear hug. He and Andre had played football together at San Juan Secondary Comprehensive and remained friends through the years.

After exchanging small talk, Andre said, "Listen, Moony, I need a bump key."

"What for? Yuh turning to a life of crime?" Moony joked.

"Anything gotta be more profitable than driving taxi," Andre laughed. "Adam lock a door in the house I need to open."

"What kind you need?"

"Kwikset. So you find is a lot of break-ins using bump keys?"

"That's usually what they're for. There's a lot of all kinds of crime in this country. If the PNM don't hurry up and do something about all the homicides, our people going get elected."

Andre pocketed the key and was soon heading back to Honesto's apartment. *Honesto will be at work all day like the rest of the Filipinos here. No one will hear me banging on Honesto's lock.* By now rush hour traffic had dissipated. Andre tuned in to 91.9 and leaned back to soak up the soca and enjoy the ride. *"Tonight I'm in the mood, I want to wine and behave rude / So anyting you want to do, I dare you, I dare you . . ."*

When he reached Honesto's building, Andre again parked on Jerningham Avenue. No one was in sight. He opened the trunk, pulled the rubber mallet from his sports bag, and hurried to Honesto's door. Except for the usual symphony of chirping, squawking, and whistling, everything was as still as a Sunday sunrise. Andre inserted the bump key into the lock and banged the key with the mallet. Nothing. He banged again. No luck. He listened to hear if the noise had disturbed anyone. Satisfied that it had not, he pounded again, slightly turning the key at the same time. The lock opened. Andre reached for the knob, then hesitated. *This is breaking and entering,* he thought. *No! Taking back my own money ent no crime.* Quickly he slipped inside.

He stood in the tidy kitchen and looked around. "Now where would I put that check?" he wondered aloud. He noticed that everything was orderly. Even the breakfast dishes stood drying in the rack. Impulsively, he opened the cupboards beneath the sink. Each item was lined neatly across the space, three deep. "Backups for his backups," Andre mused. "Like a buller man." No, the check wouldn't be in the kitchen or the bathroom. He walked into the dining room–living room which was as spotless as the kitchen. A light hung above the dining room table with its four chairs. Beyond a black leather recliner and matching sofa faced the wall with the flat-screen TV. On the right was the door to the bedroom.

The bed was made. Remote controls for the portable TV and overhead fan lay on the bedside table, along with a copy of *Aelred's Sin* and some journals, *Pharmacy Times* and *dotPharmacy*. Andre pulled open the drawer—miscellaneous papers neatly stacked, pens, paperclips, coins, cash. Eight hundred dollars. *I ent no tief.* He closed the drawer and opened the double doors of the armoire. Shirts hung on the left neatly grouped according to color. On the shelf below was a row of neatly folded underwear, and behind a row of neatly folded socks. On the right was a fold-down desktop. Behind the desktop were pigeonholes filled with envelopes, bills, receipts, and—jackpot!—a Ka Pau check for twelve thousand dollars. Just like I thought, Andre gloated. The check not cash yet. He do everything like clockwork: He always on time, he always stop by the casino every Friday exactly at 7:30, and he always go in the bank and send money home on Friday afternoons.

Andre rifled through the envelopes until he found one that said Republic Bank. Months earlier, he had driven Honesto to the San Juan branch to open the account. He continued rummaging until he found Honesto's passport. He pulled a chair over to the desk and taking a pen and blank sheet, he began copying Honesto's signature. The big loop on the *H*, the pointed *n*, the squat *t* with the downward cross. Printed capital M. Over and over he practiced the signature. Satisfied, he copied Honesto's account number on the sheet, then replaced the Republic envelope in its pigeonhole. He pocketed the check and passport, closed the armoire, and exited the apartment, leaving the door unlocked. *I go return soon. It not worth having to bump the lock again.*

He drove back to San Juan, to the Republic branch on Eastern Main Road. The Ka Pau check drawn on a Republic account, he figured, so Republic can check funds and cash the check immediately. He knew he was taking a chance going to the branch where Honesto banked, but he thought they would be less likely to question his cashing the check there. He parked on First Street just beyond the bank. "Showtime," he sighed, removing his aviator sunglasses from his shirt pocket and reaching into the backseat for his Boston Red Sox cap.

As he entered the bank, he noted the uniformed security guard standing by the back wall, and in his peripheral vision, the surveillance cameras. He averted his face as best he could and stood at the end of the short line. *Just like I thought. Not many people here at this hour on a Wednesday morning.* Suddenly, the security guard was walking toward him. Andre froze. The guard passed and opened the door for an elderly lady. Gotta relax, he told himself, exhaling slowly. It gonna work. Me and Honesto about the same height and coloring. I just a little taller and more built. He smiled to himself. And better-looking.

The woman ahead moved away from the counter. Andre stepped forward. *Don't say nothing yuh don't have to.* He handed the teller the check. "Cash, please."

The teller looked at the piece of paper. "Do you have an account with us?" she asked. Andre pulled the sheet from his pocket before realizing it was covered with his attempts to forge Honesto's signature. Quickly he lowered the sheet below the counter and folded it so only the account number showed. Then he placed it on the counter facing the teller. She typed the numbers onto her keyboard. While they waited, he slipped the paper back into his pocket. "I'm sorry, Mr. Manalo, but you don't have enough money in your account to cover this check. I can deposit the money into your account and you can withdraw the cash after the check has cleared."

"But why I need to wait?" Andre blurted. Easy, easy, he

told himself. "It's a Ka Pau check written on a Republic account," he continued evenly. "Why can't I cash it now since Ka Pau has an account and I have an account?"

"One moment. I'll ask my supervisor."

Andre forced himself to appear calm as he watched her walk to the back of the room and disappear. Cool yuhself. The worst that can happen is they won't cash the check. No, he corrected himself, the worst would be if the manager comes over and sees I'm not Honesto. Andre turned slightly. The security guard had returned to his place and stood idly glancing about. Just then the teller emerged with an older man dressed in a suit. She was showing him the check and talking. The man examined the check, looked across at Andre, and nodded.

The teller returned and slid the check toward Andre. "No problem, Mr. Manalo. Just endorse the back, please, and I'll need to see some identification." Andre handed her Honesto's passport. He picked up the pen attached to the silver chain and stared at the blank back of the check. The teller was waiting. Andre carefully drew the large loop on the *H*. Pointed *n*. Short *t*, down-slanted cross. Hook the final *o*'s backwards. The teller took the check and compared the signature with the one in the passport. Andre tensed, ready to bolt. Then she recorded the passport number on the check, stamped the back, and asked how he'd like his cash.

Gleefully, Andre jumped into his Nissan Wingroad. He looked around quickly. No one was watching. He removed the fat stack of blues from the envelope and fanned the bills. One hundred twenty of them. And all his. No way any of this belong to Honesto. He forfeit he right to half the winnings when he try to cheat me. He tossed the Red Sox cap onto the backseat and started the engine. All he had to do now was drive back to Honesto's, replace the passport, and lock the door.

Is still early, he thought, as he descended Lady Young Road, passed the Hilton, and approached the St. Ann's rotary. Honesto won't be back for hours. I have plenty time to drive to Ellerslie Plaza and deposit the money in my Scotiabank account. Better than carrying all this cash around. Is Trinidad. Anything could happen.

Half an hour later, his deposit made, Andre was again circling the Savannah, passing the Emperor Valley Zoo and the Botanical Gardens as he headed toward Belmont. The pink pouis were in bloom, their delicate, fleeting brilliance paralleling his excitement at everything the jackpot made possible. It ent often that justice happen, that nice guys finish first, he reflected. He swung left onto Jerningham Avenue and pulled up just before the entrance to the apartment building. He got out and scanned the surroundings. *Deserted. Nice.* Suddenly a ripe mango dropped before him. A *good omen.* Smiling, he stooped to retrieve it.

Andre knocked quietly on Honesto's door. He waited. Nothing. After double-checking to make sure he was unobserved, he slipped inside. He took the passport from his shirt pocket, marveling at how easy it had been to get his money back. *If I wasn't such a basically honest guy, I might even be tempted—* He stopped in the bedroom doorway.

"What the . . . ?" Papers and clothing were scattered everywhere. All the drawers were out, socks and underwear hanging from them. The armoire and its fold-down desk were open, the contents of the pigeonholes strewn about. Then he saw the arm.

"Oh god!" He dropped the passport and walked around the bed to where Honesto lay on the floor. His head rested in a pool of blood—geyser blood from slashed carotids. His throat

230 // Trinidad Noir

looked like it had been machete-chopped. Mechanically, Andre felt for the pulse he knew wasn't there. "Who do this?" he wailed. Call the ambulance. No, the police. He pressed 999 on his cell. Oh god. Who could do this? Motive. Someone who heard 'bout the jackpot must have brought Honesto back to the apartment to steal the money—

"Port-of-Spain Police."

Andre froze. *Motive. I have motive.*

"Hello? Hello?" *And my fingerprints all over the apartment.* Quickly he hung up and looked around wildly. From the floor he grabbed a shirt and began wiping the armoire pulls and the desk. The pen. The envelope from Republic Bank. The passport—*what I do with the passport?* Frantically, he searched for the green passport. There it was on the floor. He wiped it furiously and shoved it into a pigeonhole—then stopped. *Everyone know,* he realized slowly, *how Honesto cheat me. I just deposit twelve thousand dollars in my account. And I on the security cameras at the bank—at both banks, dressed in the same clothes . . .* He leaned against the armoire and slid to the floor, laughing uncontrollably.

# THE JAGUAR

BY KEITH JARDIM

*Emperor Valley Zoo*

In memory of Fred Busch

*I would like to be the jaguar of your mountains*
*And take you to my dark cave.*
*Open your chest there*
*And see if you have a heart.*
—Old song from Mexico's Yucatán Peninsula

M id-afternoon sunlight filtered through the silk-cotton tree and onto the jaguar, setting its rosette coat ablaze. The cat, a big male, moved in an un-broken rhythm back and forth along its cage, whiskers almost brushing the dark iron bars. The end of the jaguar's thick tail looped up a bit. His jaws were parted for the heat, and his tongue, tip curled to the roof of his mouth, floated over and under the air he sucked in and expelled with light gasps.

Roy watched Fiona lean over the waist-high fence, seven feet from the cage, stretching her back and neck toward the animal. He noted the ridges of her spine through her thin cotton top, and when the shirt slid above her jeans, he saw her smooth pale skin, the tiny footprints of freckles making their way down, he knew, to run across the right side of her hip, then up again, fading around her breasts in a splotchy sunset, like a birthmark disintegrating. Just above her hip, reaching for the back of her rib cage, was the bruise where he had gripped her last night while making love. It was blue-black and purple-tinged, like certain fleshy parts inside the jaguar's mouth.

Fiona stared directly into the jaguar's eyes. The cat stopped, instantly assessed Fiona's new position, and returned her gaze with such gravitas—eyes unblinking in his steady large head, compact muscles and limbs tensed as if to throw himself through the cage, the fence, and onto her—that she straightened, stepped back, and took Roy's arm. She tucked some loose strands of light-brown hair behind her ear.

"Why d'you suppose he reacted like that?" she asked, blue eyes startled.

The jaguar resumed strolling back and forth in its cramped cage. A fence sign gave the range of jaguars in the New World, and this one's name: *Lollipop*. No other information was available.

"Maybe he likes you," Roy said, still brooding over a tense conversation they'd had the night before. "Maybe you got too close. Like with De Souza?"

She released his arm. "But he was more beautiful than ever when he did that." Fiona sighed with pleasure now.

"Really?" Roy frowned. The confines of the jaguar's cage troubled him: it was cruelty, pure and simple. "How d'you suppose he'd look if he were a man?" Roy was a little taller than Fiona, but they were on an incline with Fiona upslope, so she was able to lower her head a bit, look Roy straight in the face, and ignore him. "Bet you'd want to interview him too," Roy added.

"You *are* beginning to whine, dear," she said in the playful voice she'd used earlier to deflate last night's tension. "It's time we visited the monkeys."

Roy followed, feeling as if she were talking to a slightly troubled child. She half-spun to face him, giving her dazzling, genuine smile. He tried to resist, agitated that she could so easily change his mood. Fiona's smile, as natural to her as brooding was to him, made a silent music in his head—the twirl and dip of Gaelic dances in spring, the merry, witty violins of Ireland, greenest landscape in the world, her childhood home.

Fiona laughed—an amused appraisal of the situation, perhaps, or maybe she was nervous. Roy glimpsed the inside of her mouth, her pink tongue, and was almost undone. "Come," she said. "Come along, Jaguar Man." She took his hand, and making deliberate eye contact, said, "Roy, I'd never compromise myself like that. De Souza is a creep. So forget it, all right?"

He wasn't convinced. De Souza was a persuasive man. He wanted Fiona close by and had encouraged her to interview him. He had warned Roy that perhaps she was not only a journalist for the BBC. Possibly, based on recent scrutiny, Fiona was involved in surveillance work.

An elderly man, slim and shirtless with a scruffy beard, walked purposefully up from the alligator pond toward them. He wore a bright purple scarf, loose khaki shorts, and laceless gray shoes. Halting a few feet from them he fingered his scarf, then crossed his long brown arms. His longish hair was matted, with dusty, sun-browned patches that would soon grow into clumps. He smelled of sweat and earth, but it was not unpleasant. His arms were decorated with silver watches strapped tightly from wrists to elbows. He addressed Fiona and Roy: "Good afternoon, Mr. Gentleman and Miss Lady. Dr. Edric Traboulay, at your service. This here cat you all was observing so intentionally is best referred to as *Panthera onca*, native to the shores of South and Central America. Very rarely

do it harm humans, so please don't be alarmed, Fair One."
The man was delighted with them, especially Fiona. He
looked proud, licked his upper lip as if relishing the words
he'd just spoken, and continued. "I taught zoology at the
university—long ago." He waved a hand past his head, as
though dismissing a whole period of his life. "That was just
after the colonial administration—the British, you recall?"
He looked at Roy.

"Before my time," Roy said, wary of the vagrant. "But of
course I remember the queen's visit."

Dr. Traboulay kept his distance, as if sensing that stepping
closer would defeat his purpose. In an impeccable Oxford accent, occasionally interspersed with island dialect, he began
again. "Ah, the British! Of them I have such *fond* memories!
Do you know it was through the good auspices of Dr. William
Smith—the man who discover five, *five* of our island hummingbirds. Of the family Trochilidae. Count them." Dr. Traboulay
held up his right hand, fingers and thumb splayed, and began
to count and name the hummingbirds, lowering each finger
as he tapped it. "One, the Rufous-breasted Hermit, *Glaucis
hirsuta.* Two, the Black-throated Mango, *Anthracothorax ni-
gricollis.* Three, the Green Hermit, *Phaethornis guy.* Four, the
Tufted Coquette, *Lophornis ornatus.* Five, the Blue-chinned
Sapphire, *Chlorestes notatus*—yes!" He gasped, excited by
the memory. "Smith was the boss-man of hummingbird, *oui.* It
was because of that decent fellow that I had the good fortune
to acquire a scholarship to pursue zoological studies at Oxford
University. The *British*—" He stopped and scratched his head,
overcome by a troublesome memory. "I was going to tell you
about the expedition into the northern range of the island,
but first . . ." He grimaced and rolled his eyes. "What was it, I
wonder?" He looked at the clouds.

Roy and Fiona were both uneasy now. Roy reached for his wallet and mumbled, "It's okay," offering Dr. Traboulay several reddish notes with frolicking scarlet ibises.

"Oh, sir! You are too kind—but this is entirely unacceptable!" He raised his hand in protest. "First, I must tell you my story." He turned away, deep in thought. Roy replaced the money in his wallet.

"Poor man," whispered Fiona. "We should go."

Dr. Traboulay was muttering to himself. He went to the jaguar cage and addressed the cat in Latin. "*Pulvis et umbra sumus*," he said. The jaguar, still pacing, watched him expectantly.

Fiona and Roy eased away.

"Have you seen him before?" Fiona asked Roy.

"Not that I remember. But there're a few like him around. He probably moved up from South recently. I doubt he's been in that condition very long. A few years ago a man used to ride around the Northwest on a bicycle in a suit of silver foil. You had to wear sunglasses just to look at him. Now he's gone. Perhaps he's elsewhere on the island. Or perhaps they go in and out of these phases."

As Roy and Fiona wandered beneath the huge branches of the silk-cotton tree, they passed a man hosing an agouti cage. When he saw Fiona, he wagged the hose in front him stupidly, calling, "Sweetness. Come by me, nuh."

"Oh fuck," Fiona said, looking away.

Roy, hunching his shoulders then releasing them in exasperation, said, "Good afternoon, sir."

The man ignored him. They walked by.

"When it comes to islands, I think I'm starting to prefer England, Ireland. Even in winter. It's not just crime in general, and all the guns most people seem to have, but what men do to women here that is truly frightening. At the consulate I saw last year's rape reports. You wouldn't believe—"

"But you said you loved it here, you said—"

She held his arm. "I do, you know, but . . . maybe it helps with leaving. Come with me." Fiona had asked before.

Roy lifted his free arm and let it fall helplessly. He tilted his head and saw the sky in gaps through the silk-cotton tree, blue distances, clouds drifting. "A whole island, a whole country," he said, "its problems unassailable. I couldn't listen to poor Dr. Traboulay's story. Sounds like the British treated him better than we did."

Fiona sighed, released his arm. "I imagine with independence, people began hating him for admiring the British."

"No doubt. One of the things my father taught me was to see beyond the way anyone sounded or looked. And for a long time I was able to go anywhere on this island. I looked at people a certain way and they returned it—an unassuming manner. That was the secret. Then he told me it wouldn't last. He was right. Thank God he didn't live to see how we've wrecked things."

"Why 'we'?"

"I never did anything to stop it. I never spoke to people how my father did. Like many others, I suppose, I thought things would work out, that things had been set right. They didn't. They weren't. There was so much to do, and we never realized." He paused. "Or maybe we knew what had to be done, but just didn't get around to it, for reasons I don't even want to consider now."

"Is that why you won't leave?" They walked past cages with sleeping macaws, their long blue red and yellow tails cast down, their heads and bodies hidden in the shadowed cool of their perches. He thought of the jaguar's confined pacing, of the vagrant observing him with the devotion of the zoologist he had once been. As Roy passed the last cage, a macaw looked at him out of a wrinkled sleepy eye, then stretched and flapped its wings, moving nowhere. Had the bird been a few hundred miles southeast, say in Guyana, a natural habitat, it would soon be gliding for miles along a river before roosting high in the forest canopy. And below, on the forest floor, moving through sun-dappled vegetation, would be the jaguar impatient for a night of no moon.

Roy shrugged. "Maybe, in a way, I've already left." Once again, involuntarily, he thought of De Souza.

"Stop," Fiona said. "Not now, with so few days left."

"What does it matter?" he said. "We've had our time, our chance."

"Oh . . . please."

"I'm afraid I don't have your restraint, my dear."

Her eyes glistened, but her voice was calm. "Please stop." Taking his arm, she ran her long fingers along its inside. Goose bumps raced the length of his arm, swept up onto his shoulder, tingled his neck, and ended below his left ear. It was like being caressed from beneath the skin, as though his blood were tickling him. Yet he resented this pleasure, resented even her voice sometimes. As their last days burned themselves out, thoughts of facing the island's confines alone caused him to resist her. And he resented that, as did she. Their lovemaking had become infrequent, but more passionate. They gripped and bit each other, hard. Orgasms were dramas of minor brutalities.

"It's all right," he said, circling an arm around her waist. They stopped and he held her close. "There's still time." Her head was bowed, hair falling on his shoulder and chest. She was sniffling, wiping her eyes. "I can't stand it when you cry,

Fiona. Please." He kissed her shoulder. The soft, thin cotton of her blouse met his lips. It tasted of the sea, the hidden beach where they had swum nude yesterday then sipped cold white wine in the shade of an almond tree. As the blue of the ocean deepened, and the sand became the color of old lions, they'd left, the green mountains darkening in the last light. In the air, in the sky, there was a sweet sadness, the old story of islands: People you loved, or felt you could love, went away. Matters of the heart were interrupted.

"Yes." She lifted her head. "There's still time, isn't there, Roy?" She searched his eyes, but he turned away.

Taking her hand, he squinted at the sky and led her to the green waterfowl pond. Tall clusters of bamboo, many of their leaves burned orange-brown, arched over their heads, rustling in a late-afternoon breeze. The golden sunlight flickered down. He remembered the colors of the jaguar and its small cage. The cat thrived on movement—swimming hundreds of yards, fishing in streams, climbing trees after monkeys, roaming savannahs, mountains.

"You can't come away with me anywhere, can you, Roy?"

They crossed a gray wooden bridge, a structure he'd known since he was a child, and two swans, one black, one white, glided from beneath, silent as sunlight.

"Look at them," Fiona murmured. "They have no room to run, to become airborne." She stared at Roy.

Their long, elegant necks, their grace, even here, captivated him.

Fiona needed to say goodbye to people, attend dinners, drop off videos, pack, and arrange shipping. Still, she and Roy spent a few afternoons on the coast, avoiding discussion about her inevitable departure. But the sea's distances, its green coast extending for miles into towering veils of haze, drew it from them. They bickered, attempting to gauge each other's feelings. Then, late at night, after one or two bottles of wine, they made their love.

Roy had hoped the zoo would be a distraction as well as settle their debate about the jaguar's range. Fiona thought the early colonists had killed them off, but Roy was uncertain. Years ago, the zoo manager told him that jaguars had never inhabited Trinidad. Yet the island was only a few miles from South America, and jaguars were excellent swimmers. Roy's father used to tell a story of a jaguar crossing near the mouth of Guyana's Demerara River, a distance of over two miles. And surely jaguars had roamed in pre-Columbian times, before the land connection to South America sank. Roy thought by now more information would be available. The current zoo manager—a young, worried-looking East Indian in sneakers, khaki trousers, and a blue open-necked shirt—didn't know.

"Man, like you is the first person I ever hear ask such a question, yes. You all from foreign?" Roy was about to answer when the manager turned to Fiona, and no response was required. Fiona winked at Roy as the manager spoke freely. "I think it might have had one or two that was here. I hear a story that one drift across from Venezuela on a clump of trees, but some fellers in South shoot it fast. If that was happening regular before Columbus reach, maybe the Carib Indians kill them out. And what they didn't kill, the Spanish would have kill, while killing the Caribs. As for jaguar bones, maybe no one ever really look." He laughed regretfully. "It had all kind of madness in this place, yes. People who didn't want to kill people they was living with here wanted to make money off them. Was that come first."

Roy thanked the manager as someone yelled, "Boss! The bush doc reach *again!*"

"Oh God, man. Not Daniel in the Den of Lions." The manager, looking back at Roy and Fiona, started in the direction of the big cats. A dark, barebacked figure was hastening away, silver glinting along his brown arms.

"Excuse," the manager said. "Poor old fella, his mind not too good. Last week he enter the lion den and start telling them about Africa. Good thing we had feed them already." He tapped his head, smiled at Fiona, and jogged off, shirt collar rising around his ears like little wings, his buttocks undulating in their tight trousers.

Still earlier that afternoon, in hills overlooking the western coast, Roy headed from his mother's secluded home to Fiona's apartment. He considered his mother. Two years into widowhood, abandoned by her husband's friends, ostracized by island women who guarded their too-contented husbands with a furtive wickedness, she had emigrated to Miami where two of her sisters lived. She had sold half of her husband's business interests and signed the rest over to Roy with the stipulation that he consult her before selling. Roy wanted to sell for a fair price to Norman De Souza, Minister of National Security, but the minister preferred the current arrangement he had with Roy, whose direct participation had been deemed "necessary for continued success." It was a matter of security, he had said, until Roy would agree to sell at a significantly lower price. *They are the ones you say no to,* Roy's father had written in his diary, which Roy discovered only after De Souza had intimidated him into laundering money through his businesses. *Learn to see. Watch closely. Then learn to "play no," not say it. Or better, misunderstand them. Act the fool. It's your only chance.*

Roy mulled over Fiona's imminent departure, steeling himself for its inevitability, and pondered why she had come to the island. Six months earlier, the BBC had sent Fiona to Trinidad to research a documentary on the impact of drug trafficking on the island's economy. She liaised with the British Consulate where she met Roy at a symposium on money laundering. De Souza had introduced them. Later, when De Souza realized he couldn't sleep with Fiona, he became uneasy with her questions. He couldn't understand her lack of fear. *Don't you read the newspapers, darling? One doesn't pry into the drug trade. Do you know where you are? This isn't jolly old England, you know. And even there now . . .*

But at the symposium, an elegant sense of class and decorum had prevailed, an awareness of everyone's importance, and especially of one's own importance. New information was presented: thirty to forty percent of the island's dollar was drug-based; some five to ten metric tons of cocaine were shipped through each month, with fifteen to twenty-five percent distributed on the island; drug-shipment interdiction hadn't increased in five years; money laundering was now so lucrative that it had become impossible to arrest anyone notable; major crime connected with the drug trade, prostitution, and arms-trafficking had risen significantly in the last five years. Suggestions for solutions followed: combine police and army patrols; allow American/British armed forces to enter sovereign waters and airspace; secure hotlines for reporting suspicious activity—at this, Roy noticed some men in the audience smile.

Roy watched De Souza—two rows ahead in a pale gray Armani suit, jowls appropriately puffed over his collar, gold signet ring glinting—as he scribbled away in a notebook. His profile registered the concern of the powerful under the

242 // TRINIDAD NOIR

public gaze. A national television report following the symposium featured ten seconds of footage of politicians, businessmen, and De Souza and Fiona shaking hands. Fiona was to "produce a tourism documentary with a keen interest in safety."

At the reception, Fiona meandered toward Roy and De Souza. *Have you met Miss Hamilton, Roy?* De Souza had asked softly, then grinned.

*Not yet,* Roy said, wanting to be far away from everyone there.

*She's with the BBC.* He chuckled. *I'm going to be showing her around, of course. Ah, Miss Hamilton.*

Roy turned. She was tall and wore green slacks and a black blouse, low-cut. Her eyebrows were long, shapely. Eye contact was instant. Her hand reached toward him, so he had to look at her eyes immediately. She stared with intense, brief passion, like someone who'd fleetingly glimpsed horror—the expression concentrated in her gray-blue eyes, moist and unblinking. She might have been on cocaine, Roy mused. Then, with unmistakable poise, she glanced at De Souza, who had been staring at her prominent and flushed breasts. *Delighted to meet you,* Fiona said to Roy. The tight grip of her handshake made him curious.

*And you,* Roy managed to say.

*The minister has told me all about you.* Fiona lifted a glass of wine from a silver tray as an indifferent waiter strolled by. De Souza was not liked.

*And have I been good?* Roy asked, playing along.

*That depends,* De Souza said, *on your plans.* The minister winked at Fiona, his eyes unable to convey their boyish charm so overused of late.

*And what are your plans?* Fiona asked Roy.

Roy shrugged, trying to smile like a good-natured fool. *Up to my partner here. Is there anything we can help you with?*

*Matters of safety*, Fiona said.

The minister was scanning the room. *I can't seem to get a drink*, he complained. He snapped his fingers at a waiter who appeared to be deliberately avoiding him.

Roy gave her a week. She called after four days.

Roy drove under towering roadside trees, dipped below the view of distant sea, and began to smell the village at the foot of the hills, wood smoke and the sweet stink of garbage. A natural stream ran alongside the road. A small reservoir that had once been the water source for the village lower down and the wealthy houses in the hills was now abandoned. The village depended on the stream which began high in the mountains, in mist-cool, fragrant forests he'd seen as a boy; an evergreen, seemingly pre-Columbian world existed there, though today it was higher in the mountains and further away. Fantastic flowers, variously spurred, lobed and pouched, abounded. Some were epiphytes, bulging with purple, red, and blue. As a teenager, he'd been reminded of their textures and colors when he first saw between the legs of a woman. In a somewhat intoxicated, trancelike state in the dimly lit room, he'd stroked her and whispered, *Botany.*

*What?* She'd lifted her dark, beautiful head.

So he'd breathed her name. *Annalee.*

*Up here, silly*, she'd replied.

The land, rising steeply on either side of the road, held bush and trees, but these trees were smaller than the old-forest ones Roy had passed higher up. Sections were planted with vegetables and fruit trees. Shacks rested on stones and bricks. Overhead, the treetops met and the entire area was shaded, and the stream, wider here with occasional glints, trickled and swished. Roy crossed a narrow bridge. Below, dark-skinned young women sitting on rocks were washing clothes. Others, scantily clad in bras and panties, were bathing. Two of the bathers waved and smiled. And shaking themselves, they asked if he wanted them.

After the bridge, after the stream and women and cool shadows, the road entered hard sunlight. The land opened and dwellings became concrete, but the sense of hardship remained. Houses, little more than the shacks he had seen earlier, were close. Few were painted. Around a bend, boys ran and shouted at him, moving their cricket game in the road just enough for him to pass. One spat on the windshield as Roy slowed. "Gone!" another yelled.

Then Roy saw Freddie moving smoothly and quickly, tall, too slim, dreadlocked Freddie, resident drug dealer, called Red Boy when he was a child, and now a member of an armed gang with political connections. As children, he and Roy had hunted in the green mountains. Freddie waved for Roy to stop and ordered the boys back. "Them don't know, eh," Freddie nodded. "Times change."

"Freddie." They touched hands.

"Pass some water on the windshield, boss."

Roy hesitated, then sprayed the windshield. Water and light thickened on the glass, and the world went briefly out of focus.

Freddie pulled a rag from his pocket, saying, "Leave the wipers. Lemme show them little bitches we is friends." Roy felt foolish watching his childhood friend who'd taught him to make slingshots wipe the glass in front of him. He glanced at the boys. They stood apart, silent, mystified, and respectful. Freddie wrung the rag and said, "Gervase."

"Freddie?"

"Come." Freddie tucked the rag back into his trousers, leaving most of it exposed to dry. A boy of maybe twelve stepped forward, trembling. "*Come*, I say!" Freddie shouted.

Gervase, head lowered, moved closer.

Roy shifted and said, "Freddie . . ."

"Chill, breds," Freddie replied, raising a palm. Then to Gervase: "Watch Mr. Gonzales's son. You hear your mammy talk 'bout Mr. Gonzales, right?" Years ago, Roy's father had given Freddie's parents financial assistance.

Gervase nodded.

"You hear Moses talk 'bout him, right?"

Gervase nodded again.

"And you hear I talk 'bout him too, not so?"

The boy nodded once more.

"This is Roy, Mr. Gonzales's son. Watch him."

Gervase raised his head and looked at Roy, who acknowledged him with a half-smile.

"Gone," Freddie said.

Gervase turned but was unable to miss the slap from Freddie's heavy hand. It caught the back of his head just beneath his right ear. He staggered, dropped to his knees, then rose and ran up the road.

Freddie reached for Roy's hand on the steering wheel and held it between his palms. He bent to Roy. "Praise," Freddie said. "Praise. I remember your father, I remember you."

"Okay," Roy said, wanting to go.

Freddie asked, "How the Lady? De Souza talk with you lately?"

Roy told him Fiona was fine, and that he hadn't spoken with De Souza. Should he have? "Let you know later, breds." Roy thanked him and drove off.

Fifteen minutes later, in her apartment in a sealed-off

compound whose entrance was guarded, Fiona greeted Roy. He had been thinking about Freddie and his and Fiona's discussion about De Souza the night before.

Fiona stared. "Are you all right?" Roy's face was drawn. His arms rose for her and they embraced. "Roy," she whispered. "Roy, talk to me."

He did, but not about his father, Freddie, or De Souza. Then, after a cold drink, they went to the zoo.

It was 4:30. They were sipping beer at a table outside the tuck shop, half-hoping the zoo manager would return so they could learn more about Dr. Traboulay. Lovers had carved devotions into the old wooden tabletop. Fiona's elegant middle finger circled the lip of her beer bottle carelessly, then slid to the label loosened with condensation.

Roy watched her intently. "Did you interview De Souza?"

"I did." Her eyes were mischievous.

"I knew it." Roy sat back, crestfallen. "Doesn't sound like a good move to me, especially since he wants to get you into bed."

Fiona's expression changed. "At one point the phone rang, and he had to step out. From the look on his face I knew there was no surveillance in the room. Also, he couldn't return in less than two minutes. And, of course, there were the steps, creaky wooden ones . . . dear things."

"You *went* to his *house*?"

"Of course, darling."

Roy shook his head and huffed. "Who did you have call?"

She shrugged her shoulders, winked.

"He must really regret the day he met you."

"Do *you*?" Fiona lifted her face.

But Roy asked, "What did you find?"

She gave him her dazzling smile, exactly like the one at the jaguar's cage earlier, and tapped her temple. "When he returned, he was completely flustered. We chatted a bit; I asked a few more questions, then I got up to leave. He walked me to the door." Fiona drank the last of her beer. "He tried to kiss me."

Roy paled. He glanced around and stood. "Let's get out of here. All these cages make me sick."

"Oh?" Fiona put her bottle down and rose. "Oh," she said demurely. She took his arm. "Kiss me."

Roy didn't. He was unsure where she was going with this.

Fiona said seriously, "He actually *did* try to kiss me."

Roy stepped away. "Stop it." But his words lacked conviction. Something else was bothering him. "Did you go through his desk?" he asked, facing away from her, staring into the confines of the tuck shop.

"He grabbed my tits, shoved his hand between my legs, and tried to drool on my mouth. I kicked him where he deserved."

Roy tried to stay calm. "Oh, so you didn't go through his desk?"

"Can't you ask something else?"

"We should go." He took her arm and began striding to the exit.

"Okay. I'm sorry I didn't tell you before. I was just doing my job. Didn't think you'd be so interested."

He jerked her to a halt. "And *what* do I have to do to show I'm interested, *really* interested, Fiona, tell me."

"Are you jealous?"

Roy didn't reply. A heavyset man in hiking boots, new jeans, and belt, his brand name jersey a dark navy-blue, appeared. His right hand worked a toothpick protruding from his mouth; the left was half-inserted into a front pocket. He nodded the typical island greeting, one stranger to another on a pleasant afternoon: "All right."

"Okay," Roy replied.

Fiona glanced at the man as Roy pulled her along, increasing his pace and not looking back. They passed the waterfowl pond. At the exit, they hurried through the turnstile, Fiona whispering to Roy, asking if he'd brought his gun, Roy ignoring her. He hit his knee on one of the lower bars and cursed. As they got in the car, under the massive spreading branches of a samaan, Fiona was visibly nervous, glancing back at the exit. Roy drove, thinking of somewhere peaceful, close by.

"Roy, what's wrong? Are we being paranoid?"

"Tell me."

She was silent.

The parked car ticked with heat from the winding ascent. Roy and Fiona leaned against a low rock wall. They were alone. A burned-out building, roofless, its peeling concrete pillars intertwined with vines, stood to their left. He could see several valleys of the northern range descending to the gulf. Hovels, set on the valleys' slopes, faded in and out of the hazy air. Those that didn't fade were closer, below them in the fold of this valley. The scent of kerosene fires, garbage, and dust drifted up the hillsides. Subdued reggae and Baptist bells mingled, made a steady throb, like that of a distant party, one he'd been hearing since childhood. As though once begun at the foot of the hills, the party could never cease, must overwhelm the hills and valleys, beating on and on, its hovels eating into the earth of the island.

Before them the land sloped down to the city far below,

and to the harbor, where the bulks of several shipwrecks lay side-up. Long feathery grass, green and brown-tinted and like young sugarcane in texture, rippled in a light breeze. It moved in great spreading greens down the hillside, dry-brown tints reflecting gold, a child's version of a sea. They both watched it. Some of the last mountains of the Northern Range, the highest on the island, rose dark and silent behind them, the beginning of another world. Beyond the mountains lay the sea and the deep blue air of the Atlantic.

"Are you involved with De Souza?" Fiona asked quietly, staring at the gulf.

"I'm acquainted with him. We see each other at meetings, conferences, like the one where we met. You know that."

"That's not what I'm asking."

Roy shrugged. "The rumors are there. Trinidad is loaded with them. How can people not make assumptions? It's how the island amuses itself, Fiona." Roy hesitated. "There's no evidence on De Souza. You couldn't have seen anything in his house. And even if you had, you wouldn't have taken it."

"Damn right, I took nothing. But I saw something."

He waited.

"An address book with names of members of the judiciary, the business elite—your father among them—and contacts in Antigua, Curaçao, St. Maarten. There were also Russian names, fax numbers, cell phone numbers—many crossed out, some not—and odd names, like nicknames or codes."

Roy scratched the side of his neck, gripped the skin between his thumb and forefinger, and pinched. "So De Souza, who once did business with my father, and does on occasion with me, who's presently buying paint for condos he's sprucing up in South— and don't ask me where he got the money—De Souza, who was at the signing of the drug treaty with the Americans three years ago, this De Souza, you think, is a criminal? And as for the Russians, they're everywhere these days. Look at what they've been through. I mean, so what if De Souza has those contacts. He should. He's in government and he's a businessman."

She was quiet before asking, "Roy, do you love me?"

Vultures, their wings fixed like black machetes, glided southward over the ruined restaurant. For the last five hundred years, Roy thought, this image was the most consistent for the Caribbean and South and Central America.

The tall grass rustled near Fiona. She shrank back against Roy. Out of the bush, separating it with a walking stick, and head held high, walked Dr. Edric Traboulay, his wristwatches reflecting the last of the afternoon sunlight.

"Ah! We meet again! I am presently experiencing a period of reasonable clarity," he announced. "Those hummingbirds I mentioned earlier, *these* were the mountains Dr. William Smith and I climbed in search of them, but more to the east." He waved the stick in the general direction. "Funny, but I still can't recall the story I wanted to tell you at the zoo. My mind, these days, makes its own random selections. Anyway, during the dry seasons of the 1950s, we did not experience such arid conditions as occur today after every Christmas season. Hence, we were able to travel comfortably as there were few fires during that time." He stood the stick in front of him, resting his hands on its gnarled end, his watches glinting in the light like the arm-sheaths of a knight. Roy wondered if the watches worked. Dr. Traboulay looked up at the mountains, his eyes soft, as if lost in some fond memory. Thin cuts from the tall grass crisscrossed his upper arms and ribs.

Fiona said, "You're back, sir." She glanced at Roy, unsure of everything around her.

"Please, Miss Lady and Mr. Gentleman, I mean no harm. I don't often get to talk to such nice people. How, may I ask, did Lollipop seem?"

Roy said, "Who?"

"Oh! Forgive me. The jaguar, his name is Lollipop—at least that's what *some* people think. Someone removed my sign last month. I made another then, but the new manager was reluctant to put it up. He said it did not cater to the public's tastes. What, I ask, is wrong with a little poetry by Blake?"

"'*Tiger tiger, burning bright*'?" Fiona asked, relaxing.

Dr. Traboulay's face lit up. "Precisely, my dear! Just because Blake was writing about the Indian tiger does not mean the poem cannot be applied to Lollipop, a name I strongly recommend they change. But, alas, the manager will not hear of it. I haven't given up, though. Imagine calling a jaguar *Lollipop*. You might as well name him *Popsicle*, or *Kit Kat*, names not worthy of the status of the jaguar. Surely this is obvious." Dr. Traboulay, chin up, awaited response.

Fiona said, "I agree."

"It's a very beautiful animal," Roy added.

"Exactly. You both are educated," Dr. Traboulay continued, "unlike these foolish politicians, little boys they are. I'd send them back to school if I could. Nothing but a bureaucratic herd determined to master mediocrity—and *worse*."

"And I'd help you," Roy said, thinking of De Souza while edging to the passenger side of the car where Fiona had left the window down. "Perhaps you can tell us another story," he suggested. Roy's cell and a revolver were locked in the glove compartment. He slipped his hand into his pocket, and when Dr. Traboulay turned, he quickly removed the keys and unlocked the glove compartment. He stayed leaning on the car door.

"Everywhere I go these days, I recall another story, though details, some quite significant, often elude me," Dr. Traboulay said. "My walk here was filled with memories, many I'd not recalled for ages. Chapters of my life sailed through my mind, around every corner, under every tree . . . They came to me out of the blue, literally." He laughed. "I am rather partial to the odd cliché, now and then, if you'll excuse me." He walked toward the ruined restaurant. "For instance, this relic. I mean—" He broke off, became flustered, mumbled to himself in Latin, then reverted to the local dialect. "Jew man get he place burn down. Investigation say is arson. Police commissioner tell the Jew man to leave. *Just so.* And the insurance get seize." Now he said, "The ways of the business community on this island have never ceased to amaze me."

Watching Dr. Traboulay's back, Roy got the revolver and cell from the glove compartment. He dropped the cell on the seat and pocketed the gun. Fiona noticed the gun and gave Roy a questioning look. "Just to be safe," he whispered.

She slipped an arm around Roy's as they joined Dr. Traboulay, who raised his stick at the ruins. "Allow me to tell you something about this restaurant. It was at the height of its popularity in 1960, shortly before Marlene Dietrich came out with, 'Where Have All the Flowers Gone?' I remember . . . memories are everywhere you turn. Too many for me now, though." Dr. Traboulay sighed, began again: "I was a waiter, had started working here in the mid-1950s, when I met Dr. William Smith at the bar one afternoon. Quite by chance we spoke about hummingbirds, about the fauna and flora of the island. He hired me as his assistant the following week. The restaurant gained some notoriety when Ernest Hemingway visited one evening. He was on his way back from Peru. Very decent to me he was! He asked many questions about the island, its natural history. He was returning to Cuba, and when I asked if he was sympathetic to Fidel Castro, he smiled and said yes, it was time. Sure enough, four years later—confusions within confusions." Dr. Traboulay waved a hand past his head. "There was a picture of Ernest and his wife over the bar. I have never met such a free spirit. There was something remarkably human, good about him—and, as I learned after his death, something mean and cruel. People were so eager to judge his character. His work suffered as a result. Is nothing sacred? Sad the way he died. But they say there's nothing quicker than a gunshot to the head. Is that not correct?" His tone was somber. He looked at Roy.

An early evening cool encircled them, a wind fresh with earth and sea, flowing down from the green mountains. The tall grass swayed. The haze of gray-white light over the gulf was gone. The horizon of sea and sunset was shades of gray, pale blue, and gold, with hints of lavender. Far to the south, pulsing out of the almost purple late-afternoon land, orange flames from the oil refinery became visible; they seemed to be tongues lapping through from another dimension, like devils testing a new frontier. All was quiet. The Baptist bells had subsided as the dusk deepened. The sounds of dogs were softer, more intermittent. The scent of wood smoke and kerosene was gone, breezed away. The certainty of night came upon them. Roy sensed something of what the conquistadors must have felt during their first nights on the island: the absolute promise of an infinity of tomorrows, to which no one would belong, of course—but the conquistadors would not have thought that; they had believed themselves righteous men, engaged in an ordained enterprise, one commandeered by Her Catholic Majesty, and, therefore, approved by God. All the world's tomorrows belonged to them.

"Are either of you partial to oysters?" Dr. Traboulay was regarding the ruins sadly, lost in his own thoughts. Fiona, trying to enjoy the view, had shifted closer to Roy.

Roy said, "I imagine most people are."

Dr. Traboulay, moving his head slowly from side to side, said, "They tasted better in the days of the restaurant, more like a clean sea." He held up his hand, curling the fingertips to caress his palm as he studied them. "The sea bed, actually. In the days of this restaurant, we had such oysters. They had more life then. The salt was better."

"Do you still eat them?" Fiona asked. "There must be somewhere the sea is still okay."

"Yes, but . . . but . . . it is not the same . . ." He tapped the side of his head. "It is horrible, sometimes, to *know* things. I learned too much. The British were great collectors of knowledge. And they shared it with me. But then came independence, and—and—it was good. Yes, it was. But only for a while, only for a while. The new rulers came to hate everything, including the knowledge on which my profession is built. To them it was colonial knowledge, you see. They hated it all, especially with the oil boom. There was nothing we could not buy. They set me up at the university; they ruined my life. I was a flaneur in my profession, in the strict French sense. Then, almost overnight, the nation—if that is the right word for a place like this—became a flaneur in the strict English sense. And so we remain, lapsing, a ghetto country, adrift and in awe of Almighty America when it pleases us. And so," he waved at distant hovels in the valley, at the sea changing into a last shade of blue like the night, and the orange tongues of flame, brighter now, in the far south of the island, "we remain slaves, occasionally bringing a glimmer of amusement even to the most liberal eye." Dr. Traboulay shuddered and slapped his matted head repeatedly as if trying to shake out something inside. Again he reverted to local dialect. "It have too much thing inside this head. Mankind is a sinful beast, yes." He moved toward the bushes from which he had emerged earlier. Roy watched, hands in pockets. "Excuse me," Dr. Traboulay said, "I must visit my aunt. I shall return shortly." He nodded and disappeared into the tall grass.

"We should be going soon, I guess," Roy said, relieved.

"It's odd, but I think I'd feel better about that poor man, about the world, if I knew he was really angry about something. It's so sad to be damaged like that."

"Maybe he was angry. A long time ago." Roy, hands still in his pockets, gazed at the distant gulf. He thought Fiona would question him, but she didn't.

Suddenly Dr. Traboulay reappeared. He went to the rock wall, hoisted himself up, and sat. Then he bowed his head, clasped his hands, and began to mumble. Before him the gulf reflected the deep clear indigo of the evening sky. Lights in the valley showed, little pieces of brightness cluttering their way down to the capital, down to the sea; and there, except for the ships in the harbor and beyond, these ships like signals of isolation, they stopped.

"He's praying," Fiona said. She blinked several times, then wiped her eyes.

The cell chimed. Roy went to the car and answered, leaning against the car door, watching Fiona to his left in front of the ruins and Dr. Traboulay some ninety feet ahead on the wall. Freddie's voice was crisp, more alive than earlier.

"Boss," Freddie said, "Souza call. He head hot. Like jumbie hold him."

Roy swallowed. "I'm listening."

"Miss Fiona do something. He in a state."

"A little misunderstanding. Nothing to worry about. I'll see about it."

"Better hear this first," Freddie said, his voice rising. "Souza say you *don't want to know* what Miss Fiona really wrap up with."

Roy tried to think. "Tell him not to be concerned. I know what he's worried about, and I've checked it out. All harmless."

Fiona began walking over to Dr. Traboulay. A strand of her hair lifted by the wind caught the last light and curved around her face, across the tip of her nose. She stopped near the doctor, leaned against the wall, and spoke. Roy could not hear her.

"Well, boss," Freddie said, "that is you and he business."

A pause.

"You know I will help you how I could," Freddie continued. "But is only so far I could go, you understand. Me and the fellas watching out for you, but Souza like he watching everybody these days. Best thing to do now is get the lady out fast."

Roy coughed, thinking.

"Boss?"

"You have anything on a Dr. Traboulay? Vagrant fella, educated, maybe mad?"

"I hear about him. They call him Watchman, for all them watch on his hand. Know the time all round the world. He does be all about, but he in North a year now. He know plenty thing, like history nuh, and about bird and animal. It had a fella like that in the Bahamas fifteen years ago. He cause plenty trouble. Fockin' man was suppose to be blind, yes, but he was workin' for the DEA. Anyhow, Souza calling you just now, eh."

"Right. Thanks."

Roy walked around the car twice, counting to himself. Fiona and Dr. Traboulay hadn't stopped talking. The cell rang again. He counted to five before answering.

"How are we, Roy?" De Souza's smooth slow voice filled his ear.

"There's a problem?"

"In our business, there's no such thing, Roy, only solutions. Kind of unfortunate, but there you are."

Silence.

"How was the zoo?" De Souza asked.

"Needs maintenance, as usual. It's one problem that'll never be solved, but it works fine, doesn't attract much attention. Which is the way I thought we liked things."

"Do you recall, Roy, the time I took you to meet God in Miami? Recall, if you can, the movie theater for the special preview, the scent of the people, especially the women, Roy. You said—and I've never forgotten this—that if heaven is a place, this is how it would smell. To me it was the scent of—how shall I put it?—utmost security. Power. Of never having to worry about anything. Rolex watches shining in the dim light. The women were *heaven scent*. I laughed when you said that. You've always had a way with words, Roy, words and women. It's a talent you should use a little more wisely, especially when it comes to Fiona." He sensed De Souza thinking: a series of faint sighs, but lately combined with some static, which was unusual for De Souza's connections.

"So how is He?" Roy asked. "How is God?"

"He still resides in Miami, and knows your mother socially. It's not a very warm acquaintance, despite her devotion to the church. It's an appropriate one, however, unlike yours with Fiona."

"Exactly what's on your mind, De Souza?"

"There're a few matters I'm concerned about."

"I assure you there is nothing to worry about. Fiona told me everything. It's nothing but schoolgirl drama." Roy winced. "She still has a bit of a crush on you."

Fiona and Dr. Traboulay were now silhouettes against the dark-blue light, talking to one another. The doctor had straightened from his hunched position and now faced Fiona, who stood attentively a few feet away, arms folded.

"Good. Very good, Roy. Now tell me about our resident zoologist. Or is it anthropologist?"

"Harmless," Roy said. "For Christ's sake, you're really tense. Get a massage or something."

"I'm leaving the matter entirely in your hands, Roy. I'm leaving for Miami tomorrow. I'm taking the good word to Him. I have faith in you. As does He." De Souza coughed. "Roy?"

"Here."

"I did warn you about our mutual lady friend."

"Yes. Say hello to my mother."

Roy tossed the cell onto the car seat and began walking toward Fiona and Dr. Traboulay.

The zoologist was speaking: "It was Conrad, my dear, who said, 'All ambitions are lawful except those which climb upwards on the miseries or credulities of mankind.' To that we must add the animal kingdom, and the remaining beauty of this island. If we lose it, we lose ourselves." The doctor's words trailed into the evening air.

It was cool. The mountains were dark, austere.

*Roy, do you love me?* He was trying to think.


The jaguar stopped pacing. The zoo's nocturnal captives were restless in the dark. He sensed their movements, confined as his own, and stood tall on his hind legs, front paws against the cage, observing. The moon had not yet risen. A scent of salt lingered on the sign the man had attached to the upper part of his cage. No one had been around then, and the man, who spoke Latin—sounds similar to those that accompanied the first genuine intrusion into the jaguar's environment over five hundred years ago but that afternoon a gentle music—had given him salt, which the jaguar licked from his palm. Then the man attached a black wooden sign onto the jaguar's cage, weaving a strong cotton string, tied to nails in the board, around the bars. Now in the night, the jaguar, standing seven feet tall, his nocturnal instincts aroused, was looking through the bars, his heavy head and jaws near the sign. Occasionally, smelling a faint hint of salt, the jaguar licked the sign, his eyes half-closing, affectionate almost.

The moon rose.

In careful white script, the sign read:

*For centuries, the jaguar has been associated with human fears and desires. In Mesoamerica, around 1200 B.C., Olmec art was dominated by human-jaguar forms resembling werewolves. After the Mayan conquest, images of the jaguar,* balam, *thought to be the manifestation of the night sun under the earth, guarded tombs, temples, and thrones. The Aztec culture's warrior elite was called the Jaguar Knights. Aztec tradition included human sacrifice, in which jaguar-headed altars received the still-beating hearts of victims. The word* jaguar *comes from Amazonia, where Guarani Indians tell of a beast,* yaguara, *that attacks with one leap. The jaguar frequently subdues its prey in such a manner, killing quickly by biting into the skull or neck as opposed to strangulation, the preferred method of*

*most large cats. The jaguar is South America's most pow-*
*erful predator, and it grows larger in southern Amazonia;*
*some males measure eight feet from nose to tip of tail and*
*weigh over three hundred pounds.*

*This jaguar's title is Lord of Olmec, after the Olmec*
*culture. Call him Olmec.*

*I remain yours faithfully,*

*Dr. E. Traboulay*
*Resident Zoologist and Conservationist*


Toward an opening in the trees on the other side of the
zoo, the *yaguara* was looking, his gaze as steady and penetrat-
ing as though he had sighted prey.

Had the *yaguara* been able to leap through the cage,
through the air, and into the trees and beyond, across the
night sky, flying in a magical bound to what lay in the distance
across the sea, he would come to the coast of South America.
He would land on a long wide and beautiful beach, the moon
lighting it as if its sand were made of salt or crushed diamonds.
He would run along the beach, hearing the sound of waves,
enjoying the scent of sea and the soft sand beneath his paws.
Soon he would angle toward the jungle, running to its dark
green billions of leaves tinted by moonlight. And there he
would be.

*Yaguara.*

# ERIC'S TURN

BY RIAN MARIE EXTAVOUR

*Tunapuna*

Eric's lips pulled back and he inhaled sharply as the liquid heat slid over his tongue. He blew strands of steam from the soup, and sipped the next spoonful cautiously, letting it trickle to the back of his throat. He gazed intently at each spoonful of the murky yellow liquid with the occasional dumpling, carrot, and oh-so-rare corn. The warm soup pushed against the cold in his body, temporarily evicting the uninvited guest and making him shudder. He would not feel so cold if he had worn his blue jacket, but after Jerry had jeered at him last week about the "old rag" causing the office staff to erupt in laughter, he had decided it was time to leave it behind. For three months he had succeeded in hiding the shredded lining of the overused pockets, but now the shoulder seams were beginning to tear, and a week ago the zipper refused to align.

At the time he had simply shrugged his shoulders, bowed his head, and chuckled along as he usually did. Answering Jerry would only lead to more humiliation. He certainly wasn't going to ask them to adjust the air-conditioning. Besides, the jacket was the only thing he had left of her. Wearing it not only kept him warm in the office, but it allowed him to feel closer to her. It was the one thing she had not taken when she left, and every day he would breathe into it trying to catch a remnant of her perfume. Now the jacket lay at home bundled under a cardboard box waiting for his return.

"Ey, Mopey Dick, you call the football association yet?" a voice asked. "The minister waiting on the budget." Ryan stood over Eric's desk cradling a stack of folders and tapping his foot.

To Eric, this gray-brick, two-story office complex housing the ministry felt like a prison with its creamy walls and sleepy sentinels, too old or too fat to run after any perpetrator. Its manicured presence seemed to mock the neighboring Regional Corporation to the back, whose yard was littered with mud-caked tractors, backhoes, and dumptrucks. In front, the busy Eastern Main Road bustled, slowing only on Sunday evenings and holidays. Eric felt trapped. His release would come later at his favorite bar, Spektakular-4-Rum—the only place that would still give him credit. As long as he hid there, the pressures of wife and work remained at bay.

"No, I'll get to it after lunch," he answered, turning his back to Ryan.

"I'll let her know," Ryan replied smugly before walking off. Eric's failure would be another feather in his colleague's cap of ambition. Maybe this time the minister would understand and send Eric back to the messenger department.

No one in the office understood how he had been promoted to clerical duties. He was disorganized. His work was always behind schedule causing delayed payments of community funds. This embarrassed the entire department that, prior to Eric's arrival, had prided itself on its efficiency. For the five months that Eric had worked in this office, he had pretended not to notice the cold stares and sudden silences whenever he appeared. He was certain they were all conspiring to get him transferred, and he also knew that this current post was the head messenger's way of getting rid of him after years of trying.

So Eric kept to himself. Whenever anyone approached his

desk, he would cover the papers in front of him. He never used the lunchroom, and he remained at his desk unless he had to go to the men's room or grab a bite to eat. At 12, when most of the staff was carpooling to Fai's in upper Tunapuna or to the Valpark Shopping Plaza, Eric was never included. The corn soup lady in the market lower down the main road was Eric's only option on days when he did not pack a lunch. Fortunately, the walk gave him a chance to get out of the office—away from Ryan and Jerry and the others.

Eric passed the butter-colored fire station with its silver training tower and fire tender. The adjacent police station had recently been renovated, but the demolished cars to the front and side made it seem like a car dump. Eric stepped forward to cross Pasea Road then jumped back as a car screeched past, its driver trying to catch the light. He ignored the expletives thrown his way and crossed. The snackette on the opposite corner was open, but Eric knew that the plastic-wrapped products would not be sufficient to stave off these hunger pangs. Only corn soup would fill the emptiness and keep him warm in the office.

He walked past vendors with clothes hanging and a man selling leather shoes from the back of a station wagon, offering his wares to passersby. A female vendor straightened her display of panties and bras as a maxi-taxi boomed past with laughing schoolchildren, then stopped abruptly to board another as irate drivers honked and swerved to avoid colliding.

Today Eric left for lunch earlier than usual, so there was no line at the corn soup stand and no need for meaningless bits of conversation with strangers. Good. He needed to think about how to execute his plan. He paid for his soup, covered the Styrofoam cup, and hurried back to the office. Before crossing Pasea Road, he paused and looked southward toward the Palladium Cinema. Its silver-gray gate was pulled shut. Cara loved the cinema. Eric thought of the many evenings they had enjoyed cuddling in the warm darkness with only the light from the screen before spilling onto the sidewalk with the crowd after a four-hour matinee. Once, during their courtship, they had left the cinema around midnight and walked through the dark alley that emerged at the back of the market. They had leaned against a wall to kiss, but had run off when a stranger approached from the shadows demanding money. Later they had laughed off their fright. That seemed like a lifetime ago. After they had married, trips to the cinema became a task to Eric and soon waned.

Now Cara would not be around to comfort him after a trying day, to help him laugh off the pressure. Before their separation, she had been there to listen to how he was given the most difficult projects to work on, and how the others had used every opportunity to report him. She had made him feel like he belonged—somewhere. Her soft voice would calm him, and she would bring him a cup of warm milk, sit beside him, and rub his shoulders until he fell asleep. But this time, she would not be there to tell him it was all right, that they just did not understand him. Eric decided that today was the day. He could wait no longer. If she refused to come back . . . No, she would come back. She loved him.

Later that afternoon, as he sat at his desk thinking of the empty house awaiting him that evening, his eyes brimmed with tears, and it took extra effort to breathe. Why had she left? Why? And who would take care of him now? How could she be seeing another man? She belonged to him. As he thought of her, the room became blurry and seemed to spin. His breathing became rapid and deep as though he had been running.

"Oh, geez, look at Eric's face," a voice whispered.

"Oh no, not again," someone answered.

"This is the second time this month," said another.

"I hear he have a heart problem."

More voices joined. Indistinct figures moved in front of him. Their voices became merely a buzz under the sirens sounding in his head. Eric placed the Styrofoam cup on the desk and laid his head next to it, panting to catch his breath. His hands began to shake. The tremors moved upwards until his entire body was shaking. He bit his lips to hold back sound, but a whimper escaped, signaling an avalanche of choking sobs that caused his chest to heave. He raised his head gasping for air, but as he did, the swivel chair rolled back from under him and he slipped to the floor. He curled up in a corner between the wall and his desk and rocked. Various feet appeared under the desk, and someone was calling his name. His sobs became guttural moans, silencing the voices. Someone came around the desk and bent over him, calling, "Eric! Eric . . . Eric . . ." It was Jerry. Grabbing the man's arm and clutching his own chest, Eric cried out Cara's name, closed his eyes, and let his body go limp.

When he opened his eyes, he was lying on the lounge chair in the ladies' restroom. He was not alone. A woman, her back turned, was pouring liquid into a small bowl. The ascending cane rows that led to a small bun at the top of her head and the small gold hoop earrings were familiar. He knew she would come. He had not been able to bear removing her name as "next of kin" on his employment file. Besides, she was the only real family he believed he still had. During that heated argument with his sister Kathy last Christmas, he had been warned never to come near her or her family again.

"Fine! Spoil them if you want. You go see," he had warned. "You know that is not how Daddy bring we up!" Eric believed that Kathy's children needed discipline. He had tried to explain this to her after punishing his six-year-old nephew for running around the Christmas tree. "That licking ent going to leave no marks, but he go remember not to do that again! What you worried about?"

But Kathy and her husband felt differently, and the three had argued until she finally asked Eric to leave. That was the last time he had spoken to Kathy. But it hadn't mattered. He still had Cara.

The fluorescent bulb directly overhead gave the restroom a whitish-gray cast. Eric stared at the small back and tiny waist of the woman across from him. His Cara. She was still the petite woman he had married, a woman who always took care of herself. As she turned around, he quickly shut his eyes again. She was more beautiful than he remembered. When he felt the cool damp of the cloth she placed on his forehead, he reopened his eyes slowly. His eyes searched to meet hers. He smiled, and she sighed and smiled back.

"Hello, Eric," she said softly.

"You came," he murmured. "I knew you would." He reached out, took her hand, and placed it against his chest. Her lips curved into a half-smile, but her eyes misted with concern. She still loves me, he mused. He did not need to hear her say it. She was here and that's all that mattered. It meant that they could go home together. She would take care of him and make him feel safe again from the cruel world.

"An ambulance coming and I called your sister," she said, carefully placing his hand at his side.

"I don't need an ambulance," he replied, raising himself on the makeshift cot. "I need *you*. Let's just go home and—"

"It's over, Eric," she said as gently as she could. "You can't come home with me. The judge said."

"What the hell the judge know? He know me? He know you?" Eric lay back as she placed the bowl on the counter.

Surprised by the strength in his voice, she realized that the call about Eric's possible heart attack had made her drop her guard. "Calm down, Eric," she coaxed. "You're not well." He threw back the cover and sat up in the cot. The concern in her eyes turned to bewilderment. "But, I thought . . . your heart . . . the office called . . ." she stammered.

"The only thing wrong with me, Cara, is that this heart mash-up," he declared. Fixing his gaze on her, he added softly, "And only you could fix it."

"So, that is why I here? Nothing wrong with you? You make these people call me from work because they think you dying, and nothing wrong with you? I can't believe this. What kind of game is this? You wasting my time." She moved to the chair where she had placed her purse. Her lawyer had warned her to stay away, but she believed that Eric had had a heart attack.

"Give me another chance nah, babe," he pleaded, grabbing her wrist. Cara looked at the hand grasping her. He still wore his wedding band, this man to whom she had promised herself years ago when she had thought that he was the most sensitive, mature man she had ever known. In the eyes of an eighteen-year-old surrounded by comparatively immature boys of the same age, those qualities were enough for her to consider his proposal. It had been a chance for her to escape the watchful eyes of her mother and the endless duties thrust upon her as the eldest of six girls. She believed that Eric was misunderstood and needed comfort, needed to be handled with care. Her family did not approve, but she was adamant, and for ten years she had coddled, cooed, and coaxed this man.

Her mother thought he was too quiet, and the first time Eric beat her, her mother had simply shaken her head and said, "Well, and you want to take man?" It was a question she would hear each time she ran home after Eric's abuse. After the third or fourth beating, Cara bore the next five years quietly. She would tell herself that he only drank to get away from the pressures of work. She never believed that he meant to hurt her.

"He just forgets himself when he drunk," she told one co-worker who asked about her bruises. It was only after Eric kicked her in the abdomen while she was pregnant, causing her to miscarry the three-month-old fetus, that her mother offered Cara her old room if she needed a place to stay. That was a year ago. Since then, her mother had made her register at a local center for abused women. Cara would tell Eric that she was going to her mother's house to help out, but when he called one day and she was not there, they argued and he accused her of seeing another man. Nothing she said could change his mind. Six months after joining the center, Cara left Eric.

Now she was troubled. She could only imagine the depth of his pain and confusion, and she was unsure whether to explain again that she was not with anyone else and that she cared only about him. She was no longer convinced that she could help him. Eric would have to decide for himself that he needed help. "*Another chance?* I hear that before. And we try, Eric. I try with you, with your jealousy and your drinking, and—"

"I will make things better. I go stop drinking. Don't leave, Cara," he begged.

"You need help. The last time you say that, I go back home, and the very next Friday you come home drunk, and you bus' my head," she replied, trying to pull away. "The mark still there."

"You not going nowhere," he said, standing and tightening his grip on her wrist. "I didn't say you could leave."

"Eric, you're hurting me," she winced, her eyes filling with fear.

"You 'fraid me, Cara? Your own husband, eh? Look at what they do to we! That you 'fraid the man who love you," he said, shaking his head. "I would die for you. I would kill for you," he added softly, gazing into her frightened eyes. She stood frozen.

Suddenly, as if awakened from a trance, she threw her weight back and jerked her arm once again, hoping to surprise him and run to the door, but he held her firmly with a smirk on his face.

"Where you think you're going? We're not finish here. You forget I know you? All my life I trying to please everybody. But I could never get it right. Always the misfit. Not again, you hear? Is my turn now!" he bellowed. "I go show them who is man! I taking back what is mine!"

Cara glanced again at the door and prayed that someone would come to the restroom. Where was the ambulance? She had to think of some way to calm him. "You're right, Eric," she said, steadying her voice. "I understand, but you need to see a doctor to make sure everything okay."

He tilted his head, looked down at her, and decided to relax his hold, allowing her to pry her wrist free. "I don't want any doctor or ambulance or anything. I just want you," he said miserably, staring at his hands. "I don't know what does happen. Sometimes I does get so damn vex at everything," he added apologetically.

"But you need to stay in control, Eric," she said. She picked up her purse to leave, but when she reached the door, his six-foot frame blocked her. His hands were behind his back, and she heard the click of the lock. "Eric, what you doing?"

"I not ready for you to leave, Cara."

"But I need to check to see if the ambulance reach," she said, struggling to keep her voice calm.

"Cara. Don't leave nah," he begged. "I just want some time with you. Come, please?" He reached for her. She darted from his grasp, tripped over the rug, and fell onto the cold floor. Eric loomed above, one hand reaching down to her. His other hand was in his pocket. "Babe, come. Let's work this out, nah," he said gently, pulling her to a sitting position. "I can't do this without you."

"Eric, you're not well," she repeated, shaking her head. "One minute you're sweet and gentle, the next you're a raging bull."

"I'm real sorry I hurt you, Cara. I just love you so much, I can't live without you. Tell me what I doing wrong and I will fix it."

"You really want to get better, Eric?" she asked cautiously.

"Yes, darling, but I don't know what does get into me sometimes. Only you could help me, Cara." He searched her face. "Stay nah? For me, please?" The fury in his eyes that accompanied his tantrums was gone. Before her stood the sad little boy who had lost his way. In the early years, she had been the only one who could talk him out of his rages, the only one who could once again find that little boy beneath the wrath. Things had been so different then. Maybe she should give him one more chance, but she would need to bring in someone else to guide them through it.

"Okay, Eric. But you have to promise to go to counseling," she warned.

He smiled. "Anything for you, babe. I just want us to be together again." She reached out and took his hand, letting him pull her up until she stood next to him. He beamed as he led her across the room where they sat on the lounge chair. "Here," he said, drawing his hand from his pocket. "I want you to wear this." He held a ring between his thumb and index finger.

Trembling, Cara reached over and carefully took the faded gold band. She placed it in her palm and stared at its slightly warped shape. Its smooth surface was scratched, and one of the cubic zirconias was missing. It was the old promise ring he had given her in their early courting days. Tears welled in her eyes as she remembered them giggling and strolling, arms around each other's waists, without a care in the world. She looked at Eric. Blinking away the tears that threatened to spill onto her face, she sighed and nodded slowly.

"After this," he said, smiling at her, "you won't recognize your husband, and you will never leave me again."

In the roadway outside the Tunapuna Regional Complex, emergency medical technicians joked as they removed the gurney from the back of the ambulance and placed it onto the sidewalk. "Hmm, these public servants don't have enough work, or what? They dying of boredom?" Jerome said, causing Phyllis to laugh out loud.

"Either that," Phyllis answered between guffaws, "or somebody want to leave half-day."

"How long since they call we?" Jerome wiped the sweat from his brow.

"About forty-five minutes. But don't worry about that, is probably a false alarm."

"Yeah, and besides, that lunch-time traffic to pass the market was a killer."

"Never mind that you had to finish eat your sandwich first," Phyllis teased.

"Yeah, well, I can't lift up nobody on a empty belly," Jerome replied.

The sudden crack of a gunshot made them stop. Birds flew from the nearby treetops. A second report rang out. Seconds later, a man raced out of an office, leaned over the balcony, and shouted for them to come. They quickly shut the doors of the ambulance and raced to the bottom of the staircase. They dragged the gurney up the stairs and squeezed through a glass door, past wooden cubicles in the air-conditioned office space, and finally stopped outside a restroom where a frightened cleaning lady wearing rubber gloves and an apron pointed to the door.

"They in there," she said quickly. "They put him in there after he pass out and he wife come to see about him. I was going to empty the garbage and I come and find the door lock and then I hear—" She stopped. There was no need to say more.

Phyllis tried the door. She looked at Jerome, shook her head, and stepped back. Gripping the gurney by one end, he rammed the wooden door. The lock broke. The door gave way, and splintered wood fell to the ground. Inside, a woman lay across a blood-soaked rug. Her eyes stared blankly as blood oozed from a small hole in her left temple. Behind her, on a lounge chair, a man slumped to one side. A black-red wound started at his jaw and ended where the bullet exited through his skull. The area behind the man was sprayed dark red, as if a child had dipped a toothbrush in paint and then turned it on the wall. Beneath the chair lay a small gun.

The medical technicians blocked the doorway to prevent the staff from barging in, but one woman who had pushed through the crowd peered over Jerome's shoulder into the room. She screamed and then collapsed. Someone said she was the man's sister.

"Allyuh can't do anything?" the cleaning lady asked, looking from Jerome to Phyllis. "They might still be alive."

"We can't do nothing here, nah, lady," Jerome replied. "Just call the police."

# LUCILLE

BY ELIZABETH NUNEZ

*St. James*

Lucille, who lived next door to me, was my best friend in Trinidad, and it seemed I alone knew she wore her surname like an albatross around her neck. It was Smart. She was Lucille Smart, and obvious to anyone, painfully so to Lucille, she was anything but, though, I must admit, in no way duncier than I. We both had to repeat the Exhibition class and were dangerously close to thirteen years old when we eventually won coveted seats at St Joseph's Convent Secondary School. But perhaps Lucille was actually smarter than I was. Perhaps it was the burden of carrying around that surname that wore her down, chipped away at her confidence until she began to believe the rumors whispered about her: Lucille Smart is not smart; Lucille Smart is duncy.

Lucille was a Smart because her father was a Smart, but she was not the same Smart as her older brother and sister who were the children of her father's deceased first wife. The year we took the Exhibition exams for the first time, her brother, Antoine Smart, won an Island Schol, a scholarship given by the colonial government to the smartest secondary school student on the island. Antoine was admitted to Oxford where he was studying languages, but he already spoke three: English, of course, as well as French and Spanish. He had studied French at l'Alliance Française on Victoria Avenue, and by the time he was eleven years old, he was practically fluent. Lucille also studied French at l'Alliance Française, but at twelve going on thirteen, she could barely string together words in a sentence that made any sense. Antoine did not have to spend much time studying Spanish either. He had a friend from Venezuela, and within months he and Pedro were huddled together exchanging jokes in Spanish and laughing, Lucille believed, at her expense. Antoine indeed was a true, authentic Smart. And so was his sister Suzette, Lucille's half-sister. She won the Jerningham Silver Medal in fifth form in the same year that Lucille and I finally won an Exhibition, eclipsing our victory by her triumph. After all, we had sat for the Exhibition twice; Suzette won the Jerningham Silver Medal on her first try.

But Lucille's burden was not only the cruel irony of being permanently welded to a name that so perfectly suited her siblings and was so perfectly unsuitable for her; it was the seemingly added unfairness of being darker than her sister and brother. For in a society where lightness of color was prized, she was considered unattractive, at least less attractive than her light-skinned sister who had the good fortune of having a light-skinned mother. Lest the reader come to the conclusion that Lucille was overly sensitive and paranoid, here are some facts: Lucille and Suzette went to the same secondary school. Suzette was invited to join the school choir where all the girls, coincidentally, were as light-skinned, if not lighter-skinned, than she. Lucille, who to any rational right-thinking person had a better singing voice than Suzette, failed the audition for the choir. Suzette was assigned to one School House where, again, all the girls were of the same complexion. In Lucille's School House, all the girls were dark-skinned. Suzette played lawn hockey, went sailing at the Yacht Club with other girls in her class, and at Carnival played in the band where the darkest girl was merely tanned. Suzette kept a wide berth from Lucille in school, though she was friendly enough with her at home.

In those days, mothers kept a strict eye on their daughters, especially their daughters who biologically had passed into womanhood, as Lucille and I had when we entered secondary school. The notorious Boysie Singh and his minions were said to be trawling the streets for young girls. It was alleged that they would cut open the chests of girls our age and take out their hearts to rub on the hooves of their racehorses to make them run faster. True or not, we believed this, and our mothers rarely allowed us out of the house after 6 o'clock when the sun abruptly descended below the horizon and the streets turned ominously pitch-black. But Lucille and I were duncy, and to help us keep up with the rigorous curriculum in first form, our mothers arranged for us to take private lessons from a retired school teacher whose house faced the Mucurapo Cemetery, half a mile from where we lived. Usually our lessons ended at 5:30, which gave us enough time, walking briskly, to get home before the brief twilight turned to night, but sometimes we would arrive when the porch light had been turned on and our mothers were at the gate waiting for us.

It seemed we not only had to be wary of Boysie Singh on the prowl, but also of boys, all boys. My mother's instructions when I had my first period were straightforward and simple: "Keep away from boys!" I didn't quite know what she meant. Unlike girls today who are the age I was then, I had no idea how babies were conceived. I took my mother's directive to mean I was to keep up the adversarial stance Lucille and I had long established with the boys in our neighborhood. They liked teasing Lucille about her name, and since I was her friend, they teased me too. Besides being dark-skinned—I was as dark as Lucille—we were both skinny, and so were unappealing to boys who would get tongue-tied when the buxom, wide-hipped girls passed by. They treated us like their younger brothers, playing tricks on us, their favorite to take advantage of Lucille's fear of the cemetery.

Lucille's fear was not the garden-variety fear of ghosts walking on their graves in the cemetery. Her fear had a logical basis, logical if one believes in spirits or at least the ability of humans on this side of the world to communicate with the dead. I am sure this is not how Lucille's mother would put it if asked about the prayers she said for the dead. Lucille's mother was a devout Catholic. She believed, as Catholics believed at the time, and perhaps still do, that her prayers for her dead relatives had the power to remit some of their time in Purgatory if they had the misfortune, as most of us will, of dying with venial sins on their souls. Indulgences, the Church called these gifts that the living could bestow on the dead, and one could earn them for their dearly departed if one said such and such prayers and put such and such coins or paper money in the collection basket. Chaucer, of course, had lots of fun with this practice. In the third form, brash teenagers, testing the limits of our religious beliefs, Lucille and I spent many a happy hour reciting lines from *The Pardoner*, our favorite being the Pardoner's unabashed admission that he would make people believe they were kissing the bones of saints when what he had offered were the bones of sheep: *For myn entente is nat but for to wynne, / And nothyng for correccion of synne.*

My mother had no patience with my cynicism. There are no atheists in fox holes, she would say to me, shaking her finger in my face whenever I voiced criticism of the Church. And she proved her point when I dropped to my knees the first time an earthquake shook our house. I was not an atheist by any means, but I resented the hours I had to spend in church every Sunday and on the holy days. Lucille, like me, was not religious but, unlike me, she never challenged her mother's beliefs. Every night she obediently joined her siblings in her mother's bedroom as her mother led them in prayer for Mummy Alice. Mummy Alice was how Mrs. Smart referred to her stepchildren's dead mother. All Souls' Day was special. On that day, according to Mrs. Smart, the souls of the dead gathered near their graves, anxiously awaiting Indulgences. So every All Souls' Day, Mrs. Smart took the children to the cemetery, to the grave of Mummy Alice. I would go with Lucille because, of course, Lucille was my best friend. Mrs. Smart would give each of us several candles. She would light them for us and we would stick them, one at a time, into the earth on the mound of Mummy Alice's grave. Soon Mummy Alice's grave would twinkle and glitter with pretty flickering tongues of fire and even I was inclined to believe that Mummy Alice stood their smiling with gratitude and appreciation.

In the year Lucille and I failed to win an Exhibition, we were so ashamed that younger girls had won and so desperate for help that we decided that the next All Souls' Day, when Mummy Alice supposedly came out of Purgatory to hover over her grave, we would make a bargain with her. For a whole year, we would put half our weekly allowance in the Indulgence box at the entrance of the church if she would ask God to help us. Hoping to seal the bargain, we placed extra lighted candles on her grave.

To this day, though rationally I know better, I still wonder if it was the force of nature or, as Mrs. Smart proclaimed, the arrival of Mummy Alice that suddenly caused a powerful wind to swoosh across the cemetery, bypass all the other graves, and slam into the lighted candles on Mummy Alice's grave. Most of the candles went out immediately, but the flames from a row of them, close to where Lucille was standing, reached up to the edge of her dress and set it on fire. Her mother, who kept a bucket of water nearby for such eventualities, quickly put out the flames. Lucille did not get burned, but whether she believed it was Mummy Alice or the wind that had set her on fire, she developed a mortal fear of the cemetery.

News traveled fast in our neighborhood, and it was not long before the local boys learned what had happened. But this much I could say for the power of the Indulgences we earned for Mummy Alice with our money and our candles: we both won an Exhibition the next time we took the exams. Yet neither Mummy Alice nor the Smart name could save us from failing Latin and Math in the First Form. On the walk back home from the after-school lessons, which our parents hoped would stir dormant gray cells in our brain (surely, with her last name and accomplished brother and sister, Lucille's cells were simply resting; in my case, my mother's hope was an act of faith), we had to endure the taunts of the boys. They would hide behind the cemetery wall, waiting to terrorize us, especially on days when no matter how often I repeated the convoluted Latin verb declensions I never could get them right, and so our lessons lasted close to 6 o'clock. "Boo!" the boys would shout over the cemetery wall as we made our way home in the dusky twilight. We would run, but they would race behind us, stopping just short of our homes. "Lucille Smart ent smart!" they would shout. "She friend duncier. Devil come from the grave and bring the fire from Hell to burn she dress!"

Did Lucille believe their taunts? It is hard not to lose confidence in one's intelligence when test scores prove malicious boys right. But I did not believe in all that stuff they said about the Devil and the fires of Hell and I wanted to pay them back for scaring my friend.

The rainy season that July, toward the end of the school

year, was worse than any other in the memories of our parents. According to the rhyme we sang to herald the coming of the rains, July should have stood by. *June too soon / July stand by / August come it must / September remember*. But the thunder and lightning and powerful winds came in July. There was no standing by. For four days it rained, and when it stopped, much of the earth from the tops of the cemetery graves had eroded. Lucille was not with me when I passed the cemetery and noticed something white and hard and round lodged in a corner between the wall and the rails of the gate. It was the head of a skeleton! I am not a particularly brave person, but I could not bear to see my friend breaking into a cold sweat each time we passed the boys. I had to stop them. When I saw the skull in the corner of the cemetery wall, my already overactive imagination went into overdrive. Our English teacher had told us that we would be reading *Hamlet* in the Second Form, and Lucille, being an avid reader (though, paradoxically, her competence in every subject except English cast doubt on her native intelligence), couldn't wait that long. I confess I did not share her enthusiasm, but I listened as she told me the plot. The cemetery scene piqued my interest. *Alas, poor Yorick!*

I don't remember the excuse I gave Lucille for leaving our lessons early that day, but I must have been persuasive for she never suspected I had devious plans. I got to the cemetery early, before the boys came, mounted the skull on a stick, and hid behind a headstone near the cemetery wall. Just as the boys began taunting Lucille, I raised the skull and began such a hooting and a bellowing I almost scared myself and certainly scared them. They ran for their lives.

I wish I could say that from then on life was wonderful for Lucille. By the Second Form, my brain cells became active, not radically so, but enough that I was able to pass all my seven subjects in the O Level exams in the Fifth Form and was promoted to Lower Sixth to sit for A Levels. Lucille barely passed five subjects. I am convinced it was the pressure of high expectations that stunted her potential. I believe she was so terrified of failure, she was afraid to try. It is curious that only by daring to risk failure do we get the chance to succeed. Lucille never dared. Her father, however, banking on the Smart name, was not deterred, and he was able to persuade the principal of our secondary school to admit Lucille to Lower Sixth.

Boys, of course, came back in our lives. By the Fifth Form we had begun to blossom: breasts, hips, thighs, and legs. Lucille, struggling behind me in class, overtook me by wide margins in each of those areas. Her dark skin with its red undertones glowed like a ripe governor plum. The boys noticed and vied for her attention. In Lower Sixth her grades continued to slip, though more drastically. Caught up with the rigors of the curriculum for my A Level exams, I could no longer find the time to help her. Lucille turned to the boys, basking in the adoration they showered on her. Was it because at last she found the approval she had longed for all her life that she didn't seem to care when she wasn't promoted to Upper Sixth? A few months later she left for the States, and it was years before I heard from her again.

I know now where Lucille went and what she was doing while I was sitting for my A Level exams. Lucille, who longed for attention and approval, not for what she did but for who she was, succumbed to the hot passion of a boy who did not love her. Ashamed when she became pregnant, her parents squirreled her away to a distant great-aunt in Harlem. Hers is too much a Caribbean story, a story noir, not of guns and daggers, not of high crimes and misdemeanors that cause havoc on the corporeal frame, but a story noir nonetheless, of crimes and misdemeanors against the spirit that feeds *"the canker* [that] *galls the infants of the spring / Too oft before their buttons be disclosed."*

# PEACOCK BLUE

BY VAHNI CAPILDEO

*Fort George*

When your blood fills with bubbles as you come up too fast to the surface from that kind of depth, that's when you die. Maureen didn't think of herself as a water sports girl. Twelve months after the honeymoon at the neighboring island's safe resort (one block down from the unsafe resort where the hurricanes call in on their way north), that was when she and Vikram started their deepsea diving. That's their code name for sex like you wouldn't believe.

It's always like that now. Something breaks and then a million bubbles fill the space she used to call her brain with blue champagne and her eyes scream out to smile. The first time they went to that kind of depth was right after the first big fight. Even a drunk Vikram is not unsteady on his feet, but a Vikram holding their three-month-old (count it, a wedding-night conception) to his chest saying, *Is a reflex. I go dive off the cliff, the babba go close he little eyes an' hold he breath, and then we go come back up safe an' sound. That way he won't ever fear the water. Do not fear! Vikram is here* is not Maureen's idea of someone steady enough to lean on. But it was the deliberate use of dialect that drove her wild. They had met abroad at university. She struck the first blow. *Not in front of de child,* her big man had begged. *Put my child down,* Ms. Maureen had ordered. And the child had been dumped in the bassinet,

284 // TRINIDAD NOIR

and (not in front of the child) they had incurred each other's gratitude and forgiveness. As any policewoman could have told her, though no policewoman did, it was her fault. So they made a home, the married lovers.

If the red planet Mars could lift extra color from the vertically aligned points glowing on top of that hill, the points would win out, redder. What else is up there, anyway? A view you'd do better to find in a stack of shopping-mall postcards?

Up there is the national broadcasting station; is an anarchic geographical condition that makes mobile phones yield up and die halfway through their new national anthems; is a road running from named to nameless that you wouldn't be driving your Toyota Hilux up in a hurry—with or without an invitation—to the isolated mansions where a catalogue's worth of electronic amenities flashes constant through the earthquake and thunderstorm power-cuts, for such houses have their own generators, satellite dishes, and stashes of fire-arms that a slender woman can manage two-handed, her feet spurning rugs that must have driven three generations of a weaver's family blind, azure into amethyst, blood-red into terra-cotta, shipped here to get crapped on by geckos that turn themselves azure, amethyst, blood-red, and terra-cotta in one blink-free flick of the tongue, but still crap black and white.

Requisite woman stretches her long legs in her long skirt. The skirt fabric is officially known as "slinky." Pity that nobody is there to see why. A genuine crocodile-skin bag emits its silent visual crackle on the teak bar. A choppy little wind makes racing silks of the pool. Similar purplish patterns were recently invoked on the soft skin behind the knees beneath the slinky.

Requisite woman is slender no longer. Four hours hill walking per day "for the sake of her health." Now she is built. You wouldn't call that a beaten look.

The garden hose coils up quietly.

The lady knows how to treat herself. That dash of lavender in the citronella candle. How about that more-than-a-dash of vodka in the grenadine cocktail with the ruby glass cocktail stirrer tipping back in it. Angostura. Jeezanages! Another stirrer smashed! Just seven left in the set. Get another, order another, go abroad just to buy another. Go abroad and why come back?

"But he will always come back." Maureen knows to be tender with beautiful things. Vikram has been a Beautiful Thing surprisingly long, even after the second babba, conceived in fury, blessed their home.

"Look at him now," she giggles. It's not the violence. It's not the betrayal. It's his vulgarity! Ducking behind next door's washing line to have bareback sex with the forty-six-year-old, grizzle-chopped maid. Mr. Not-in-Front-of-the-Children. As if children playing in the upstairs veranda won't cast a glance next door. Is that beautiful? Telling the doctor it couldn't be from him that his own wife . . . and then the injections. "It was very uncomfortable," she enunciates. But the children turned out all right.

True, things go sweetly. Only sometimes they have what Vikram calls "ding-dong quarrels" and the old people call "Tobago love." Season in and season out, Tobago love stays in fine flower.

Maureen sips the drink and smiles. Mica-flaked lips glitter at the smashed ruby glass on the poolside tiling. She pulls her skirt up above her knees. One leg uncoils. See the Beautiful Thing's latest artwork? It aches to be critiqued. Bitterness sets in, the chlorine aftertaste to every kiss. (Sip, and sip again.)

This stuff is damned expensive. But he wouldn't want me to have to work. *You can disconnect the wife from the household, but the family'll keep transmitting to her brain.* A sober Vikram maxim. Lucky lovers' move, to their fortress hilltop, away from Vikram's poisonous clan. "I made a cry for help. And nooo-body heard me." What was that his mother had said?

"Look at you! How you get those hard calves? You were a small-small girl when I saw you on the airplane steps five years ago! You become an old hardback woman now! Watch yourself, or you will find you have to think about . . ."

"About cosmetic surgery, like Kirti?"

"Hush your mouth! Who told you that? Kirti is blessed with a natural beauty. Ever since young she has used the aloes from my garden. You want me to bring you some aloes? You could plant them in your garden, or keep them in the fridge and use them fresh. I could keep bringing them for you, if you want to do that and spare yourself the trouble of plant-ing them. I don't mind. True, I don't mind. Aloes is good for all kind of things. But what happen, child? You not listen-ing to me! So, sweetheart, where you going to celebrate your anniversary? Somewhere nice? Tea at La Boucan? Dinner tête-à-tête at Apsara? You know how I am happy to mind the grandchildren, if you two young things want some time to go out and enjoy yourselves while you are young—not like me! Where Vikram taking you for your anniversary?"

"I'm glad you mentioned his name—" Petal the Matri-arch suddenly solidified, ten times denser. Her voice softened. That was a rawhide whip in it.

"Listen to me. If you have something to say about my son, remember this. He loves you so much, it even makes me—his mother!—jealous. Imagine that! When I love you like if you were my own daughter! Vikram is a very loving boy, but he is not per-fect. I don't know what kind of men you had when you were abroad, or how many, and don't tell me—I don't care for you to tell me. I know you feel you are modern young people with a modern marriage. All I know is that you are the apple of Vikram's eye. You hear me, sweetheart? You believe that? The apple of his eye." Petal the Matriarch was satisfied with the ensuing silence during which her daughter-in-law's mouth had closed again after opening in a way that it had never quite opened before.

That was then.

"And you know," sings Requisite Woman to herself, "Petal is the ideal mother-in-law. She would do anything for the grand-children. We are family. She is right."

The glass arcs. Maureen drinks to women's solidarity. *Nice girls don't snarl in the throat. Let that sound be a sob from the womb. Quick, not the glass too! So many things smashed up, he will notice! Sa-a-a-ve it.* A couple of tries before Maureen gets a grip, then the Murano is upright on the—

"But who the hell put the table there?" The glass is saved. It's the footing that goes. Muscular bottom, aflower with bruises, makes slinky-clad contact with marble. And—just like that—she sees it.

Candlelight and fairy lights shine into the pool, but the shining snake has the starring role. *Neat, how the tail thrashes. The head's elevated on that segment of body—so long, would you call it a neck? It's no bad swimmer. Still doesn't look pleased to be in the water.*

"You, too, in at the deep end! Poor thing. I wonder what you did in your pas' life to end up in our pool in all that stink-stink chlorine. But you're a mapipire. A poisonous one. Death in what, twenty minutes? The hospital people would never find the way up this hill in time. And my mobile might cut out and I forgot again to pay the damned blasted bill for the land line. What would Vikram say in this situation? Do not fear, snake, Maureen is here. If you do something bad, it's not your fault. Nobody meant you to be in the water."

Flat of the hand on the marble, she pushes herself up, small of the back against the table. The fall has doubled the old pain. For a split second, woman faced with snake is filled with a rare sense of mastery. Lord of creation! But a semi-Hindu lord, animated by a sense of identity with the creature. "Snake," says the woman, "you are lucky. I know. I am like you. I am not going to hurt you. Listen to me, snake. I did not grow up in Port-of-Spain." The snake's eyes flash. It's going somewhere fast, though not out of the water. "I am a country girl from Sangre Grande, snake, who did well at school and went abroad to university. I fell in love. Now here we are at home. You cannot know what it is to love, snake. Count yourself fortunate."

The snake's flat head reminds the woman of her long-dead, beloved Sangre Grande old ladies, their oiled hair flat under the *orhni*, their English hissing and thudding, moved by an older, more complicated language translated from but not spoken. The flash of the eyes.

"Should I save you, snake? If I were my uncles, I would take a long stick and crush your head fast-fast right there where the neck gets thick. That is where you have your li'l reptile brain and reptile soul, snake. You would not twine up the stick and sting me. See, I have a long stick. But you don't have to swim so fast. Take a rest, snake. You take a rest though I cannot."

Vikram rounds the corner of the house soundlessly, navy on navy, evening on denim. A drunken wife is disgusting. There had been no whiff of drunkenness about Maureen the student. A good girl to present to the family and marry, yet more able than a home-kept virgin to appreciate a steady man. Vikram considers himself no drinker. He began during the engagement. There was so much to reconcile. He hates the idea of himself as the athlete who's started drinking. Early swimming sessions almost abolish the night, and day, before. If only he could make sure that day would always break on him in the blue water.

And does his wife feel his eyes on her? Of course not. How long will she harangue this freestyle mapipire? Even a snake can hold her attention more than her husband. He knows he cannot make her pay. His beautiful wife is an emotional bankruptcy. Give her a chance, a minute or two. Hasn't she promised to notice him first and forever? Beautiful Things, if they are male, do well with a touch of cruelty in their good looks. Vikram is no exception. If Petal the Matriarch could have seen her son, she'd have had cause to insist on just how handsome he is.

"It is not good for me to have a drink, snake, and it is not good for you to be in that pool. I do not give satisfaction as a wife and mother. I know that. But you, snake, I can save you and I can tidy you. Let me tidy you up now." Maureen totters toward the long pole, the one with the net on the end that the yard boy uses for fishing out dead leaves, belly-up lizards, and whatever unwelcome floating objects you don't care to have your cocoa-buttered shoulder brush up against in the predawn chill. Those are crazy steps the high-heeled Spanish sandals are making. The Clinique nails press lustrous on the white-painted wood pole. Holding it, the arms swing the body out of balance.

"MAUREEN!" One foot in the air, mouth open, she skids and lunges to a stop. "MAUREEN!"

"Hello, darling." Graceless, she scatters the fire that alcohol stitches to the edge of a sexy voice. She topples onto her bottom and giggles.

"What the hell you doing, woman?"

His wife gets up surprisingly fast. Her grip on the stick appears martial. "You want this?"

"No. No . . ."

"Here, you want this? Port-of-Spain man, Fatima Boys' School athlete, you want to take the snake out of your own pool?" She nears at a prowling crouch. The stick lashes across his shins. "Hold onto it, man! I am giving it to you! You can't take it? Hold onto it!"

What should be clear tumbles dark. Somewhere in the same pool is the snake, thrashing. Water is bitter on his corneas, bitter bile runs in his gullet. Maureen is not visible through the splinters of water and night light, and the sense of the unwanted thing nearing.

It is she crying out. "Let me help you . . ."

She is on her knees, wetting the slinky and stinking of chlorine, trying to scoop a snake into her net. Her ears are filling with husband-voiced curses. She is on her knees screaming as the pole is snatched from her hands by a dripping hero. The snake is on the tiles among the ruby glass splinters. He is beating the snake on the back of the neck with the pole. He is beating her with the same pole. One kick and she's in the pool. Then they are in the water together. A million bubbles blueing out her brain, the kissing is beginning.

The Northern Range is green no longer. Much of the rain forest burned down in the last dry season. The police and the army were busy all day and the water trucks exhausted just taking water to people who complained on television that they did not have any. You could study the deforestation and the erosion and everything else, but who listens? What to do? It's better not to worry your head and beat yourself up about that. Petal the Matriarch watched the burning mountains. "The colors real pretty, you don't find so? Like sunset all through the day."

At the edge of the Port-of-Spain Swim Club pool, Vikram stands. Rain or shine, every day that there is not thunder and lightning, he likes to stand as he is standing now, on the diving board. He must have bought that swimsuit in the States—skintight peacock-blue. His cousins wouldn't be seen dead in anything except baggy swimshorts of a nondescript color. But from the neck down, it is so obvious that Vikram is no pretty boy. Suave, yes, but not a sof' man. He real macho.

Open-air electric-blue laid out in an oblong, and Vikram dives into it. Speed and perfectibility—the white sky shattering announces his departure from the air with a thousand gongs. Bubbles tumble. Deep in the water, Vikram turns with strength. He reemerges all brightness.

That girl he married does not know when she's lucky. Like she doesn't remember she married a man she could talk to. You should see Vikram at a family get-together. You know the way women stand about in groups by themselves? Well, he will go over and talk to the women. He can talk about anything—scandal, international politics, people living abroad. And he will tell the women that looking pale doesn't mean looking good, that they should not be afraid of getting a little suntan or putting on a little weight, that the most beautiful women in the world are from this country. He offers to top up their whiskey if they are the kind of educated women who drink because they still feel they have something to prove. Vikram is a bit of a radical since he got back from Away, a little bohemian. He knows how to debate, in dialect and in formal English, and he knows how to respect a woman's intelligence. Whenever Cheryl or Ambika is at one of these dos, he will talk with them 'specially now and then during the evening. You should hear the kinds of things they discuss. Legalizing abortion! Turning a blind eye to homosexuality! But you know, he can be very nice to the children. Even when they grow up and go away, they will always remember him for the little books and things he used to bring back for them when he was studying. It's so nice when you see that happen in a family.

When Vikram has dived, he is alone. Maureen should be there to watch him. Even six months ago, before she started drinking and getting ideas, she would have been there on a deckchair, wearing sunglasses and one of those dresses that make her look like Miss Brazil. She has a sense of style, though she went to live with her aunt in England and then to Art College, which is why she hardly knows Trinidad at all.

Vikram loves Maureen too-too bad. He dwells on the nice figure she had when they met. Maybe it fooled Vikram up, how Maureen tossed her hair and shoulders and giggled, wriggling string-bean legs. Poor Vikram is a boy, after all. Despite her veneer of intellectualism, he must have seen what she had in common with the girls at home, the most beautiful girls in the world.

Maureen and Vikram have been living apart for all of three days. What is there for her to do alone in that house on the hill? Hog it all to herself and her third, barely-there, pregnant bump? She and her days' worth of dirty plates on the floor, waiting for her husband to return and fetch and carry and pick up after her, as if he had nothing better to do? And like any nice boy, isn't her husband hard to convince that he has nothing better to do? Three days' worth of convincing has not convinced him back up the hill.

You should see how patient he is. It must be twenty times in the last three days that he has had this conversation:

"So how come you are the one to move out?"

He shrugs. "She threaten me with lawyers, police, all kind of thing, I don't know. Sometimes I'm afraid she hasn't . . . adjusted . . . so well. But if this is how she feels for the moment, this is how she feels. She is my prin-cess and she must have her space."

Who could believe ingratitude like Maureen's? It's true she did not throw his clothes out on the lawn, or pull a gun on him, or change all the locks. If she'd wanted an excuse, she had one after the thing with the maid that they both tried to hush up. But it's ungrateful of her to allow him to just leave voluntarily. If Vikram was intent on leaving for her sake, and Maureen loved him, why didn't she lock up the house and abandon it and follow? How could she be so ready to abandon her born children and let their grandmother take them away?

Why is she not there as she used to be—with that naughty-but-nice English-girl look, not straightforward—waiting to offer him a cool drink, pink and green in a rock crystal tumbler, a nip of something else in it. And his clean-cut refusal.

"It's only temporary. She needs her space." Vikram speaks in his American voice, a voice that conveys hurt, together with the smile where the eyebrows quirk up in the middle while the corners of the eyelids droop—a good face set against a bad fate.

"You mean she let you leave? What a bloody selfish cow!" shouts Ambika, who spent a year at the English college with Maureen.

"Maureen looks so quiety-quiety, but you can never tell," Auntie Kirti mourns, frowning at Ambika's strong language. "Your wife really string you along, boy. She is ungrateful. *Nee-makharam*. A taker. What space she need so? Maureen should be minding her family. She even have a place to live here if it wasn't for you? But what you worrying about her for? I can see you worrying. Here, you want something else to eat? Take something nah, take something and eat nah, you need your strength for your studies. For your job."

"You stupid or what?" Petal the Matriarch scorns her mealy-mouthed sister. "The bitch good, yes. She eh play she lucky! She lucky for true! My son leaving she with the marital home while he traipse back long-face and tail between he legs to his mother's house? And I minding she children since I don't know when and I don't know for how long! But what kind of blasted arseness is this? You stay here as long as you want, Son. Your welcome will never wear out here. I went to college in England too, for well longer than she, but I know I come back home for Independence, I not going to talk like she. She have house and land and children and husband, and now she have she space."

Women of the generation of Petal the Matriarch can use bad words without shocking anybody. They started doing so forty years ago, after their marriages, when they acquired their own homes. But Petal makes "space" sound so deeply obscene that everyone is quiet for three seconds.

"He get thin, eh? How you looking so thin? How she have you so? Like she bewitch you! Look how thin he get! But what happen, like Maureen never used to feed you? Come and eat, boy, sit down and ree-lax, sit down and eat."

"He's not any thinner than he wants to be, Auntie Kirti," Ambika drawls. "He's always down the gym, watching his figure." She taps her cigarette into a red-and-black plastic ashtray on an ivory inlaid table. The Matriarch looks outraged.

"I have a little paunch," interjects Cheryl. She places her glittering hands on either side of the concavity around which she has strung a belt. "You see? I am getting a little paunch."

"How much do you weigh?" asks Ambika, with interest.

"One hundred and twelve pounds. You know, eight stone."

"And you are how tall? What, five-foot-four? You shouldn't weigh more than a hundred and four pounds. That is your ideal weight."

Anyone can see how Vikram misses Maureen—misses her enough to get vexed. But he won't say anything. He won't do anything. He is a gentle man.

"You don't worry, Beta," says Auntie Kirti. "What that girl did was totally out of order. But you don't worry about her. I have told my maid to get a taxi and go up there and spend two hours a day every morning until that girl is up and about again."

"People don't expect a young lady to get into those sorts of state, do they?"

"Mind your own business, Ambika. I am concerned for the girl," croons Cheryl. "It seem to me she has not adjusted well. Maybe she will need to go away for a little while until she feels better."

A single woman soon to be dispossessed of her social status, Maureen tries to think that she is safe. That day when the yard boy walked into her bedroom pretending to ask her an ordinary question—she felt too miserable to move when he came in, too sick to know when he left, and she was too wise to tell anyone how he and his friend materialized on another day when she was lying there unbathed and in a tangle of cotton and grief. Since then she hasn't trusted the so-called instinct of self-preservation. No, since before.

Maureen knows that someone like her does not really require help. She will not buy a guard dog. How could she manage that kind of beast? She does not talk to the police more than she has to. The police are her in-laws' friends, and they already check up on her. She knows, when she hears the lock of the back door going. And even the best private security firms would not bring a helicopter to her hill. But armed service is not always what a girl needs to feel secure.

One little thing she can do, and she has done almost straight away, is to have the swimming pool emptied. That gives her a reason to send the yard boy on a few weeks' holiday. *So nice of him to stay and work for her without wages, when she is so difficult.* Without the pool needing chemicals and things fished out of it, and with Kirti's fearful polisher doing her daily stint, the property is kept up at a decent standard. Any more snakes can go in the pool next door.

Vikram keeps smiling. "She needs her space."

"You need to get out more, talk to some men, boy. Maureen had you shut up there in that house until, like, you gone stupid over she? Why you don't drop in on Jay and Eduardo this evening? I know they would like to see you."

Ambika's drawl. "Eduardo is a barbarian."

"Shut up, Ambika. Isn't that what you foreign-educated girls like to say to your elders—*shut up?*" Vikram's ears are packed with bubbles when the womenfolk talk. He can think only of the fresh start in the morning's electric blueness.

Received wisdom has it that on or near the equator, the day

vanishes abruptly, gold to black, without nightfall. At eleven degrees above the equator, for those who care to perceive it, there is a violet hour. Whiskey has been on Vikram's breath for about three and a half hours by now. His tan is deep, acquired by poolsides that are not his own. His anger surges. The new moon is strung out like a hammock, white by the red of the broadcasting station's three-point glow.

Does Vikram need an invitation to his own house? It is not without an invitation that the borrowed Toyota Hilux ransacks a path, on full beam, to the heights where that house and wife of his are located. A tipsy giggle ripped apart by mobile phone crackle. "You don't swim for me anymore? Swim for me tonight." Then the flatline tone. No hope of a workable signal on that hill.

There are some lessons that a good man would hope not to have to teach. Vikram is equipped with tools for the teaching.

Such ridge-top trees as stayed unburned make ink etchings on the tropical dusk.

Vikram knows this road's ups and downs. He switches off the engine and the lights. He inches. He coasts. But he can hear singing and talking. That must be in his head. The radio is not on and nobody is about in the neighboring houses, except the high-ranking army couple whose voices are raised as ever on their veranda, a gun making punctuation in the air, all present and correct.

Vikram stops outside his own land. He knows what he has come to do. "My babba. My *baby*." He is sobbing and shaking. He is all alone with the feeling of being a man who means harm. This is hateful. He switches on the pinpoint torchlight of his mobile phone—all it is good for in this place where its waves cut up voices.

First, can't he cool his head? He rubs some whiskey on

his forehead. He takes out his wallet and looks at the photo of Maureen, small smiler in an alien landscape. His Beautiful Thing face reasserts itself over its breakup. (*Handsome*, the Matriarch says . . .) He can't cool his head? The Clarks come off and the Pringle socks. The dark jeans too, he folds them neatly. Those as well? Yes. Now there is only the shirt, only the white vest. The athlete, stripped. It is night, but he needs the touch of blueness. Poised at the edge of the pool, he lets it sink in before he speeds up—the feeling of perfectibility, the anticipation of brightness. It shatters white as the moon, whiter than day.

There is a cry at the moment of no contact with water.

There is a female cry following hard upon the sound of his cry. Maureen.

Will she offer to help? She was expecting something to tidy up now.

If you look at certain hills in other countries—territories that are northern by latitude though seldom by title—any green that you can see might as well be called purple or blue or brown or Venetian-red. The reflections and weave of things prevent the tongue from settling on any adjective, except as a compromise between the dullness of the naming language and the dazzled eye. Here in Trinidad it is different. The green is green. Except when rain gathers, then it is darkness. And except at dawn, when amethyst and terra-cotta slip a glory that is almost cold on the nation's three defining lines of steep terrain.

Not far from these houses is the kind of area where you see the steps that go nowhere. These concrete or stone steps may go straight up any hill or mountain in Trinidad. You may have seen them, for example, on the North Coast Road, cut into the ferrous rock. On your left you will have had the precipice—the vines, the trees, and the drop down to the gorgeous dangers of the bathing beaches. Your car, like all the other cars, will have been taking the winds and speeding, hoping not to meet another vehicle going the opposite way around a turn. On the right there will have been the chuckling of rain forest—at certain times of year, a waterfall that runs where nobody knows, under fern flooring. On such a route you may have seen the steps starting in a clearing, but then just going—up. Could the end of that vertical be where the true Rastafarians live, those enlightened yogis tenderly raising their pumpkin, plantain, cassava, and marijuana, with as little disturbance as possible to the earth they cleanly and illegally hold? I doubt that's how it is, but I like the idea of it.

Then again, maybe you haven't seen those steps. Maybe you took the north coast road, like most of us, dreaming of arrival—a whole ocean, peacock, electric blue.

# DARK NIGHTS

BY JUDITH THEODORE

*East Dry River*

A ll eyes of the waiting commuters followed the pair of shorts with the cheeks exposed and the long thin legs that carried them. Three-inch stilettos gave movement an added bounce. The spandex short top with diamond-studded heart motif on the chest was hardly noticed, so interesting was the lower half. Her companion attracted some glances, but her tight mini halter dress drew fewer comments.

"That girl is not sixteen yet, I'm sure. Where was the mother when she left home?"

"Why is she leaving home this hour of the night anyway?"

These comments were loud enough for the teenager and her companion to hear. They ignored them except for an extra thrust of the hips and approached the last car in line. The long legs stretched into the taxi, then shifted so that the cheeks slid along the seat. The chunky legs with the elevated gym shoes entered next and made the same motion on the seat while the owner tugged at the tight dress. A male passenger followed and caused some more shifting of cheeks. The taxi was now full. The driver reversed, shifted, and sped away, humming softly to the reggae music playing on the radio. "Everybody going to St. James?" he asked, glancing over his shoulder. Three passengers said yes.

The two girls chorused, "No, we're stopping off in Woodbrook."

"I was thinking of passing on the avenue," the driver explained.

"No problem then. We're coming off at Murray Street." Except for the low music and soft humming of the driver, no one spoke again until the girls reached their destination, paid, and alighted.

"Thanks, drive," the young woman in the mini dress said as she closed the door. "But Effie," she turned to her friend as they started up Murray Street, "you never finished telling me why your mother slapped you last night and ripped your dress."

"Why you ask me that now, Maggie? I don't want to spoil my good mood."

"I was really feeling bad, girl. She really cursed you stink and got on ridiculous," Maggie answered with genuine concern.

"You know my mother. You should be used to that. Don't worry."

They reached the park, where some other young women called out to them.

"Where you think those two are going?" the driver asked no one in particular.

"They're going to work," the male passenger in the back shrugged. "Look where they dropped off. Look how they're dressed."

The woman in the front seat, who had her arm resting on the window, shifted position and shook her head. "I think it's a real shame the way those girls parading the street at night and standing at street corners. I thank God for mine. I know they are home right now doing homework."

The man sitting between the woman and the driver stared straight ahead and remained silent. The others chatted with the driver for the remainder of the journey. They mainly discussed the demerits of prostitution, condemning the lifestyle. The woman was the first to reach her destination. She exited the taxi with a cheery, "Good night to all."

"I won't say I never went with one of them," the driver confessed as soon as the car was in motion again, "but that was when I was young and just doing it for the experience. I know better now."

The man in the backseat cleared his throat and looked out the window. After a few moments, he broke the silence. "I used to hang around some friends who did that for a living," he admitted. "I don't lime with them now. When I used to be around them, I went with them. But I was a friend—although I would pass a little change."

The man who sat next to the driver sucked his teeth and burst out, "That is why I didn't say anything. I know man is man. I don't know who you all fooling."

The car was silent again.

Two blocks from the park, a car stopped. A man got out and slipped through the gate. A few minutes later he emerged. He drove slowly down Roberts Street. Two women standing at the corner opposite the park called out to him. He pulled over, rolled down his window, and stretched across the passenger side.

"You're doing anything tonight?" Effie asked.

"I'm in the mood for a lot. Come in. Let us negotiate."

"I'm not making a move till we settle on job and price. And I don't have time to waste." Effie glanced at another car slowing down across the road. The vehicle stopped and was quickly approached by two women from the park.

"I'm paying for the night," the man said with an air of confidence.

Effie leaned on the window and looked him in the eye. She picked up a whiff of cologne she recognized. "That is twelve hundred dollars," she said boldly.

"One thousand, baby. We'll discuss the other two hundred at the end of the night." Effie opened the door and plopped down on the seat. Maggie pulled out her small notebook as they drove off and recorded the license plate number—*PVM 2025*.

On and on she walked, more steadily now, more urgently, more confidently. Each time her heel then toe met the dusty asphalt, the acquaintance was briefer. The utter solitude of her journey was only broken by tiny flickering yellow lights, some close, some distant. They comforted her, amused her, distracted her long enough for her to forget her fear. She tried a few times to catch them but gave up because she felt silly waving her arms about. How would she know if she caught one, anyway? Would she feel a furry spot on her hand, or would it be a gooey mess? She could only tell by touch since she could see nothing except these luminous companions. No tree or shrub was outlined. No moon shone, and there were few stars. She kept a steady pace and made as little noise as possible. She had already encountered one stranger who had mumbled, "Night," his breath almost knocking her out with its alcohol content. She briefly felt intoxicated herself. Suddenly she saw a light in the distance. It was small at first, then grew larger as it approached. It almost seemed to be rushing toward her. As she slowed her steps to delay the inevitable, her breath quickened. She felt strange as she realized this, the drumbeat in her chest echoing her anxiety. Abruptly she sank to her knees, her eyes on the light. Within a few feet of her, it veered to the left.

She sprang up like a blade of grass momentarily stepped on, determined to reach her destination. This time heel and toe barely met the asphalt. She considered running but did not want to attract attention. Despite her terror, running was not an option.

Eventually she discerned pairs of low moving lights crossing in opposite directions. Not many, but enough to let her know she was approaching a junction. Soon she could hear the passing cars. She slowed to her normal pace and strolled to the main road. The drum pounding inside her need not be apparent to all. She entered a bar and bought an Apple J, which she drank quickly and then bought another and left. She stopped a taxi and headed into town.

Effie did not return to Murray Street. She went to her friend Pat's. Pat was not there, so she slept on the porch. She had no intention of returning home with all that money. If Effie got home before her mother, she hid her earnings in various places in the house. Otherwise her mother, who worked the area around Queen's Royal College opposite the Savannah, took what she believed was her share. This time, despite Maggie's warnings about taking too many risks with clients, Effie had stolen all the money she had found at her client's home and more. This time, she had taken two plastic bags of cocaine.

"I ran out the house as soon as he fell asleep. I had to walk about a mile to the main road in these heels, and then while I was walking, the electricity went out. Talk about bad luck. You could imagine my fright. Then I saw car lights coming toward me. I swore it was him, then the lights swerved off. That was so scary."

"So, Effie, you mean to tell me you stole money again? You will get caught one day."

Sucking her teeth, Effie looked skyward, shifted her weight, and lifted her little handbag higher on her shoulder.

"I always tell you, Effie. I'm a prostitute, but I'm not a thief."

"Guess what? He had cocaine and I took that too," Effie announced boldly.

"What! Are you crazy?" Maggie exclaimed. "You went too far this time, girl. What do you intend to do with that?"

"I gave one parcel to Marlon to sell. He is selling already, so I offered him a cut."

"So you will trust Marlon to give you the profits?"

"Marlon knows I'm not afraid to use my knife." Effie pulled the weapon from her bag and flicked it open.

"What about me? Now I can't go back for a long time. You did the thieving, but I was with you, so what am I supposed to do when that man comes looking?"

"I'm giving you a cut too. He had five thousand dollars in the house—well, that is all I found. We can work Chaguanas till the heat is off. And," Effie added, "don't worry about his reporting it to the police. When his wife comes back from vacation, what reason will he give her for going to court?"

"All of that traveling to and from Chaguanas eat up my hard-earned money. The last time we worked Chaguanas, I had to raise the cost of jobs and got less clients."

"New chicks in town always make a hit, so don't panic," Effie assured her. "I'm giving you a cut, I tell you. You could buy more sexy outfits and put in a new weave so we will blow away the Chaguanas posse."

It was 11:15. The sun was making its presence felt. People lined the wall of the building opposite the Royal Gaol for shade. A few leaned against the curved wall of the prison looking expectantly at the gates. Finally, the gates opened and the released prisoners emerged, some moving toward familiar faces. A dark-skinned youth dressed in black jeans, a white Sean John jersey, and gym shoes, and carrying two large plastic bags, strolled through the gates. He wore dark glasses. He took a quick gulp of his soft drink, threw back his shoulders, and swaggered down Frederick Street.

Meanwhile, a young brown-skinned man was walking up the same road. He was dressed for the office in black pants and a long-sleeved white shirt, and his hair was neatly cut. Not far from the prison, his face broke into a smile as he recognized the ex-con and embraced him. "How was your stay inside, breds? How is the life?" he asked as they headed down Frederick Street, arms around each other.

They spoke quietly as they walked. The office worker took the soft drink while the ex-con tied a plastic bag onto one of his pant loops. Removing his sunglasses, the ex-con looked around casually, then placed them in his pocket. The office worker finished the soda and threw the bottle away. They turned and crossed Park Street onto Piccadilly Street.

"I got to go back to work now. I'll check you later, breds."

"Sheldon, boy, you hug me up, drain my soft drink, and you leaving me just so?"

"You know if I was holding, Carl, I would give you a purple note, even a blue note, but I skating on passage till payday."

"I know you have my back, Sheldon. Hold a ten nuh. Later."

Sheldon took the ten dollars Carl handed him and hurried back to work. Carl walked until he reached the housing development on Nelson Street commonly known as the Plannings. He had lived here when he was younger, but in his early teens his family had moved to Maloney. He still spent a lot of time in his old neighborhood, where he had relatives and many friends. He noted nothing had changed in the last four years.

Marlon spotted Carl from his second-floor window and raced down to meet him. He threw his arms around him, slapped him on his back, bounced his fist on Carl's chest, and offered his open palm which Carl slapped. "So you just fly, bro," he said, leading the way to the apartment. Marlon bounded up the stairs two at a time while Carl took the steps singly. Inside, Marlon made a show of dusting off a chair for Carl while calling into the kitchen, "Ma, come and see who here."

"Carl, God bless my eye," Marlon's mother exclaimed, hugging him. "You just come out?" She moved to the door to check that it was locked. "Well, you in good time. I now take off the pot, so you must eat something."

"Thanks, Ms. Noble. I will take a little taste," Carl said shyly, shifting in his chair.

"A little taste? Only a little taste of my food?"

"Well, when I pass by my two aunts in the next Plannings, I sure they will want me to eat too," Carl explained.

"Boy, when last you had good home-cook food? Eat here, eat there, eat all you can. Don't be shy."

"All right, Ms. Noble, dish out what you want." Carl smiled as Ms. Noble bustled over to the kitchen.

As soon as his mother was out of earshot, Marlon pulled up a chair close to Carl's and spoke in low tones. "What type of piece you want, a nines or a .38?"

Carl shook his head. "I not in the life again. I had plenty time to think in prison, and it not making sense. I plan to go to church."

"Carl, you was going to church with your mother when you was in the life."

"I was fooling myself, not the Lord," Carl said, searching Marlon's face for understanding.

"This is our way of life," Marlon argued. "What job you will get? How will you survive?"

"I will trust in the Lord for my survival."

"You still need a piece to protect yourself," Marlon insisted stubbornly. "You don't have to commit any robberies, but you made plenty enemies, and they will be coming for you."

"I will ask for forgiveness and trust in the Lord."

"Boy, like they mess with your brains in prison. Like you gone off. Before you reach to ask for forgiveness you will get a bullet. A man must have a weapon for protection in these times."

"That is the chance I will take," Carl said quietly. "You don't know what it is to be locked up for four years. I don't want to go back there again. I will not go back there again."

Ms. Noble brought out lunch then and they all ate.

"Yes, Ms. Noble, you outdo yourself today. You have me licking my fingers," Carl said, eating the last piece of breadfruit with relish. "That was the best oil down I taste in years."

"The best? Boy, that was the *only* oil down you eat in years," Marlon joked.

"True. We didn't even get that on Christmas Day. One apple per man for Christmas," Carl reflected soberly. "Thanks, Ms. Noble. I really appreciate that meal, my first meal of freedom. When they tell me I could leave, I bought a soft drink from the prisoners' canteen. I just wanted to walk down the road doing something natural."

"You see how it feel to be free again? Just hold on to that and don't do a thing to end up there again," Ms. Noble advised. She cleared the table and returned to the kitchen.

"Where you get money for soft drink?" Marlon asked Carl.

"The authorities give me my money for good behavior and prison work."

"So what is your plan now?" Marlon asked.

Carl rose. "I'm heading to Maloney after I check my aunts." He called goodbye to Ms. Noble as Marlon unlocked the door. Marlon followed him downstairs.

"So what you going to do when that money run out? I can give you a parcel to sell to start," Marlon offered.

"Marlon, you don't understand," Carl said, raising his voice. "I finish with that life." He left and headed for the apartments on Duncan Street.

Carl walked slowly, savoring the old neighborhood. The cracked pavement and garbage strewn in the drains was just as he had remembered. The noise from the corner bar was as raucous as ever. Small children peered from windows to relieve boredom. A pack of dogs rounded the corner after a bitch in heat. A young woman strutted down the street toward him wearing a tiny tube top and a short denim skirt. Carl thought something about her looked familiar. They passed, and both turned at the same time to look over their shoulders. They recognized each other, and slowly walked back examining each other's faces. Carl searched his memory, then blurted, "Effie!" Before him stood the teenage version of the little girl who had lived in the apartment opposite his aunt. He had no sisters and had sometimes regarded Effie almost as a little sister.

"That is you, Carl?" Effie almost shouted. "I heard you was inside. It's good to see you. How long you come out?"

"This morning. You didn't go to school today," Carl commented, observing Effie's outfit. When he had last seen Effie, she was excitedly telling everyone she met that she had passed the Secondary Assessment Examination for a "prestige" school. Carl remembered the joy he had felt at her success.

"I leave school a long time now," Effie answered flatly.

"But I hear you were doing good in Convent."

"I was doing good in school, yes. Then I started to feel like I shouldn't be there. I felt like the other girls were treating me funny." Effie crossed the road to the shade of a shop at the corner. Carl followed, looking her over.

"Why you feel the other girls treat you funny? I'm sure you didn't dress like this to go to school."

Effie laughed. "No, my uniform was neat as ever."

"What happened then?"

"You don't know what I do?"

"No. What?"

"I work in the night."

"Where, KFC?"

"KFC don't sell roast fowl."

Carl stared. "Effie, don't tell me you working on the streets. Why?"

"My mother started bringing her men home to have a time with me when she was pregnant with my last sister. I couldn't concentrate on my schoolwork again. I hated them big sweaty men. I used to feel dirty when I went to school, so I drop out. It's two years now. After a while I decided to earn my own money. I get accustomed to the life now."

Carl felt the pain behind Effie's bravado. He easily recognized it, having seen so much of it in prison. He had acted the part himself until he had decided to accept and deal with his reality. He sensed Effie was in no mood for a lecture, least of all from him. He made a mental note to find a time to give her that lecture. Pictures of the pretty brown-skinned girl, her wavy hair pulled back into a ponytail, flashed in his mind. He could hardly believe this was the same girl. Effie had straightened her hair. It fell straggly around her face whose once chubby cheeks were now sunken. Sadly, he realized how much older she looked than her approaching seventeenth birthday. He made a silent vow to make a difference in at least one life.

"Girl, you couldn't go by anybody for help?"

"I beg some friends to stay by them, but she used to come around and curse in front of they house. My friends tell me I have to go back. She used to meet me outside my school and slap me up, so I moved out a few times."

"Nobody tell the school principal?"

"I didn't tell my friends the real reason I wanted to leave. I used to feel shame. I wouldn't tell my principal that. Only Maggie from next door to your aunt suspect, and when she ask me, I tell her everything."

"Maggie!"

"Yes. I know she doing the same thing, so I feel comfortable talking to her. I started going to Woodbrook with her. She show me how to operate."

"So what your mother doing these days?"

"She still working the QRC area. I don't go by her territory, and she don't come by mine, except when she want to slap me up for some stupid reason."

"What you call a stupid reason?"

"Just imagine, a few nights ago she made a big scene in front of my friends, accusing me of stealing money she had in a radio to pay for the new fridge. I didn't even know she hide money in the radio. She tear my dress. In any case, I already gave her money to pay for the fridge. She just like to take advantage," Effie said, her voice betraying her hopelessness. Carl looked beyond Effie's face to the apartments opposite, to the mildewed walls and peeling paint, and the exuberant feeling of freedom he had felt earlier faded.

* * *

Early-morning light struggled to overcome a steady rain. A woman walked along Besson Street to Piccadilly Street on her way to work, sheltering the rain with an umbrella. She bumped into a man leaning over the wall of the Dry River. Startled, she stepped aside and apologized. The man fell heavily to the ground but he uttered no sound. When she saw that his shirt was blood-soaked, and that the blood had run down the wall and mixed with the rain to form a red puddle on the pavement, she screamed. Then she ran to the next corner and stopped. Her screams had been heard. People started trickling from apartments. Soon a small crowd gathered, and the woman edged back to see the body. It was a young man.

"He not from around here. Anybody know him?" someone asked.

"I don't recognize him." A woman with her hair in rollers stepped into the street to walk around the body.

"It's a good thing my heart isn't bad, or Lord, I would have fall dead too. I bounce the man leaning on the wall and he fall *boup* on the pavement."

"So it's you who scream?" the woman in curlers asked.

"Yes, it was me," declared the woman. "My hair stand up straight on my head. I am still shaking. Oh-oh, look. The police cars coming. I didn't see and I don't know." She left to take up her 7 a.m. shift. With the police on the scene, the crowd thinned. But the body was still there when more city dwellers awoke and children wended their way to school. Three hours later, the DMO arrived to declare him dead.

"I gave you a contract and the man is still alive," a voice hissed. "You killed the wrong man. I want the job done. I don't expect to have this conversation again."

Sheldon was shocked to overhear this conversation from his boss's office. He was certain his boss thought the office was empty. He slipped noiselessly out the door and found himself walking more briskly than usual to City Gate where he clambered up the stairs of the transit hub and descended quickly down the exit to the Maloney maxi-taxis. He pushed among the crowd to get a seat in the first one that drove up. He sat at a window and jerked slightly as the taxi pulled from the line. Soon they were speeding up the priority bus route. He smiled wryly as he reflected that he, who was always advising young men in his neighborhood to keep away from crime, was working with someone involved in criminal activity. He pondered his next step. He needed the job, but he knew he would be uneasy in the office after what he had overheard.

As the houses of Maloney Garden came into view, Sheldon mused at the contrast between the serene rows of pastel buildings and the violence in the community. Hardly tranquil, an air of controlled rage foamed, seethed into a fog that enveloped the area and followed the bad boys like a dark cloud. Sheldon strove to be in Maloney but not of Maloney. He prided himself on being a role model to the youth of the community simply by getting a job and going to work every day.

When he reached his stop, Sheldon found Carl sitting on a culvert opposite the small shop at the corner near Carl's home. Carl listened to Sheldon and felt in his heart that he knew how his friend felt.

"Who my boss had a hit out on, and for what?" Sheldon wondered aloud.

Carl shrugged. Sheldon knew he could no longer work there. A familiar car was speeding toward them. It was his oldest brother's car. Actually, Balo was his half-brother. In her teens, Sheldon's mother had become pregnant, and

Balo had become a father figure for Sheldon.

Balo pulled over and jumped out, shouting, "They—kidnap—Reshi!" His panic was palpable as the words spurted from his mouth in gasps. He was sweating and his large frame trembled. Reshi had been on his way to meet his sister at school yesterday. He never turned up. Today, Balo had gotten a call for ransom.

"Sheldon, come with me. I want to go and search."

Sheldon was stunned. "Search where?"

"I get some tips, so I going on that."

"You call the police?"

"No. The kidnappers say don't involve the police or they will kill Reshi."

"You want us to go looking just so, without protection or anything?"

"You forget I am a businessman. I have a gun. That is protection. I more damn vex than anything."

Sheldon was worried. "Balo, I want to help, but this sounding out of my range."

"That is your nephew they have, boy. Both of you grow like brothers. Listen!" Balo clicked voice mail on his phone. Sheldon and Carl listened to the message, then Balo replayed it.

Sheldon turned to Carl who had said nothing. "You would come with us?"

"I know people who do that kind of work," Carl replied slowly. "I don't want to be on that run nah, Sheldon."

"Who side you on? Your old bandit friends or decent people?" Sheldon demanded.

"Call the police. That is the best plan. If they want to kill, they will kill, police or not," Carl reasoned.

Balo was livid. "No police, no police! I will go alone if I have to!"

Sheldon followed Balo into the car. He sat in front and looked at Carl as Balo started the engine. Reluctantly, Carl got up, walked to the car, and got in.

"I gave you some time. You make a new plan yet? This is the last time I calling you on this."

"I already made the hit and I expect the rest of my payment, just like the last time. You gave me a name and I killed the man. And I took serious risk to leave him where he would be seen so close to my home."

"That's the only thing you got right."

"I was even in the crowd after he was found this morning."

"You'll get paid when you complete the job."

"My job complete. He was driving a red car just as you said. I even did as you suggested and made a call about a kidnap to throw them off the scent for a while."

"You got the right name, but the wrong man," Sheldon's boss barked into the phone.

"To get the right man will mean a new job and new pay," Marlon insisted.

"Don't cross me, boy. But I can compromise. I'll make a partial. Meet me at the usual in twenty minutes."

Marlon hung up his mobile phone. He locked the apartment door, and as he started downstairs, Effie approached.

"Marlon, if you don't have all the money now, just give me some. I see customers coming all the time. You must have it." She collected some of the profits from the drugs she had given him to sell.

Effie and Marlon walked out of his building. Marlon was talking on his phone again. A car slowed just as they reached the pavement. The front passenger window rolled down and shots rang out. Marlon grabbed Effie and used her as a shield.

She slumped in his arms, bleeding from the neck. He let her go and ran back to the building, collecting three bullets in his back.

*Didn't expect to get two birds with one shot. Hope she made good use of the money and coke she robbed me,* the driver of car number PVM 2025 thought as he pulled away. He had been surprised to see Effie and felt a tinge of regret, if only for a moment. Sheldon's boss did not like to be challenged. He knew Marlon would be nearing their meeting place and was right on target for perfect aim. Getting Effie in the bargain was almost unreal to him.

As Balo's car turned onto Prince Street, a piercing scream cut through the air. Before the apartment building, Ms. Noble threw herself on Marlon's body. "He was a good boy!" she cried, beating her arms on the paved yard. "He was a loving son. Why? Why?" Then Carl saw Effie lying on the pavement and sprang from the car. He knelt and cradled her head, weeping uncontrollably. He felt cheated of his chance to reform Effie. It was too late now to ask Marlon about the kidnapping. Carl had recognized Marlon's voice on the ransom message.

"Three for the day," one onlooker from the gathering crowd observed. Instinctively, Balo inquired about the other. A third corpse had been found dead leaning over the Dry River. He and Sheldon sped to the Forensic Science Centre, where that body had been sent. The pathologist opened a large metal drawer and rolled out Reshi's bloody body. Balo's hand tightened around the gun in his pocket before he fainted.

# GITA PINKY MANACHANDI

BY T‌IPHANIE Y‌ANIQUE

*Chaguaramas*

The children's coffins are from West Africa. He imports them. They are in shapes that a child's body would be happy to lie in—living or dead. One is shaped like a sneaker. It sits in the middle of the room as though a giant lost it in a stroll through the building. It is white and has a Nike swoosh on the side. The laces are made of cloth, but the rest of it is made of wood. There is also a lollipop one, the candy part painted in blue and green and yellow swirls, the stick—where the child's legs would go—painted an authentic bone-white. Corban's favorite is the airplane coffin. It has only one wing. It's a tiny replica of the BWIA Tri-Star in the military museum further down the peninsula. Many years ago the coffin was commissioned by a family who didn't need it when their son recovered. It's a coffin for a one-armed child. He likes it because he knows no one will ever buy it.

The store is never crowded, so often, when the proprietor, Anexus Corban, and his friend, Father Simon Peter, are there together, they can talk as candidly as two men with unforgivable secrets. Simon is not from the island. He's from a little hot country he cannot forget. The coffins here remind him of home. Simon Peter sits at the stool reserved for him. "How is business, Corban?" The answer is always the same. "Well, *you* know, Father." He doesn't say this flippantly. Corban is Catholic and believes priests are magic men—they are clairvoyant, they are conjurers and soothsayers. "You bring me luck. Without you, this place would be looking to close down." And Father Simon always says the same thing: "My friend, don't worry. When the good Lord takes people, He likes it if they bring some art with them." But before they can go through this usual routine, two girls in school uniforms walk in.

"School project," the blonde one says as she waves her notebook at Corban. He knows they are lying. He knows that even though he is running an honest and important business, for some his shop is just a curiosity. Like everyone, the girls are attracted to the children's coffins, but the dark-haired one slinks away to the Mexican coffins that are closer to the counter, where there is less light.

Corban comes from behind the counter where he displays folded silk shrouds that look like nightgowns and tiny prayer books from every God-fearing religion he knows. He asks the girls if they need some help.

"We're picking our coffins," says the brown girl.

The other opens her eyes at her and interjects, "For a history project."

From the ties of their uniforms, Corban can tell they are seniors from the International School.

Father Simon is annoyed at them. They do not go to a Catholic school. They are not supporting the shop. They are an interruption from his favorite part of the day. He tries to overcome this. "What is the topic of the assignment?"

"Death," the fair one says.

"The history of death?" asks Father Simon with what sounds like disbelief.

"The history of mourning," the brown-skinned one says. She is thinking that this place is like a museum of death. No, no, a gallery of mourning. She sees a simple wooden coffin, the kind that devout Syrians sometimes get buried in because it is all pine. It's all natural and will go back into the land without harm. The girl likes this idea in theory, but the coffin looks very sad to her. She cannot picture anyone she loves in it.

Her name is Gita Manachandi. When her parents gave her that name they expected it would stay put until she married, when it would turn to her husband to rename her—last and first name both. A brand-new name for her rebirth into wifedom. But Gita did not stay put and she did not always go by her given name. And she was certain she would never go by any husband-given name either. It was not that she did not like the name Gita. It was just that early on, her best friend had begun calling her Pinky because of a mistake, as is the case with the birth of so many nicknames. Perhaps *Gita* too was a mistake. She became Pinky in the second grade when her family moved to the island and Leslie Dockers asked her her name and she said it timidly, sucking on her little finger. Leslie couldn't make out the name but from then on called her Pinky. And that was that. In the classroom and in her home she was Gita. In the playground and in the street she was Pinky.

She and Leslie Dockers were a pair. Their mothers had approved of the friendship when the girls were young because each family felt the other would help with assimilation to island life. The Manachandis thought that Leslie's family was Creole—the white French they had heard were native to the island. The Dockers thought Gita was a Trini Indian. But neither family was actually from the island—the Manachandis were from Mumbai by way of Toronto and the Dockers were from Leeds. By the time anyone began to question the need for this friendship, it was too late.

Now Leslie is caressing the satin lining of the lush Virgin coffin as though she might climb in. It is open to show the brown Virgin de Guadalupe emblazoned on the inside. Leslie stares at the image as though she knows the woman. Then she realizes that this Virgin looks like her friend's dead mother. She stands in front of it so Pinky cannot see.

But Pinky has wandered over to the airplane coffin with her pen and notebook ready. She stoops down to better see into the tiny glass windows. She puts her fingers into the coffin via the emergency exit door and touches the soft inside. Corban thinks she might get her finger stuck. It has happened before. He clears his throat.

"It's so small and perfect," Gita says, removing her hand with a slow reverence. "There's even a cockpit in there by where the head would go. How much it cost?"

"A lot," answers Corban guardedly.

But Pinky is bolder than she seems. She lingers as though she were a real customer. She asks questions like, "What kind of person would buy a one-winged plane? Where did you get it? When people come in, do they bargain?" Then she pulls out her money and buys some marigolds in a tiny clear box. They are fresh and soft.

The flowers are the same color as the gold satin of the Virgin coffin, and when Gita slips one of them in her hair, Father Simon feels a shiver between his shoulder blades and warmth at the back of his knees. This girl looks like the Virgin.

"It's so beautiful in here," Pinky says, as Leslie hisses at her to leave. "It's like art." The girls are on their way to get ready for dancing.

Gita was pretty smart by all definitions, but no one thought there was anything special about this. She was a hard worker.

She studied with the ferocity of someone in love. And this *was* special. She was respected for her tenacity by the American and Trinidadian teachers and sought out for guidance by students. Her parents, who imagined her growing up to be someone important's wife, approved because her study habits meant she would be a desirable catch—a woman who could bear smart and studious sons. Gita did not see it this way. She imagined that she was growing up to be an obstetrician-gynecologist. In her dreams, she treated the poor Indian women from South and slipped them birth control while their husbands waited in the lounge. Gita was often mistaken even by Trinis for being Trini. Her parents thought this was a bit of an insult. They had never cut cane. They had never been indentured. Those island Indians had children who spoke loose and didn't go to Hindu classes on Saturdays. The girls didn't think twice to date African or Syrian boys. But Pinky did not take it this way.

Up until the first two weeks of her senior year, Pinky's routine was the same.

"Gita! Get up, my daughter. Gi-ta!" She was the only child and much was made of her. Her mother would tug on her toes until Gita pulled her feet away and bolted upright. She would go to the shower which was her shower alone. As she got older her showers became longer, and by the second week of being a senior in high school, she was taking forty-five minutes—something of a crime on an island where rain water was often stored under the house like treasure. She liked the water scalding, despite the heat of the island. Her mother would come and knock on the door: "Too much heat! You're going to wrinkle young!" Then Gita would blast on the cold water and squeal, turning circles under the shower so that she could erase the wrinkling. For many years she stepped out of the shower and reached for her towel without even glancing

322 // T<small>RINIDAD</small> N<small>OIR</small>

at herself in the bathroom mirror that covered an entire wall. But since becoming a senior and since Leslie had lost her virginity last year, Gita had become more interested in her own body, and more brave with it.

Now she would step out of the shower and dry herself off with the delicate pats her mother had taught her would not dry out the skin. When the steam evaporated, Gita would hang the towel up and walk slowly to the mirror. She would look at herself as she brushed her teeth and arranged her hair. Sometimes, if she was thinking of Mateo Diaz, she would look serious and sexy like she imagined Leslie might when doing it with Benjamin Jamison. Then she would blow a kiss to her reflection, but this would be too much and she would collapse into giggles. Her uniform would be laid out on the newly made bed when she emerged.

Every morning, Gita and her father ate an elaborate breakfast together. Mrs. Manachandi stayed in the kitchen doling out her experimental dishes, like steak dosa, for the class she taught on Indian/Americana fusion. Gita was always her father's daughter. He imagined that she would marry the son of one of his fellow managers at the Alcoa Aluminum dock. As each son returned from the U.S. or U.K. with his business or architectural or mechanical engineering degree, Mr. Manachandi would scrutinize him. But often the young men didn't return at all. And when they did, there was often a scandal with some unknown girl met during the ringing nights of Carnival. The young man would marry hurriedly or be ruined for Gita by the burden of a bastard child. Still, Mr. Manachandi knew that Gita would have to be witty and up on national, regional, and global politics to win the best mate. He thought it would also serve her well to know the value of aluminum. How when the smelter plant was built it would be like gold to the island. Like bauxite had been to Jamaica. He would read all the protest articles in the paper to her. Father and daughter would take turns arguing the side of the softhearted environmental activists or the tough-minded board members at Alcoa. Pinky was good at both. She could argue against the carbon dioxide poisoning with passion. She could argue the side of industry and jobs with coolness. Mr. Manachandi was proud of raising a daughter who could see all sides. Secretly, he wished that she would come work with him at the aluminum dock like a son.

But this had changed in the second week of Gita's senior year of high school. She and Leslie hung about in the school courtyard and talked about college. Leslie would go over to UWI—despite the ISPS education. So would Gita. Leslie, because it was cheaper than leaving the island and her grades weren't good enough to get her an international scholarship to a stateside college. Gita, because—though she was a sure thing for a full Barnard grant and even had Spelman as a backup—her mother didn't want her to go away to college. Too many girls came back with African-American fiancés or with ideas about never getting married.

"There's Benji," said Pinky, pointing with her chin across the school pitch where a pickup game of football was in progress.

"Screw Benji."

"Why?"

"He horned out on me over the summer."

"How do you know? He was in Atlanta all summer."

"Grapevine, Pinky."

"Why you ent tell me, girl. We need to get you a next man."

"I ent tell nobody. We need to get *you* a man, period."

"Good luck."

"I telling you. Fine-ass Mateo is all over you."

"Mateo's a idiot."

"But he's fine and he can dance and you're smart enough for the both of you."

"And what I going to do with him? He can't even drive his car without crashing it. Good luck getting a black guy to pass my parents' husband meter."

"He's half-black. Just tell them he's a dark-skinned Spaniard. A Moor or something."

"They'll think of Othello and worry he'll kill me when we're married."

"Pinky, really. Stop thinking stupidness. You practice first with boyfriends. Don't even think about husband. Boyfriends are more fun anyway. Husbands are sooo boring. You ent noticed?"

Pinky nodded. "Do you think you'd ever do it, like, on the kitchen table?"

"Do what?"

"You know."

"Oh, you slut." Leslie paused and looked out at the boys across the schoolyard. "Yeah. I think I would. Would you?"

"I guess if my husband wanted to."

They nodded together. Leslie had only done it three times with Benji before school let out and he went to Atlanta to spend the summer with his mother. She said it hurt every time but she expected that if they'd kept doing it all summer, by now it would feel good. Pinky had shrugged. She didn't like the idea of waiting for it to feel good. Why can't it feel good right away? It feels good to him. She imagined that when she became an obstetrician-gynecologist, she would make sure it felt good for all women all the time.

Leslie picked up her school bag. "You want a drop to the institute?"

"Sure."

"Hey, we gone," called Leslie to the guys playing on the green.

Mateo dribbled the ball between his ankles until he was a few feet away from them. "Hey, I going see you ladies at Anchorage tonight?" His voice had become deep over the summer and to Pinky it sounded rich and matched the musky way he smelled.

"Maybe," said Leslie.

Mateo was looking at Pinky. "You too, Pinky!"

"No. I'm bagged up."

"Sneak out," said Mateo, rolling the ball back and forth under his foot in a smooth movement. Pinky laughed at his suggestion. She flipped her hair and then felt stupid for doing so. Someone on the pitch shouted at Mateo to get back in the game or send the ball.

In the car, Leslie didn't look at her friend as she maneuvered out of the tight space. "Really, Pinky. I sick of giving you the business secondhand. I mean, I go with you to all the Divali stuff but you never come to the club. 'Bout time. You's seventeen, woman."

"Screw you. Divali is a religious thing. The club is not."

"It could be."

"Whatever." But she wanted to go. Maybe tonight she would have that fight. She would cry and ask her mother why she'd brought her here to this island only to tell her she couldn't be a part of it. Or maybe she would ask to stay over at Leslie's in Glencoe. The last time she'd asked, her mother had said she was too old for sleepovers.

At the gate they kissed on the cheek before Leslie drove

off. Pinky walked past the guard, who stared at her instead of nodding as he normally would. The campus at the hospitality institute seemed more beautiful today, the yellow bougainvillea blooming out extra, and so Pinky did not notice the difference in the air until she walked into her mother's culinary classroom. There was one student sitting quietly at the long teaching table; another was leaning into the sink as though washing her hair. Gita stood in the doorway and felt the lightness drain out of her. The girl from the sink straightened as though in pain, walked over to Gita, and touched her face with the palm of her hand.

"Gita, girl. You need to call home."

Gita went to the front desk to make the call. No one answered. When she hung up, the phone rang and the receptionist picked it up. The woman nodded into the receiver without looking at Gita.

A half an hour later, Gita watched as a man who worked with her father at the loading dock drove up in her dad's sedan. The man didn't come out to get her but leaned over and opened the door to the passenger side for her to get in.

"What's going on, Uncle?"

But he just shook his head quietly and drove toward Port-of-Spain. When they turned into the hospital parking lot, Gita could feel her bowels growing tight. *Not Dada*, she thought. She held her belly as they walked through the lobby and back toward the emergency room. Her father was sitting in a solitary plastic chair. When he saw her, he turned away as though she had insulted him. She went to him anyway.

"Dada?" She put out her hand. He moved from it. Gita turned and walked past her father's friend, who was just standing there dumb, and went to the nurse's station. They called for a doctor. The one who came was young and Indian, and she wore her hair in a ponytail like a student.

"Are you Gita?" the doctor asked.

Gita nodded.

"Come, let's sit over here."

Gita followed her to a far end of the room.

"Did you know that your mother was ill?"

"Just tell me."

The young doctor narrowed her eyes. She seemed to be either scrutinizing Gita or fighting back her own tears.

"Your mother died this afternoon. Your father is very up-set and wanted me to talk to you. I want you to know . . ."

As the doctor talked, Gita heard her father let out a loud wail. She turned to look at him. He was watching her and weeping. At that moment Gita decided that no, she would never become a doctor.

Gita's mother had not been buried in a coffin. She had been cremated. Her ashes were sent to Mumbai to her family, as was the custom. Mr. Manachandi didn't mind this. The presence of the urn would only make him think his wife was dead.

Mr. Manachandi talked to his wife at night. Gita would walk past the door and hear his side of the conversation. The first time, she thought he was on the phone, but then he said, "Ey, Leela?" and there was no audible response. He seemed quite normal otherwise. His did not miss work at the dock. He did not crash the car. He did not become edgy or volatile. He simply talked to his dead wife at night. He simply slept on only one side of the bed.

But at breakfast Mr. Manachandi had stopped asking his daughter about aluminum and smelter. One morning, he looked past her shoulder and into the kitchen where his wife should have been cutting lakatan bananas into bowls of maple syrup. "The hospitality institute used to be a navy hospital. A hospital, and they couldn't even save Leela."

Gita stared at her father but did not know how to tell him that he wasn't making any sense.

He focused his eyes and looked now at his daughter. "Are you going to college?" he asked.

And Pinky realized that she had only had that conversation with her mother. She was aware of the betrayal when she answered, "I've been thinking of Barnard."

He nodded. "That would be a good school for you." She lowered her head and felt that pain in her bowels again. Her mother was dead and now she would get to go to Barnard.

"What will you do, Dada?"

"I will stay here," he said softly. And if he had been talking more loudly, he might have finished his thought as well. *I will stay here because I am waiting for your mother to come back.*

Gita's mourning was different. Her mother died and suddenly her own life began. Suddenly she could spend the night at Leslie's. Suddenly no one scrutinized her clothes when she went out . . . didn't check the length of her skirts or the transparency of her blouses. Suddenly she could go to Barnard or Spellman. But she was no longer sure if she wanted to go anywhere at all.

Gita mourned her mother by going to the coffin shop in Diego Martin. She had watched the shop from across the street. She noticed that mostly women went in. That many of them were older women, perhaps burying parents. She would stand across the street and watch them and her stomach would hurt. Perhaps she was getting an ulcer. On the fourth day she'd invited Leslie.

"That place is creepy, Pinky."

"Come on, Les. I just want to see inside."

"Why?"

"Because."

"I don't think it's a good idea."

"Come on. I'll go with you to Anchorage tonight. I just want to see. You ent curious?"

"Tonight is Base night. And no, Pinky. Not at all curious. And you're never coming, anyhow. Even with Mateo begging you. It's nearly the end of the semester, but I swear, if you go he'll ask you to be his woman."

"I'll go. Now come on."

"Fine. But I still don't think it's a good idea." Leslie brought her friend's face to hers. "You okay?"

"I'm good," Pinky said, pushing Leslie's hand from her face. "Just curious."

She and Leslie went to the coffin shop. They pretended they were there for an assignment. "And this one?" she'd asked Corban. "The airplane with one wing?"

And she would have stayed there among the funeral things for hours, forever, if Leslie hadn't said, "I'm leaving you here if you don't come now."

Pinky bought some fresh marigolds from the nice older man on the way out and put one behind her ear. In the car, Leslie moved the rearview mirror so Pinky could see herself. "Tonight, you get Mateo Diaz." Pinky nodded. Yes. She would.

As she was getting dressed, and her father was reading his first installment of the *New Yorker*, Gita shouted through the door that she would be staying at Leslie's for the weekend. "Will you be okay, Dada?"

"Yes, my love," he called back. He turned a page. Smiled at a cartoon.

"I'll call tonight and tomorrow."

"You don't have to," he said.

Pinky pursed her lips and walked out into the living room. "But you'll be alone."

Without looking up from his magazine, Mr. Manachandi waved his hand dismissively in the air. "Not really, you know," he said. "Not really."

That night, Pinky wore a dress to match her name. A magenta dress that wasn't even hers. "The sluttiest thing I own," said Leslie, laughing. But Pinky didn't laugh. She looked at herself in the mirror and thought of her mother in her red wedding sari. In the picture, her father wore a European suit and had thick sideburns. Her father looked like a child of an era, her mother looked era-less. She was not sure which was better. Now she looked at herself in the mirror and puckered. Her dress was spandex and it stuck and stretched. It was open at the back and ended above the knees. There was a slit at the left thigh. Pinky thought that she would never look like this again. But in the next instant she said out loud, "This is what I always want to look like."

The club was not the hot smoky place she had expected. It was cool with AC inside and there was a big balcony out by the water. "Scope the place out first!" shouted Leslie, as the entry bands were fastened around their wrists. "Stay away from the nasty old men."

They walked in. They kept their backs straight. They flipped their hair. Leslie had taught her the screw face. This club was about attitude. Don't smile unless you see someone you know, and then hug and air kiss, and if it's a guy, wait for him to offer a drink. Never say no to a free drink. And never buy your own drink. It was a masquerade. They were pretty. They were desirable. Everyone was supposed to know it. When you dance, make sure you're not next to a girl who can dance better than you. Make sure to establish eye contact with a good-looking guy, but let him come over to you. Dance even when you're tired. Dance even if you're sweaty and tired. Take off your shoes if you need to, you can keep them behind the deejay booth. Only stop dancing if a guy offers you a drink. And then ask for something good. What's good? Get, like, a Sex on the Beach. Or a Fuzzy Navel. Or a Blow Job. No, don't get that. That's taking it too far. Never get what he's having. Man drinks taste nasty. Like Long Island Iced Tea. Disgusting. That's a get-drunk drink. You just want to look good when you're holding the glass. In fact, stick to Sex on the Beach. It matches your dress. And me. I'll get Blue Lagoons all night.

The old men against the walls watched them like a movie.

Outside on the deck, Pinky and Leslie drank their colorful drinks bought by forgettable boys and cooled off with the sea breeze. Pinky's hair was plastered onto her face. It wasn't so hot inside but they had been dancing and sweating. The deejay had played hip-hop and rock but not calypso yet. Pinky didn't really know how to move to hip-hop or rock. She was waiting for soca. "They play it last," explained Leslie.

"No Mateo," Gita said aloud and felt relieved, and then disappointed by her own relief.

"No Mateo yet. You wait." Leslie lit a tiny black cigar with a plastic tip. She blew out over the balcony. When the bells and knocking of calypso came on, Leslie flicked her cigarillo over the side of the balcony. They left their drinks.

Inside, the dance floor was crowded. Women had their skirts hoisted and men had their hands in the air. People were dancing in the corner by the tables and on top of the couches. Women leaned on the backs of chairs to steady themselves. Leslie and Pinky didn't look for an empty space, they simply walked in and danced where they ended up. Pinky felt good now. She didn't need Mateo after all. She swung her hips and her heavy wet hair. And then, just like that, Mateo came up behind her, as though it was something he did often.

He had that rich musky smell and he held her hips in his hands as he pulled her body closer to his. Her first thought was that this was not right. Her next thought was this was very right. Everyone in the club was screaming the words to the song. Everyone was knocking hips into one another. The bass beat twice and people stomped their feet twice. Pinky put her hands over Mateo's so she could follow his rhythm.

She looked around, realizing that Leslie was not beside her. But then there she was. A white girl was hard to miss in the dark club. Leslie had her palms flat on the wall, her arms straight and stiff, and her backside was rolling on the crotch of a man who was old enough to act cool about the friction. It seemed so odd, all of this. All this display. All this. And after Christmas break they'd be back in class in their uniforms, and perhaps that was its own kind of pretend.

Mateo turned her around so they faced each other, and though this was less vulgar, because less of their bodies touched, it seemed much more intimate. He leaned his face into her neck and she felt his lips on her wet skin as if he had tapped directly onto her spine. She shivered and pulled back. And then she left the dance floor. Mateo stood there for a moment before following her.

"You okay?" he asked once they were outside.

"Yeah. Are you okay?"

"Yeah." They were quiet for several moments. "I wanted to kiss you in there."

"I know."

"Can I kiss you now?"

"I don't know, actually."

"Can I try?" She nodded. He leaned forward and she turned to give him her cheek. "If we get married," he said smiling, "we'll be doing a lot more than kissing."

"What?"

And then he kissed her open mouth and she felt his soft lips and his wet tongue and she jumped back. And she smiled and then she backed away some more and then she ran away, into the cavern of the club, her heels clinking on the deck like knocking bones. She'd had her first kiss and it had been with Mateo, and had he asked her to marry him? This was like a Bollywood movie except with real kissing. She needed to talk to Leslie.

But inside, the dance floor was a living mass of its own. It was hot and steamy now. And the people were not concerned about the expensiveness of their dresses or the intricateness of their hairdos. The floor was sticky and difficult to walk on in Leslie's heels.

Mateo had kissed her and now Gita did not know what to do. It had felt animallike. It had felt slutty. She didn't want to see him again. But she wanted to see him every day for the rest of her life. And that was silly. Did she really believe that Mateo Diaz was the kind of boy who kissed a girl and then married her? Was he? He would want sex first or at least dating a little. He would want to fool around with American girls in college and all that. Wouldn't he? Would he? Why would he say something so serious if he wasn't serious? She felt sick. Her head felt sick. She felt as though she had to get away from the crowd. "Are you tight?" someone asked. She shook her head but thought she might throw up. "Man, Pinky Manachandi is tight!"

She wandered to the bathroom, then hiked up her pink dress and sat on the toilet until she felt as though the kiss and

the drink were gone from her. When she emerged she felt better but more stupid. Had she even kissed Mateo? And had she
run away afterwards?

Someone grabbed her wrist gently. It felt protective. She
looked up expecting to see her father. The older man leaned
into her face. "You don't look so good."

"I'm not."

"You need some water." He was wearing a panama hat fitting tight and low. He offered her his open bottle.

She wasn't used to drinking. Water seemed like a savior.
She took it and drank steadily. Drank the whole bottle before
she knew it. It felt clean. It tasted sweet.

"I'm sorry, sir." She handed him back the empty bottle.

"Sir!" said the man with amusement. "Well, I haven't been
alive *that* much longer than you." Gita didn't know how to feel
about this. But now she peered at him and thought he looked
familiar. She squinched up her eyes at him. It wasn't a bad feeling, this familiarity. But it felt dark, like a secret. He squinched
his eyes back at her. Then, without smiling or saying goodbye,
he slipped into the men's room with his water bottle.

"Where you been?" Leslie's voice, suddenly next to hers,
was hoarse.

"In the bathroom."

"Were you puking?"

"I don't know."

"Mateo just tell me he kissed you and then you run
away."

"He's lying."

"Oh man, Pinky. Now what you going do? Do you like him
like that?"

"I going marry him. My dad will let me do anything. He
visits with my dead mother every night."

"What?"

"Nothing."

"Are you boyfriend and girlfriend now?"

"I don't think so." Gita watched the door of the men's room and waited for the man to come out. She wanted to remember who he was.

"You should find out." Leslie paused. "Do you even have his number?"

"Who? Oh, no. I don't think so."

"Pinky, are you high or something? What the hell! Let's go give him yours."

They walked around the club that was now playing its jazzy theme song. People were leaving. The lights went on like a wide search beam. People now looked human and raw. Some stood around and waited. Others talked loudly about heading out to a new club in Port-of-Spain that stayed open later. No one was dancing anymore. The dance floor looked like a sad, dirty place. Mateo wasn't there. Outside, they stumbled over the pebbles to Pinky's car. "I'll drive," Leslie offered.

"That's okay," said Pinky. She sat in the driver's seat of the SUV that had been her mother's. She started the engine and rolled down their windows with the automatic buttons.

"Hey, Pinky. Stop running away from me."

"Oooh," whispered Leslie from the passenger's seat. "He good."

Pinky put the car back in park and told her heart to stop slamming against the inside of her chest. Asked her brain to stop floating around in her head. She wanted really to drive away. She wanted really to wave and honk her horn like others were doing and then find the main road and then go to school in January and wait to see if Barnard had accepted her and then wait to see if she actually wanted to go after all. But instead her palms sprung water and slipped off the steering wheel.

"Can I get your number?"

She nodded but didn't turn to look at him. Her head might fall off, it felt that soupy. *Is this what love feels like?*

Mateo leaned into the car window. "Pinky, girl, I'm not messing with you. I know this has to be on the down low cause of your pops. I'm for real. However you want it, girl. Hey, give me your cell."

She kept her hands in her lap. Leslie dug through the little magenta purse and passed him Pinky's cell phone. He typed his number in. "I put in 'Mary.' That can be my code name. That way, when I'm calling no one knows it's a guy. Cool?" And then he backed off a little. "Good night, Les. You take care of my girl."

Leslie smiled and waved and reached over to honk Pinky's horn. "Now drive away, Pinky," she said under her breath.

Pinky put the SUV in gear and drove. "I have a boyfriend," she said as the sea air whipped around them on the highway. The air made her head feel less swimmy. Kept her palms dry.

"You have a man, Pinky. Now what you going do with him?"

"I have no idea."

She drove faster. She wanted the air. She and Leslie were careening into their happiness. They were nearing Alcoa, where her father worked. Pinky thought, *Father*, and then remembered the Catholic priest, and then she finally remembered where she knew the older man from. The coffin shop. She smiled. There was something funny about the man. He had been so mad when she touched his one-winged plane. He was nice to have given her water, though. Did he remember her? Is that why he was so nice? The water had been sweet.

Maybe it was coconut water. This thought made Gita laugh out loud. The laughter made her head float. Leslie glanced over at her to ask what was so funny.

But they had already gotten to the narrow loop in the road before the aluminum warehouse. Pinky turned the wheel into the dark corner. There was a sudden blare of another car's horn. Then, the invasive brights of the other car's headlights. Pinky let the wheel pull away from her. She released her hands and raised her foot off the gas. She saw the Alcoa dock and thought of it as a solitary arm reaching into the sea as in welcome.

Leslie saw her friend's hands raised above the wheel. She felt the car slam into the railing. Felt it lift as though alive and turn, turn, until upside down. Her body stiffened in anticipation. The fear was like metal on her tongue. "Hold on," she tried to scream, *hold on!*—but the words were too slow. They hit the water like a wall. The wall gave way. Then it was dark and they were underwater and they were in a sinking car and they were upside down.

Leslie released her seat belt. She reached out for Pinky, who was facing her. They were staring at each other—Leslie could tell that much. She tugged at Pinky's seat belt. Pinky did not tug back. Pinky's eyes were wide open as though she were breathing water and surprised at her new magic. Leslie's body filled with the burn of the saltwater in her chest. She grabbed at her friend's seat belt. She pulled at Pinky. It seemed like forever but maybe it was only a few seconds. Five seconds maybe. Leslie's chest hurt and her eyes hurt and she was more afraid than she had been at birth. Five eternal seconds and then she turned to open the door, but the door would not open and so she pulled herself through the window and she did not look back but swam toward what she hoped with all her heart was the surface and not further out into the ocean. She hit the air and heaved and was surprised to see the highway quiet, as if nothing at all had happened. As if Gita were not under the water stuck in her seat belt. She swam until she could climb out. Four more minutes maybe. She ran across the street without looking either way, toward the first rum shop at the edge of the village. It was closed. A minute. She ran toward a convenience store, a red open sign buzzing above the door. Five minutes. She was wet and dirty and she babbled to the register man, who nodded and handed her the phone. She didn't call the police station which was less than half a mile away. She called her parents. But all she could say was, "Mateo kissed Pinky and now she's in the water. She's in the water and it's only me on land. Just me. Help. Come help." By then the convenience store owner had used his cell phone to call the police. And by the time the police came and the firefighters came and Gita's father came, it had been almost thirty minutes.

"Why don't you go get her?!" Gita's father shouted before his car had even stopped. Mr. Manachandi left his car like a catapult and rushed past the police, who were gathered around Leslie. He jumped over and into the water.

The police did not stop him. "Part of his mourning," one said to another, and jotted the occurrence down in his notebook.

Mr. Manachandi went under and then came back up. "Help me! Please. I see her. Help me."

Then another police officer said, "Get the old man out of the water." And a young cop took off his gun and jumped in and grabbed Mr. Manachandi and hauled him out. The father looked like an animal. He looked like a wild dying animal. The firemen, who were more trained in dealing with human beings than car wrecks, told him that they needed him over here. Away from where the divers were going down to cut the body out of its seat belt. And by then Pinky had been under water for forty-five minutes.

In the ambulance, Leslie howled as though her own mother was dead.


Leslie Dockers walked into the shop and said good afternoon out of a new formality. Mr. Corban remembered her, the friend of the Indian girl, and sat more erectly in his chair. He was nervous. He was excited.

Leslie walked to the mustard-colored coffin with the Virgin emblazoned on it and caressed its satin lining with the back of her hand. She felt this one would be best, but she wasn't sure she'd have her way. She'd already convinced Mr. Manachandi that a coffin would be better than an urn.

The jangle of the door sounded again. Mr. Manachandi walked slowly into the shop, his shoulders stooped over and his hands clasped in front of him. He walked over to Leslie and stared for a second at the Virgin. He began to raise his hand to his mouth, but instead swayed unsteadily, holding onto the coffin. The coffin held the weight.

Corban cleared his throat and gestured to the stool where Father Simon usually sat. Father Simon, the magic good luck. Away on his yearly trip to the parish in Tobago. Business was always dead when Father Simon was gone.

But Corban studied a little magic of his own. Bitter herbs. Sweet potions.

Mr. Manachandi took the seat. "Something for a girl," he said.

Corban nodded with the appropriate weight of this request and came out from behind the counter. The man, Corban noticed, had a flattened gold marigold edging out of his breast pocket.

"Well, there is this one. The BWIA plane. It's odd. I never thought I'd sell it, but a girl was in here just the other day who liked it very much. I would be willing—"

"No. No. No," Mr. Manachandi began, his voice small. He shook his head and closed his eyes. "Something pure and natural," he said firmly, and then opened his eyes.

Corban put his hand to his chin and squeezed it. He looked at the blonde girl who was standing there at the Virgin coffin as though it were an altar. "Yes, I understand." He glanced about and saw the simple pine coffin. Corban knew this was not the right choice, the Indian girl hadn't liked it when she came in a week ago. But he would show the pine to the man anyway. A sale was a sale.

# ABOUT THE CONTRIBUTORS

*Brian Ng Fatt*

**LISA ALLEN-AGOSTINI** is a poet, playwright, and fiction writer from Trinidad and Tobago. She is the author of a children's novel, *The Chalice Project* (2008). An award-winning journalist, she has been a reporter, editor, and columnist with the *Trinidad Express* and the *Trinidad Guardian*.

*María José Furió*

**ROBERT ANTONI** carries three passports: American, Bahamian, and Trinidadian. He is the author of three novels, *Divina Trace* (1991), *Blessed Is the Fruit* (1997), and *Carnival* (2005), as well as the story collection, *My Grandmother's Erotic Folktales* (2000). He presently lives in Manhattan and teaches in the graduate writing program at The New School. According to his horoscope, he has "no barometer for abstinence."

*Rattan Jadoo*

**KEVIN BALDEOSINGH** is a journalist and the author of three novels. His novel, *The Autobiography of Paras P* (1996), is a social satire. *Virgin's Triangle* (1997) is a romantic comedy. *The Ten Incarnations of Adam Avatar* (2005) is an historical novel covering the past 500 years of Caribbean history. In 2000 and 2001 he was the regional chairperson for the Commonwealth Writers' Prize (Canada and Caribbean). He is also a founding member of the Trinidad and Tobago Humanist Association.

*Eric Grims*

**ELISHA EFUA BARTELS** is finally escaping the unnecessary hazards of winter and coming home to Trinbago. While in Washington, D.C., she stage-managed and performed with several theaters, including the Washington Shakespeare Company and the Folger Shakespeare Library, and was a freelance associate producer for the *Kojo Nnamdi Show* on WAMU-FM 88.5. biglove to grims and her family for continuing to support her similar endeavors in locations current and future.

*Doug Vernimmen*

**VAHNI CAPILDEO** lived in Trinidad until she moved to Oxford, England, where she studied Old Icelandic because "Vikings" wrote hardboiled prose. She now works on the *Oxford English Dictionary* for Oxford University Press. Her books include *No Traveller Returns* (2003), *Person Animal Figure* (2005), and *The Undraining Sea* (2008). Works in hand include *Dark & Unaccustomed Words* (poetry) and *Static* (stories).

**WILLI CHEN** is a Trinidadian entrepreneur, artist, and writer. His accolades include the BBC prize and Trinidad's Chaconia Silver Medal (2006). His writings have appeared in literary magazines in the Caribbean and the U.S. His works include *King of the Carnival and Other Stories* (1988), *Chutney Power and Other Stories* (2006) which was short-listed for the 2007 Commonwealth Writers' Best Book Prize (Canada and Caribbean), and *Crossbones* (forthcoming).

**RAMABAI ESPINET** is a writer, critic, and academic. Her published works include a novel, *The Swinging Bridge* (2003), a book of poetry, *Nuclear Seasons* (1991), and the children's books *The Princess of Spadina* (1992) and *Ninja's Carnival* (1993). She is the editor of *Creation Fire* (1990). A documentary on her work, *Coming Home*, was released in 2005. Forthcoming is a collection of short fiction, *Shooting Trouble*.

**RIAN MARIE EXTAVOUR** has worked as a freelance journalist for the *Catholic News* and was selected to be a fellow in Trinidad's Cropper Foundation Creative Writing Workshop 2005. She enjoys acting and singing and has appeared in Relevant Theatre's 2006 production, *Phases*, the University of the West Indies (St. Augustine) Festival Arts Chorale production of *Oliver!*, and she appears regularly with Mawasi Experience.

**KEITH JARDIM**, a jaguar who lives in the forests of Guyana and Venezuela, is the author of *Under the Blue: Stories* (2008) and *The Last Migrations: Stories and a Novella* (forthcoming). He eats peccaries and alligators, fish and capybara, the occasional moist-eyed deer, and agoutis. He knows the government of Trinidad and Tobago never had a heart.

**OONYA KEMPADOO** was born in England of Guyanese parents and brought up in Guyana. She has lived in Europe, St. Lucia, Trinidad, Tobago, and currently lives in Grenada. Her first book, *Buxton Spice*, was published in 1997 and has been translated into five languages. Her second novel, *Tide Running* (2001), won the 2002 Casa de las Américas prize. Kempadoo was named a Great Talent for the Twenty-First Century by the Orange Prize judges.

Gerard Gaskin

**JAIME LEE LOY**, a native Trinidadian, studied literature and visual arts at the University of the West Indies (St. Augustine) and is pursuing an MPhil in literature. A contributing artist to *Galvanize* (2006), she has participated as artist-in-residence at Caribbean Contemporary Arts (CCA), Trinidad, and the Vermont Studio Center, U.S. She was Exchange Programme Coordinator for CCA where for five years she experimented with video.

NO AUTHOR
PHOTO

**DARBY MALONEY** writes short stories, poetry, and is currently working on a children's Heroes of Trinidad and Tobago series which includes *Russell Latapy: The Little Magician* (2007) and *Stephen Ames: Trinidad's Ace Golfer* (2008). Darby has lived in eleven states and three countries, and currently resides in Southampton, New York and Trinidad and Tobago.

Nickolai Salcedo

**REENA ANDREA MANICKCHAND** is a twenty-six-year-old native of Trinidad and Tobago who has enjoyed creative writing since she was eight. Besides short stories, her work also includes socio-dramas. Her writing has moved from dark and negative to sweet and positive. After being baptized into theater, she began producing works that explore how to appropriately resolve these extremes. She credits her countrypeeps and close ones for her inspiration.

Arlene Moscovitch

**SHANI MOOTOO** was born in Ireland and grew up in Trinidad. She is the author of a collection of short stories, *Out on Main Street* (1993), a book of poetry, *The Predicament of Or* (2001), and two novels, *Cereus Blooms at Night* (1996)—long-listed for the Booker Prize, short-listed for the 1997 Giller Prize, and a finalist for the British Columbia Book Prize—and *He Drown She in the Sea* (2005), which was long-listed for the 2007 International IMPAC Dublin Literary Award. She lives in Canada.

Tony Akeem

**ELIZABETH NUNEZ** is a CUNY Distinguished Professor and author of six novels, including *Beyond the Limbo Silence* (1999), winner of the Independent Publisher's Award, and *Bruised Hibiscus* (2000), winner of the American Book Award. *Prospero's Daughter* (2006) was a *New York Times* Editors' Choice. Nunez is coeditor of the anthology *Stories from Blue Latitudes: Caribbean Women Writers at Home and Abroad* (2006) and executive producer of the television series *Black Writers in America*.

**LAWRENCE SCOTT** was the 1999 winner of a Commonwealth Writers' Prize for Best Novel (Canada and Caribbean) for *Aelred's Sin* (1998). He is the author of *Witchbroom* (1992), *Ballad for the New World* (1994), and *Night Calypso* (2004). His stories have been anthologized in *The Penguin Book of Caribbean Short Stories* and *The Oxford Book of Caribbean Short Stories*. His stories have also been read on the BBC. For more information visit www.lawrencescott.co.uk.

David A. Williams

**JUDITH THEODORE** was born and grew up in Woodbrook, Port-of-Spain. One of her short stories was short-listed for a local *Newsday* competition, and she was selected to participate in the Cropper Foundation 2005 Caribbean Residential Writing Workshop in Tobago. She recently completed the Playwrights' Workshop 2007 conducted by Tony Hall. She is also a member of the Trinidad and Tobago Art Society and works in various media, but has a preference for oils and pastels.

Bill Cardoni

**TIPHANIE YANIQUE** won a *Boston Review* Fiction Prize, a Fulbright Scholarship in creative writing, and a Pushcart Prize. She holds an MFA from the University of Houston. Her fiction, nonfiction, and poetry can be found in various publications including *Transition*, *Callaloo*, and the *London Magazine*. She is a professor of creative writing and Caribbean literature at Drew University, and currently is the review editor of *Calabash* and a fellow with Teachers & Writers Collaborative.

## Also available from the Akashic Books Noir Series

**HAVANA NOIR**
edited by Achy Obejas
360 pages, trade paperback original, $15.95

*Brand new stories by:* Leonardo Padura, Pablo Medina, Carolina García-Aguilera, Ena Lucía Portela, Miguel Mejides, Arnaldo Correa, Alex Abella, Moisés Asís, Lea Aschkenas, and others.

"A remarkable collection . . . Throughout these 18 stories, current and former residents of Havana—some well-known, some previously undiscovered—deliver gritty tales of depravation, depravity, heroic perseverance, revolution, and longing in a city mythical and widely misunderstood." —*Miami Herald*

**BROOKLYN NOIR**
edited by Tim McLoughlin
350 pages, trade paperback original, $15.95
*WINNER OF SHAMUS AWARD, ANTHONY AWARD, ROBERT L. FISH MEMORIAL AWARD; FINALIST FOR EDGAR AWARD, PUSHCART PRIZE

*Brand new stories by:* Pete Hamill, Robert Knightly, Arthur Nersesian, Maggie Estep, Nelson George, Sidney Offit, Ken Bruen, and others.

"*Brooklyn Noir* is such a stunningly perfect combination that you can't believe you haven't read an anthology like this before. But trust me— you haven't. Story after story is a revelation, filled with the requisite sense of place, but also the perfect twists that crime stories demand. The writing is flat-out superb, filled with lines that will sing in your head for a long time to come."
—Laura Lippman, winner of the Edgar, Agatha, and Shamus awards

**TORONTO NOIR**
edited by Janine Armin & Nathaniel G. Moore
272 pages, trade paperback original, $15.95

*Brand new stories by:* Gail Bowen, Peter Robinson, Kim Moritsugu, Michael Redhill, Andrew Pyper, George Elliott Clarke, and others.

"Akashic's city-noir series descends upon Toronto . . . Top-shelf contributors like Michael Redhill, Andrew Pyper and fourteen others get inside of Toronto's self-loathing psychogeography for a detour to the dark side. Such attitudes among our citizenry might not make for livability or relaxed subway rides, but they are the grist for great fiction."
—*Eye Weekly*

## LOS ANGELES NOIR
### edited by Denise Hamilton
360 pages, trade paperback original, $15.95
*A LOS ANGELES TIMES BEST SELLER; EDGAR AWARD FINALIST

*Brand new stories by:* Michael Connelly, Janet Fitch, Susan Straight, Héctor Tobar, Patt Morrison, Robert Ferrigno, Neal Pollack, Gary Phillips, Christopher Rice, Naomi Hirahara, Jim Pascoe, and others.

"Akashic is making an argument about the universality of noir; it's sort of flattering, really, and *Los Angeles Noir,* arriving at last, is a kaleidoscopic collection filled with the ethos of noir pioneers Raymond Chandler and James M. Cain."
—*Los Angeles Times Book Review*

## NEW ORLEANS NOIR
### edited by Julie Smith
298 pages, trade paperback original, $14.95

*Brand new stories by:* Ace Atkins, Laura Lippman, Patty Friedmann, Barbara Hambly, Tim McLoughlin, Olympia Vernon, Kalamu ya Salaam, Thomas Adcock, Christine Wiltz, Greg Herren, and others.

"The excellent twelfth entry in Akashic's noir series illustrates the diversity of the chosen locale with eighteen previously unpublished short stories from authors both well known and emerging."
—*Publishers Weekly*

## LONDON NOIR
### edited by Cathi Unsworth
280 pages, trade paperback original, $14.95

*Brand new stories by:* Patrick McCabe, Ken Bruen, Barry Adamson, Joolz Denby, Stewart Home, Sylvie Simmons, Desmond Barry, and others.

"While few of the names will be familiar to American readers . . . there are pleasures to be found [in *London Noir*], especially for those into the contemporary London music scene."
—*Publishers Weekly*